Bierfon 2/14

D1076747

The M~~agic of a Family Christmas, His Mistletoe Bride~~ and *Under the Boss's Mistletoe* were first published in Great Britain by Harlequin (UK) Limited.

The Magic of a Family Christmas © Linda Susan Meier 2009
His Mistletoe Bride © Cara Colter 2008
Under the Boss's Mistletoe © Jessica Hart 2009

ISBN: 978 0 263 91037 7
ebook ISBN: 978 1 472 01617 1

05-1113

Harlequin (UK) policy is to use papers that are natural, renewable and recyclable products and made from wood grown in sustainable forests. The logging and manufacturing processes conform to the legal environmental regulations of the country of origin.

Printed and bound in Spain
by Blackprint CPI, Barcelona

THE MAGIC OF A
FAMILY CHRISTMAS

BY
SUSAN MEIER

Susan Meier spent most of her twenties thinking she was a job-hopper—until she began to write and realized everything that had come before was only research! As one of eleven children, with twenty-four nieces and nephews and three kids of her own, Susan has had plenty of real-life experience watching romance blossom in unexpected ways. She lives in Western Pennsylvania with her wonderful husband, Mike, three children and two overfed, well-cuddled cats, Sophie and Fluffy. You can visit Susan's website at www.susanmeier.com.

For the people at Gardners Candies in
Tyrone, Pennsylvania!
Thanks for a great tour and your help with this story!
Merry Christmas!

For my mom, who was the inspiration
for Harry's Christmas cookie painting!

PROLOGUE

"I've hired a nurse."

"Really?" Wendy Winston tried to sound surprised by her next-door neighbor's announcement, but she wasn't. Betsy's cancer hadn't responded to treatment. Wendy had been able to help Betsy struggle through the aftereffects of the initial round of chemotherapy, but her friend needed real care now. Care beyond what a neighbor could provide.

"I appreciate all the help you've given me over the past few weeks, but I'll bet you'll be glad for the break."

Fluffing the fat pillow before she slid it under Betsy's head, Wendy laughed. "You think I'll be glad to go back to an empty house?"

Betsy frowned. "I've always wondered why you didn't move back to your family in Ohio after your husband died."

She shrugged. "Memories mostly. It seemed too abrupt just to leave when he died. I needed time to process everything."

"It's been two years."

"I also have a job."

"No one stays away from family for a job."

She grinned at Betsy. "Would you believe I can't sell that monstrosity I call a house?"

Betsy laughed.

"One of these days I'll have the kitchen and bathrooms re-modeled and then I can put it on the market and go."

Even Wendy heard the wistfulness in her own voice so she wasn't surprised when Betsy said, "It makes you sad to think of leaving."

"Four years ago I settled here with the assumption that Barrington would be my home. I can't shake the feeling that this is where I belong. No matter how alone I am."

"Why didn't you and Greg ever have kids?"

"He wanted to be done with his residency before we even tried."

"Makes sense."

Wendy smiled sadly.

"But it didn't make you happy."

"If we'd done what I wanted and had a child I wouldn't be alone right now." She sighed. "Not that I only wanted a child to keep from being lonely. It was more than that. My whole life I longed to be a mom. But what Greg wanted always came first. Some days I struggle with that."

"That's one of those tough choices that happens in a marriage. Nobody's fault."

Wendy turned away. "Yeah." She wouldn't burden Betsy with stories of how her late husband had been so focused and determined that he frequently didn't even listen when she talked. She didn't want to give Betsy any more to worry about or the wrong idea. She had loved Greg and missed him so much after he died that she had genuinely believed she would never be happy again. But because he was so self-absorbed, their marriage was far from perfect.

Silence stretched out in Betsy's sunny bedroom as Wendy walked around the room tidying the dresser and bedside tables.

"You know, it won't be the nurse's job to read Harry a story or tuck him in at night," Betsy said, referring to her six-year-old son.

Wendy turned from the dresser.

"So if you want to keep coming over to do that, I know it would make Harry happy. He loves it when you read to him."

Wendy smiled. "I love it, too."

CHAPTER ONE

WENDY Winston twisted the key to silence her small car and turned to the boy on the seat beside her. Six-year-old Harry Martin blinked at her from behind brown-framed glasses. A knit cap covered his short yellow hair. His blue eyes were far too serious to be those of a child. A thick winter coat swallowed his thin body. His mittened hand clutched a bag of toy soldiers.

"I'm really sorry to have to bring you to work."

He pushed his glasses up his nose. "S'okay."

She wanted to say not really. It wasn't okay that he'd be forced to sit and play with his plastic soldiers for God only knew how long while she worked. It wasn't okay that he'd lost his mom. Or that Betsy's lawyer had been out of town when she'd died. It had been four weeks before Attorney Costello had finally called to tell Wendy that Betsy had granted her custody of Harry in her will, and another few days before social services could pull him out of his foster home and give Wendy custody—and then only temporarily.

Regardless of what Betsy's will said, Harry's biological father's rights superseded her custody bequest. But no one knew where Harry's dad was, so, for now, Wendy had a child who needed her, and, for the first time in two years, she had someone to anticipate Christmas with. Though social services was searching for Harry's dad, Wendy believed she and Harry could have as long as a month to shop, bake cookies and decorate. If it killed her she would make it the best month before Christmas this little boy had ever had.

She smiled. "I promise I'll make this up to you."

"Can we bake cookies?"

Her heart soared. It seemed that what he needed done for him was what she needed to do. They were the perfect combination. Maybe fate wasn't so despicable after all.

"You bet we can bake cookies. Any kind you want."

Wicked wind battered them with freezing rain as they raced across the icy parking lot to the executive entrance for Barrington Candies. Juggling her umbrella and her purse as they ran toward the door, she rummaged for her key, but before she found it, the right side of the glass double doors burst open.

Cullen Barrington stood in the entryway. Six foot three, with black hair and eyes every bit as dark, and wearing a pale-blue sweater that was probably cashmere, the owner of Barrington Candies was the consummate playboy. He was rich, handsome and rarely around, assigning her boss Paul McCoy the task of managing the day-to-day operations of the company while he handled the big-picture details from the comfort of his home in Miami. Cullen was also so tight with money that no one in the plant had gotten a raise since control of Barrington Candies had been handed to him by his mother.

Scrooge.

That's what she'd taken to calling the man who'd summoned her to work on a Saturday afternoon. Even though he'd surprised everyone with his offer to fill in for her boss so Mr. McCoy could take an extended Christmas vacation,

Wendy wasn't fooled into thinking he'd changed his ways and become generous. Though he'd probably called her in today to prepare before he took over on Monday morning, he'd paid no thought to the fact that she would lose her day off. She'd lose precious minutes with Harry. She'd lose the chance for them to enjoy whatever time they had together, and maybe even the chance for her to show him life wasn't entirely bad, just parts of it.

Even if, some days, she didn't quite believe that herself.

Occupied with her thoughts, she slipped on the ice and plowed into Cullen. She braced her hand on his chest to stop her forward momentum and it sank into the downy cashmere covering the hard muscle of his chest. His body was like a rock.

Confused, because she thought all rich men were soft and pampered, she looked up. He glanced down. And everything inside Wendy stilled. She swore the world stopped revolving. As dark as moonless midnight, his eyes held hers. Her femininity stirred inside her.

That confused her even more. She hadn't felt anything for a man since her husband's death, and Cullen Barrington was the last man on the planet she wanted to be attracted to. A playboy from Miami? No thanks. She'd glimpsed him a time or two in the four years she'd been working for his company and never felt anything but distaste at the way he treated his employees. She had no idea what was going on with her hormones, but it had to be an aberration of some sort.

She stepped away, and as the door swung closed behind her a bell rang.

Funny, she didn't remember a bell being on that door.

She turned to investigate and sure enough someone had tied a bell to the spring mechanism at the top of the door.

Probably Wendell, the janitor, making sure he'd be alerted if one of the executives sneaked in to check up on him.

"Why did you bring your little boy?"

She pulled off her mittens. "Oh, I don't know. Because I wasn't supposed to be working today? Because it's such short notice that I couldn't get a sitter?" She shrugged. "Take your pick."

His gorgeous eyes narrowed. He obviously didn't like her speaking so freely with him.

Wendy almost groaned at her stupidity. A single woman who might get custody of a little boy couldn't afford to be fired!

"I'm sorry. I shouldn't have snapped at you. It's just cold and I had things to do. So tell me what you want to work on and we can get started."

"I'd like to catch up on what's been going on, so I'll need production schedules and the financials. Once you help me find those, you can go home."

He didn't smile. Didn't give any reason at all for her heart to catch at the smooth baritone of his voice, but it did. Her entire body felt warm and soft, feminine in response to his masculinity.

She stepped back. She did not want to be attracted to him. It had taken her two long, miserable years to get over Greg's death. And she refused to go through the misery of loss again by being attracted to a playboy who—as sure as the sun rises every day—would dump her.

Of course, she might not be attracted to Cullen as much as she was simply waking up from the sexual dead. It *had* been two years. And she had been feeling like her normal self for at least three months. Maybe this was just a stage?

She peeked at Cullen, knowing that beneath that soft sweater was a very hard male body. Something sweet and syrupy floated through her. Moving her gaze upward, she met his simmering dark eyes and knew she could get lost in them.

She swallowed. Nope. Not a stage. It was him. She was attracted to *him*.

He turned to walk back to the office. Following him, she caught Harry's hand and brought him along with her.

"As far as the financials go, I don't want those fancy reports that go out in the annual statement. I want the spreadsheets. The nuts and bolts."

She stopped with a frown. She had access to everything, but if he was looking for the whys behind the line entries, she couldn't help him. "Why didn't you call Nolan, the accountant?"

He faced her. "Are you saying you can't get me the financials?"

"No. I have them. Everything is in my filing cabinet. But—"

She stopped talking. First, his eyes were simmering sexily again and her whole body began to hum—which made her want to groan in frustration. Second, she was making this harder than it had to be. All she had to do was find a few documents for him. The faster she found them, the sooner she'd be at home making cookies.

She squeezed Harry's hand. "I can get you anything you need."

"Thank you."

Cullen turned and resumed his walk to the executive suite. Wendy and Harry scurried behind him.

In her office, she stripped off her coat and removed Harry's. Cullen stood patiently by her desk as she rummaged through her purse for the key to the filing cabinet. Walking over, she noticed the door to her boss's office was open. Papers were strewn across his desk.

"Oh, you're already working?"

Cullen nodded. "I typed a few letters. But there isn't a printer in the office. I'm guessing I have to send my things to a remote printer, but I'm not sure which one is which."

"E-mail them to me and I'll print them."

"Why don't you just come to the computer with me and show me which printer to send them to?"

Okay. So he didn't want her to see what he'd written. No big deal. Whatever he wanted to print was probably personal. Not her business. She not only got the message; she also agreed. The less she knew about this man and the faster she got away from him, the better.

She unlocked the cabinet, pulled out the accordion file that contained the backup documentation for the financials for the year that had passed and handed it to him.

He glanced at the packet, then back up at her. Her stomach flip-flopped. His eyes were incredible. Dark. Shiny. Sexy. And the perfect complement to his angular face. He had the look of a matador. Strong. Bold. Everything about him was dramatic, male.

"Is the forecast in here?"

With a quick shake of her head, she rid herself of those ridiculous thoughts, not sure where the heck they kept coming from but knowing they were absolutely wrong. She returned her attention to the open drawer and pulled the file folder for the five-year plan. "Here you go."

"Great."

Cullen took the folder from her hands and stepped back. He'd thought that bringing in Paul's administrative assistant would make his life easier, but this woman wasn't at all what he'd been expecting. For a widow, she was young and incredibly good-looking. Long, loosely curled red hair fell to the shoulders of her thick green cable-knit sweater. Her cheeks had become pink in the cold, accenting the green of her eyes. Low-riding jeans hugged a shapely bottom.

He wasn't sure what the heck had happened when she'd fallen into his arms after she'd slipped on the ice. Their eyes had met and he'd felt a jolt of something so foreign it had rendered him speechless. He couldn't blame it on the fact that she was attractive. He knew hundreds of gorgeous women. Women even prettier than she was. He couldn't say it was because she was sexy. He knew sexy women. And he couldn't say he'd felt a jolt because he was happy to see her. He didn't know her.

But whatever the hell that jolt was, he was smart enough to ignore it.

He was also taking that damned bell off the door. The whole point of having an executive entry was so the workers didn't know when he was there or he wasn't!

"Come on. Show me how to send these letters to a remote printer."

She followed him into the office of the current company president and her little boy followed her.

"What's your name?"

"Harry."

Cullen couldn't help it; he laughed. "Like Harry Potter?"

"No, like my grandpa."

He turned to Wendy Winston. "So your father was a Harry?"

"No, *his* grandfather's name was Harry."

Confused, Cullen stopped and faced them again. He looked from Wendy to Harry and back to Wendy again. They didn't look a thing alike. So the kid probably resembled his dad which meant that Grandpa Harry had been her late husband's dad. Whatever the deal, he really didn't care. He was trying to make light conversation so the afternoon would go more smoothly. If they wanted to play guessing games, he wasn't interested.

He turned and walked behind the desk, falling into the uncomfortable desk chair. With a few keystrokes he minimized his letters and left a blank screen. He rose and motioned for Wendy to take a seat in the chair.

"Show me which printer to send these to."

She sat. "Okay. Well, you just do all the things you need to do to print—" Using the mouse, she clicked the appropriate icon to get the print menu.

When the print menu popped on the screen, he leaned down to get a closer look. The scent of something floral drifted to his nose. With a slight movement of his eyes, he took in her shiny red hair—more the color of cinnamon than autumn leaves—then let his gaze drift down to her shapely breasts.

Damn it! Why did he keep looking at her?

"Once you get this screen, you scroll to the top, click this menu to get the available printers, and choose this printer. Your documents will be sent to the printer by my desk."

He cleared his throat. "Okay. I get it. Thank you. You can go now."

She rose from the desk chair and caught Harry's hand. "I can leave?"

"Yes. All I wanted were the financials and production reports, and to know which printer was closest." He plopped down on the chair again and she turned to go but another thought struck him. "Wait!"

She faced him.

"You aren't leaving town, are you?"

She laughed and he frowned. The last review in the personnel file for Wendy Winston had described her as quiet and unassuming, but extremely capable. He'd never know that from her behavior today. Of course, the way he kept staring at her, his attention continually caught by parts of her body he normally wouldn't look at with an employee, wasn't normal either. All because she'd fallen into his arms.

So maybe that brush had affected her as much as him? And maybe he should just ignore the way she was acting?

After a few seconds of silence, she gasped. "Oh, you weren't kidding about my leaving town?"

"Why did you think I was kidding? Everybody else in this company is out of town."

She gaped at him. "Because it's the holiday! People are going to parties and visiting friends and relatives for Thanksgiving!"

"Right." Because his holiday had been uneventful he'd almost forgotten it altogether. He looked down at his papers, then back up at her. "I'm not Scrooge. I'm just trying to make sure I don't lose my source for information."

She pulled in a breath. Her breasts rose and fell. Realizing he was staring, he jerked his eyes upward, cursing himself for acting like a horny teenager.

"No, Harry and I are staying in town. Even weekends."

"Great." Forcing his mind off her sweater and to the mission he was here to accomplish, he rubbed his hands together over the keyboard. "I'll call you if I need you."

She turned and left the office. Though Cullen had thought his attention was on the family business, where it was supposed to be, he couldn't resist glancing up to watch the sway of her hips as she left.

Because her back was to him, he braced his elbow on his desk and his chin on his closed fist, letting himself watch as he tried to figure this out. He felt bewitched. But he couldn't be. They hadn't spent more than ten minutes together. And she wasn't his type. He liked blondes. And she was a widow. A serious woman, not to be trifled with.

So he wouldn't trifle. He would be the perfect gentleman for the few weeks he had to run this company, and then he'd leave Barrington, Pennsylvania, and, he hoped, never again even set foot in the town that bore his family's name.

Wendy hustled Harry into the foyer of her echoing home. Her house was a monstrosity, a five-bedroom, three-bath mansion built in the eighteen hundreds that had been updated with the times, but had gone into disrepair when the last owner had left town and let it sit empty for over a year. She and her husband had purchased it with the idea of turning it into their dream home. They'd gotten as far as ripping out carpeting and finishing the hardwood floors throughout the house, chucking wood paneling in favor of plastered walls and installing a new furnace, roof and windows. But Greg had died before they even touched the bathrooms or the kitchen, which could best be described as early-American. As in Revolutionary War.

She turned up the thermostat to accommodate the howling wind outside and pointed Harry in the direction of the kitchen.

Creamsicle, her fat orange-and-white cat, thumped down the stairs and wrapped himself around her legs in greeting.

She motioned to the cat, diverting Harry's attention to him. "Harry, this is Creamsicle. Creamsicle, this is Harry."

The cat blinked. Harry grinned. "You have a cat!"

"Yes, but he's old and moody, so you have to be nice to him." She stooped down to pet Creamsicle, who ignored Harry—which was probably for the best. "I seem to remember something about Christmas cookies."

Harry's eyes grew as big as her cat's belly. "Can we make them red and green?"

She began walking to the kitchen. "Hey, if you want to paint stained-glass windows on the church cookies, that's fine by me."

"We're making churches?"

"I have a cutter for a church. One for Santa. An angel."

She walked to the cabinet by the refrigerator. Her cupboards were knotty pine that actually made her dizzy. Especially when combined with the green-and-white print in the linoleum floor. She'd replaced the busy leaf-print curtains with simple taupe panels, removed the floral wallpaper and painted the walls a soothing sage color. But she hadn't been able to replace the cabinets or the floor and the floor/cabinet combo sometimes gave her motion sickness.

"Here's a bell, a wreath, a Christmas tree," she said, pulling the cookie cutters from the deep drawer. "Let me grab the ingredients for the cookies and we'll get this show on the road."

"Don't you think I should take off my coat first?"

She laughed, walking toward him, as Creamsicle waddled in and took his place on the floor in the corner, watching her and the newcomer.

"I don't have any kids so I'm going to forget some obvious things every once in a while." She unzipped his coat and tugged on the sleeve to pull it off then yanked his cap off his head. "Don't be afraid to remind me!"

"Okay." He pushed his glasses up his nose.

After stowing his coat and hat in the hall closet, Wendy gathered sugar, vanilla and flour from the cupboards and eggs, butter and milk from the refrigerator. Harry climbed on a chair.

"Oh, no! No sitting for you! You have to help."

He peeked up at her. "Really?"

"Sure." She handed him a measuring cup. "Fill that with flour."

Standing on the chair, he peered into the canister, then back at her. "Fill it?"

"Just dip it in." She cupped his soft little hand over the handle of the measuring cup and scooped it into the flour to fill it. "See? Like that."

"Cool!"

"I'm guessing you've never baked before."

He shook his head. "My mom didn't have time."

Wendy nearly cursed at her stupid mistake. The last thing she wanted to do was remind him of his mother, but before she had a chance to say anything, the phone rang.

Wendy walked to the wall unit talking. "You never having baked isn't a big deal. In fact, it will be fun for me to teach you. Something new for both of us." She lifted the phone receiver. "Hello?"

"This isn't the right forecast."

"Oh, hello, Mr. Barrington."

"This forecast has *draft* written on it. Every copy in the file has *draft* stamped on it. Isn't there a final version?"

"Yes." She thought for a second, wondering why her final copy wasn't in the file, but in the end decided it didn't matter. "I probably have to print you another copy."

"Great. I'll see you when you get here." He paused then added, "And don't dillydally."

He hung up the phone.

She sighed. "Harry, do me a favor and put the butter back in the fridge."

He scooted off the chair and took the butter to the refrigerator. Right behind him with the milk and eggs, Wendy caught the door as he opened it.

"This is so much fun!"

She frowned. "Getting things out and putting them away again is fun?"

"Having somewhere to go!"

"You like going to work?"

"I like going *anywhere*. My mom didn't go places." He frowned then glanced at the floor. "She was sick."

Wendy stooped down in front of him. Her own pang of loss rippled through her as she remembered Betsy. "I know she was sick. And I'll bet you miss her. But I don't think she'd want you dwelling on her."

"What's dwelling?"

"Thinking about her when she can't be here. I'll bet she'd want you to think happy thoughts this close to Christmas."

Even as the words came out of her mouth they brought a rush of memory. Her mom had told her the same thing about Greg. That she shouldn't dwell on him, their plans, their life. She remembered thinking that her mom was right and still being angry that he'd died, had left her when she'd loved him so much, needed him so much. Two years without him had taught her to be stronger, bolder and independent enough never to fall into the trap of needing a man the way she had Greg. But when her mom had said those words, she'd been devastated.

Harry, however, nodded sagely.

She rose and helped him with his coat. After shrugging into her own coat and getting her purse and keys from the table in the foyer, she caught Harry's hand and led him outside into the driving wind and freezing rain.

Ice now covered tree branches and clung to the mailboxes of the row of older, but well-tended homes. She paused in front of her little blue car, studying the icicles that hung from the door handle. It was so easy for a car to slide on ice. Walking might be safer. "I'm not sure about this."

"About what?"

"The plant isn't very far from here. We could actually walk."

But it was raining. And Harry was a little boy. A simple ten-minute walk for her might not be so easy for short legs. She frowned. "Never mind. We'll drive."

As they waited for the car windows to defrost, she said, "So do you know what you want to be when you grow up?"

"A fireman."

"That's a great job."

"I want to save people."

Wendy yanked her gearshift out of Park and into Drive. With his mother's passing so fresh in his memory, there was no way Wendy would let him go down that road. Not this close to Christmas. If nothing else, she intended to give this little boy a break from reality. A few days or weeks of comfort and joy while social services employees hunted for his dad.

"Maybe if you're good enough with the cookies, you might want to consider being a baker."

He giggled. "Girls are bakers."

"Not really." As they drove to the plant, they talked about the different kinds of jobs he could consider then she took his hand again to help him navigate the icy parking lot. This time she needed her key to get in.

When they arrived in her office, Cullen Barrington was standing by her desk, looking at his watch.

"Five minutes? I told you to hurry, but I didn't mean for you to be reckless."

"I wasn't. I don't live far." She rubbed her hands together before removing her coat. "We actually considered walking, but it's freezing out there."

"If you think you're cold, you should be me. In Miami the temperature rarely falls below sixty. I'm lucky that I remembered to bring a winter coat. Even with it I shiver."

He was trying to make small talk, to be nice, she supposed, to take the sting out of calling her into the office again, and she smiled at him. He returned her smile and her nerve endings shimmered with life and energy, even as her brain filled with silly, romantic notions. Maybe this incredibly handsome man wasn't a Scrooge after all? Maybe beneath that playboy exterior was a nice guy? Then all these feelings she had of drowning in his dark eyes wouldn't be wrong. Maybe she'd get to kiss that mouth, be held in his strong arms—

Luckily, he had turned and didn't see her shaking her head to clear those thoughts. They were ridiculous! Even thinking about getting involved with someone like him was dangerous. He probably practiced being nice to seduce unsuspecting females like her! She needed to keep her feet firmly grounded in her real world. She was strong now, independent, not dreamy as she had been when she'd fallen for Greg. Cullen needed one little thing printed, the forecast, then she and Harry could go home and bake.

She slid onto her desk chair, turned on her computer, hit a few keystrokes and the room went dark.

CHAPTER TWO

"WHAT did you do?"

So much for thinking that deep down inside he was a nice guy. "I didn't do anything!"

A childish whimper floated to Wendy. Her office didn't have a window, so when the lights went out, the room became pitch-black.

She bounced from her seat. "Harry, everything's fine. The ice probably brought down a power line or two."

"Damn."

That had been Cullen.

Sliding her fingers across the edge of her desk, she began feeling her way to Harry. Instead, she bumped into Cullen's thighs. Once again solid muscle greeted her and she jerked her hands away. It seemed fate was determined to find ways for her to touch him.

"Sorry!"

He cleared his throat. "It's fine. I think Harry's about two paces to your left."

She found her way to Harry. Putting her hand on his shoulder for security, she said, "Here's what we'll do. It's still light outside, so we can open the drapes in Mr. McCoy's office." She squeezed the little boy's shoulder. "Is it okay for me to go and do that?"

Harry said, "Yes."

"Okay. You stay here." She carefully navigated past her desk, praying Cullen hadn't moved in the thirty seconds she'd spoken with Harry.

"Don't you have a flashlight or something?"

Cullen's voice came from behind her, thank God.

"I'm sure there's one in maintenance. Would you like to walk through the dark plant and then down the dark-as-night steps to the basement to get it?"

"Very funny."

In another few seconds she found her boss's desk and walked to the window behind it. Running her hands along the curtain, she found the pull string and opened the drapes. Pale light filtered in, but it was enough that she could see Harry and Cullen.

"If you guys want to sit in here, I'll—"

Before she finished her sentence, Harry raced into the office. She stooped and caught him as he threw himself at her. "Are you okay?"

"Yeah," he said, but he hugged her fiercely.

Looking away, Cullen scrubbed his hand across his mouth. "Now, what do we do?"

"It depends on how long it takes for the electricity to come back on." She rose and grabbed Harry's hand. "Benny Owens works just inside the door to the plant. He has a radio. It runs on batteries. It's a mandate of our safety manual because in an emergency, we can tune it to the local station and hear what's going on. There are five of them in strategic locations throughout the building. Benny's is the closest."

"Makes sense."

"I'm the most familiar with the plant layout so I'll go and get the radio." She stooped in front of Harry. "Do you want to stay here with Mr. Barrington or come with me?"

He glanced at Cullen, then back at her, pulled in a big breath and said, "I'll keep an eye on him."

Wendy laughed, rose and tousled his hair. The kid certainly caught on fast. "This should only take about five minutes."

Standing in the semi-dark room with the uncomfortable little boy who'd promised to keep an eye on him, Cullen frowned. One minute turned into two. Two turned into three. Harry began to squirm.

"Don't worry. Your mom will be back soon."

The little boy peered up at him. "She's not my mom."

"Your aunt?"

He shook his head. "She's nothing."

Cullen frowned. "Nothing?"

Harry pushed his glasses up his nose. "I'm a frosting child."

"A *frosting* child?"

"You know. Somebody else has to take care of me until portal services decides what to do with me."

"Portal services?"

Exasperated, Harry said, "The place that puts kids in a home."

"Oh! *Social services*. You're a *foster* kid."

He nodded. "Yeah. My mom died."

Cullen's heart stopped. Sadness filled him. Hoping he'd heard wrong, he said, "Your mom died?"

He nodded again.

Cullen bent down to talk to Harry on his own level. "Mine did, too."

"Really?"

"A few months ago. January." He shook his head in wonder. Time had certainly flown. "It's been almost a year, but I still miss her."

"I miss my mom, too." He caught Cullen's gaze. "She was sick though. Everybody says she's happy now."

Cullen nearly cursed. At the wake when people had told him his mother was in a better place, he'd believed it. But it was cruel to tell this little boy his mom preferred leaving him to staying with him.

"I'm guessing you don't have any aunts or uncles?"

He shook his head.

Though he hesitated, half afraid of the answer, Cullen asked, "Where's your dad?"

Harry shrugged. "He's around somewhere." Then he flapped his arms in exasperation, as if this is what he'd seen and heard adults do when they talked about his dad. "We'll find him eventually."

The kid was just a tad too observant.

The light from the window in Mr. McCoy's office thinned as Wendy walked farther into the building, but when she reached the main corridor, emergency lights were lit. She scrambled to the door and into the plant. At Benny Owens's workstation, she snatched the radio and quickly made her way back to Cullen and Harry.

The second she stepped into the office, Cullen caught her gaze. His normally bright eyes were soft, sincere.

"Harry was telling me about his mom."

"Oh." She glanced at Harry, who looked up at her with a smile. "You okay, little guy?"

Still smiling, he nodded.

Whatever had happened between the two of them, Harry was okay. He might have even gotten afraid in the dark again and Cullen had taken care of him. Surprising, but good. She turned to smile at Cullen in thanks, but when their gazes caught, that funny feeling happened in her stomach again. Only this time, her chest also tightened. It became hard to breathe. She sort of felt as if she were drowning in the deep pools of his eyes, once again overwhelmed by the strange instinct that deep down he really was a nice guy—

The church bell across the street rang twice, jolting her back to reality.

"Must be two o'clock," she said, brightly, trying to pretend nothing *had* happened because nothing had happened. So they'd looked into each other's eyes? It wasn't a big deal.

Setting the radio on her boss's desk, she said, "I forgot about the emergency lights. The corridors are well-lit. The plant has emergency lighting, too."

She turned on the radio and slowly moved the dial until she found the local station. The announcer said, "The mayor is telling everybody to just sit tight—"

She glanced at Cullen. "Either I have perfect timing or this is an emergency broadcast that's repeating."

"To repeat… Trees and power lines are down all over town. Route 81 has been shut down due to accidents."

Cullen cursed.

She faced him. "What?"

"That's the only highway out of town. The only way to get to my hotel."

"I'm sure it will be open before you want to go back."

"Since I can't work without a computer, I want to go back now."

"Good point."

They both glanced at the radio.

"I'm sorry to say, folks," the announcer said, "the power

company is warning that this is going to be an all-nighter. Get out your candles, light your fireplace, and be careful."

The announcer stopped talking and a song floated from the radio. Wendy shifted away from the desk. Technically, she and Harry could leave. They could even bake their cookies. She had a gas stove. And a fireplace. They could roast marshmallows and sleep in sleeping bags on the living-room floor.

This could actually be the most fun day of his stay with her.

She put her hand on Harry's shoulder, took another step back, easing toward the door.

It almost seemed wrong to leave. Almost. The truth was she didn't know Cullen Barrington. And she was attracted to him. The first man since Greg. That left her feeling odd enough. When she added that he was a playboy, out of her reach, the man who owned the company she worked for, in front of whom she'd prefer to be on her best behavior, not walking around a dark old house with a flashlight… Well, it was for the best that she not invite him to her home. She shouldn't feel guilty for leaving him to figure out what he'd do for the next twelve to twenty-four hours—in the dark—when she not only had light and warmth, she could also cook dinner.

While he sat in the dark? Slept on the floor with his jacket for a cover?

Damn it!

Why couldn't her conscience just shut up long enough for her to get to her car?

"Do you want to come with us?"

His head jerked up. "Where are you going?"

"As you said, we can't work in the dark. So Harry and I are going home. I have a gas stove and a working fireplace in the living room. Even my hot-water heater is gas. We can be without power for a week and the only thing we'll miss is television."

"I don't watch television."

"Then you should be fine."

He growled as if annoyed with the inconvenience of humbling himself to go to the home of an employee, and she said a silent prayer that he'd be stubborn enough—or maybe independent enough—to decide he'd rather sit alone in the office, maybe reading files by the emergency lights in the corridor, than go with her.

Please, God...

He pulled in a breath. "Okay. Fine. Let me get my coat."

CHAPTER THREE

THEY stepped out into the parking lot and Cullen motioned to the right. "That's my rental car."

"And it's a fine car," Wendy said, "but with power lines down, we can't drive. We don't want to become part of the problem."

Cullen ignored her sarcasm in favor of more pressing concerns. "Part of the problem?"

"We could get halfway home, come across a tree that's down and either have to leave our cars in the middle of the road or drive back here and walk anyway."

She faced him. Sunlight sparkled off the thick ice on the trees surrounding the parking lot, encircling her with a glow that made her look like a shimmering angel. He shook his head to clear the haze, but there was no haze. She truly sparkled in the icy world they were caught in.

"So what do you say we skip the first few steps we know might not work, and just walk?"

Great. Maybe a little exercise would help him get himself back to normal around her. "Fine."

"Good. You can carry Harry."

He gaped at her. "Carry Harry?"

"It's a ten-minute walk. And he's a forty-pound kid. Are

you telling me that rich guys are too soft to carry forty-pound kids?"

He snatched the little boy off the ground and hoisted him to his shoulder. Not that he took her bait about him being soft. He liked Harry. Who wouldn't? The kid had suffered the kind of loss that would flatten most adults, yet he was taking it like a man. He deserved a little special treatment.

"You have a smart mouth."

She grimaced. "Not usually."

He didn't want to hear that. He didn't want to know that she was behaving out of character in his presence. It was confirmation that she was attracted to him, too. If they were attracted to each other and about to spend the night together that might be trouble. Of course, if she was being smart with him it could be because she didn't like the attraction any more than he did—which should make them perfectly safe.

Occupied with his thoughts, Cullen slipped on the ice and bobbled Harry, who squealed with delight. "This is fun!"

"Always happy to oblige," Cullen told Harry, before he leaned toward Wendy and whispered, "Italian loafers weren't made for walking on ice."

"It's a very short walk. Ten minutes tops." She pointed to the grassy strip beside the sidewalk. "But if I were you I'd walk in that."

He stepped into the bumpier grass and found the footing a little more solid. Harry groaned. "Darn."

With his hands on Harry's thighs, holding him on his shoulders, Cullen shook his head. "Kids. You think the weirdest things are fun."

Harry giggled. Cullen's spirits unexpectedly lifted, but he told himself to settle down. He might want to make Harry's life a little brighter, but he wasn't here for fun and games. He had to work with Wendy Winston for the next few weeks. He had to be nice to her, but he also had to keep his distance. He didn't want to accidentally start a relationship that would have to end when he left.

He stayed quiet the rest of the way to her home. Walking on the grass, he managed to slip only a time or two, but that provided Harry with a few laughs, and Wendy with something to talk about with Harry.

Suddenly she turned up an icy walkway to the right, and Cullen stopped.

Oh. Dear. God.

"Come on."

Swallowing back a protest, Cullen carefully navigated the walkway and the five icy stairs to the wide front porch. They stepped inside a freezing-cold foyer with beautiful hardwood floors, a new paint job and a modern table holding a ginger-jar lamp and a stack of unopened mail.

She stripped off her coat. "As soon as I light the fireplace and turn on the oven, the downstairs will be toasty warm." Heading for the kitchen, she called over her shoulder, "If you're cold, don't take off your coat until the place heats up."

He slid Harry to the floor. The little boy immediately shucked his coat, found the hall closet and tossed it inside. Cullen grimaced. He'd look like a real wimp if he stayed in his coat, so he shrugged it off and followed Harry into the kitchen.

Wendy beamed at Harry. "Oh, you took off your own coat!"

Harry nodded. "I saw you put it in the closet before so I know what to do now."

Cullen caught the exchange but he was too busy staring at the kitchen cabinets to comment.

Wendy winced. "I know they're ugly."

"My father hated them, too."

Her pretty green eyes widened. "This was your house? Your family was the rich family that left town and neglected it?"

"That would be us."

"And your mother is responsible for this floor?"

He shrugged. "It was the eighties. Linoleum was all the rage."

"Yeah, but now I'm stuck with it. I should shoot at least one of you."

Cullen heard her, but didn't respond. Memories of conversations over breakfast with Gabby, the Barrington's housekeeper, came tumbling back.

Are you ever going to learn to make pancakes?

No.

I like pancakes!

Little boys aren't supposed to get everything they want. Makes them spoiled.

Gabby hadn't been mean about it. She'd laughed. She was a fun, easygoing woman who sometimes even sat at the table and ate scrambled eggs and toast with him before she drove him to school.

"I asked if you wanted anything to drink."

Hearing Wendy's question, he spun to face her. Standing by the open refrigerator, she held a pitcher of something pink. "What is it?"

"Pink lemonade."

"Got any bottled water?"

"I have tap water."

"That's fine."

"Glasses are in the cupboard." She pointed at the one by the sink. "Help yourself."

Walking to the sink, he watched her pour a drink for Harry and one for herself then carry eggs, butter and milk to the center island after storing the lemonade. He tried to remember his mom even being in the kitchen, let alone cooking, and not one memory surfaced.

"We're baking cookies, if you want to help."

He turned at Wendy's question. Her smile was forced. Her eyes not as bright as they had been. She obviously didn't want his help and he wasn't really in the mood to remember things that only made him a weird combination of angry and sad.

"No, if you have a book somewhere I wouldn't mind passing the time reading."

She relaxed. "I have a roomful of bookcases stuffed with just about anything you could want. Third door…"

"On the right. I know. It used to be a library and office. That's why there are built-in bookcases."

"Okay. Just open the drapes. When it starts to get dark, we'll break out the candles and flashlights."

"Great."

He entered the library feeling a mix of nostalgia and disappointment. His mother had worked in this room every night and most weekends. But Wendy didn't have a desk and leather chairs. Instead, a chaise sat by the bay window. A well-worn yellow comforter lay across the foot. The room that had been a place of work was now a place of peace and quiet. He scanned her titles, found a thriller by a favorite author, and settled in on the chaise.

After an hour, the scent of fresh-baked cookies drifted into the room. He closed the book and inhaled deeply before rising from the chaise and walking into the kitchen.

"Smells good in here."

Green icing on the tip of his nose and flour across one cheek, Harry grinned at him from his chair beside the kitchen island. "I'm painting stained-glass windows on a church."

Cullen laughed. "No kidding!"

Wendy looked offended. "Hey, I can get pretty fancy with my cookies."

Glancing at the rows of already painted cookies on the far end of the island, Cullen nodded. "So I see."

Harry nodded. "You paint one, Mr...."

"This is Mr. Barrington," Wendy supplied.

"Since we're kind of in close quarters and unusual circumstances I think you might as well call me Cullen."

"Okay, Cullen!" Harry said, handing him a cookie. "You paint this one. It's a bell."

"I see that."

"So paint it."

"With frosting," Wendy qualified. "But you should also wash your hands first."

He was going to say no. He'd never done anything like this in his life and he was too old to start now. But just the mention of the word *frosting* squeezed his heart. Unable to catch every word said about him, Harry had repeated what he thought he'd heard and had called himself a frosting child. In a way he was. He was a sweet little boy left in the hands of a cold, sterile system. How could Cullen turn away the request of a child who'd just lost his mother?

"Okay."

He washed his hands, picked up his cookie again and chose a paintbrush from those assembled beside the colorful cups of frosting. He watched Wendy dip her brush into the yellow icing and paint the bell she held a bright yellow, then switch brushes to add red icing to create a bow. He mimicked her movements, except he dipped his brush in blue. He covered his cookie in pale-blue frosting and painted the bow shape at the top white.

Harry approved it with a smile. "I like it."

"I like it, too, but you know what? I'm kind of getting hungry."

Wendy said, "Let me finish up here and I'll make hamburgers."

"Actually, I make a great hamburger. You said your gas stove will work, right?"

She nodded. "That's how we made these cookies."

"Then you guys just go ahead and keep painting. I'll make burgers and by the time you're done, dinner will be ready."

Wendy smiled. Cullen's heart tripped over itself in his chest. Now that they were in a comfortable environment, he'd begun thinking of things a little more normally. But that wasn't necessarily good. Instead of envisioning off-the-wall images like sparkling angels when he looked at her, he was now thinking how he'd like to kiss the lips that had pulled upward into a smile. They were a soft reddish color. Untarnished by lipstick or gloss. Very real. Plump. Tempting.

But that was wrong. They'd be working together for the next weeks. Visions of angels were one thing. Actually wanting to kiss his employee was another. Anything he said or did could turn into a sexual-harassment suit. He had to stop this and stop it right now.

He walked to the refrigerator and pulled out the hamburger. "What's going to happen to everything in your refrigerator if the power stays out for a long time?"

"If we don't open the refrigerator often, lots of it will be okay. Plus, I have blocks of ice in the freezer for times when this happens. It acts like a big cooler. Everything in there will stay frozen and I can put the important things from the refrigerator in there, if I need to."

"You're pretty smart."

Holding a cookie she'd just painted with bright-red frosting, she laughed. "Yeah. Right."

Happy to have their minds back on work, he said, "You are. All your performance appraisals say that."

"You read my performance appraisals?"

"I read your file this morning. You are my administrative assistant for the next four weeks. I figured I'd better know who I was getting."

"Oh." She placed her cookie on the aluminum foil that lined the far end of the island and reached for another one. "So, how did you learn to cook?"

He grimaced. "Our housekeeper taught me."

"That's right. Your mom was the last company president."

He nodded. "My dad owned an investment firm and my mom ran the factory, so my parents were overly busy. Our housekeeper was the one who fed me, nudged me to get dressed, drove me to school…" He pointed at the stove. "And taught me to cook. Nothing fancy, just the basics. Eggs. Hamburgers." He shrugged. "That kind of stuff."

"So that makes you pretty handy to have around the house."

He laughed. "And also a good roommate for everybody in college."

"Where did you go to school?"

He could tell she was only making casual conversation, but he nonetheless felt odd, as if he were bragging and he winced. "Harvard."

"Ah. Right."

"Where'd you go to school?"

"Community college for two years, then I met my husband and realized I could be an administrative assistant while he did his internship at the local hospital. When he died, I probably should have gone back for a degree." She shrugged. "But I just never found anything I wanted to study."

"I'm sorry. I didn't mean to pry."

* * *

With her focus on choosing the next cookie to paint, Wendy shrugged again. "It's all right." She said the well-practiced words easily, but the emptiness that shuddered through her contradicted them. Still, as she'd told Harry, she shouldn't dwell. She'd moved on. Gotten tougher, smarter. "It's been two years since Greg died."

Surveying the cookies to be painted, Harry casually said, "Cullen's mom died this year."

Wendy spun to face the stove. "Now, *I'm* sorry."

"As you said, it's all right. She actually died in January. So my dad and I are pretty much beyond it."

Finished patting the hamburgers into shape, Cullen poked through cupboards, looking for a frying pan. Wendy watched him, feeling a shift in the funny catch she got in her heart every time she looked at him. Hearing about his mom's death reminded her that he was as human as everybody else. But was it really good to begin seeing him as a normal man? Wasn't it wiser to continue thinking of him as a super-good-looking but unapproachable playboy?

By the time the hamburgers were ready, Wendy and Harry had finished painting their cookies, and laid them on the island to dry. Wendy pulled paper plates from the pantry and handed them to Harry.

"Since we're not sure when we'll get power again, it's probably a good idea for us not to dirty too many dishes."

Harry scurried to the round table in the corner of the room and arranged the plates in front of three chairs. Cullen set a platter of hamburgers in the center.

Wendy found the plastic cutlery and carried it to the table along with a bag of hamburger buns and a bag of potato chips. "We can eat reject cookies for dessert."

"Sounds good to me," Cullen said, pulling a seat up to the table.

But Harry stopped him. "I want to sit there!" he said, shifting Cullen to the left, to the place beside Wendy.

Wendy looked over at the little boy. He didn't seem upset. He seemed to genuinely want the seat on the end. So she said nothing. They passed the hamburgers and buns around the table, then the chips. Pale light filtered in from the windows in the top half of the back door. The sun was setting.

"I think I might need to get a candle."

"Do you want some help?"

"No, I'm fine. I just have a feeling it'll be dark before we're done eating." She rose from the table and found the big round candles and matches she kept for times the electricity failed. She lit one of the fat beige candles, set it between the hamburgers and the chips and took her seat again.

As they ate, the light from the window faded and the candle's light replaced it, creating an unfortunately romantic glow. Wendy stole a look at Cullen. He was stealing a glance at her. A sizzle of electricity arced between them. Time stood still as they simply stared into each other's eyes.

"My head looks like a watermelon," Harry said with a giggle, pointing at a shadow cast by the flickering candlelight.

Wendy laughed. It was exactly the comic relief they needed. "So does mine."

Cullen turned to see the wall behind him. He laughed. "So does mine."

Harry settled into his seat again. "I like this."

One of Cullen's black eyebrows rose. "Eating in the dark?"

"No. Laughing."

Wendy glanced at Cullen, again just as he looked at her. This time, instead of chemistry sparking between them, understanding did. This little boy had spent the past months of his life not doing anything, not going anywhere, probably never laughing.

Cullen rose and unexpectedly grabbed Harry, hoisting him over his shoulder and tickling the strip of belly exposed when his T-shirt rose. "Yeah, well, if you like to laugh so much how about this?" He tickled him again and Harry giggled with delight.

Wendy's heart melted in her chest. Never in a million years would she guess somebody like Cullen could be so perceptive, but he was and she was grateful.

"I have a good idea," she said, rising from the table. "Why don't we throw away these dishes and take the cookies into the living room? The fireplace is already lit. We'll put our sleeping bags down on the floor and make popcorn."

Cullen swung Harry to the floor. "Or we could tell ghost stories."

As Harry's small feet touched down he said, "Ghost stories?"

Cullen smiled evilly. "Oh, I know plenty. I spent some time in Gettysburg."

Harry's nose wrinkled. "You were in prison?"

Cullen and Wendy both laughed. Wendy said, "No! Gettysburg is a famous battlefield. But rather than ghost stories," she said, giving Cullen a look, hoping he'd understand, "why don't we tell funny stories?"

Harry jumped up and down. "I love funny stories!" Then he raced out of the kitchen, toward the living room.

Obviously realizing his mistake, Cullen rubbed his hand across the back of his neck. "Sorry. I forgot his mom just died or I never would have mentioned ghosts."

"That's okay. I've slipped up a time or two myself today."

He glanced around. "Have you got any marshmallows?"

Dipping into the pantry and then out again, she displayed

a bag of fat white marshmallows. "I always keep a bag on hand in case I ever want to make s'mores."

"We'll start toasting those over the fire and tell funny stories and he'll forget all about the ghosts."

Wendy smiled her agreement, but her smile faded when he turned away, gathered the catsup and mustard and walked to the refrigerator as if it were very normal for him to be in her kitchen. In a way she supposed it was. This had been his home. But she had the oddest feeling that he was right where he was supposed to be.

And so was she.

Blaming that feeling on the fact that they both called this house home, she shook her head, told herself to stop acting like an idiot and carried the marshmallows to the living room where Harry eagerly awaited her.

They spent the next hour roasting marshmallows and teasing Harry. Then Cullen realized he'd not only have to sleep in his uncomfortable clothes; he'd also have to wear them the next day unless he went to his car.

Wendy grabbed two flashlights from the kitchen and met him at the front door.

"Are you sure you're okay with this?"

"It's a ten-minute walk to my car, remember? I hadn't yet checked into my hotel, so I can grab my duffel bag and be back in twenty-two minutes."

As he spoke, he smiled down at her, and she suddenly knew why she kept getting these odd feelings. In the office when he was Cullen Barrington, owner of Barrington Candies, he was an unapproachable playboy. But here in this house where he was comfortable, with a little boy he couldn't resist being kind to, she was seeing a side of him she would bet few people—if any—had ever seen. And she was beginning to like him.

She quickly looked away and stepped back. She didn't want to like this guy. At least not romantically. This time next month, he'd probably be on a beach or in a casino. There was no sense forming an attachment. But more than that they came from two different worlds, saw life two different ways, probably had totally opposite beliefs about most things. Liking him was just wrong.

"See you when you get back."

He opened the door and pointed at his Italian loafers. "Wish me luck."

Wendy couldn't help it; she laughed. "Luck."

While he was gone, Wendy went to the storage room and found the two sleeping bags that she and her husband had used on camping trips. Because there were only two, she grabbed blankets from the linen closet and brought them along, too.

After she and Harry laid the open sleeping bags on the floor to serve as a cushion, they covered them in blankets. She took Harry upstairs, helped him wash up and eased him into his pajamas. On the way back to the living room they stopped in the library and found a tattered copy of *A Christmas Story*.

By the time Cullen returned, she'd begun reading it aloud to Harry. Cullen took his duffel bag upstairs and returned dressed in sweatpants and a T-shirt. Not interrupting her reading, he slid under the blanket on the other side of Harry. She read a few chapters until Harry's eyelids began to droop and eventually closed completely.

Wendy slid the blanket up to his chin. He snuggled into the pillow.

She glanced over at Cullen and whispered, "This wasn't exactly how I'd hoped our first night would turn out."

"This was your first day with him?"

She nodded.

He laughed softly. "I don't think Harry minded." He pulled

in a breath. "And I have to thank you, too. I'd have been sleeping on your boss's lumpy couch tonight if you hadn't come to my rescue."

"It's nothing."

"No, another employee might have been too intimidated to invite me. I appreciate that you not only opened your home, but you didn't make a big deal of it."

Cullen rose from the makeshift bed and tossed another log on the fire. Levering his hand on the coffee table, he lowered himself to the floor again, but as he pulled his hand away he jarred the table enough that the silver bell decoration in a Christmas flower arrangement rang.

Hearing the bell, Harry squeezed his eyes shut even more tightly.

Please, let Miss Wendy and Cullen get married and adopt me.

He made the wish quickly, just as he had the other two times he'd wished.

The first time he'd wished they'd get married and adopt him had been at the door of Miss Wendy's work, when she'd slipped on the ice. He'd seen her and Cullen look at each other funny like Jimmy Franklin's mom and dad looked at each other, and he knew they could be a mom and dad. *His* mom and dad. So he'd wished and when he was done wishing the bell rang.

Then, when she came back from getting the radio, she and Cullen had looked at each other funny again, he'd wished again and church bells had rung.

He snuggled more deeply into the pillow, a plan forming in his head. What if he made the wish every time he heard a bell ring? He'd tried to wish that his mom would get well and that wish hadn't worked. But maybe that was because he didn't have a bell? So this time, he'd wish every time he heard a bell. And maybe his wish would come true.

CHAPTER FOUR

WENDY woke first. Sunlight poured in from the big window behind the sofa. Guessing it was probably around nine o'clock, she sat up and her back protested.

"Floor's not the most comfortable place to sleep," Cullen whispered.

"You can say that again." She pulled in a breath and smiled ruefully. "My coffeemaker's electric, but if you'd like some tea, we can make that."

"Anything with caffeine is fine."

She rolled over to lift herself off the floor. On the other side of Harry, Cullen did the same.

While Cullen went upstairs to change out of his sweatpants and T-shirt, Wendy boiled water for tea. He returned to her kitchen dressed in dark trousers and a black-and-beige-striped sweater. Her stomach took a tumble. He was so damned good-looking.

She turned back to the stove, poured boiling water over tea bags in two cups and brought them to the table.

"You were very good with Harry last night," he said.

"You're no slouch yourself."

He laughed. "Thank you." He toyed with his tea bag. "So what's the story with him?"

"Right after he and his mom moved in next door, his mom was diagnosed with cancer." She dipped her tea bag in and pulled it out, testing the strength of her tea. "I started visiting once a week to see if she needed anything and soon I was helping her get through chemo. Eventually I was doing pretty much everything at her house." She smiled at the memory. "Including reading Harry a story every night and tucking him in."

"So social services considered you a good candidate to take him in while they look for his dad?"

She snorted a laugh. "Not even close. His mom gave me custody in her will."

"Oh."

Cullen's voice was full of such happy surprise that Wendy shook her head. "Don't get excited. His biological father has first right to custody no matter what Betsy's will says."

"But I can tell you'd really like to be the one to raise him."

She nodded. "I think I could be a great mom. I already love Harry and the thing he needs more than anything right now is just plain love."

"I'm surprised you don't have children of your own."

She licked her lips, so tempted to be honest and confide in him. But she knew the bond they'd formed over the past twenty-four hours was an aberration, so she'd tell him the basics and keep the heartache to herself. "My husband and I were waiting to be more financially secure to have children."

He inclined his head in acknowledgment, holding her gaze as if he knew there was more and waited for her to admit it. When she stayed silent, he said, "So the bottom line is your arrangement with Harry is only temporary."

The fact that he didn't probe or push relieved her as much as disappointed her. She supposed she secretly hoped he wanted the bond, but not pushing her to elaborate proved he didn't.

"There are lots of ways this could play out. They could find his dad and his dad could take him. Or they could find his dad and he could tell them he doesn't want Harry—"

Cullen's eyes widened. "Doesn't want Harry?"

She shook her head. "Harry told me he hasn't seen his dad in so long he doesn't remember what he looks like. He thinks he's in prison."

"That's not good."

Avoiding his gaze, she bobbed her tea bag in and out of the hot water in her cup. "In any event, I have him until they find his dad."

He caught her gaze. His dark eyes were serious and sincere. "That's too bad. I think you're a good pair."

She smiled. "Thanks."

The kitchen became silent as Wendy pulled her tea bag from her cup and added milk and sugar. After taking a sip, she said, "What about you?"

"What about me?"

She shrugged. "I might not have spilled the entire story of my life, but you now know things lots of people at the plant don't know. I think it's only fair you tell me something about yourself so we can keep each other's secrets."

"Honestly, there isn't much to tell. When my parents finally retired, five years ago, they moved to Miami with me, and my dad and I started a small investment firm."

"You have a job?"

"Of course I have a job."

She shook her head. "I'm sorry. I just pictured you in Miami boating, going to parties, taking private jets to Vegas to gamble."

He laughed. "I can still do all that. Rather than create a big firm like my dad had here in Pennsylvania, we kept our Miami firm small. I make appointments when I want them. Schedule myself off a lot. So your guess isn't too far off the mark."

She said, "Ah," and their gazes caught. The sizzle from the day before returned. But this time they both knew it was pointless. He was a strong man who clearly arranged his life the way he wanted it. Just as her late husband had done. Because Greg was so determined, so forceful, so focused, so sure of what he wanted, she'd lost the opportunity to have what *she* wanted…children with him. She vowed she'd never get involved with that kind of man again.

Plus, she might be bolder now, but she was still a small-town woman whose fondest wish was to get custody of the little boy next door. Even if she wanted to take a risk with her new-found independence with someone as clear about his life goals as Cullen seemed to be, she was too simple, too average to fit into his extravagant, exciting world.

They couldn't be further apart if they tried.

The refrigerator motor started. The microwave beeped. The kitchen lights popped on.

Wendy pulled away from Cullen's gaze. "Talk about timing."

He laughed and glanced down at his half-empty tea cup. "Yeah."

"So, are you ready for coffee?"

He shook his head. "I'll get some on the way to the office."

"Do you want me to come in?"

"I'll be fine." He rose from the table. "If Harry's awake I'll say goodbye."

She nodded. Cullen turned and walked out of the kitchen.

Wendy put a pot of coffee together and dropped four slices of bread into the toaster.

A few minutes later, Cullen returned to the kitchen, carrying his duffel bag. "He's still asleep."

"I'll tell him you said goodbye."

"Okay." He turned and headed for the foyer and the front door. A polite hostess, Wendy followed him.

He faced her with a smile. "Thanks for everything."

Her nerves spiked with the sense that his leaving was all wrong, even though she knew it wasn't. There was no reason for him to stay. No reason for her to ask him to stay, except that she enjoyed his company, and they'd already figured out there was no point to that.

Wendy pulled in a breath. "You're welcome."

"I'll see you tomorrow."

She nodded.

He caught her gaze. She smiled slightly. He didn't seem to want to go any more than she wanted him to. A second spun into ten; ten seconds stretched into half a minute. Finally, with their gazes clinging, he lowered his head and touched his mouth to hers.

She wasn't so much surprised by the fact that he'd kissed her as she was by the power in one brush of his lips across hers. The electric sparks they'd been throwing to each other for the past twenty-four hours all congealed and shot lightning through her.

He slowly pulled away, his eyes bright, his expression as dumbfounded as she felt.

"I'll see you at the office tomorrow."

She whispered, "Okay."

And then he was gone. He wouldn't be this warm, this open, this honest with her at the candy factory. She'd never see this Cullen Barrington again.

Wendy was glad for the distraction her curious six-year-old provided. She let him help make eggs and toast for breakfast, then bundled him in his jacket and mittens and took him to the mall.

"What are we shopping for?"

She smiled down at him. "I have three brothers and a mom, so every year I buy each of them a Christmas gift."

"Cool."

"If you're still with me at Christmas, I'll be taking you to Ohio with me for the holiday."

His blue eyes widened. "Out of town?"

She laughed. Everything was an adventure to this child. "Yes."

"Cool."

She laughed and he tugged on her hand to get her attention again.

"Do you think we could buy a bell for Creamsicle?"

"A bell for Creamsicle?"

Behind the brown-framed glasses, Harry's big blue eyes blinked at her. "Yeah."

"Why do you want him to have a bell?"

He tilted his head. "Because it's Christmas?"

"Oh, a *Christmas* bell!"

He smiled. "Yeah."

"I'm not sure he'll wear it, but he does wear a collar. So why don't we look for a new collar with a bell?"

Harry nodded eagerly. "Okay!"

They found a bright red-and-green collar for Creamsicle, complete with a small red sleigh bell. Harry tucked the little bag into the pocket of his jacket with a smile. They shopped for another hour, ate dinner at a local fast-food restaurant and returned home.

Harry immediately yanked the cat collar from his jacket pocket. "Here, Creamsicle!"

"He's not going to come," Wendy said.

Harry ignored her, running to the steps and calling upstairs. "Come here, Creamsicle!"

A few seconds later the rotund orange-and-white cat came thumping down the steps. At the bottom, he wound around Wendy's feet, then Harry's.

Wendy smiled. "He likes you."

Harry peered up at her. "I know." He crouched down and tried to work the buckle on the old collar.

Wendy stooped down beside him. "Here. Let me. I forgot how old this collar was. It was probably time to replace it anyway."

She made short order of the old collar and helped Harry slide the new one around Creamsicle's neck. The cat nudged them both as if saying thanks, and walked away.

Harry frowned. "It doesn't ring."

"It's a small bell. So Creamsicle will have to do something like jump for it to ring."

The little boy considered that then grinned. "That will make it special when it rings, right?"

"Exactly."

Harry's grin grew. Wendy shook her head and led him into the kitchen for a snack. She'd never seen a kid who got such pleasure from little things the way Harry did.

Tired from the day out, Harry fell asleep on the sofa and Wendy carried him up to bed.

When she returned downstairs, she tuned the television to one of her favorite shows, but without the distraction of Harry, her mind drifted back to that kiss with Cullen.

She pressed her fingers to her lips. It was hard to believe that a man like Cullen would find her attractive, let alone that he'd kiss her. But she did eventually make some sense of it.

In their discussion over tea, they'd realized how different they were. They both knew nothing would come of this attraction, so maybe he felt safe in kissing her? He probably considered it a one-time thing. A chance to give in to the attraction, albeit a little, just for a taste.

The very notion made her dreamy and she sighed heavily. Was it so wrong to want a little romance in her life? Just a little. Just something to make her believe that someday she would find somebody else.

Realizing the television show wasn't going to hold her attention, she walked back down the hall to the library, found a book and went to bed.

Because she read most of the night, she woke late and the morning routine she'd envisioned with Harry went to hell. The twenty minutes they had before Harry had to be at school were pure chaos. She'd called the principal on Friday morning, after she'd gotten word that she would get Harry on Saturday morning, and had had them reactivate his records. He was actually returning to the very class he'd left. That part of things worked out so well that she couldn't let him be late for his first day back. She quickly dressed Harry and herself and headed out the door to drive him to school.

She took him to the office where one of the administrative assistants walked him to the room he already knew. Happy that she'd gotten him to school on time, she breathed a sigh of relief, then realized getting him to school on time had made *her* late. She thanked the principal and raced out of the building to her car.

Even driving as fast as was allowed on the quiet streets of Barrington, she was twenty minutes late for work.

At her desk she shucked her coat and scarf, waving silent

hellos to coworkers who said good morning as they passed her door, and walked to the open door of Cullen's office.

Dressed in a dark suit with white shirt and pale-blue tie, he looked as good—as yummy—as he always did.

"Sorry I'm late."

He glanced up from the computer. Their eyes met. Everything female in her burst with life and energy just from the look in his beautiful dark eyes. It was all she could do not to sigh with longing.

Instead, she cleared her throat. "Harry and I had trouble getting accustomed to our morning routine." There was no way she'd tell him that she'd overslept because she hadn't been able to sleep the night before because she'd been thinking about how he'd kissed her. He might be attracted to her, but he'd made his choice. And she'd made hers. Attracted or not, they weren't a good match.

"Ah. First day of school."

"I was lucky enough to get him back into the class he was in before his mom died."

"That's great." He glanced down at his desk then up at her again. "Did you tell him I had to leave? That's why I didn't say goodbye?"

She nodded. "He wants me to invite you to dinner."

He laughed. "Tell him thanks." He paused then added, "But just between you and me, I don't think that's a good idea."

Staring into his dark eyes, she wanted to sigh with disappointment, but they'd actually come to this conclusion at the breakfast table Sunday morning. They were attracted, but different. Too different really to have a relationship. No matter how good the kiss at her door.

"Okay." She took a careful step into the room. "Is there anything you need me to do this morning?"

"I'm fine for now." He caught her gaze again. "But I'd like you to walk with me into the plant when I make my morning rounds."

"To introduce you?"

He nodded.

She smiled. "Okay. Just let me know when you're ready."

She left his office extremely proud of both of them. They were adults who knew better than to give in to silly chemistry. There were too many differences between them. They came from two different worlds. Wanted two different kinds of lives. So they were being smart. Savvy.

It was nearly lunchtime before Cullen had her guide him through the plant. He'd already met with the supervisors, so his trek around the manufacturing floor was to give the regular employees a chance to get comfortable with him.

They stepped through the door separating the office from the cooking area and were immediately immersed in the scent of chocolate. The men by the kettles grunted greetings, but otherwise kept to their work. The men watching the assembly line where chocolate poured over creamy centers, smiled and said, "Hello."

But the female candy packers visibly stared as Wendy introduced him to the group in general.

"These are the first-shift packers."

Cullen smiled and nodded. "Ladies."

"Good morning, Mr. Barrington."

"And back here we have shipping and receiving."

A titter of giggles followed them as they walked away. Wendy pressed her lips together to keep from laughing herself. Cullen had just made himself the object of everybody's fantasies and today's lunchtime topic of conversation.

After visiting the remaining departments, they returned to their work space.

Cullen paused by her desk. "They all seem like very nice people."

He said it as if that surprised him and Wendy gaped at him. "Of course they're nice!"

He rubbed his hand along the back of his neck. "Yes. Of course."

With that, he went into his office and closed the door. Wendy stared at it for a few seconds, thinking his comment was odd, but shook her head to clear it of any thought of Cullen. It was better not to get too involved, especially not to try to figure him out. Plus, it was time for her to go to lunch.

In the small lunchroom, she pulled her brown bag from the refrigerator and made her way to the table where her two friends sat.

"He's cute!" Emma Watson said before Wendy even sat down. Ten years older than Wendy, Emma was a short brunette, married with two kids.

"Yes, he is."

"And you're single," Patty Franks reminded her. A fortyish blonde, recently divorced, Patty continually tried to get Wendy to hit the bar scene with her.

Wendy laughed. "He is a rich man with an exciting life in Miami. What the heck would he want with a little Pennsylvania bumpkin like me?"

Emma and Patty exchanged a look. Emma sighed. "Uh, Miss Pennsylvania Bumpkin, it seems to me you were married to a doctor. I'm guessing you have to know you're the kind of woman a rich guy wants on his arm."

Wendy gaped at her. "You think I want to be on some guy's arm?"

Patty pressed her hand to her chest. "I would kill to be able to attract a guy like that. You should be dressing a little better," she said, pointing at Wendy's simple red sweater. "Wearing perfume. Tempting him."

Wendy's mouth fell open. "Are you nuts?"

"I saw him looking at you," Emma said slyly. "He likes you."

Wendy felt a blush creeping into her cheeks. Maybe she and Cullen weren't as good at hiding their attraction as they believed. A little honesty was the only thing that would nip this in the bud. "Even if we were attracted, think it through. We aren't suited."

"I'm almost tempted to ask you to pretend you are." Patti leaned close to Wendy and whispered, "We could use a spy. There's a rumor going around that he's actually here to close the plant."

Wendy gasped. "That's not true!"

Emma said, "How do you know?"

"Yeah," Patty seconded. "How do you know?"

"Because I know."

"You don't think it's odd that Mr. McCoy suddenly decided to go on vacation?"

"No."

"Or that *the* Cullen Barrington decided to step in for him?"

It *was* odd, and Cullen had behaved oddly on Saturday morning, not letting her see the letters he'd typed. Plus, there was the matter of the missing final copy of the forecast.

She gave herself a mental shake. The company made too much money for Cullen simply to close it. With the profits the company made, the Barringtons shouldn't even be considering selling it. But she couldn't tell her friends that. She knew how much money the company made because she typed the financial reports. Confidentiality precluded her from discussing what she saw.

"No, I don't think it's odd that Mr. Barrington is standing in for Mr. McCoy. I think he has his reasons. He could be here simply because it's been five years since his family were directly involved with the plant. They might have decided it was time one of them was."

"Maybe. But you can't explain away the fact that we haven't gotten a raise since his mom retired. No raises usually means things aren't going well. Now that the Barringtons are in Miami, they don't care about us. They could close this factory—" she snapped her fingers "—like that."

"No. Stop!" Wendy held up her hand. Patty was interpreting the facts all wrong, but Wendy couldn't talk about what she knew from typing confidential financial statements. With everything going on in her life, she also didn't have the quickness of mind to make up an alternative story. "I don't have the brain power to think about this right now. Even if I would date him to spy for you guys, I can't. My plate is full with Harry—"

Patty put her elbow on the table and her chin on her fist. "Really? There's a good chance they'll find his dad tomorrow and Harry won't be an issue."

Only Emma or Patty could be this brutally honest with her, and though right at this minute she wished they couldn't, she also saw Patty's point.

"I just don't want to see you lose a good opportunity," Patty said. "Guys like Cullen Barrington only come along once in a lifetime. If you're not following up on your attraction because of Harry, you could be making a big mistake."

She shook her head. "There's no point to following up when we don't want the same things."

"How do you know you don't want the same things?"

Wendy glanced over at Patty. Damn the woman was quick. But Wendy was quicker.

"Did you look at him? His clothes scream designer names. My clothes are from a discount department store. I don't fit into his world. That is, if he'd even want to make room in his world."

Emma sighed. "You're a pessimist."

Wendy took a bite of her sandwich, chewed and swallowed then said, "I'm a realist." She glanced around to make sure no one else was paying attention then she added, "You guys know what happened with Greg. I let him make all the decisions because he was so sure of where he wanted to go and it cost me the opportunity to have a child."

Emma frowned. Patty rolled her eyes. "So don't let this one make all the decisions."

Wendy toyed with her sandwich. "Not all men are like Greg, but Cul—Mr. Barrington is. Just from the way he works, I can tell he's a man accustomed to giving orders and getting his own way." She wouldn't tell them about his investment-counseling business, about being able to arrange his life any way he wanted, that would prove they'd had a private conversation. As much as she loved Emma and Patty, the gossip would spread like wildfire and Cullen's stay would be hell for both of them. "I want a man who wants a partner, not arm candy."

"Arm candy." Both Emma and Patty grinned.

Emma said, "How appropriate for a guy who owns a candy factory."

"You guys are hopeless." She pulled in a breath and changed the subject. "Things went very well with Harry this weekend."

Emma grinned. "So how does it feel to be a mom?"

"I wouldn't know. I'm not letting myself feel too much. Just as you said, they could find Harry's dad tomorrow."

The buzzer sounded, signaling the end of the lunch break, and Wendy made her way back to her desk and resumed her typical Monday chores. Around two o'clock, Cullen stepped out of his office and handed her some notes he wanted typed. When he returned to his office, he left the door open.

Wendy immediately went to work on the notes. She typed them quickly, e-mailed them to his computer, printed them and slid the hard copy onto his desk.

Without looking up, Cullen said, "Thanks."

Happy that they were behaving like a typical boss and assistant, she returned to her desk and went back to work.

On Tuesday everybody still gossiped about why *the* Cullen Barrington would stand in for the plant manager. Finishing up the Christmas rush might be the reason. But that only spurred more questions that rumbled through the workers on the plant floor. Why had Mr. McCoy taken a vacation during their busiest time of the year? Had he been fired? Was the plant about to close?

Wednesday at lunch, Patty and Emma speculated that Cullen had asked Mr. McCoy to take a vacation and was there as a spy of some sort. That made Wendy laugh. "I can understand you wanting to spy on him. But why would he spy on us? What could he possibly be looking for?"

That stopped Patty cold and made Emma frown in consternation.

At lunch on Thursday they decided he was looking for ways to make his father and himself more money from the factory, and that, Wendy had to concede, made at least a bit of sense.

It actually calmed the gossip, until Emma said, "And if he doesn't, we're history." Then that rumor caught fire and spread throughout the factory.

On Friday the conversation mercifully turned to everybody's plans for the weekend. Patty had a date. Emma was taking her kids for pictures on Santa's lap. Wendy's heart stuttered with joy at just the thought of getting Harry's picture taken on Santa's lap. Also, involving Harry with other kids, especially for a holiday reason, was a good idea.

"Can Harry and I meet you at the mall at about one o'clock?"

Patty rose from the lunch table. "Sounds great. I can't wait to meet him."

"You'll love him."

Wendy made her way back to the office amazed that within six short days she'd not only gotten the hang of thinking of Harry first, but also that the rumors of the plant closing seemed to have died down, if only for the weekend.

At about a quarter to three she heard a noise, looked up and saw Randy Zamias walking into her office.

She pulled in a breath. "Mr. Zamias."

Tall and thin, wearing a neat-as-a-pin brown-tweed suit, Harry's case worker took the remaining steps to her desk. "Ms. Winston."

Because she didn't have a seat in her office to offer him, she rose. "How can I help you?"

"I'm afraid I have some unfortunate news."

"News?"

"Yes, we've located Harry's father."

Her heart stopped. She told herself that Harry would be better off with his biological father, but Harry didn't remember his father. Fear coursed through her. "You have?"

Randy cleared his throat. "Unfortunately, he's dead."

This time the world spun. "That's…" She swallowed, as mixed feelings danced around inside her. Even as her heart swelled at the prospect of getting Harry, it also broke for the little boy who now had no parents. "That's sad for Harry."

Randy pushed his glasses up his long, thin nose. He pulled in a breath. "He was killed in a fight in the prison yard three years ago."

Right about when Harry said he'd last seen his dad. Wendy fell to her seat. "Oh, my God."

Randy sighed heavily. "Betsy had been informed, but by that time she'd divorced him." He shook his head. "There's a lot Betsy didn't tell us when we visited her."

Wendy could only stare at him. The knowledge that Harry's dad was dead was difficult, but she understood Betsy's reasons for not being forthcoming with Mr. Zamias. She had been ill and protecting her child.

Cullen stepped out of his office. He looked from Randy to Wendy and back to Randy again. His eyes narrowed. "Can I help you?"

Wendy quickly said, "This is Mr. Zamias. He's Harry's case worker from social services." She motioned toward Cullen. "And this is Cullen Barrington."

Randy's entire demeanor changed. He went from being a stiff and formal prude, to being awestruck in the blink of an eye. He stuck out his hand to shake Cullen's. "Mr. Barrington! Such a pleasure to have you back in town."

"I'm only here for a few weeks." Cullen turned to Wendy. "Are you okay?"

"Mr. Zamias just told me that Harry's dad is dead."

Cullen looked shocked. "Oh. I'm sorry."

Randy frowned. His beady brown eyes narrowed. His voice dripped with disdain when he said, "So it appears custody falls to you, Ms. Winston."

Not knowing what to say, Wendy stayed silent. She knew Randy Zamias wasn't thrilled with the way she'd demanded the rights granted to her by Betsy's will while social services searched for Harry's father. But with the news of Harry's dad's death, she became Harry's guardian. End of story.

"Don't get smug," Randy said, folding his arms on his

chest. "The will may give you custody, but because Harry was in our system, we can check up on him. Check up on *you*."

Wendy suspected Randy was only blustering because she'd challenged him, but before she could say something conciliatory to smooth things over, Cullen walked to Randy and slid his arm across his shoulders. "If it makes you feel any better, I've been interacting with Harry since he's been in Ms. Winston's custody."

"You have?"

"Yes. If you're concerned about this transition period, I'm in Barrington until Christmas. I can continue to help out while Harry gets adjusted."

"That does make me feel better."

"Great," Cullen said, leading Randy to the door.

Watching the exchange, Wendy didn't know whether to be grateful or appalled. Cullen had taken the entire discussion out of her hands. He hadn't even given her a chance to be her own diplomat. If she had any doubts that Cullen was exactly like Greg, he'd just eliminated them.

The second Randy was out of hearing range, Cullen spun to face her. "What the heck did you do to get on his bad side?"

"When Betsy died, Harry was put into foster care because I didn't know about the will. None of us did." She pulled in a breath and caught Cullen's gaze. "When her lawyer finally contacted me, I immediately petitioned the courts to get Harry while they searched for his dad."

"You made him look bad to his superiors."

"I wasn't saying he made a bad decision, just an ill-informed one. None of us knew about Betsy's will. It wasn't anyone's fault that Harry had gone into a foster home. But I didn't want Harry to be with people he didn't know when he could have been with me." She paused. Though it felt odd to thank him for high-handing her, she knew she had to. "I guess I should thank you for smoothing things over."

"Save your thanks. I might just become a thorn in your side. Since I told old Randy I'd help with the transition, I'll have to take Harry up on his offer of dinner every few nights."

"That I can handle." Sort of. She wasn't happy he had insinuated himself into her life, but she did know his offer had given Randy a graceful out in their situation and he probably wouldn't bother them. Harry was all hers to raise—

She stopped her thoughts as a terrible realization occurred to her. With Harry now officially in her custody, everything to do with the little boy was her responsibility.

She looked at Cullen again. "I have to tell Harry that his father is dead."

CHAPTER FIVE

"Do you want me to be there?"

Wendy bit her lip, considering that. Cullen had promised Randy Zamias he would be part of things while he was in town, but she didn't want Harry to see Cullen in such an important role that he'd grow to depend on him and have a hole in his life when Cullen returned to Miami.

Still, this was a delicate situation and the more people Harry had around him for support, the better.

She glanced at her watch. "I've hired a babysitter who's been staying with him after school until I return from work. I'm trying to decide if it's better to let him have another afternoon of thinking he's got at least some family, or if I should just go home and be honest."

"Let's go be honest."

Leave it to Cullen to make the decision for her. In another twenty seconds she would have said the same thing. Yet, he beat her to the punch. Still, in this case, it really didn't matter. Harry would appreciate having Cullen around when he got the news about his dad. Anything else was irrelevant.

"Okay. Let's go."

They drove their separate cars to her house. Wendy parked

in the driveway beside the babysitter's SUV. Cullen parked on the tree-lined street in front of her house. The ice from the storm over the weekend had melted. Broken limbs had been cleared away. The sun smiled down from a bright-blue sky, but the air was cold, promising that before too long there would be snow on the ground, a sparkling white blanket for Christmas.

She walked into her warm kitchen, where Mrs. Brennon was setting a mug of steaming hot cocoa beside a plate of iced Christmas cookies for Harry's after-school snack.

"Mrs. Winston!"

"Hi, Mrs. Brennon. I know I'm early today but I really need to talk with Harry."

Cullen walked in the kitchen door behind her.

Harry's face instantly brightened. "Cullen!" He bounced off the chair and raced to Cullen to hug him around the thighs. "I missed you."

Cullen stooped down. "Hey, kid."

Harry glanced at Cullen's topcoat, black suit and silk tie. "Were you at work?"

Cullen nodded. "Yeah. With Wendy."

Wendy tapped Harry's shoulder to get his attention. "Why don't you and Cullen eat those cookies while I spend a minute with Mrs. Brennon?"

"Sure!" Taking Cullen's hand, Harry led him to the table.

Wendy directed Mrs. Brennon to the front foyer. She explained that they'd gotten the news that Harry's dad had passed away and they needed to tell him.

Mrs. Brennon's eyes filled with tears. "How sad for that sweet little boy."

"I know."

The babysitter walked to the closet and pulled out her winter coat, mittens and scarf. "I'll just be on my way then."

"Thanks. We'll see you on Monday."

Mrs. Brennon said goodbye and exited through the front door.

Wendy took a deep breath then walked into the kitchen. Cullen had removed his topcoat and hung it on a hook beside the door. He sat at the table eating cookies with Harry.

"Hey, guys."

"Hey, Wendy." Harry peered at her above his glasses. "Cullen likes my cookies better than yours."

"Well, yours were definitely prettier." She took another breath. "How about if we go into the living room for a minute to talk about something?"

Harry grabbed two cookies. "Sure."

He scrambled into the living room ahead of them. Without speaking, Cullen and Wendy followed him. He bounced onto the sofa. Wendy sat on one side. Cullen sat on the other.

"Randy Zamias from social services came to see me today." Harry wrinkled his nose. "He's bad."

"No. He's trying to look out for your welfare," Wendy said. "But he also had some news."

When Harry didn't answer, Cullen touched his forearm and Harry faced him. "About your dad."

Harry looked at Wendy. "My dad?"

"Yes, honey. Randy was searching for your dad and he found him. But he's… Well, he's…"

"He's like my mom, isn't he?"

Wendy nodded. "Yes. I'm sorry. He died."

It took a few seconds for that to really sink in, and when it did, Harry's little face crumpled and tears welled in his eyes.

Wendy took his free hand, as Cullen grabbed the cookies that were falling from his other hand. Harry hadn't seen his father since he was three. Technically, he'd lost his dad years ago. Wendy knew his tears weren't so much from loss, but from fear. Now he was totally alone.

"But this really doesn't change anything. You and I are together. I'm your mom now."

His head down, Harry said, "But it's just us." Tears dropped to his blue-jean-covered thighs. In the silence, Wendy could hear fat Creamsicle thump down the stairs and amble into the room.

Over Harry's bowed head, Wendy met Cullen's gaze. She didn't have a clue how to respond. She knew exactly what Harry meant. He had lost everyone in his life. With only her as a guardian, how could she promise him that he wouldn't someday find himself alone again?

Cullen gave her a look that nudged her to be honest. To say what she felt.

"No matter what happens, I'll be here for you, Harry. I love you."

Creamsicle picked that exact second to jump up on the sofa and into Harry's lap. He nuzzled his nose against Harry's chin. As he did, the little red bell on his collar finally rang.

Harry's head jerked up. He looked from Cullen to Wendy and back at Creamsicle again. Then he rubbed his face in the thick fur of the cat's neck. "Thanks, Creamsicle."

Wendy's heart splintered. She'd never known her ornery cat to be affectionate with anybody but her, but right at that moment she was abundantly glad he'd taken to Harry.

"Okay," Cullen said, rising from the sofa. "Since this has been a bad day, I'm going to take you both out to dinner."

Harry sighed. "I don't want to go anywhere."

"Then," Wendy said, deliberately brightening her voice, not really angry with Cullen for trying to cheer Harry, but noticing again that he never asked. He simply told. "Why don't we make something fun for supper? Like spaghetti?"

Harry's sullen expression didn't change.

Cullen said, "Or hot dogs? We could roast hot dogs here in the fireplace. My dad and I used to do it all the time."

That perked Harry up. "You did?"

"Sure."

"And then we'll make s'mores," Wendy added, leading the men into the kitchen.

They managed to keep Harry entertained all evening, tiring him out so much that when he finally took a bath and went to bed, he fell asleep immediately.

As they closed the door on his bedroom, Wendy began to feel guilty for judging Cullen so harshly. His behavior that evening had proven he truly liked Harry, and only wanted what was best for the little boy in her care. She should appreciate the fact that Cullen had smoothed things over with Randy and invited them to dinner. After all, it wasn't as if he were high-handing her into a relationship. He was being kind to her little boy.

Walking down the stairs, Wendy said, "Thanks for your help."

"You could have handled it."

That made her feel a little bit better. "Yeah, but your expertise about roasting hot dogs in the fireplace definitely came in handy."

Thinking he would be leaving, Wendy walked to the front door, but Cullen passed her and returned to the living room. He grabbed the paper plates and chocolate-bar wrappers from the s'mores. As he straightened from the coffee table, he turned to the fireplace mantel and he stopped.

Setting the candy-bar wrappers on the paper plate, he walked over to the mantel, and lifted the picture of Greg holding a fishing pole.

"Is this your husband?"

"Yes."

"He was a fisherman?" he asked brightly, obviously pleased they had something in common.

Realizing he'd gotten the wrong impression, Wendy snorted a laugh. "Not at all."

"So there's a story behind this?"

"Not really. More like a boring joke. Not something you'd be interested in." She gave what she hoped was a conversation-ending reply, grabbed the napkins from the coffee table and gathered the unopened chocolate bars and graham crackers.

Now that it had sunk in that she was really Harry's mom, she had yet another reason not to get involved with Cullen. Forget about the fact that he was her boss and they weren't a good match; too much involvement between her and Cullen meant Harry could be hurt when he returned to Miami. As long as he was just a guy who came to dinner once or twice to visit Harry, Harry would be okay. But if Harry saw her and Cullen being romantic, he'd get all the wrong ideas and a little boy who'd already suffered enough hurt in one lifetime would once again be disappointed. It was best to keep things simple between her and Cullen.

In her peripheral vision, she saw him shake his head, just before he turned and walked through the foyer toward the kitchen.

Carrying the candy bars and graham crackers, she followed him. He dropped his trash into the receptacle, while she stored the extra chocolate and graham crackers in the pantry.

By the time she walked out, Cullen stood by the back door with his topcoat in his hands. Not wanting him to leave with her refusal to talk hanging in the air between them, she took them back to neutral conversational ground. "Thanks again for your help."

Shrugging into his overcoat, he nodded. "It's not a problem."

His voice was gruff, as if her refusal to talk had annoyed him, so she smiled and said, "Still, it's very kind of you to be so good to Harry."

"I'm good to Harry because I like him." He spoke softly, and Wendy quickly glanced over at him. "I like you both."

His unexpected statement left Wendy with no chance to stop her automatic response to it. Her cheeks flushed. The air in the room evaporated. Joy coursed through her veins. All of which was ridiculous. They could not have a relationship. She shouldn't even *want* a relationship with a playboy who would disappear from her life when his work in Barrington was done. But with Harry in the picture, it was doubly wrong.

She quickly turned to the sink again, grabbed a paper towel from the wall-mounted roller and dried her hands. Keeping her voice light and friendly, she said, "We like you, too."

She heard him take the few steps to the counter and wasn't surprised when she felt his hands on her shoulders, or that he turned her to face him. "No. I mean I really like you. I feel so at home here."

Not knowing whether to be relieved or disappointed, Wendy laughed. "You *lived* here. Of course, you feel at home here."

He shook his head. "This was hardly a home. My parents were rarely around. Which was actually good because when they were here they fought."

"Your parents fought in front of you?"

"They weren't much on the decorum of fighting." He took a breath, as if he couldn't believe he'd actually admitted that. "My dad wanted to leave Barrington. He knew he could start an investment firm anywhere. But my mom didn't want to leave her friends. The people who depended on her for their jobs."

Wendy's eyes widened. "That's why you didn't want to go into the plant alone?"

"No. I've simply never been on the plant floor before. I didn't know anyone and I didn't want to scare anyone. The first morning, when I saw everybody peeking into your office to say good morning in the few minutes before you came into my office to explain why you were late, I knew you were the perfect person to introduce me around."

That made sense, but she suddenly realized they were standing close, his hands still on her shoulders. Memories of their kiss came tiptoeing back, causing her lips to tingle and her breathing to falter. He was the first man to kiss her since Greg. She'd been alone so long. Empty for so long—

Neither of which made wanting him right. Especially when he was so wrong for her.

She cleared her throat. "I guess I'd better finish cleaning up so I can get up on time for Harry tomorrow."

He grinned. "You slept in? That's why you were late Monday morning?"

"It wasn't funny. I'm trying to be a good parent to Harry, and the very first time he was supposed to be somewhere I slept in."

"Oh, Wendy," he said, wrapping his arms around her and pulling her close. "You are only human."

The feeling of being held by a man flooded her system. The joy of the emotional connection with someone who seemed genuinely to like and understand her nearly overwhelmed her. Then the scent of his aftershave filtered to her and she realized her breasts were nestled against his chest. Their thighs brushed. Strong muscles braced her softer form. They fitted together perfectly. And she so wanted to fit with someone again.

She took a breath to bring herself back to reality. She and

Cullen *didn't* fit. He was a playboy. She wouldn't get involved with a man who wouldn't be interested in anything permanent. By Christmas day he'd be gone. If she depended upon him too much, grew accustomed to having him around, or, God forbid, actually fell in love with him, she'd find herself with a broken heart on Christmas morning.

She pulled herself out of Cullen's warm embrace. "Thanks for your help tonight." She motioned to the door. "I'll see you on Monday."

Time suspended for the few seconds it took for Cullen to get her message. It looked as if he might say something, then he turned on his heel and headed for the door. "Good night, Wendy."

"Good night, Cullen."

She said the words softly, but it really didn't matter. He'd already walked out and closed the door. The soft click echoed through her empty kitchen.

Busying herself with finishing the dishes, she ignored the emptiness. She was glad he could help her through some of the initial difficulties with Harry. She wasn't too proud to refuse the assistance that a scared little boy needed. But she was also smart enough not to get sucked into the daydream that she might be the woman to tame the playboy who owned the company where she worked. She was even smarter not to get involved with another man who would dictate, not discuss. She'd been hurt once and she wouldn't let it happen again. She had everything she wanted now. A child. And she would never risk hurting Harry.

She dried her hands on a paper towel and threw it in the trash before heading for bed. If she was so smart and had done all the right things, why the hell was she so damned disappointed that he hadn't argued, but had simply gone?

Which proved she really didn't mean anything to him.

CHAPTER SIX

CULLEN just barely caught his flight to Miami. Exhausted from the week of almost nonstop work, he fell asleep two minutes after takeoff, and woke when the wheels touched down at Miami International. But part of him was glad. He'd never felt as odd as when Wendy showed him the door that night. She'd kicked him out. *Out.* After he'd helped her! And told her the thing about his parents that he'd never told anyone. That they fought. Often. If he'd stayed awake, he would have spent the entire flight fuming about that.

Hoisting his duffel bag off the carousel in baggage claim, echoes of the odd sensations he'd felt when she pointed at her kitchen door rumbled through him again. He reminded himself that he had already been in his coat and she probably had been tired. Walking out into the balmy Miami night, he decided that she hadn't so much kicked him out as gotten him moving.

In his Mercedes, he lowered the convertible top and exited the airport, letting the wind whip through his hair as he made his way to the house on the beach that he shared with his dad.

But he couldn't stop thinking about Wendy, about how the emotion of the situation had caused him to hug her and her to cuddle into his embrace. What he'd felt in those few seconds was different than anything he'd ever felt with a woman.

He frowned. Maybe *different* wasn't the right word. *Expanded* was better. He felt all the usual male/female things he felt when he held a woman, but there was more.

Over an icy weekend, they'd both helped Harry adjust to living with her. She'd told him bits and pieces of her life. He'd told her bits and pieces of his. Together they'd told Harry about his dad, then helped him get through the difficult evening with hot dogs and s'mores.

Of course he felt close to her. He typically didn't get this involved in *anybody's* personal life. When he pulled her into his arms, he wasn't simply wooing an attractive woman, he was holding somebody he knew. Somebody he liked. The velvet of her skin was warm and familiar. The questions in her eyes echoed his own. In a few short visits, they'd become so close that he swore he could feel her heart beating.

Then she'd kicked him out.

With a growl of annoyance, he reminded himself he'd already figured out that she'd done it because she was tired, but he suddenly realized that wasn't what bothered him. The real problem wasn't being "kicked out." It was being kicked out after her refusal to talk about her husband.

Driving along the coastal highway, wind in his hair, the perfect world around him glittering with lights, the ocean a peaceful rumble to his left, he wondered if she hadn't kicked him out *because* he'd asked about the picture. Which was really rich since *he* was the one who had the right to be insulted. It had been years since her husband's death and his question had been innocent, yet she wouldn't answer it. He'd automatically told her things about his family. He'd answered every damned question she'd asked him. But she didn't want to talk about her husband.

He slapped his hand on the steering wheel. Damn it! What did it matter? He'd never pursue her. She was a serious woman and he was a flirt. A guy who liked to have fun. Were it not for Harry, they'd probably never even speak outside the office.

Maneuvering his car onto the driveway that led to his rambling two-story stucco house with windows that rose to the sky, Cullen told himself to relax. Really relax or his dad would figure out something was wrong and wouldn't let Cullen rest until Cullen spilled the whole story. And then his dad would be angry. He'd think that Barrington, Pennsylvania, was sucking Cullen in the way it had his mom. The memories that would be dredged up would ruin Christmas. So, no. He absolutely, positively would not let on that anything was bothering him.

Because nothing *was* bothering him. He accepted that Wendy didn't want to talk about herself. It was just another proof that he and his family didn't fit into the town that bore their name. He didn't know why he'd been so foolish as to think Wendy might be different, but he'd gotten the message. From here on out he wouldn't ask her questions about her life and he'd keep his own life off-limits, too.

The house was dark and quiet when he entered the echoing foyer. Assuming his dad was asleep, and without turning on a light, he carried his duffel bag up the curving cherrywood stairway and walked down the hall to his suite of rooms. He was determined to forget all about Wendy Winston and Harry Martin and spend Saturday and Sunday enjoying himself on his boat, soaking up the sun before he had to fly back to frosty Barrington on Monday afternoon.

Wendy let Harry sleep in on Saturday morning. When eleven o'clock came and went with Harry still asleep, she cancelled her plans with Emma and her kids. He woke about noon, sullen and cranky, and Wendy gave him a lot of leeway, letting him work out his feelings in his own way. On Sunday when he was still moody, she ordered pizza and let him watch football on television. But Monday morning when he refused to go to school, she knew he had to snap out of this.

She took a firm hand and got him dressed and fed him. After she walked him to his class, she explained his situation to his teacher, then spent another few minutes in the principal's office, telling the story again, making sure Harry would have sufficient support.

She arrived at work over an hour late, only to discover Cullen wasn't there. Breathing a sigh of relief, she got busy with her typical Monday-morning duties and forgot all about her temporary boss.

When Cullen hadn't arrived at noon, she took her lunch, expecting him to be in Mr. McCoy's office when she returned, but he wasn't. Worried now, she called his hotel and discovered he'd checked out. Assuming he'd gone to Miami for the weekend, she relaxed, until another hour went by. If he had no intention of returning until Tuesday, he should have let her know. She was, after all, his assistant. She scoured her desk for a note, then scoured his. Nothing.

At three, she began to fear that maybe something had happened. He could have been in an accident. By the time he strolled into her office after four, every nerve ending in her body was sitting on the edge of her skin like glitter.

"Where were you?"

His eyebrows rose at her tone. "Excuse me?"

She combed her fingers through her hair. "Sorry. I had a bad weekend and when you weren't here and there wasn't a note—" She fisted her hair in her hands this time. "I just panicked and thought you must have been in an accident. I'm sorry."

He shucked his overcoat. "No. I'm sorry. You're right. I should have let you know I would be going home for weekends and not returning until late Monday."

"It's almost quitting time. You shouldn't have bothered to come in at all."

He laughed. "You *are* in a mood."

She sighed. "Harry had a bad weekend."

"I'm not surprised. He lost his mom and spent a month in foster care. When he was finally given to you—someone he knew and felt safe with—he was told his dad was dead."

His instant understanding made her so damned glad to see him that she was sure it showed on her face. They might be different. They might even be unsuited. But he absolutely understood her and what she was going through with Harry.

She busied herself stacking the pages she'd just pulled from the printer, turning her face away so he couldn't read anything into her expression. "It has been an awful month for Harry."

"My offer of dinner is still open. Remember, I promised Randy that I'd look in on you."

"And you can. But I—" She glanced over and totally lost her train of thought. He always looked positively yummy, but two days in the sun had given his skin a warm glow. He looked rested, relaxed and so damned sexy that her heart skipped a beat. Her own skin flushed with color but not from the sun, from being flustered and tongue-tied. God, she was an idiot. Not just attracted to a man who was out of her league, but also unable to hide it.

"I—"

His eyes narrowed. "You what?"

She pulled in a breath that caused her breasts to swell beneath her warm pink sweater and Cullen suddenly realized what was going on. She hadn't kicked him out of her house on Friday because she was moody or tired or even unwilling to talk about her husband. She *liked* him. He'd worried all damned weekend for nothing.

He grinned. "You want to orchestrate my visits, don't you?"

She wouldn't look at him again. "I just want to make sure that you're not around so much that Harry misses you when your work here is done."

He stepped closer. "Ah."

"Now you're making fun of me."

He slid his index finger under her chin and lifted her face so that she would look at him. "No, I'm just curious about why you're afraid of me."

"I'm not afraid of you."

"Of course you are," he said, holding her gaze, noting that her pretty green eyes had flecks of gold and that her skin was a smooth, perfect pink.

He gave her points for not yanking herself away from him and breaking eye contact, even as he wondered why he was forcing himself into a situation that was totally wrong. He knew as well as she did that two people who were this attracted couldn't have a lot of contact or they'd spontaneously combust one day and do something they'd both regret. Yet here he was, pushing.

"Or I could simply be too busy with Harry to add another thing to my life."

Her gaze flicked down for a mere second as she said that and he knew that if she wasn't out-and-out lying, she was at least only telling him a half truth.

Before he could stop himself or once again remind himself of all the reasons he shouldn't be insinuating himself into her life, he said, "We both know this isn't completely about Harry, so why don't you tell me what's really going on? On Friday night you were fine and then suddenly you kicked me out. Let's start there."

She pulled away from him and rounded her desk so she could stand behind it, almost as if she wanted protection. "You're a playboy. Anything between us would mean very little to you. But even if you weren't, you're too much like my husband."

He'd been all ready to argue her concerns about him being a playboy until she mentioned her husband. "What?"

"You're like my husband. Greg was a wonderful person. And he always seemed to know the right thing to say…the right thing to do. So much so that I never argued when he made all our decisions." She finally glanced up from the papers she was stacking. "That cost me the chance to have a child of my own with him. Had I pushed for the one thing I truly wanted, a baby, I wouldn't have been alone when he died. I would have also proven myself a capable parent. Nobody would wonder whether I could care for Harry."

This time Cullen took the step back. "You're saying you don't want me around me because I'm like your husband?"

She raked her fingers through her hair. "Yes. No. Because for me this isn't about you and me. It can't be. It has to be about Harry."

"Why?"

"You don't think he'll miss you when you return to Miami?"

And suddenly he got it. They were talking about Harry, but she was also talking about herself. *She* would be hurt when he left. *She* would miss him.

He took another step back. Away from her. The events from Friday night came back to him in a rush. He couldn't help himself from being romantic with her, from touching her, from wanting to kiss her again. Now, she was telling him she didn't want to be involved with him because he reminded her of her husband. Which should—and did—put the appropriate fear in him. Tighten his chest. Make his heart speed up and his stomach tighten. *She was seeing him as a husband.*

And he was a bachelor. She'd even gone so far as to accuse him of being a playboy. He liked Miami. He loved nightlife. He wasn't wild about responsibility so he chose his responsibilities carefully.

But the way he was behaving around her reminded her of a husband.

He took another step back. "I'm helping Harry through a tough time in his life. He needs me because he knows I understand him because my mother also died recently. But by the time I leave, he'll be adjusted to you, secure with you. He'll miss me a bit, but not for long."

"Really?"

The trust in her eyes nearly was his undoing. No one had ever looked at him like that.

He pulled in a breath. Took another step back. He'd never *wanted* anyone to look at him like that.

"Take it from a guy who had to get adjusted to a lot as a kid. Once Harry feels secure with you, I could fall off the face of the earth and he'd be okay in a day or two. It's in this transition time as he's adjusting to living with you that he needs someone he thinks understands, and that's why I'm making myself available."

She smiled and nodded, and Cullen turned on his heel, eager to escape to Paul McCoy's office, but he stopped and faced her again.

"For the record, I would never deliberately hurt anyone."

It was as close as he could come to telling her that he understood her fears. She didn't want his advances, didn't want to get too close because she would be hurt when he left.

He got it.

Now he just had to stop himself from acting on all the impulses that raced through him whenever she was around.

Harry's mood improved greatly on Tuesday morning. Wendy made him oatmeal, sprinkled it with cinnamon and sugar and promised him a trip to the mall after school. She didn't downplay his sadness or his fear of being alone, but rather, tried to show him he was secure with her by feeding him and taking him to school. She promised him the trip to the mall to demonstrate that life went on by making plans for the future.

Walking into work, on time, she experienced a swell of pride until she glanced into Cullen's office and saw him sitting behind Mr. McCoy's big desk.

She knew she'd scared him silly the day before by telling him he reminded her of her husband. She'd done it on purpose. He liked her. She liked him. Their chemistry could go off the charts if they let it, and he didn't seem to have a practicality switch or understand that they were opposites. He might be the if-it-feels-good-do-it type, but she wasn't. If they got involved, he'd have a good time, maybe be sad when he returned to sunny Miami, but in twenty minutes on his boat he'd forget all about her. While she'd be left in snowy Pennsylvania with a broken heart.

No thanks.

She understood that Cullen being in Harry's life in Harry's time of trouble was a good thing. She also got Cullen's point that by the time he left Pennsylvania, Harry would be adjusted. Though he'd miss Cullen, he wouldn't pine for him because he'd be secure with Wendy by then. So it was good for Cullen to be involved with Harry. His point had been made. But she'd also made her point with him. He had to stop giving in to their attraction.

She didn't even poke her head into his office to say good morning. Instead, she stripped off her coat, hung it in the small closet, and went straight to work. A half hour later, he strolled out of his office and stopped in surprise. "Oh, you're here."

She smiled her best administrative-assistant smile. Friendly, but not personal. "I've been here a while."

He angled his hip on her desk and made himself comfortable. "So everything went well this morning?"

"Yes. Harry's back to being his typical sunny self." She pushed her chair back, rose and took some papers to the filing cabinet, putting some distance between them.

"That didn't take long."

Deliberately occupied with filing so she wouldn't look at him, she said, "As you said, he's becoming secure with me."

"You sound like the girl giving the morning news when you talk like this."

"Really?"

Cullen was about to say yes, but he stopped himself. *This* was the reason she would miss him when he left. Because of one icy night together they'd bonded enough that making conversation came naturally. Easily. And, for two people totally unsuited to each other, they really were beginning to like each other too much. He'd already decided to rein in his romantic impulses, but he now saw the reining had to include private conversations.

Without replying, he returned to Paul McCoy's desk. He tried to read the numbers on the production reports, but he couldn't focus, and soon they blurred on the sheet in front of

him. Before he knew it, he was thinking about how nice
Wendy looked in her blue sweater. With a growl of annoyance,
he rose and walked to the window, shifting his thoughts in a
direction they were allowed to go: Harry. But thoughts of
Harry naturally segued to Wendy again.

He glanced out at her. She sat at her desk diligently typing
on her computer keyboard. She'd make a terrific mom, and
that made his heart swell with respect for her. He liked Harry.
In fact, he saw a little bit of his own loneliness and insecurity
as a child when he looked at Harry. Knowing exactly how
Harry felt, if he had one wish, it would be that Harry could
feel safe and secure. Always. For the rest of his life.

He turned back to the window. He didn't trust wishes. He
trusted in his own abilities. Even as a child, he'd quickly
realized the only person he could count on was himself. So if
he wanted to help Harry, it couldn't be with a wish. It would
have to be with something substantial he could do—

Returning to his desk, he grabbed the phone and punched
the intercom numbers for the human resources director. There
was something he could do. And that something might even
be why fate had brought him to Barrington.

When Poppy Fornwalt answered her phone, Cullen said
simply, "I want the detailed wage reports for the past six months."

Wednesday morning, Harry dressed himself for school and had
toast ready for Wendy when she ambled into the kitchen.
Pleased, thinking her life was finally settling into a routine, she
hugged him and he proudly served her toast with strawberry jam.

Off in her own little world, contemplating how great life
would be now for both her and Harry, she drove to work and
was surprised out of her reverie when Poppy Fornwalt called
her down to her office.

She entered with an enthusiastic hello, and dark-haired, blue-eyed Poppy looked up with a smile. "Close the door."

Wendy swallowed. "You don't normally ask anybody to close the door unless it's bad news," she said, as she pulled the office door shut behind her.

"Or unless we're going to talk money."

She took the seat in front of Poppy's desk. "Money?"

"You really must have impressed Mr. Barrington."

Her eyebrows rose. "Impressed Mr. Barrington?"

"He's giving you a twenty-five percent raise!" Poppy all but bounced out of her seat with joy.

Wendy's mouth fell open. "Twenty-five percent?"

"Yes!" Poppy cried. "And isn't it wonderful timing? He wants it backdated to last week so you'll have extra money in time for Christmas!"

Her heart sank and the world spun, as her head filled with a truly awful conclusion. She'd brushed him off, so he was offering her money? This time her stomach turned over. Was he trying to buy her with a raise? "Oh really."

Poppy's happy expression faded. "You should be dancing."

Wendy pulled in a breath, working to react naturally to what appeared to be good news, but what was, in reality, the worst possible news. "I'm dancing on the inside."

"Wendy, everybody knows you recently got custody of your neighbor's little boy. Maybe this is his way of helping."

Wendy forced a smile. "I'm sure it is."

Poppy handed some forms across the desk. "Here's your paperwork. It has all the numbers. Your raise will be on this pay. Mr. Barrington simply asked that we keep this between us."

Wendy rose. "I'm sure he did."

Poppy apparently didn't catch the note of dismay in Wendy's voice because she rose, grabbed Wendy's hand

and squeezed it. "I'm so hoping this helps you with your little boy."

Wendy smiled. She would look incredibly ungrateful if she didn't show some appreciation. "It will. Thank you, Poppy."

"Don't thank me. Thank Mr. Barrington."

"Oh, I will."

Wendy left Poppy's office, not sure if she was furious or ashamed. Particularly since the Barringtons had held raises to cost-of-living raises for the past five years. Being singled out to get a raise when everybody in the plant needed and deserved one, only made Cullen's generosity stand out all the more. If anyone heard about this she'd be a pariah.

By the time she reached her office, she was breathing heavily. She stormed through the open door, into Cullen's office and slapped the paperwork for her raise on his desk.

"What is this?"

He glanced up, took in her angry expression and his brow furrowed. "It's paperwork to give you a raise?"

"I know!" Tossing her arms in the air, she pivoted away from the desk.

"And yet you're angry."

She spun to face him. "What do you think that money is going to get you?"

"Get me?"

"Do you think I'm going to sleep with you for this?"

The expression in his eyes went from confused to fiery in the beat of her heart. "You'd better stop talking and let me explain." Real menace dripped from his words.

Her blood ran cold at his tone. Dear God, he was the boss! He could fire her, call security and have her escorted off the property. And she had a child to think about!

"I checked into your salary to see if I could help you out

since you now have a son to support." He sat back in his chair, tossed his pencil to his desk. "I certainly wasn't intending to pay you to sleep with me."

Her cheeks flamed. The room spun. It was so hard to breathe she wasn't even sure she could speak, but there was no turning back. "You're still treating me differently, showing me favoritism. Even if I was wrong about the reason—" she swallowed "—you can't give me and no one else a raise without making it look like I did something to get on your good side."

"When I checked your salary I saw everybody's. No one in this plant has gotten above a cost-of-living raise in five years. Which is why everybody will be getting a raise similar to yours in January."

Embarrassment coursed through her. She wanted to faint or die, but knew she couldn't do either. She fell to the seat in front of his desk. "Everybody?"

"Yes. When I saw those numbers I was actually glad I was forced to take a real look at what was going on here. My dad and I check the big-picture figures when we get our profits every quarter, but we never looked at the details. Your situation forced me to do that."

"Oh, God." She squeezed her eyes shut.

"You don't trust me. I get it. Personally, man to woman, I'm not to be trusted. I'm not looking for what you want. You probably couldn't live the way I live. But don't ever question my business judgment again."

She swallowed. "I'm sorry."

He sat back on Paul McCoy's tall-backed black leather chair. "I'm not going to tell you it's okay because it isn't. But I am willing to forget about it and move on."

"Thank you."

"And don't tell anyone about the raises."

She looked up, confused.

"You need yours now. Don't tell me you don't. But accounting and human resources need time to process everyone else's. So, on my order, they did yours now. But I don't want anyone to be offended or upset. So please, keep this all under your hat until everyone's raise is announced in January."

She frowned. "But then no one will know you're the one who authorized the raises."

He picked up his pencil and glanced down at the papers in front of him again. "There's no point."

"Sure there is. It's Mr. McCoy who's run such a tight ship that we only got cost-of-living raises. He claimed the plant couldn't afford more. So when he gets back, he'll get the credit for giving everyone their raise."

"This isn't about who gets credit." He didn't even look up. "I was only giving you what you had worked for over the past four years. You may go now."

Dismissed, Wendy rose. She'd put the last nail in the coffin of their friendship, and felt like a complete fool.

CHAPTER SEVEN

THAT night, after tucking Harry beneath a soft comforter and kissing him goodnight, Wendy ambled into her living room. In need of a little comfort herself, she made a fire in the fireplace, found a book and curled up on her sofa.

She read for only twenty minutes before the events of the day weighed down on her. She hadn't meant to insult Cullen. She'd thought she was protecting herself. Which was just more proof that they were too different to get involved. So different she'd seen his kindness as an attempt to buy her favors and embarrassed herself.

Wondering what he saw when he looked at her, at her life, she glanced around his former home. Her sofa and chair were simple beige. The area rug atop the hardwood floors she and Greg had refinished was a modern print in soft yellow, cream and green that brought the room to life. The walls had been painted a pale yellow.

It was a soothing room, a calm room, but it wasn't elegant. She couldn't even imagine the kind of home he lived in in Miami. But he hadn't looked down on her or her things the Saturday he'd stayed with her. He'd joined in her fun with Harry, working to make Harry happy. He'd slept on the floor without complaint and even cooked for her and Harry.

She frowned. Technically, with the exception of kissing her, everything he'd done had been for Harry. When he'd stepped into the conversation with Randy Zamias, when he'd said they shouldn't wait to tell Harry his father had passed, when he'd volunteered to take them out to dinner—all those things had been for Harry. And maybe he hadn't been pushy or domineering, simply desperate to help? As out of his element with the little boy as Wendy had been, he'd made a few mistakes.

So had she.

Yet she'd taken everything personally. Forgetting, or maybe not even noticing, that at the office and in their private conversations, he'd always been a perfect gentleman.

Running her hands down her face in misery, she rose from the sofa to make a cup of hot cocoa, but a blood-curdling scream sounded from upstairs. She dropped her book to the coffee table, raced upstairs and burst into Harry's room.

Sitting in the center of the bed, Harry sobbed. He wasn't wearing his glasses and she could see the tears that poured down his cheeks. She sat on the edge of his bed and he leaped into her open arms.

"It's all right. It's all right."

Sobs racked his small frame and he clung to her. "No, it's not!"

"Did you have a nightmare?"

"Yes."

"Well, I'm here now. You're safe."

"I want Cullen."

Surprised, she pulled in a breath. Not only did it sting that her comfort wasn't enough, but also she wasn't really sure Cullen would come. "It's late. He's at his hotel."

"He said if I ever needed him I could call."

"I'm sure he meant it but it's—"

"I want Cullen!"

He clutched her upper arms tighter and pressed his face in her shoulder, his tears wetting her T-shirt.

Wendy stroked his soft hair. She had to at least try. "All right. I'll call him."

Cullen didn't ask for details. Hearing Harry had had a nightmare and was inconsolable, he raced to Wendy's house. She opened the door before he even knocked. She didn't mention their argument. He didn't either. What happened between them was between them. What happened with Harry wasn't just separate, at the moment it was the only thing that mattered.

"How is he?"

As she led him up the stairs, Wendy said, "Once I called you he stopped crying. So it must have been the right thing to do."

"Let me see what's going on."

He stepped into the little room that had been his own when he and his parents had lived in the house. The bright-blue walls he remembered had been repainted a soothing blue. Trains and dump trucks decorated the comforter. The base of the lamp was in the shape of a football.

Sitting up on the bed, partially covered by the thick blanket and sliding a small plastic car on his thigh, Harry said, "Hi, Cullen."

He sat on the bed. "Hey." He ruffled Harry's hair. "What's wrong?"

Without looking up, he said, "I had a nightmare."

"What kind of a nightmare?"

Harry shrugged.

"Monsters?"

He glanced up. "No."

"Then what?"

"Kids at school."

"Are the kids at school bothering you?"

He shrugged again. "Some."

"Just some?"

"Just one."

"Who is that?"

"Freddie."

"Is he hurting you?"

"No. He just told me I was an organ and nobody wanted me."

Not feeling the need to tell him *organ* was probably *orphan*, Cullen reached over and hugged Harry, then drew him onto his lap. "Wendy wants you so much that she was willing to go to court for you. Why do you think Randy Zamias gives your mom so much trouble?"

Standing just outside the doorway, Wendy leaned against the wall. She wondered if Cullen had slipped up in calling her Harry's mom, but doubted it. He was a very smart guy. He realized Harry needed reassurance, continuity and he was giving it to him in the most subtle way.

Harry twisted to look up into Cullen's face. "Because he wants me?"

"No. Because he needed to be sure the right person has you."

Running the car up his pajama-clad thigh, Harry said, "Did kids tease you when you were in school?"

Watching Cullen's facial features harden, Wendy's brow furrowed. She'd never considered what it might have been like for him to live in the town where his dad's grandparents started the company that provided jobs for nearly everyone in town and his mom was the president who ran it. But it must not have been a joyful experience. Otherwise, his expression wouldn't have gone from sympathetic to hard in an automatic reaction he hadn't had time to stop.

Thinking back to his first day at the plant, she remembered that he wouldn't go onto the plant floor without introductions and none of the employees had treated him normally. Men had grunted hellos. Women had giggled.

Wendy had treated him normally, but only because he'd stayed at her house the night of the ice storm. And she wasn't from Barrington. She'd only moved here four years ago. She had no idea how he'd been treated as a child.

"Yes, kids teased me. But not for the reasons you think. My mom was sort of everybody's boss. When I got into third grade, the kids thought it would be cool to hit me and stuff."

Wendy smiled at the way he brought the language of his conversation to Harry's level.

"Our neighbor down the street, my dad's partner in the candy store, waited for me one day after school and set them straight."

Harry's eyes widened. "He did?"

"Yep. He handed me a brand-new ball and bat, with nine mitts. Enough for an entire team."

"Wow."

"Then he told the kids who'd gathered around us that if we wanted to become a Little League team he would coach us."

"Wow."

Cullen laughed. "He'd coached his own kids, but they'd outgrown Little League and he hadn't."

Wendy tilted her head to the side as a clear image of that day formed in her head. She could see eight-year-old Cullen being teased and tormented, and a family friend stepping in to help him because apparently neither of his parents had noticed.

A shudder of sadness passed through her. He'd been as alone as Harry. But he probably hadn't been an easy mark.

She couldn't imagine that even as a child he'd let anybody push him around, but she also knew most children weren't equipped to defend themselves against a gang.

A sudden realization swamped her. He'd spent most of his life in this town alone, a child constantly being forced to prove himself. Only she had treated him normally. Until Friday night when he had asked about her husband and tried to kiss her a second time, then everything had changed. She'd put her back up and refused to talk, wanting to protect herself. But even though she had explained that, she had nonetheless become another person from Barrington who treated him coolly. Then she'd made the ultimate mistake by accusing him of trying to buy her. Lord, could she have been any more wrong?

Harry shook his head. "Freddie already has a mitt."

"And you don't need to buy gifts to make friends. You said only he teases you. Do the other kids like you?"

He nodded.

"Then you're just going to have to ignore Freddie."

Glad he hadn't told Harry to punch Freddie, Wendy breathed a sigh of relief. Fighting wasn't the answer. But she also wouldn't let Freddie get off scot-free. She'd have a discussion with the principal in the morning.

Harry began rolling the little car along his thigh again. "Do you miss your mom?"

"Sure. But not the same way you do. I don't need my mom to take care of me. You do. So part of what you feel is fear. Especially fear of being alone."

He nodded.

"Wendy's not going to leave you alone. All you have to do is believe in her."

Harry looked up. His blue eyes connected with Cullen's

dark ones. The trust that Wendy saw in them nearly stole her breath. "Okay."

"And any time you get afraid, I want you to call me."

"Okay."

"In fact," Cullen said, reaching over, opening the bedside-table drawer and retrieving a pen and a little tablet. "This is my cell phone number."

Harry grinned. "You have a cell phone? Jimmy Johnson has a cell phone."

He placed the tablet and pen on the bedside table. "Well, now you have my number. You can call me any time. Day or night."

They were quiet for several seconds before Cullen said, "Do you think you can sleep now?"

"Yeah."

"I'll tuck you in."

Rather than laying him down, Cullen switched the mood of their discussion by tossing Harry to the bed. The little boy landed in the middle, his head slightly askew on the pillow. He giggled then said, "Thanks, Cullen."

"Hey, any time."

Cullen pulled the covers to Harry's chin, kissed his cheek and ruffled his hair. "Go to sleep now."

"Okay."

"Okay."

Wendy ducked out of the doorway before Cullen turned in her direction. She raced down the steps as quietly as possible, ran into the living room and fell to her couch, not wanting Cullen to know she'd listened in.

A few seconds later he appeared at the doorway. "I think I have him settled."

"Thank you."

"He only wanted reassurance that everything's going to be

okay." He rolled his shoulders, as if to loosen their tightness. "I gave him my cell phone number."

"You didn't have to do that."

"I don't think he'll bother me. He's in school all day so he doesn't have a lot of access to a phone. Even after school he's with a babysitter until you get home." He met her gaze. "But if he wants to call me forty-six times a day until he's comfortable, I can handle it."

She smiled slightly, feeling like a real jerk for being so wrong about him. "Thanks."

"You're welcome." He turned and walked into the foyer. Wendy scrambled from the sofa and to the door before he opened it.

"I know this was a huge imposition, so I appreciate it."

"Again, you're welcome."

The foyer became quiet. Wendy searched her brain for something to say, but there was nothing, unless she wanted to apologize once more for misunderstanding about the raise. And she didn't care to bring up that particular misery again.

Not sure what else to do, she looked up and found him staring at her, studying her.

She knew he was probably wondering how she could be so dense, and she shook her head. "Look, for two people who got off on the right foot, I know I've made a real mess of things."

"It's okay."

"No, it isn't. You've been nothing but nice to both me and Harry and I've been…well…odd." She pulled in a breath. "You're not like my husband. Not that he didn't have his good points, but when he died, leaving me alone, I got angry. I obviously jumped to some wrong conclusions about you and I'm sorry. I don't normally take that anger out on people."

"But it made you cautious."

She nodded.

"Maybe you *should* be cautious."

She smiled. "Are you warning me off?"

"Yes."

The seriousness of his voice caused her stomach to tighten. She caught his gaze again. His dark eyes virtually glowed, sending a sizzle of electricity through her. If she touched him, she had the feeling he'd be lost.

"I'm not the kind of guy to settle down and you are absolutely the kind of woman to settle down. Even if you didn't have Harry, I would know it. But that doesn't stop me from wanting you. And you're not too far off the mark about me being pushy. When I want something I go after it. And right now I want you."

She licked her lips at the severity of his tone and took a step back.

"Forget all about your first impression and stick with the worry that I'm enough like your husband that you shouldn't get involved with me. We'll both be happier, if only because you don't want to get hurt and I don't want to hurt you."

Swallowing, she caught his gaze. "You don't have to warn me. I can take care of myself. I'm a big girl."

"Not big enough to play in my league."

With that he turned and walked out of her house. Wendy stood in her foyer a long time, every cell in her body tingling. Not just because he was an attractive man, but because he'd admitted that he was so attracted to her he was having difficulty stopping himself from doing what he wanted.

She absolutely knew that feeling. Just being in the same room with him made her blood hum in her veins. She hadn't felt this good, this alive, in years. Though the Miss Goody Two-shoes in her told her to back off, the promise in his soft voice and sensual eyes told her not to listen. She wanted this, and for once in her life she didn't want to walk away wishing things could have been different. For once in her life, she'd simply like to enjoy the moment. Do what she wanted to do instead of what she knew was the "right" thing to do. For once in her life she didn't want to be Miss Goody Two-shoes.

But she didn't really know how to be anybody else.

CHAPTER EIGHT

THE next morning, Wendy met Patty and Emma by the time clock. Patty tapped her forearm to catch her attention. "You know, you haven't really spoken much since you got Harry. Everything okay?"

Punching her time card, Emma added, "You didn't bite off more than you can chew with that little boy, did you?"

Wendy gasped. "Oh, no! I love everything about having Harry in my life."

"Then what?" Emma asked.

Wendy licked her suddenly dry lips. Part of the problem she was having with Cullen was that she hadn't talked about any of this with her friends. The only input and opinion she had was her own. Lately, she was beginning to think she wasn't all that smart when it came to men.

Patty growled, "Come on, spill it."

Catching Patty's arm and nodding to Emma, she moved the three of them to a quiet corner. "Okay. The problem is Mr. Barrington."

Both Patty's and Emma's eyebrows rose. "He's a crappy boss?"

"He's a great boss and he's even been helping me with Harry."

"Oh, really?"

"Harry and I met Cullen the Saturday before he took over for Mr. McCoy."

"The day of the ice storm?"

Wendy winced. "The day we lost power."

"Oh, you little devil! He stayed at your house, didn't he?"

"Yes, and that's why Harry got so close to him."

"And you, too?"

She sighed. "And me, too." Glancing around to make sure the hall was clearing and no one could hear, she took her voice down to a whisper. "Last Friday night, he tried to kiss me and—"

Both Emma and Patty's eyes widened.

"—then we had a bit of a disagreement about money. I more or less accused him of trying to buy me."

This time their mouths fell open.

"Girl, when you decide to have a life you pull out all the stops."

"No kidding. The problem is he's a really great guy. And I'm afraid he's never going to speak to me again because— well, I'm an idiot. I keep taking everything he says and does the wrong way." She shook her head. "But I think he's wrong about a few things, too. He says we're not good for each other because he doesn't want to settle down, but I'm not so sure I want to settle down either right now."

Patty gasped. "You want a fling?"

"Maybe."

"So," Emma said, leaning closer, her eyes bright with excitement, her voice a low whisper. "What are you going to do?"

"I don't know."

"Well, I know," Patty said, grabbing Wendy's hand to make sure she paid attention. "You're going to really listen when he talks, stop jumping to conclusions and stop comparing him to Greg."

Wendy winced. "You figured that out."

"Yes."

Patty glanced at the clock on the wall. "Two minutes to get to the wheel." She sighed. "If we had more time I'd give you real advice, because I saw the way he looked at you. For now, just listen—really listen—to what he's saying and take your cue from that. For God's sake, don't push him, but don't miss the obvious."

Deciding that was probably the best course of action, Wendy headed for her office. When she arrived, Cullen was rifling through the file cabinets in front of her desk.

"Good morning."

Without looking away from the files, he said, "Good morning. So, how was Harry this morning?"

Normal conversation. Thank God. This she could handle. "He was great. Happy as a clam. I reminded him to ignore Freddie, and he grinned."

Cullen shook his head with a chuckle. "Kids. They're very resilient."

"I have a feeling Harry has spent a lot of his life accepting things he couldn't change."

"Yeah, me, too." He paused a second then said, "Are you busy today?"

"Just the usual. But my job title is assistant to the president, so if you need me to do something, your work comes first."

He rubbed his hand along the back of his neck. "I don't really have work for you to do. Actually, I have nothing on my calendar today for myself." He caught her gaze. "So I thought maybe you'd come out with me this afternoon and help me choose a gift for Harry for Christmas." He paused.

"The kid's had it so rough the past few months that I want to buy him a great gift. Something that makes him feel special." He paused. "That is, if it's okay with you."

She nearly cursed herself for being such a hard case that he worried it might not be okay for him to buy Harry something for Christmas. "Of course you can buy him a gift!"

"And you'll help me?"

This was her perfect opportunity to fix the mistakes she kept making with him. Away from the office, away from Harry, they could simply be themselves.

"Sure. I'd love to go shopping."

"I understand there's a mall—"

Before she nodded in agreement, a thought struck her. She wasn't the only one who had made some mistakes about Cullen. The employees had been gossiping ever since he arrived and most of what they'd said had been way off base. When they got their big raises in January, she wanted the people in the town to realize Cullen had been the one who saw the problem and rectified it. Since job confidentiality precluded her from telling anyone he, not Mr. McCoy, had instigated the raises, the best way to help everyone figure it out for themselves would be to get him out among the townspeople. Soon they'd see him for the nice guy he was and know he'd been their benefactor.

"The mall's too impersonal. We should stay in town. There are a few small shops that have some interesting gifts." She slid onto her desk chair. "You're very important to Harry. A gift from you should reflect that."

"I was going to get a dump truck."

She laughed. "You can buy him a dump truck. But let's look around town. See what else might strike your fancy."

He pulled in a breath. "Okay."

"Okay."

He turned to go into his office, but she had a second, even better idea. "We could have lunch at the diner first. Kill two birds with one stone."

He faced her with a scowl. "I don't know."

"Why not?"

"I usually go back to my hotel—"

"Really?" She swallowed back the surprise of that and added, "That's quite a drive for lunch. Let me introduce you to the ladies at the diner. They'll take care of you. Then you won't have to go so far every day."

Cullen was suspicious of Wendy's *they'll take care of you* claim until they stepped into the diner. In the years he'd been out of town, it hadn't changed one iota. Heavy-duty floor tiles in pale brown were flecked with enough colors that they didn't show the dirt from the foot traffic. Chocolate-brown stools rimmed a beige counter. Booths of the same chocolate color lined three of the walls. Tables filled in the center space.

But what he'd missed most in the years he'd been away, without even realizing he was missing it, was the smell. The scents of chicken, pie, French fries, hamburgers, butter and cinnamon mixed and mingled and wafted through the seating area.

Waitresses in pink uniforms dashed from table to table and into the kitchen. Dodie, the same cashier/hostess who'd manned the cash register when he and his parents had come here to eat on special occasions still stood behind the counter, her pink uniform stretched around her round tummy.

"Well, as I live and breathe! Cullen Barrington."

"I didn't think you'd recognize me."

Dodie batted a hand. "Handsome devil like you? Are you kidding?"

He laughed.

She grinned, but her smile quickly faded. "I heard about your mom. I'm sorry."

"Thank you."

"How's your old man?"

"He's fine. The warm weather agrees with him."

"Warm weather agrees with all of us." She peered at Wendy. "And don't think I don't see you standing there, missy. How's that new boy of yours?"

Wendy laughed. "He's great."

"You're going to make him a wonderful mother. You don't let social services push you around."

Wendy shook her head. Dodie knew everything. "I won't."

"Good. Find yourselves a seat. I'll send Mercy over to get your orders."

At the booth, Cullen helped Wendy with her coat and hung it on the hook at the end of the booth along with his topcoat. She slid onto one side, he slid onto the other.

Taking a menu from the holder behind the salt and pepper, she said, "I didn't realize you knew Dodie."

He grabbed a menu, too. "Everybody knows Dodie."

She smiled. "And she knows all of us, too."

His eyes on the menu, Cullen said, "That's the one thing about a small town that's good and bad. Everybody knows everything."

"I think it works in our favor more than it works against us."

"Your family didn't own the town's major employer."

"True." She paused when the waitress came over. Cullen deferred to her and she ordered a salad. He ordered a hot roast beef sandwich.

When the waitress left, she picked up the conversation where it had left off. "So, how was it?"

"Living here?"

She shrugged. "Living here. Living with a mom who was company president." She frowned. "Why was she the one running the company? The company was founded by your dad's grandparents. Why didn't your dad take the job?"

"He didn't want it. All along he wanted to hire a competent manager, move south and enjoy life."

"So what happened?"

"He married a local girl. He met my mom his last year in college and it was love at first sight. They kind of got married without really talking about what they wanted out of life."

Though Wendy and her husband had had a good marriage, it was only because she'd never complained when Greg had totally controlled their lives. "I basically did the same thing."

"Then you understand my dad's disappointment when she wouldn't leave her friends."

"She wouldn't leave her friends?"

"She was afraid that an impersonal manager wouldn't treat the people of the town well."

Wendy shrugged. "In a way she was right. Mr. McCoy hasn't given raises in five long years."

"Yeah, but that doesn't change the fact that my father was miserable. So he hid himself in his work. He started an investment company and grew it until my mom retired."

Which was why a neighbor had to coach Cullen's Little League team. His mom felt it her duty to ensure that her friends at the candy factory were treated right, and his dad hid in his work. No wonder Cullen understood Harry's loneliness.

The waitress came with their drinks and silverware, silently set them on the table and left again.

He nodded at Mercy. "She's not much of a talker."

"She's new. And probably afraid of you."

He snorted a laugh. "Right."

"I'm serious. Everybody's afraid of you or suspicious of why you're here. I figured out last night that the way everybody treats you oddly is part of why you don't want to live here."

"No. I don't care what the people of the town think of me. I don't want to live here because I have a life in Miami. A life I love."

A shiver of caution tripped down her spine, reminding her of how different they were; how they wanted different things out of life. Still, worries like those were irrelevant. She already knew their differences. Yet, she still liked him. A lot. She hadn't even been slightly attracted to a man in so long it felt wrong not to follow up on what she felt for Cullen. And if that led to an affair, it led to an affair. She wasn't going to be Miss Goody Two-shoes anymore. But she wouldn't get her heart broken because she'd go in with her eyes open. No expectations.

"All the same, it wouldn't hurt you to spend a little time with the people your company supports."

"Is that what this is all about?" He motioned around the diner. "Getting me out among the people?"

"No. Yes." She winced. "I think you have a poor opinion of them from your childhood and they have a poor opinion of you since nobody got a raise after you took over."

"That was Paul's doing. Once my mom retired, my dad wouldn't let her even peek at the books, afraid she'd become overinvolved again. Paul was making money for us and we chose to let him do whatever he felt necessary. Now that we know he was a little heavy-handed with the employees, we're fixing things."

"*You're* fixing things. Everybody thinks the no-raise policy came from your family and you're the living, breathing person in Barrington getting the blame. You need to get the credit."

He laughed. "Once again, I don't need the credit."

She toyed with her silverware. "Have you ever stopped to think that maybe *they* need you to take the credit?"

His face twisted in confusion. "How's that?"

"Just as Harry needs to learn to trust me, these people who depend on you need to know that you're trustworthy."

Cullen said nothing.

"Do you want them to spend the rest of their lives wondering if they'll have a job next year?"

"Why would they think that?"

"The rumor has run rampant for years that no raises means no profits, which means there's no reason to keep Barrington Candies open."

"Our profits are fabulous! Why do you think we never sold out when we decided to move away?"

She shrugged. "Everybody felt your family was sentimental."

"Wow." He leaned back in his seat. "Nobody ever leaked the numbers?"

She shook her head.

"*You've* seen the financial reports. Are you telling me you've never even tried to reassure your friends that everything was fine?"

"Of course I did. I'd say things like, 'we have nothing to worry about.' But no one believed me." She pointed across the table. "You, they'd believe."

He closed his eyes and puffed out a breath. "I'm really going to have to do this, aren't I?"

She grinned with delight, her confidence in him blooming. "Yes."

"Damn. I'm not much on PR."

"You'll live."

He laughed and opened his eyes just as Mercy arrived with their food. After she set the dishes in front of them, Cullen looked up at her with a smile. "Thank you, Mercy."

She smiled shakily. "You're welcome, Mr. Barrington."

"You can call me Cullen."

Her eyes widened, but she didn't call him Cullen. She said, "Okay," then scurried away.

"How was that?"

"That was a wonderful beginning."

He picked up his fork and dug into his hot roast beef sandwich. "Just so you know—I'm not doing this to get credit for the raises. I'm doing this so people get comfortable with the idea that their jobs aren't going away."

"You won't be sorry."

"I'd better not be."

When they stepped out of the diner, a faint sheen of snow covered the cars parked on Main Street. A light breeze tousled the feathery tinsel wrapped around the streetlights. The silver bells on light poles jingled.

"Where to?"

"We've got three choices. Perry's Toys, Mac's Hardware or Truffles."

Cullen nearly laughed at the thought of Mac's Hardware until he remembered the hardware store had been the best place to buy trains. Then he heard her mention Truffles, the candy store his father half owned. He was a partner with their former neighbor, Jim Edwards, in the store that sold Barrington Candies as well as toys, gifts and greeting cards. Though Cullen had spent many an afternoon trailing behind Jim when he had coached the Little League team, or watching as he arranged toys and candy displays, he hadn't seen Jim in years.

"Let's go to Truffles."

They walked side by side down the sidewalk, passing shops decorated for the holiday with brightly colored lights and tinsel. The airy snow danced around them, as if refusing to fall. The scent of cinnamon and apples wafted from the bakery. He felt the strangest urge to take Wendy's hand and tuck it in the crook of his elbow, but he knew that wasn't only silly, it would start tongues wagging. So he kept his distance, but it didn't feel right. When he was with her he had the oddest urges to protect her from the snow, warm her hands with his own, tell her his deepest, darkest secrets.

All of which were wrong. They were too different to consider their attraction anything more than a potential affair and she wasn't the kind of woman to have affairs, though he knew she was weakening. The night before he'd seen the light in her eyes. They had chemistry stronger than any he'd ever experienced. It was hard enough for him to resist it. Maybe she couldn't. Maybe she didn't want to?

No. He wasn't even going to *think* in that direction. It wasn't right. She would miss him when he returned to Miami, and be hurt that he hadn't even considered staying. And he wouldn't even look back.

When they reached Truffles, he opened the door and a bell jingled.

"Good afternoon, Mr. Edwards," Wendy called.

Cullen stopped just inside the door, memories of his childhood washing over him. The store didn't have typical shelves. Instead, three-tiered tables were arranged around the showroom floor. The bottom tier of the first table held short, cuddly elves. The middle tier had slightly taller Santas. The third tier held a tall music box.

Each table was similarly appointed. Short toys, candy boxes or holiday decorations nestled on the first tier. Taller items sat on the second and the tallest on the third.

Red and green ribbons had been entwined with tinsel and looped along the walls. Holly and evergreen accented with fat red velvet-ribbon bows lined the counter.

The curtain separating the showroom from the storage room slid open and Jim stepped behind the counter, wiping his hands on a red-and-green towel. "Good afternoon, Wendy—"

He stopped, peering through the little round glasses on the end of his nose. "Well, Cullen Barrington! Your dad mentioned you'd be in town."

Cullen stepped over to the counter and shook Jim's hand. Short and bald, wearing a red plaid work shirt and jeans, Jim looked ten years older than Cullen's father, though they were the same age. "Nice to see you, Jim."

"You know the missus will shoot me if I don't ask you to supper tonight."

Cullen patted his tummy. "I'm afraid I had a hot roast beef sandwich at the diner."

Jim laughed. "One day soon then?"

"I'll call Rosie," Cullen promised.

Nodding his agreement, Jim said, "So what can I do for you?"

Wendy said, "Cullen would like to buy Harry a Christmas gift."

"The little boy you brought here the other night?"

She nodded.

Jim brightened, tossed the towel to the counter and came out from behind it. "We have some fabulous gifts for a six-year-old."

As Jim scurried to the front window display, Cullen

watched Wendy's eyes light up. She was so pretty. So innocent. And darned near as easy to please as Harry.

He thought about the last time he'd been shopping. He'd
gone to a boutique in Miami, stepped into a room scented with
roses, was given a cup of spicy tea and told what he would buy
his latest lady friend. Because it was all the rage. Because it
had a price so high he wasn't told the price. He didn't see it
until he signed his credit-card receipt.

"Here you go."

Jim pulled an old-fashioned fire truck from the display.
"He'll love this."

Wendy's mouth fell open in awe. She spun to face Cullen.
"Oh, he will! As we were driving to the office the Saturday I
got custody, he told me he wanted to be a fireman."

"And it's got a bell," Cullen said, finding a little string tab
and tugging twice to make the bell ring. "I don't know what
it is with that kid and bells but he loves them."

Wendy laughed. "It's true. When Harry and I walked here
the other night, he did nothing but chatter about the bell on
Creamsicle's collar."

Cullen stared at her. Mesmerized. Smitten. Her eyes were
alight with joy, her cheeks flushed. Her lips plump and
kissable. His fingers itched to skim her jaw, tilt her face up
for a kiss.

To distract himself, he lifted the little truck to examine it.
"It's not very big."

Jim chuckled. "It's a replica of the one we have at the
firehouse."

"It's a small-town truck?" Cullen peered at it from all angles.

"He'll love it," Jim assured him.

"Okay. I'll take it." He handed the truck to Jim and turned
to walk back to the counter. "And don't tell me it's free."

Scurrying behind the cash register, Jim said, "Not on your life! The same rules apply as when you were a kid. Just because your dad owns half this store, that doesn't mean you get everything half off."

Cullen shook his head and turned to Wendy. "My dad had a thing about making me responsible." The second the words were out of his mouth, he snapped it shut. Why did he constantly confess his secrets to her?

"And yet you survived."

And why did her response always make him laugh? Make him feel normal, as if his past was just like anybody else's, riddled with ups and downs that were part of everybody's growth from child to adult?

Jim rang up the sale, telling Cullen a price that caused his eyes to narrow. "I thought you said there was no discount."

"There isn't. That's the price."

Handing his credit card across the counter, Cullen glanced around the store, his gaze automatically finding Wendy. Standing by one of the three-tiered tables, she examined a row of Christmas ornaments, all of which she returned to the display. He took in her serviceable gray wool coat, plain white mittens and simple black boots.

He wondered when she'd last spent money on herself and knew it had probably been a long time ago and even then she'd purchased the sensible items. The mittens that matched every coat or jacket. The boots she could wear everywhere.

He'd love to buy her a fancy coat, leather gloves, high-heel boots to be worn only on special occasions. Without any trouble, he could envision her face lighting up when she opened the packages. She wouldn't fake an "oh" or "ah." Her surprise would be genuine, her pleasure sincere.

The thought filled him with indescribable warmth that

tingled through his bloodstream. Without even closing his eyes he could see them together on Christmas morning. Harry surrounded by wrapping paper. Wendy's face wreathed in smiles. While he sat on the sofa, one arm stretched leisurely across its back, a cup of coffee in his free hand, enjoying the show taking place in front of a sparkling Christmas tree by the crackling fire in the fireplace.

Disappointment that he couldn't be around on Christmas Day brought him back to reality, but he stopped it in its tracks. He was an adult, and he knew the truth about life. A person couldn't have everything he or she wanted. Which was actually good. Because the things we wanted didn't always turn out to be so wonderful. So it was best to hold back. Not wish. Simply accept that our visions of life were always happier than reality.

Still, that didn't mean he couldn't surround Harry with presents and buy as many things as he wanted for Wendy. That was, after all, how he lived. From a distance. He'd buy the gifts, envision their joy and imagine it as he sat on his boat, soaking up the sun, fishing with his dad.

That was reality.

He signed his credit-card receipt, took his package and walked over to Wendy. "Ready?"

She smiled and he smiled, though he knew she hadn't a clue. He would put that smile on her face again on Christmas morning. He might not sit on her sofa and watch, but he would know he had made her smile.

The odd warmth filled him again only this time he recognized it. Contentment. It was as if he'd figured out that the real reason for his trip to Barrington was to meet her and make her happy, and he had zeroed in on how to do it. Finally, finally, he'd figured out why he always had a sense that he was supposed to be around her.

"Ready when you are."

They stepped out into the cool December afternoon and Wendy automatically turned in the direction of the factory again. Cullen caught her arm. He wouldn't risk buying something she didn't want…or even a color she didn't like or a style she didn't care for.

"We're not done yet."

She glanced up at him. "We're not?"

But he also couldn't tell her he was buying her gifts. She'd refuse them before he even had a chance to shop. He had to watch what she paused beside, what she examined, what she sighed over. But he couldn't do that if she wasn't in a store. "Let's spend a little more money on Harry."

"Why? You bought him exactly what he wants. You don't need to spend more."

"I just—"

He stopped. The confused expression on her face banished the warm, fuzzy feeling of contentment. What was he doing? They didn't really have a relationship. He didn't really know her. And as for figuring out that the real purpose of him being in Barrington was to buy her gifts—well, that was idiotic. Gifts, like a raise, could be misconstrued, and hadn't they already had enough trouble because of misunderstandings? She'd warned him off at least twice. He'd warned her off the thought of having a fling the night before. This cat-and-mouse game that continually tried to pull him in was going to get her hurt, and he refused to let that happen.

"No. You're right."

They walked the length of Main Street in silence, the snow swirling around them like ballet dancers enjoying the notes of a perfect song, the scents of pies and cookies enticing them, the low hum of sporadic traffic hardly penetrating his consciousness. Try as he might to keep his distance, he was ultra-aware of Wendy. He wanted to take her hand, enjoy the quiet walk.

He always loved his time with her. Always felt happy, normal and wonderful around her. Which was undoubtedly why he yearned for a kiss. The season was romantic. But his feelings around her and for her were new and special. No one had ever made him feel like this and for that reason alone he'd love to explore whatever it was that hummed between them.

That was the real bottom line. The thing that kept nagging at him. He'd never felt this way about anyone and it seemed wrong not to at least enjoy it while it lasted. This happiness might not be permanent, but she wasn't a child. She was twenty-six. A widow. If she wanted to have a fling, who was he to decide that they shouldn't?

Maybe if he stopped trying to give her gifts to assuage his hunger and was honest with her, they could have something wonderful for the final two weeks he was here?

CHAPTER NINE

"CULLEN?"

Standing on Wendy's front porch, feeling like a gangly teenager who'd finally found the nerve to visit the girl he had a crush on, Cullen had to work to hide his embarrassment. Which was crazy. His relationships were always short-term, for fun. He shouldn't feel any differently just because the woman he was pursuing lived in Pennsylvania.

"Hi. I...um...came to see how Harry is."

The little boy in question appeared from behind Wendy's knees. His wispy yellow hair floated on his forehead to the rim of his glasses. His smile was wide and welcoming.

"Hi, Cullen!"

Wendy stepped aside and invited Cullen into her foyer. "Hi, Harry!" he said, picking up the little boy and looping him over his shoulder.

Harry whooped with delight, and Cullen surreptitiously glanced at Wendy. She didn't seem displeased that he'd come to visit Harry, but he hoped she'd be even more pleased when she realized that the real reason for his visit was to have some alone time with her.

"We were just about to get Harry ready for bed."

Which was exactly why he'd timed his visit for later in the evening.

"Why don't I read Harry his bedtime story?" And after that he and Wendy would be alone and he could either see for himself that she wasn't so nice, so perfect, so wonderful, and that all these emotions swirling around him were ridiculous, or she'd get the message that to him sexual attraction meant exactly that. Sexual attraction. Not love. Certainly not marriage. And they'd get involved. On his terms.

Wendy shrugged. "Sounds good to me." She turned to go up the stairs. Harry followed her. Cullen followed Harry.

Stopping in the hall outside Harry's door, she pointed to the bedroom. "I'll get the bath ready. You two get a clean pair of pj's from his dresser."

Harry obediently walked into his bedroom, directly to the dresser. He opened the drawer, pulled out a pair of pajamas, left the room and headed for the bathroom.

Cullen smiled. That was easy.

Watching through the open bathroom door, he saw Wendy pull off Harry's T-shirt. Over the little boy's head she called, "There are three library books in the bottom drawer of his bedside table. Pick one. He'll be in in a minute."

Cullen went to the bedside table, sat on the bed, and opened the bottom drawer to find three worn children's books. He pulled out the last book, leafed through it to make sure he hadn't made a bad choice and decided he'd be okay with the story about a pig in a puddle.

Tossing the book to the bed, he rose and shrugged out of his leather jacket. He hung it across the back of the chair tucked under a Harry-sized desk and walked to the window.

Outside, the dusting of snow had turned into an inch of fluffy white that sparkled in the streetlights. Car windshields were covered. A coating clung to bare black branches of the big trees in the front yards in Wendy's neighborhood. The quiet, peaceful scene almost made his plans feel all wrong.

Almost.

Small-town women weren't any less sexual than those in the big city. They were simply more discreet, and he could be discreet.

"All set," Wendy said and Cullen turned to see her standing behind Harry who grinned at him.

"I'm all set, too."

"I found a story about a puppy in a puddle."

Harry rolled his eyes. "You mean a pig in a puddle."

Laughing, Cullen walked to the bed. "Same thing."

"No, it isn't!" Harry looked horrified. "There's a big difference between a pig and a puppy."

Struggling with a smile, Wendy grabbed Harry's doorknob as she left the room. "I'll just leave you two alone for now." She closed the door behind her.

Harry scrambled under his covers, took off his glasses and set them on the bedside table. Cullen sat on the bed.

Twenty minutes later, with Harry fast asleep and Cullen's tongue about tied in a knot from all the rhyme and alliteration in the storybook he'd read, Cullen walked down the steps. He casually tossed his jacket over the coat tree in the foyer and walked into the living room where Wendy sat.

Now things would get interesting.

She looked up from the book she was reading. "How did it go?"

"He's out like a light." He casually walked to the sofa and sat beside her. Not so close as to appear inappropriate, not so far away that he wouldn't accomplish his purpose.

"I think I should stay awhile, though, make sure he doesn't have a nightmare and wake up."

She set her book on the coffee table and reached for a round yellow pot. "Hot cocoa. Would you like a cup?"

"Sure."

She poured some into one of the bright yellow mugs on the bamboo tray and handed it to him.

"Smells great." But she smelled even better. The scent of her floated around him. He guessed it was shampoo. Every time she moved, her long red curls danced and shifted, sending the aroma of something light and floral swirling around him. All his hormones cheered. He'd absolutely made the right decision.

"It's from scratch."

"From scratch?"

"I made it myself. I boil cocoa, butter, sugar and vanilla until it makes syrup, then I add whole milk."

He took a sip. "That's really good."

"I don't make it often because it's fattening and probably full of cholesterol."

But tonight was a special night. Damn it. She didn't even have to say the words. He got the message. Because he felt it too, the strange sense of being in the right place at the right time enveloped him. No matter how he tried to keep things purely sexual, something else hummed between them. And that "something else" wasn't what he wanted out of life. He knew that "something else" let people down. He didn't want to be let down the way his parents had been. He didn't want to let Wendy down the way her husband had.

He leaped up off the sofa. "You know what? It's getting late. Harry'll probably be fine." He headed for the door. "I'll see you in the morning."

She rose from the sofa, gave him a confused smile. "Okay."

* * *

Cullen didn't say another word to her. He grabbed his jacket and ran from her house. Wendy dropped her head to her hands. She was such a klutz. A ditz. And the worst of it was, this time she had absolutely no idea what she'd done wrong.

She ambled to bed, miserable.

Friday morning, he barely spoke to her and he left for Miami before noon. Emma and Patty took an early lunch, and Wendy missed them, but she wasn't ready to share anyway. She was growing a tad tired of looking like an idiot. Not just to Cullen, but to her friends.

Saturday morning, Emma and Patty surprised Wendy with an early-morning visit.

Motioning for them to enter her kitchen, she said, "What are you two doing here?"

Emma held up a box of doughnuts. "We've brought food."

"So you'll spill the beans," Patty added as she shrugged out of her coat and hung it on the peg by the door.

Still not quite sure she was ready to talk, Wendy took the box of doughnuts to her kitchen table. "Spill what?"

Patty glanced around. "First of all, where's Harry?"

"Watching cartoons."

"Good."

"Yeah, because now we can get into the juicy stuff." Patty walked to the table. "I saw his car here Thursday night."

Wendy frowned. "What were you doing out in this part of town?"

"Forgot my inhaler at work," Patty said. "Had to call Wendell to let me in."

"Oh."

"So," Emma prodded, sidling up to Wendy as she poured three mugs of coffee. "What happened?"

Wendy glanced over at Emma. "Nothing."

"Oh, come on." Patty sat on one of the chairs at the round kitchen table.

Handing Emma one of the mugs of coffee, Wendy said, "It's true. He came to check on Harry, read him a story, took one sip of the hot cocoa I had made while he was reading and bolted."

"Bolted?" Emma sat beside Patty. "Interesting choice of words."

"Because it's true. He ran as if his feet were on fire."

Patty grinned at Emma. "Very interesting."

"Very embarrassing. I'm guessing the cocoa sucked."

Emma leaned closer to Wendy. "I'm guessing he hadn't come over for cocoa."

Patty leaned in, too. "And you confused him." She shook her head in dismay. "Who offers a man like Cullen Barrington cocoa? It's like saying you're homespun—which means you want a home—which he probably interprets as meaning you want marriage."

Wendy gasped. "I didn't mean that!"

"Of course you didn't." Emma sighed. "You hardly know the man. You shouldn't want to marry him."

Patty shook her head. "You are really rusty."

"Rusty?"

"On dating. Which is why we're here. Monday morning you're not going to look like Suzy Snowflake."

"Or Sandy Secretary," Emma agreed. "He's interested, but you keep confusing him."

"So we're going to help you pick your outfits for next week, so you stop sending mixed signals."

Wendy bit her bottom lip. "I'm not sure this is a good idea."

Both friends put their folded arms on the table. "Why?"

"Because he…he's…"

"Different," Emma supplied. "We get it."

"He's not going to settle down with you." Patty snagged a doughnut. "But you need to get back into the real world."

Emma also took a doughnut. "Consider him practice."

"And if you're lucky, you'll get lots and lots of *practice*."

Wendy hid a shudder of pleasure. She told herself nothing could come of this, but just as quickly reminded herself that Emma was right. Even if nothing happened between her and Cullen, she needed to practice even simple things like how to make small talk, what drinks to serve and even how to dress. She wouldn't make a big deal out of this. She knew the truth. Cullen wasn't the kind to settle down.

But a little voice in her heart reminded her that plenty of flings had turned into the real thing. Practice or not, she liked him. There were so many things to like about him. And maybe…just maybe…

She shoved those thoughts away, telling herself she shouldn't wish for things that couldn't be. But try as she might to think of spending time with Cullen as only a trial run, she liked him. And she could very well end up hurt.

But playing it safe had gotten her hurt, too.

There was no easy answer.

She pulled in a breath. "All right, I'm in. Just don't make me look like somebody I'm not."

Cullen spent the weekend on his boat, soaking in the tropical sun, reminding himself that *this* was where he belonged.

When he returned to Barrington Candies late Monday afternoon, he kept his head down. He plowed through Wendy's office and only grunted hello as he strode by. He even closed the door.

He didn't get involved with women like Wendy. Normally, he didn't even want to. Not because they were somehow wrong, but because he was fair. They were looking for something he couldn't give, so he unselfishly let them alone.

So why the devil couldn't he just do that with Wendy?

He had absolutely no idea, but he did know that his innate sense of fairness would keep him in line. A bit of sexual desire would not be his undoing. He could control the crazy urges he had to touch her and taste her and kiss her. And by God, he would!

After hanging his leather jacket in the closet, he strode to his desk. In keeping with Wendy's suggestion that he behave a little more comfortably with the workers as a subtle reassurance that their jobs were safe, he'd chosen to wear corduroy trousers and a green sweater over a white shirt, and was amazingly comfortable himself. He reminded himself that was because he typically worked in casual trousers and lightweight shirts, in beachfront restaurants or on boats, persuading investors to trust him with their money. He wasn't the kind of guy who liked being stuck in an office—though he couldn't say he'd been unhappy here at Barrington Candies. In fact, he'd been amazingly happy.

He growled at himself. Told himself to stop. One woman couldn't change how he felt about everything in his life!

Tuesday morning, he arrived in the office when Wendy was away from her desk. The minute his butt hit the chair, he put his head down and set his mind on the production figures from the day before. He didn't surface until eleven o'clock, when he needed to see the five-year plan again. Hitting a button on his phone, he buzzed Wendy.

No answer.

He tried again.

No answer.

With an annoyed sigh, he rose and walked into her office

only to find she wasn't there. Thinking she might be in the clerical area, and sorely in need of a short walk to stretch his muscles, he walked out.

Remembering Wendy's suggestion about helping the employees grow accustomed to him, he smiled. "Has anyone seen Wendy?"

A pretty brunette glanced up at him in surprise. "She's on the factory floor, doing a quick safety audit."

"Thanks."

She nodded eagerly, obviously happy to have been called upon.

Cullen headed for the factory floor. He knew that in their small company employees did a lot of double duty. It wasn't a surprise that the employee who probably kept the records for the safety equipment was the one who walked through the plant to make sure everything was where it was supposed to be.

But he really couldn't wait until she was done to get the reports he needed. He opened the door to the plant and the scents of chocolate and peanut butter that had floated on the air all morning hit him in earnest, making his mouth water. But he forgot all about the sweet temptation when he saw Wendy at the other end of the floor.

Wearing a black skirt and crisp white blouse, she looked coolly efficient. That thought registered and then floated away when his eyes ran the length of exposed leg. He'd never seen her legs before. Realizing he was staring, he gave himself a mental shake and began walking toward her.

For Pete's sake, he partied with women in thong bikinis! How could he be so startled, so affected, by the sight of a woman's calves? It was ridiculous. And if he didn't stifle his reactions, stop giving her these signals, she'd be the one to do something about their attraction, he wouldn't be able to resist…and he'd end up hurting her.

"Hey, Mr. Barrington?"

He stopped and turned toward the sound of his name.

Standing by the Ferris-wheel-like apparatus that distributed assorted candies for packing, and wearing a white coat and a hairnet, a woman in her fifties smiled at him.

"Are you going to the company Christmas party Friday night?"

He took the few steps over to the candy wheel. "Actually, I didn't know there was a Christmas party."

"It's sort of employee-sponsored. We save the proceeds from the vending machines all year and in December we have enough to have a Christmas party."

She gave him the name of his own hotel as the venue for the party, but he hardly paid any attention. Paul McCoy couldn't even spare a few thousand dollars of the company's money to host a Christmas party for the people who worked for him all year? He was an abysmal general manager. Cullen intended to call his hotel that afternoon and pay for the party, and he also intended to have a few choice words with Paul.

"Sure. I'm going."

She grinned and waved a piece of candy at him. "Want a Peanut Butter Bite?"

The *no* that should have tripped off his tongue, tripped over itself. He hadn't had a piece of Barrington's Candies in at least ten years. The scents wafting through the factory combined with a vivid memory of the taste of sweet chocolate and smooth peanut butter, and somehow moved his feet closer to the packing cylinder.

"Actually, my favorite is caramel."

A younger woman stretched her gloved hand to the distributor and plucked off a piece of candy. "Here you go."

His mouth watering, Cullen took the chocolate-covered caramel she handed him. He popped it in his mouth and groaned.

"I'd forgotten how good this was."

The packing ladies giggled.

"Want another?"

"Maybe one for after lunch."

The first packer snagged a piece and set it in one of the little brown paper cups that lined the Barrington Candies boxes. "Here you go."

He smiled at her. "Thanks."

From her position in shipping at the back of the factory floor, Wendy watched Cullen, crossing her arms on her chest, pride swelling inside her. She wasn't entirely sure why he'd come onto the plant floor, but unlike his first trip to have her introduce him around, his demeanor was totally different. And he'd accepted candy from strangers.

She wanted to giggle, but didn't want to call attention to herself, which might shift the attention of the employees milling around her to Cullen. He was doing so well building the employees' confidence in him that she didn't want to ruin that.

She pulled in a breath and let it out slowly. He was such a good guy. Really good. The affection he had for Harry could be explained by Harry's charm. But the gracious way he'd agreed to ease the employees' worries about the company closing was all Cullen. He was a good-hearted person. A nice guy.

A nice guy who wouldn't even look at her now.

She watched him laughing with the packers, accepting the various pieces of candy they handed to him, until ultimately Jennie Ferguson gave him a box in which to store his goodies.

Wendy smiled at his silly behavior. He wasn't simply a good person; he was a fun person. Fun had been missing from her life for two long years and in a little over two weeks, Cullen had her toasting marshmallows, making cocoa from scratch, Christmas-shopping and kissing again. For the first time in months she'd actually thought about sex. Not because of a physical need but because of him. This gorgeous, sexy, sweet guy had her tiptoeing into uncharted territory. But she was a small-town girl with so little experience she constantly made mistakes with him.

Before anybody noticed her staring, she turned and began taking inventory of the items in the first aid kit in shipping and receiving.

Like Patty and Emma, she'd thought for sure he had come to her house last Thursday night to see her. But he couldn't even sit with her for two minutes after he'd read Harry's story. Now, he wouldn't look at her. She suspected he hadn't yet noticed that Emma and Patty had given her a makeover. And if he had, he'd probably realized she was dressing up for him and that was why he was keeping his distance.

This time she'd made a fool of herself without even opening her mouth.

She couldn't remember the last time she'd been so disappointed. So embarrassed. Seeing him laughing with the candy packers, her humiliation grew. She was the only person he seemed nervous around. Because of their damned attraction. Because he realized she wouldn't mind having an affair with him. Because she was now strutting around in skirts instead of slacks, wearing makeup…making a fool of herself!

He'd warned her off. But she couldn't take a hint and now she felt like an idiot.

* * *

With a box of assorted chocolates under his arm, Cullen glanced in the direction of shipping and receiving and didn't see Wendy.

He turned to his candy posse—which is what they'd told him to call them since they intended to make sure all his chocolate needs were met for the rest of his stay. "Anybody see where Wendy went?"

"She left through the side door," Annette said, pointing to the opposite end of the plant floor. "Probably on her way back to her office."

"Thanks."

He arrived in Wendy's office, smiling. After his encounter with the ladies in packing, he now understood that most of the people in this town were happy-go-lucky and generous with their time and attention. He didn't have to worry about Wendy. She wasn't falling for him. She was simply being nice to him because that's the way people in this town were.

Walking into her office, he displayed his box of chocolates. "Look what I got."

She didn't look up from her work. "That's nice."

"How can you say that's nice when you didn't even see what I have?"

"You have a box of chocolates."

"How do you know?"

"I saw you talking with the ladies in packing."

He thought about that for a second. She should be dancing for joy that he was doing as she asked, mingling, making himself seem normal, putting everybody's mind at ease that he and his father had no intention of closing the factory.

Yet she was angry. Why would she be angry that he talked with the packing ladies?

His eyes narrowed. Unless she was jealous?

A sweet pang of self-satisfaction danced in his belly. But he stopped it. That was ridiculous. First, she didn't seem like the kind of woman to be jealous. Second, he didn't want her to be jealous. Now that he understood what a bad idea it would be for them to have an affair, he wanted their relationship to be strictly professional.

"They're all very nice," he said softly, not quite sure what else to say.

She rose from her desk and walked with the safety binder to the filing cabinet. Sliding it into position with the other binders, she said, "Wasn't I the one who told you that?"

Her clipped tone made him sigh. "All right. What's wrong?"

"Nothing. I have work to do."

The sharp tone was a downgrade from the clipped tone. Whatever had her angry, it was getting worse. "Why are you angry?"

She spun to face him. "I'm *not* angry."

He took a step closer, set his candy on top of the filing cabinets and touched his index finger to the red spots flaring on her cheeks. "These say otherwise."

But as the words came out of his mouth, he realized she wasn't angry. She really was upset.

His index finger hovered above her soft cheeks, so it was a natural movement when his hand shifted to cup her jaw.

Her big green eyes blinked up at him and his pulse scrambled. He didn't take the time to evaluate the situation. Didn't give himself an opportunity to issue the three thousand warnings that were ringing like bells in his brain. The sweet syrupy feeling tightening his chest had him under its spell. It urged him to shift forward, just brush his lips across hers.

He did and wasn't sorry. Her taste was sweeter than a

thousand candies. Her soft mouth responded to his, naturally, honestly, sending another pang of need through him.

His hands fell to her waist, nudging her closer, and she melted in his arms.

But it was the way she melted with total trust that brought him to his senses. If they got involved, one way or another he would let her down. Even if things worked out the way she wanted and they fell in love, he knew love didn't last. His parents had sniped at each other for nearly forty years. When his mother had died, Cullen had actually struggled with the worry that his father had been relieved. Though he'd cried at her funeral, the next day he'd been off on his boat and soon he was out at parties with friends. In a week, it seemed that Cullen's mom had been forgotten by everybody but Cullen. There was no way he wanted that for himself. But more than that, there was no way he wanted that for Wendy.

He pulled away. She blinked up at him, her pretty green eyes bright. Her lips were glistening from his kiss.

He squeezed his eyes shut in misery. "I'm sorry. I shouldn't have done that. I don't want to give you the wrong impression. But most of all I don't want to hurt you."

CHAPTER TEN

STANDING by the filing cabinet with her lips still tingling from his kiss, Wendy watched Cullen race into his office. She noticed that he'd forgotten his candy but wasn't about to take it in to him. She was too stunned.

Not because he'd kissed her, but because he couldn't help himself. She hadn't made a fool of herself. He *liked* her, but he didn't want to hurt her.

She should feel that he was noble. She should even appreciate it. But part of her was annoyed. Maybe she and Cullen weren't meant to be together forever, but she needed this. She needed a few days or weeks with a man who truly couldn't resist her to make her feel strong and sexy again. He was leaving on Thursday of the following week. They didn't have enough time left together that she'd be paralyzed with pain when he left. So everything could be okay.

But she wouldn't be the one to pursue him. She refused to make a fool of herself. The embarrassment of the past few days had burned that lesson onto her brain.

She went back to work.

He went back to work.

And they didn't speak for the rest of the week, except when he needed something.

* * *

Friday at lunch the employee cafeteria was abuzz with the news that Cullen intended to attend the Christmas party. Sitting at her desk that afternoon, Wendy watched him, saddened that a wonderful opportunity was slipping through her fingers. Still, she couldn't be the one to make the first move. Especially not at the Christmas party. Too many people would be watching. Too much chance that her coworkers would see her embarrassment if he rejected her.

At five o'clock she dashed home, thinking she'd have to remind Mrs. Brennon that she was cooking dinner and babysitting that night. She found the plump older woman humming at the stove, stirring a pot of something that smelled like beef stew.

"You remembered!"

Mrs. Brennon nodded. "How could I forget dinner with such a handsome young man?"

Sitting at the table crayoning the pictures in a thick coloring book, Harry peered at Wendy over his glasses. "She means me."

Wendy walked over and hugged him. "Of course she means you."

"You scoot now," Mrs. Brennon said, waving her arms at Wendy. "You have a party to go to."

Wendy raced to her bedroom. The party began at seven. She needed an hour to dress. And there was the matter of the thirty-minute drive to the hotel. She didn't have a second to waste.

She quickly stripped and showered but spent far too long twisting her long hair into bouncy curls with the curling iron.

Realizing she had about ten minutes to get on the road or dinner would already be started, she raced to her closet. And stood staring at the dress she'd purchased the week before with Emma and Patty's guidance.

She pulled out the simple sleeveless red sheath and

examined it, wondering if she should wear it. They'd picked it knowing it would attract Cullen's attention. Short enough to reveal a bit of leg, but not embarrassingly short. Snug enough to cruise her curves but not too tight.

Would it be enough to attract his attention?

And if it wasn't, would she lose her patience and ask him to dance?

Could she risk another rejection?

Not entirely sure how to dress for this event, since he'd never attended a company Christmas party, Cullen decided on a plain black suit, a white shirt and a gold tie. That was about as festive as his wardrobe got when he was traveling. But when he stepped into the hotel's ballroom and saw that most of the men wore suits and ties, no tuxes, he relaxed.

He took a drink from a passing waiter and saw Wendy in the back of the room chatting with some people from shipping and receiving. The sleeveless red dress she wore was particularly flattering to her figure, and he let his gaze ripple from her head to her toes, pausing to take in the length of leg she exposed.

She'd never looked prettier or sexier, so he turned and walked in the other direction. Not because he wanted to avoid her, but because he needed to be careful around her. Especially in a room full of witnesses. If he lost control and kissed her again, that would be the talk of the factory on Monday morning. He still had almost a week to work here and the prospect of being teased or gossiped about didn't thrill him. Worse, Wendy had to work with these people forever. He wouldn't embarrass her.

The ladies in his candy posse corralled him and he accepted their invitation to sit at their table for dinner. Which was good. He'd avoided yet another opportunity to get too close to Wendy.

After dinner, the band shifted from dinner music to dance

music. Telling his posse that he needed to mingle, he excused himself and headed for the bar. He was stopped by so many people that the band finished their first set, took a break and began playing again before he actually made it.

He ordered a Scotch and suddenly found himself standing by Emma Watson and Patty Franks. "Good evening, Mr. Barrington."

"Good evening, ladies. Are you enjoying yourselves?"

"Yes. Thank you."

Patty blinked false eyelashes at him. "I haven't seen you dancing yet tonight."

"I sort of got waylaid."

"That's no excuse," she said with a laugh. Just when Cullen was absolutely positive she was about to ask him to dance, she shifted slightly. Wendy stood behind her. "I'm sure Wendy would love to dance."

From the way Wendy's eyes widened with fear, Cullen not only knew her friends had surprised her, but also that dancing with him was probably the absolute last thing she wanted to do. But because she was afraid, not eager, he knew they would be safe together. Saying no or making a fuss would only call more attention to them than if they simply complied and danced to one song.

He held out his hand. "Would you care to dance?"

She swallowed and looked at her two friends who were smirking with victory before she placed her hand in his. "Sure."

He led her out to the crowded floor just as the band stopped playing a hopping fast tune and began playing something slow. He caught her gaze. "If you'd rather not—"

She grimaced. "They'll just keep hounding us until we dance, so we might as well get this over with."

Taking her into his arms, he said, "Just what every guy wants to hear."

She laughed. "Sorry."

She fit so perfectly and felt so good that Cullen nearly groaned. Luckily, Wendy tilted her head back and said, "You're a big hit."

He laughed. "Thanks to my love of candy and my candy posse."

"Rumor has it you paid for the party."

He shrugged. "It's the least my father and I can do."

"Well, that gesture's gone a long way to improve employee morale."

"Nobody thinks the plant is closing anymore?"

She shook her head and gave him another sweet smile. "No. Thank you."

"These people should be thanking you."

She shrugged. "Not really. I was just being a good assistant. Filling you in on things you should know."

He pulled back, caught her gaze. "You really can't be that good."

Her pretty face scrunched in confusion, as her eyes lit with laughter. "What do you mean *good*?"

She truly didn't get it. She didn't understand that she was beautiful, sexy and intriguing enough to draw a jaded man like himself to her and then sweet enough to make him almost believe in Christmas wishes.

"You're very nice to people."

"No. I simply treat people the way I want to be treated."

He groaned. "Stop."

Wendy tilted her face up to him. "Stop what?"

"Stop being so nice."

She laughed. "I'm not always nice."

The look in her eyes told him exactly what she was thinking. He was the person she didn't want to be "nice" with and he could almost envision the naughtiness she hinted at. The temptation to kiss her was nearly overwhelming. But she wasn't one of the pampered socialites he typically dated. He couldn't be flippant with her—tease her, take her home and make love until dawn—then go back to being her boss on Monday morning.

Still, he might not be able to make love with her or even kiss her, but he couldn't stop himself from dipping her on the dance floor, and was rewarded with a giggle.

"Stop that," she admonished, but her words poured out through a laugh. "This isn't *Dancing with the Stars*."

He laughed, too, and whirled her around. He might not ever get to sleep with her, but why couldn't they spend this last hour of the evening simply enjoying each other's company? If there was one thing he'd learned about her in the three weeks they'd been together, it was that he was always himself, always had fun in her company.

The night suddenly felt young and full of possibilities. No one had ever made him as happy as Wendy did.

The thought that she'd become so special to him caused him to ease back a bit, once again not wanting to start something he couldn't finish. But he suddenly realized that this might be the one and only time in his life when he'd allow himself to feel this close to someone. In Miami, he'd go back to dating spoiled socialites. His life would be all about hiding who he was, what he cared about, so no one could get too close. He *wanted* this. He wanted this hour of simply having fun. He wanted it enough to convince himself that if he returned to his typical boss self on Monday morning, the way Cinderella's coach returned to being a pumpkin at the stroke of midnight, she'd take this night for what it was—one fabulous hour filled with joy—but she'd also realize anything more wasn't to be.

Wendy felt the shift in him. Rather than being stiff and polite, he relaxed. His arms wrapped around her possessively. His cheek pressed against her temple. She could match the soft puff of breath near her ear to the gentle rhythm of his chest rising and falling against hers.

At first she stiffened. If she misinterpreted this, she would make a huge fool of herself. But he tightened his hold and pulled her closer. He smelled so damned good that she weakened. Her bones seemed to melt and she cuddled closer.

When the song ended, she pulled back, out of his embrace, but he caught her hand and stopped her. "There's no reason to leave the dance floor."

Her heart kicked into overdrive. "You want to dance again?"

The band began playing another slow tune and he smiled. "Yes."

She swallowed. "Okay."

By the end of the second dance, Wendy felt gooey inside. They didn't have to speak for her to feel them growing closer.

The band started a fast song and Cullen grabbed her hand. Thinking he was leading them to the bar, she was surprised when he walked out of the ballroom and into the brightly lit lobby. Using his room key card, he opened a door that led to a dark and silent atrium.

She stepped inside. "Wow."

"There's a pool just beyond that garden." He pointed to a large circle of tropical plants beneath a skylight that revealed a million stars twinkling in a sea of black sky. "It's locked to anyone but hotel guests."

Her eyes widening, she spun to face him. "We're not—You're not thinking of swimming—"

He laughed. "No. I don't want to swim. I just wanted some privacy."

She stepped away. "Oh."

"You don't have to be afraid."

"I'm not afraid." She walked over to the circle of plants that hid the pool from view of anyone in the lobby. "I always wondered how they got these to grow here."

"Climate control and sunlamps."

She tilted her head. "That makes sense."

"Yep."

This time his answer came from directly behind her. His hands fell to her shoulders and he turned her around. "I also didn't bring you here to talk about the plants."

"What do you want to talk about?"

He shrugged. "I don't know. Your plans for the future."

Her heart stuttered. Her pulse scrambled. She nearly asked him why he'd be concerned about her future, but didn't want to look needy. Silly. There were only two reasons he would ask. One, he was worried about her. Or, two, he wanted to be part of her future and wondered if he fit into it.

She liked number two better.

Considering what she'd say, she caught his gaze. "I…um…have to take care of Harry. That's my number-one priority."

"Anything else?"

Suddenly feeling flirtatious, she stepped away. "I want lots of things."

He followed her, but she continued to stay just out of his reach. "Like what?"

"Well, I'd like to fix up my house."

He grimaced. "You want to stay there?"

She turned to face him, let him catch up to her. "Yes. It's a beautiful house."

"No. It's a solid house. A sturdy house. With a little work it might be beautiful."

"All the more reason to keep it. It's dependable. I can make that house a home for me and Harry."

Holding her gaze, Cullen tilted his head. "Yes. I think you can."

Then he kissed her and she didn't hesitate to wrap her arms around him. He was staying at this hotel. In one short elevator ride they could be behind closed doors with no worries that anyone else in the hotel with a room key could pop in on them. Then she'd have him all to herself.

Just the thought made her heart skip a beat and filled her with fear. She didn't just want a fling. Cullen was perfect. Wonderful. She'd fallen in love with him. And it appeared he was falling in love with her, too.

He pulled away slowly. His voice was a mere whisper when he said, "Let's get out of here."

She nodded. Cullen caught her hand and led her into the lobby, but instead of heading for the elevator he walked her to the coat room. At first she was confused, then she remembered that the coat room would be locked by the time she came downstairs, and she'd either have to ask at the front desk to be let in to get her coat, or slink home without one.

But instead of slinging her coat over his arm, he helped her into it.

"Party's about over," he said, taking her hand and leading her to the hotel entrance. "This way, we'll miss the crowd."

They walked in silence across the cold parking lot. A

million thoughts swirled through her head. But she said nothing because she had no idea what he was doing.

When they reached her little blue vehicle, she said, "Why did you walk me to my car?"

He caught her hand, lifted it to his lips. "Come on, Cinderella. You didn't really think I was going to miss this opportunity, did you?"

He said the words as he bent to kiss her and Wendy's head spun. With one coaxing swipe from the tip of his tongue she opened her mouth to him. He drew her so close that their bodies melded together and she cursed her black wool winter coat. The kiss went on and on, warming her blood, making her forget her own name, and suddenly he pulled away. Stepped away.

"Good night."

Her breath puffed out in confusion, until she realized he probably knew she had to get home to Harry. She smiled. For once his noble gesture really was a noble gesture. She also couldn't really argue with him. As much as she'd love to walk back into that hotel with him and finish what they'd started, he was right. Harry needed her. Plus, they had at least the week he was in Barrington to follow up on this.

Maybe more.

She couldn't stop her heart from wishing that maybe, just maybe, what had started this Christmas could extend throughout the year.

But that was a wish for another night. Tonight, she simply wanted to bask in the joy that he really did like her, as much as she liked him.

And they had another week.

* * *

Cullen flew home to Miami on Saturday morning.

"Are you home for good?" his dad asked, not looking up from his newspaper.

Cullen carefully set his briefcase on the counter. "I have a few more days to finish out, Dad."

"Uh-huh." His dad's voice dripped with skepticism as he folded the paper and tossed it aside. "We got a call from Paul McCoy last night. He quit."

All the breath rushed out of Cullen's lungs. "What?"

"He lied to us. He wasn't on an extended vacation. He had bypass surgery. Seems that the whole process left him feeling life's too short to work it away and he's choosing not to come back."

Cullen fell to one of the breakfast-nook chairs. His immediate reaction was that he could run the factory, but he stopped it. Even the *suggestion* would infuriate his dad—which was probably why his father was behaving so oddly. Plus, he'd be giving up the life he'd created here in Miami. The life he loved.

The lust still racing through his blood from a few simple kisses the night before reminded him that maybe he could love another life. As clear as a bell, he could see himself marrying Wendy, fixing up the old monstrosity that had been in his family for generations before Wendy had bought it, and raising Harry.

A bubble of joy formed in his chest. As if the entirety of his life had been leading him to this moment. This decision.

His father's voice brought him back to reality. "I already called an employment agency. They're setting up interviews for Sunday afternoon and Monday morning at your hotel."

"That was fast."

"I offered the recruiter a bonus if we could have a firm yes from someone before Christmas."

"That's not much time."

"It's a week. The economy is down. Lots of people are looking for work. Some people will consider a shot at this job their Christmas miracle."

And suddenly Cullen saw the truth. "You don't want to risk me staying."

Donald Barrington pulled in a breath. "I'm seeing some signs I don't like, Cullen." He reached for his coffee. "Don't get me wrong. I'm not so prejudiced that I don't know that there are some nice people in Barrington. Good people. But the truth is that that factory sucks Barringtons into a black hole that never lets them out. Look what happened to your mother."

"I'm not my mother."

"No. You're not. You're more like me. You'll find a woman that you really love and who you think loves you, and *she'll* tie you to the factory. You might not think so at first. You'll be so far in lust with her you'll think you'll be happy forever. But one day you'll get bored with the factory and you'll suggest you hire a replacement so you can come back to the life you love here, and she'll say no. She doesn't want to leave her friends. And you'll start noticing she cares more about her coworkers than she cares about you and you'll wonder if she ever cared about you at all."

Cullen licked his suddenly dry lips. He never realized how much his relationship with Wendy was like his parents' relationship. "I can always get a divorce."

"And never see your child? That's how she'll hold you, you know. She'll convince you to have a child or two and then tell you that if you move you'll never see your child again."

He swallowed. "Was that what mom threatened?"

"Yes. Not because she intended to ask a judge to preclude me from seeing you, but because she knew I'd be moving thousands of miles away. She didn't have to threaten me. School would keep you in Barrington. And I'd see you in the summers. If I was lucky."

"You stayed married for me?"

"Yes."

Cullen's stomach sank and his world spun. So many things that hadn't made sense suddenly did. His father had stayed for *him*. He might not have coached Little League or even spent inordinate amounts of time with him, but he'd kept the bond so when they finally could move away they'd have time together. As much as Cullen wanted.

And now Cullen was considering abandoning him. For a woman he barely knew. A woman who'd already worked some kind of magic on him to get him involved with the employees and to like them.

Donald Barrington rose to get another cup of coffee, bringing Cullen out of his reverie. "I was going to do the interviews but if you want to—"

"I'll do it."

He didn't believe Wendy had faked her feelings for him, but they didn't know each other well enough for him to say they wouldn't end up like his parents.

He wouldn't take the job of running Barrington Candies, but he did owe her an explanation. He simply didn't know how or when he'd make it.

CHAPTER ELEVEN

CULLEN arrived so late on Monday afternoon that Wendy would have missed him if she hadn't been a few minutes behind in leaving for the day.

Just the sight of him made her heart sing. "Hey."

His voice was soft and solemn, when he said, "Hey."

"What's wrong?"

"Nothing." He paused. "I'm just tired."

"After traveling from Miami, I suppose you have a right to be tired."

"Yeah." He pulled in a breath. "You go on home. I have everything I need."

"You're working?"

"Yeah."

"Okay," she said, understanding, but unable to stop the swell of disappointment that poured through her. Now that the weekend was gone, they had three days—three short days—to see if they could have something before he returned to Miami—and he'd scheduled himself to work one of those nights.

It didn't make sense, unless she'd misinterpreted everything on Friday night. After all, they'd only shared a few mind-blowing kisses. A guy like Cullen Barrington probably kissed hundreds of girls. What had been magic for her might have been normal for him.

"I'll see you in the morning," she said lightly, leaving the office with her dignity intact. But her heart hurt. She didn't know if he was really busy or backing off, and she was too inexperienced to figure it out. Worse, the situation was too fragile to call Patty for an interpretation.

"Hey, Wendy. Can I ask you a question?"

Wendy turned from the dishwasher with a smile for Harry. She didn't have any idea what was going on with Cullen, but she did know she couldn't let it affect Harry. "Sure."

"Can we go see Santa tonight?"

She'd totally forgotten about the trip to see Santa. The news of Harry's father's death had completely wiped it off her radar screen, and time was running out. With only four days until Christmas, if they didn't go see Santa soon, their chance would be gone.

Miserable or not, she needed to take him to see Santa. Plus, getting out of the house might get her mind off Cullen.

"Sure. Why not?"

"Yes!" Harry said, doing a victory hand pump.

"Go upstairs and change your shirt and comb your hair, while I finish the dishes."

"Okay."

Harry scrambled off his chair and raced into the hall and up the stairs. He passed his room and stopped in front of Wendy's. With a quick look behind him to make sure she hadn't followed him, he darted inside and rifled in his jeans pocket for the scrap of paper he'd torn out of his notebook.

As Harry picked up the phone, Creamsicle ambled into

Wendy's bedroom. He plopped beside Harry's feet, his bell chiming.

"There's no point in ringing that bell if they're never together," Harry said as he punched the number for Cullen's cell phone into the phone on Wendy's bedside table. Cullen answered on the second ring.

"Hey, Cullen!"

"Hey, kid. What's up? There's nothing wrong, is there?"

"No. Wendy's taking me to see Santa tonight."

Cullen settled more comfortably against the headboard of his hotel-room bed. He'd just finished his final interview. After talking with fifteen various and sundry potential plant managers, he'd decided that Tom Ross had all the qualifications they were looking for. Cullen had not only given him a tour of the plant, Tom had also accepted the job. He had to work out a two-week notice, but after the rush for Christmas, Barrington Candies closed for two weeks for the holiday, so Tom would be available the first day Barrington Candies went back to work.

His head spinning from the hectic pace of the past two days, Cullen could use a few minutes of mindless conversation with the little boy he'd miss more than he'd ever imagined.

"That's great. Are you going to sit on his lap?"

"Yep. And somebody will take a picture of me."

"It's usually an elf."

Harry laughed. Cullen smiled. The kid was too damned cute.

"So if you want to, you could come with us."

His chest tightened. He'd pay good money for a little more time with Wendy, real time, private time, but he'd started the process of distancing himself from her that afternoon. It wasn't a good idea to give her the wrong impression. He knew firsthand what happened to a marriage when love left. He didn't want what his parents had. A miserable shell of a relationship where they argued more than they talked.

And he was already half in love with Harry. That's why it was so easy for him to understand why his dad had stayed, why he hadn't divorced his mother and moved on. He didn't want to lose touch with his son. He and his dad might not have had a perfect relationship, but his dad had been there every night. When Cullen became a man and his father and mother had moved to Miami to be with him, they'd had a relationship to build on. Cullen could see himself doing the same thing for Harry—staying with Wendy even after the love died, if only to keep enough contact with Harry that they could have a relationship when Harry became an adult.

It was better to stop things between him and Wendy before he got to the point where he fell in love, made some bad choices and ended up hurting everybody.

"I don't think so—"

"Really?" Harry's happy voice shifted to unhappy without missing a beat. "You should see Santa, too."

"Santa stopped bringing me presents years ago."

"But if you're there when I'm talking to him, you'll hear what I want when I tell him."

Cullen stifled a laugh. The little dickens was making sure that he got everything he wanted for Christmas. "What if I want to surprise you with my gift?"

"What if you're so old you don't know what to get me?"

This time Cullen did laugh. The kid had a point. Wendy had approved the fire truck he'd already purchased, but one fire truck was hardly a good gift for a kid who'd had such a rough year. He wanted to shower him with presents, but he knew they should be gifts Harry wanted. Plus, if he continued to be impersonal and businesslike with Wendy tonight, he could drive home his point about their relationship. Friday night had been fun, but it was over. If she asked why he was distant, he could actually tell her that without worrying that one of her coworkers might overhear. He could make a clean, honest break with her.

He might also get a chance to tell her about the new plant manager. He didn't want her to walk in the Monday after Christmas vacation and discover she had a new boss—a boss Cullen had hired—yet Cullen hadn't told her.

He owed her that much.

"All right. What time are you going?"

"We're leaving as soon as I get a clean shirt on."

"Then go get a clean shirt on."

Walking to the closet to retrieve his jacket, Cullen was hit by a bolt of uncertainty. He'd never been around Wendy when he didn't melt a little. She made him laugh. She made him happy.

He squeezed his eyes shut. At one point his mother had made his dad happy. She'd made him laugh. And he'd made all the wrong choices in his life, mostly to ensure he didn't lose his only child.

And Cullen had had a front-row seat not only to his dad's misery, but to his mom's. So, no. There was no worry he'd make the same mistakes his father had.

The mall was alive with Christmas music and happy people. Holding Harry's hand, Wendy guided him toward the roped-off area where Santa sat. Two elves guarded the break in the ropes that served as an entry. A rotund man wearing a red suit and fake white hair and beard sat on a gold throne. Two more elves stood by his side. One held candy canes. The other held a bag of toys. Previews of things to come, Wendy suspected.

She expected Harry to race up to the display, instead he held back.

"What's wrong?"

He blinked up at her then pushed his glasses up his nose. "There are no bells here."

She laughed. Sometimes his mind worked in the weirdest ways. "Bells?"

"You know. Silver bells like the song."

"Oh! Well, silver bells are only a part of Christmas. Just like you don't see Santa everywhere or elves in every decoration or display, silver bells aren't mandatory."

Even as she said the last, she saw Cullen striding toward them from the far end of the mall. At the same time, a man dressed in a reindeer suit stepped over the green velvet ropes into the Santa display. The collar of sleigh bells that he wore jingled merrily.

Harry grinned up at her. "Never mind. Everything's okay now." He turned to Cullen as he approached. "Hey, Cullen!"

"Hey, Harry!" He smiled at Wendy. "Wendy."

Her heart skipped a beat. He was here! Maybe she'd misinterpreted what happened between them that afternoon?

She stopped herself. She was *not* going to be "that" girl. The one who embarrassed herself over a man who really didn't want her. He'd hardly spoken to her that afternoon. She'd felt a distance between them. Something had been wrong. She couldn't assume he was here to see her. It was probably a coincidence they were at the mall at the same time.

"Hello, Cullen."

"I hope you don't mind, but Harry invited me."

She looked down at the little boy. "You did?"

He nodded. "He needs to know what I want for Christmas, too."

She was glad Cullen had made a special effort for Harry, but that only made his dismissal of her more obvious. Why had he romanced her on Friday night if he didn't want her? No. That wasn't the question. The real question was why had she fallen for everything he'd said Friday night? He was a playboy. She knew it. She should have protected herself. But she hadn't, and now her heart ached.

But tonight wasn't about her. She had a son to raise, and tonight he wanted to see Santa. She'd think about this, berate herself, feel bad tomorrow.

"All right. Let's go." She pointed at the short line by the Santa display. "It must have been a smart idea to come on a weeknight because there's no line."

Harry looked at Cullen. "You can't hear from back here. You have to come with us."

"Sure. Lead the way."

Harry danced over to the booth behind the green velvet ropes, Wendy and Cullen on his heels. The reindeer at the cash register told Wendy the price of the picture and she reached for her purse but before she could even open it, Cullen handed the man enough money for two pictures.

Her heart twisted in her chest at the thought that he loved Harry enough that he wanted a picture of him to remember him by. But that only meant she'd have to be doubly careful that his kindness to Harry didn't make her starry-eyed again.

Handing Cullen's change to him, the reindeer leaned forward and his collar of sleigh bells jingled merrily. Harry squeezed Wendy's hand.

She laughed. "You really like bells, don't you?"

He nodded solemnly. "I love bells."

A tall thin blonde in a red velvet outfit that looked more like a French maid's uniform than an elf suit walked over and caught Cullen's arm, walking him to Santa. Behind them, Wendy experienced a twist of jealousy. *That* was the kind of woman a man like Cullen Barrington belonged with. Sexy and not afraid to flaunt it. Not a crazed assistant whose fondest wish was to create a real home for a six-year-old boy who'd lost his mom, who wouldn't wear a French maid's outfit on a lost bet and who preferred hot cocoa to hot toddies.

She had to remember that. She had to accept the reality that they might be attracted, but they weren't a match made in heaven, and she had to stop wishing for things that couldn't come true.

When they reached Santa's throne, the old man called, "Come on up, little boy, and my photographer, Frenchie, will take your picture."

Harry scrambled up the steps to Santa's throne. Frenchie ambled to the camera sitting on the tripod about six feet away.

"That's certainly an apt nickname," Wendy murmured.

Cullen faced her. "Excuse me?"

She cleared her throat. "Never mind."

"No. You said something. What was it?"

"I said her nickname is appropriate."

Cullen studied her for a second then laughed and shook his head. "Women. Dress another woman up in something scanty and you all turn into the preacher's wife."

She sniffed the air. "This is a child's display."

"Yeah, but I'm guessing old Frenchie brings in her fair share of single dads and this is a money-making enterprise. Santa's not here out of the goodness of his heart."

She couldn't argue with that, but she didn't like the hot string of jealousy threading through her. So she kept her mouth shut. The song being piped through the intercom system ended and was quickly replaced by "Silver Bells."

Harry beamed. Wendy gave him a thumbs-up signal.

"What was that for?"

"He likes bells."

Cullen laughed. "I've noticed that, too."

"It's probably a normal kid fixation."

He nodded. "When I was six I loved the garbage truck."

"Really? I loved the mail truck."

"You liked getting surprises."

"That's better than wanting to see the trash leave."

Cullen laughed again. "Though I can't deny that I loved watching the trash disappear, I have to confess I was more in love with the hydraulics."

"Really?"

"Why are you so surprised?"

They turned simultaneously; their gazes caught and clung. Memories of the Christmas party danced like sugar-plum fairies through her head. Especially the goodnight kiss. She felt the warmth of it to her toes. Remembered every delicious sensation and the way her softness melted into his strength. And knew from the way his eyes heated that he was remembering it, too.

"I guess I shouldn't be surprised."

The words came out as a soft whisper as she fought the urge to step closer, to satisfy her curiosity about him with a hundred personal questions, to tell him all her secrets and dreams.

"No. You shouldn't." His words were soft, too, filled with an emotion she couldn't identify, though she could see the struggle taking place inside him from the way his eyes flickered. He liked her, maybe even wanted to love her, but something stopped him.

A burst of desperation overwhelmed her. She *loved* him. She loved everything about him. And he absolutely wanted to love her. But something held him back. Still, every time they had a personal conversation a chip of his resolve fell away. If they had enough time together, he wouldn't be able to resist the pull. He'd fall in love, too. But they didn't have time. He would be leaving in a day or two.

Holding his gaze, she drew in a soft breath and did something she hadn't done in at least a decade. She made a wish. Not that he'd love her, but that he'd stay. Not forever, but long enough for them to give what they felt a chance. She didn't want to live her life wondering if her chance at true love had gone because he didn't have enough time to realize he loved her. She wanted to know if he was the one…or if he wasn't.

Then if he loved her, *they* could go to Miami. They could move to the moon. She didn't care. But he'd be going alone if they didn't have at least another month together, maybe two.

She wished it. She opened her heart to the universe and wished, just as the reindeer stepped out of the booth, his sleigh bells jingling.

"Cullen Barrington?"

The man tapping on Cullen's shoulder caused Cullen to break eye contact with Wendy and he was glad. He could feel himself weakening again, longing for something that couldn't be.

"Skinny?"

Richard "Skinny" Pedrosky laughed. Now six feet tall, with a body obviously built by hours in a gym, sandy-brown hair and blue eyes, Rich was no longer the ugly-duckling runt he'd been in high school.

"Most people call me Rich now."

"I'll be damned!" Cullen said, extending his hand for shaking. "How are you?"

"I'm fine." Without missing a beat, he added, "Who's your friend?"

"Oh, this is Wendy Winston. She's my admin while I'm in Barrington running the factory."

Leaning forward to take the hand Rich extended, Wendy smiled. "It's nice to meet you."

"Please tell me you aren't here because you have a child visiting Santa."

"I do."

"Damn," Rich said. "All the good ones are taken."

Wendy laughed. "I'm not taken. I was awarded custody of my neighbor's son when she passed a few weeks ago."

Rich said, "Oh, I'm sorry." But the gleam in his eyes didn't match his words.

Something hot and angry bubbled up in Cullen's stomach. He told himself to settle down, told himself it shouldn't matter that another man was interested in Wendy. It didn't quite work, but Rich shifted his gaze from Wendy back to Cullen, forcing him to school his expression into one of complete apathy, as if it made no difference one way or another if Rich flirted with Wendy.

"I hear your plant manager resigned."

"What?" Wendy gasped her reaction before Cullen could reply.

He turned to her. It wasn't how he'd planned to tell her, but he'd wanted an opportunity and this was it.

"Mr. McCoy was close to retirement age. He actually took vacation to have bypass surgery."

Her eyes widened in shock.

"He's fine, but he decided life was too short to spend it working and he won't be back."

"Wow."

He watched her delicate features shift and change as she processed that. Finally she said, "I guess I'm not really surprised. His taking time off in December was odd." She raised her gaze to meet his, her eyes so full of hope that Cullen froze.

"Do you have a replacement?"

The question hung in the air between them. Their gazes held. The world around them shifted to slow motion, and for Cullen all sound stopped. He knew what she was thinking. He could take the job. They could explore what they felt for each other. He could help raise Harry.

He swallowed. Even though he'd already counted himself out, even though he knew he'd someday hurt Wendy if he pursued this attraction, it was suddenly all so tempting.

Once again, Rich interrupted. "Yeah, Cullen," he said, shifting just slightly to stand beside Wendy, giving Cullen an instant vision of what they'd look like as a couple. "That's actually why I'm glad to have run into you. I'd like to be considered."

Cullen's world spun. He felt like a sorcerer overwhelmed by a mystic vision of the future. They looked good together, perfect. Even as half of him screamed in protest, the logical half really could see their future. *Wendy's* future. Security with somebody stable. A real father for Harry, instead of a man who couldn't even be sure he was capable of staying for the long haul. If he gave in to everything he felt for her and they failed, she'd miss her opportunity with someone like Rich, someone who was right for her.

The reindeer walked over and tapped Cullen on the shoulder, the bells of his collar jingling pleasantly. "Hey, your kid wants you to look at him."

Red-faced, Cullen quickly turned and waved at Harry. But Harry wasn't upset, as Cullen had thought he would be. Instead he grinned. "I'm telling Santa what I want. You should be closer."

Rich stepped back. "I didn't mean to interrupt. Is there somewhere I can send a résumé?"

Cullen nearly told him not to bother, he'd hired a replacement already, and then he remembered the vision. Wendy would be happy with Rich, and a man who truly liked her would want to see her happy. Though he'd given the job to someone else, if that candidate didn't work out, Rich might.

"Send it to my hotel."

As Rich nodded and turned away, Wendy realized Cullen had answered her question about having a replacement by telling Rich to submit his résumé. If he had a replacement, he wouldn't need more résumés. Cullen would be staying long enough to do interviews and make the decision.

Her wish had come true.

He might not be staying forever, but they had time.

She nearly lost her breath with joy, but Santa's laughter brought her back to reality.

"Ho. Ho. Ho. Little boy! Before we get to presents, I have to ask you if you were naughty or nice this year. Do you really want your parents to hear your answer?"

"Oh, they're not my parents. And they know I've been nice," Harry said as Cullen and Wendy approached the platform of Santa's throne. He leaned closer. "My mom was sick. I wasn't allowed to do a lot so Wendy and Cullen are making it up to me."

Santa said, "Oh, well, I'm sorry to hear that." He caught Cullen's gaze, then Wendy's. "I'm sure these two nice people won't let you down."

"We won't," Wendy said, stepping close enough to pat Harry's knee. "Go ahead. Tell Santa what you'd like for Christmas."

Harry gave a long rambling list. Wendy surreptitiously glanced over at Cullen and could see from the expression on his face that he was memorizing it. Her heart swelled. He was such a good guy. Now that he was staying, she could allow herself the feelings she had for him, and maybe even start showing him how she felt.

Harry finished his list. Santa laughed and winked at Cullen and Wendy. "There you go, little boy. Don't forget to be good these last few days before Christmas!"

"Oh, I will!" Harry said, scurrying off the man's lap and over to Wendy and Cullen. "Did you catch all that?"

"I did," Cullen said, scooping Harry off the floor and over his shoulder.

Frenchie quickly printed and framed Harry's pictures in simple cardboard frames and handed them to Wendy.

"But you know you're not getting everything, right?"

"That's why I have such a long list."

Wendy wasn't exactly sure of Harry's rationale, but it made her laugh. How could she not feel giddy? She'd have lots of time with Cullen. At least long enough for him to find a replacement for Mr. McCoy. Now all she had to do was use that time. Not waste it. Get herself some better clothes, some perfume, and take every opportunity to show Cullen they belonged together.

And considering that they were already together, this was one of those moments she wasn't going to let pass.

"How about a pretzel?"

From his perch on Cullen's shoulders, Harry said, "I want cinnamon."

Cullen hesitated for a second, and then said, "I'm a simple cheese and mustard guy."

"Me, too," Wendy agreed.

He slid Harry to the floor. "You two get a bench. I'll get the pretzels."

The number of mall shoppers seemed to have doubled while Harry sat on Santa's lap. Wendy scanned the densely populated concourse, looking for an empty bench and found one. Catching Cullen's gaze, she motioned to the bench, he nodded, and she and Harry trotted off to the seat.

After a short wait in line, Cullen walked over with the pretzels. "Cinnamon and sugar for you." He handed a pretzel and napkin to Harry. "And cheese and mustard for you."

Wendy took the pretzel he handed her. "Thanks."

Without meeting her gaze, he said, "You're welcome."

He sat on the far end of the bench, with Harry between them. But, again, Wendy wasn't dismayed. Something hummed between them. With the time they now had together, everything would fall into place. She simply had to have faith.

Wendy took a bite of her pretzel, chewed and swallowed. Smiling over Harry's head at Cullen, she said, "This is good. Thanks."

Harry grinned up at Cullen. "Yeah. Thanks."

A tall girl with purple hair, wearing black and white striped tights, an oversize sweatshirt and a ring of sleigh bells around each ankle walked by. The cacophony of tinkling bells caused Harry to look from Wendy to Cullen and burst into another round of giggles.

Cullen peered at Wendy over Harry's head. Wendy shrugged.

"What's with you and bells?"

Harry glanced from Wendy to Cullen and back at Wendy again. "I use them to make wishes."

"Wishes?" Cullen asked, his brow wrinkling in confusion. "What kind of wishes?"

"When my mom was sick, I would wish every day that she would get better, but she never did."

Wendy's heart splintered in her chest. "Oh, Harry," she

said, tapping his forearm to get his attention. "That wasn't your fault. Not all wishes can come true."

"I know," he said solemnly. "But this time I have a plan." He looked from Wendy to Cullen. "Every time I hear a bell ring I make a wish."

Cullen chuckled. "That's very cute, but you can't put too much stock in wishes."

"But you can't stop wishing altogether!" Wendy disagreed. She believed in wishes. She had to. *Hers* had just come true. She couldn't let Cullen's opinion steal Harry's natural sense of wonder. Particularly in light of his already difficult life.

"Some wishes are wonderful and prove that sometimes life can be magical. What did you wish for?"

Harry peered at her over his glasses. "I can't tell you."

"Sure you can," Wendy said, clasping his hand reassuringly. "Because, just like with telling Santa what you want for Christmas, sometimes wishes come true because other people in your life make them happen for you. But that means the people in your life have to know what you want."

Cullen frowned thoughtfully. "You know what, Harry? She has a point. Shared wishes have a better chance of coming true because people who love you will try to make them come true."

Harry blinked up at them. "Really?"

They nodded.

"You want me to tell you?"

"Yes."

"Okay." He pulled in a breath. "Every time I hear a bell ring I wish for you two to get married and be my mom and dad."

Wendy's heart just about burst in her chest. "Oh, Harry!"

Cullen shifted his feet uncomfortably.

Harry looked from her to Cullen. "So, I told you. Can you make it come true?"

"Look, little guy—" Cullen paused to pull in a difficult breath. "The other reason it's good to tell adults your wishes is so that they can help you not get your hopes up. Wendy and I aren't going to get married. I'm leaving in a couple of days."

"But you said—"

"We said that sometimes grown-ups can help your wish come true. Not always." Wendy swallowed, and her eyes filled with tears. He wasn't staying? He *had* to stay. He had to find a replacement. How could he be leaving?

Cullen caught Harry's attention. "Wendy and I are friends. But that's it. I live in Miami. Very far away. I'm going home the day before Christmas Eve. There isn't enough time for Wendy and me to get to know each other enough to fall in love."

Their eyes met over Harry's head and to her embarrassment, Wendy found herself blinking back tears. Tears for Harry. Tears for herself. She was so stupid. She knew all this. Plus he'd never said he was staying to find Paul McCoy's replacement. She'd assumed he would be, because it was the answer to her foolish wish.

"That's true, Harry," she said softly.

The child gaped at her. "But you didn't know me long, and you took me and you said you love me."

"I do!"

"Then why don't you love Cullen?"

She scrambled to think of an answer but none came. She *did* love Cullen. That was why this hurt so much.

She swallowed.

Cullen balled up his pretzel paper and napkin and handed them to Harry. "Would you take this to the trash for me?"

Harry blinked, said, "Okay," and scampered off the bench.

Cullen grabbed her hand. "Wendy, I'm so sorry."

"For what? Both of us encouraged Harry to tell us his wish—"

"Not about the wish. He's a kid. He'll bounce back from this. It's you I want to apologize to."

"For what?" she asked again, fighting the stupid tears that kept filling her eyes. "All along I realized you didn't want me. We've been attracted from the second I fell on the ice into your arms." She shrugged. "We both knew it. But we also both knew it wouldn't come to anything."

He studied her face for several seconds. She knew her eyes brimmed with tears and her nose was probably red from holding back her sniffles. He had to see.

Hoping to save a bit of her pride, she switched the focus of the conversation. "I'm just a bit confused and surprised since I thought you'd be staying long enough to replace Mr. McCoy."

"I've already done the interviews." He pulled in a breath. "That's why I was busy tonight. I gave Mr. McCoy's replacement a tour of the plant."

"Then why take your friend's résumé?"

"In case Tom doesn't work out."

"Oh. Great." She struggled to take it all in and accept it, but it was too much. He'd probably known for days, maybe weeks that Mr. McCoy wasn't coming back, but he hadn't told her. If she needed any more proof that she had meant nothing to him, he'd just provided it. "That's good then."

He shifted uncomfortably on his seat and Wendy wished the ground would swallow her up. Finally, rubbing his hand across the back of his neck, he said, "Look, I'm sorry."

"You don't owe me an apology."

"I think I do. Not because I'm leaving, but because I've been trying like hell to stay away from you and sometimes I couldn't and I know I gave you the wrong impression."

"It's fine. I'm a big girl. I'll be okay."

"You're such a wonderful person, you deserve better than me. I'm ridiculously scarred. My parents had a really crappy marriage and—"

"I know. You told me. They wanted two different things. Your dad stayed because he loved your mom. But neither of them was ever happy."

"No, my dad stayed because he loved *me*. Had he divorced her and moved away he would have lost me. But both of them were miserable." He shook his head sadly. "I see it happen all the time. Friends so in love they can hardly wait to get married are divorced two years later." He caught her gaze. "I won't do that to you."

"I wouldn't do that to you."

He frowned. "You wouldn't what? Divorce me?"

"No." She caught his gaze. "I wouldn't fall out of love."

Her answer seemed to shock him, which seemed to make him angry. "How do you know?"

"I'd commit."

"My parents committed!"

"Not really. I think your parents fell in lust and when the lust was gone they were stuck. If they had really loved each other, they wouldn't have hurt each other. If you really loved me, you wouldn't have questions. Or doubts."

"I think you're talking in circles."

Wendy studied his handsome face for a few seconds, then pulled herself together. Even smiled. "No. I'm making perfect sense."

She was and because she was her common sense and strength returned. She loved Cullen enough to realize she'd never hold him. Never keep him. No one would. He was right. He was too scarred to trust enough to ever really fall in love.

She had to let him go. Freely. No regret. No remorse. He couldn't see any more tears. They couldn't have a sad goodbye on the twenty-third. He had to think she was totally okay with their situation.

She'd bear this hurt alone.

"And everything's okay."

Cullen pulled in a breath then said, "Are you sure?" as Harry turned from the trash can and headed over.

She forced a smile. "Everything's great."

Harry bounced over to them. Cullen rose and swung him over his shoulder. She saw all the love in him that he had to give, and knew with absolute certainty that he'd never give it. Not to her. Not to anyone. He'd always be alone.

And as much as she hurt for herself, she hurt more for him.

CHAPTER TWELVE

THE next morning, Wendy and Cullen didn't speak. He barricaded himself in his office and Wendy buried herself in her tasks for the day, aching with misery because she couldn't help herself, stop herself, from falling in love with a man who could never love her.

When the day was finally, mercifully, over, she hurried out of Barrington Candies and rushed home. Harry met her at the door of her house.

"Wendy! Wendy! I'm a star."

Her spirits lifted at the sight of him. She ruffled his hair. "I know you're a star."

"No, not that kind of star! I'm really a star! We're doing a play in the park the day before Christmas and I got picked to be the star. There are six sheep and three wise men, but only one star."

"So you really are a star?"

"Yes. Cullen's gonna love me!"

Her eyes welled with tears as she stooped down to his level. They'd been over this several times, and he never quite understood. "He's going home the day before Christmas Eve, remember?"

"Can't he stay one more day?"

She shook her head and appealed to Harry in a way he could understand. "His dad is all alone in Miami. If he doesn't go home, his dad doesn't have anybody to celebrate Christmas with."

Harry's happy face fell. "Oh."

"But you're still a star," she reminded him, praying that would take his mind off Cullen.

Harry's eyes instantly brightened. "That's right."

At work the next morning she immediately got down to business, keeping herself too busy to think of Cullen. At nine, he walked in, and, as if nothing were wrong, he said, "Good morning."

They were the first words he'd spoken to her since their disastrous night at the mall. She pulled in a breath and forced a smile, attempting to hide the dangerous hope that filled her heart. If he was talking, maybe they could make peace. Maybe she could talk him into staying the day to see Harry in the play.

"Good morning."

"How's Harry?"

"He's okay. He came home excited yesterday because he got a part in the Christmas play that's held every Christmas Eve in the park."

For that, he paused. "Oh, yeah?"

Pretending great interest in stacking the papers on her desk, desperately wanting to look like a normal assistant, so he wouldn't leave knowing he'd broken her heart, she said, "I think he'd love it if you'd stay long enough to see him."

She looked up just in time to see a shadow pass over his dark eyes. Had she not been holding his gaze, Wendy knew she would have missed it because it disappeared so quickly.

Turning to walk into his office, he said, "Sorry, I can't."

* * *

Cullen called the next morning, at six, according to the message he left on Wendy's office voice mail. He said he had everything caught up. There was no more work to be done. So he was going home early.

"Merry Christmas," he said, then he paused. He didn't speak for so long that Wendy was certain he'd hung up the phone, but he quietly added, "Tell Harry Merry Christmas, too. I wish I could have stayed for the play in the park."

The evening of December twenty-third found Cullen and his dad dressed in tuxedos, holding glasses of champagne, chatting with Mr. and Mrs. Chad Everly on their yacht.

Chad had been in real estate in New York City. Bonnie graced the cover of more magazines than any model before her. She was pretty and happy. Chad engaged Cullen's father in a discussion of futures that kept everybody on his conversational toes. And Cullen was bored.

He took a sip of champagne, glancing around at the models, actresses and career women, all dressed in glittering red, black, silver and gold dresses and couldn't help missing a woman in a simple red wool dress. If he closed his eyes, he could see her curly hair dancing around her shoulders, see the sparkle in her green eyes. If he focused he could even smell her perfume and remember the feeling of holding her while dancing.

"Cullen, you're a million miles away," Bonnie said, then wove her arm beneath Cullen's to slide him away from the serious conversation between her husband and his dad. "And there are at least twenty women here ready to vie for the position of your next lover."

He blinked. "What?"

She laughed. "Oh, come on. No one's so naive as to believe you'll ever take a wife."

He couldn't argue that.

"So everybody's happy to play the game." Bonnie paused by two tall, polished women. "I brought him."

Though this situation probably would have made him laugh the year before, he suddenly felt like a slab of beef. Confused by his sudden desire to look around for an escape route, he felt his cell phone vibrate in his pocket.

He smiled apologetically at the two women, reaching into his jacket pocket for the phone. "Sorry. For someone to call this late, it's got to be important."

As he walked away, he glanced at the caller ID and saw it was Wendy's number. But he didn't think it was her calling. He suspected it was Harry.

His heart twisted, but he didn't answer. There was no point in making things worse. He returned to the two women in sparkling diamonds and skin-tight holiday dresses, but suddenly thought again of Wendy's simple red dress. How not one of these women even came close to being as beautiful as she'd looked the night of Barrington Candy's Christmas party.

Annoyed with himself, he shook his head, tried to make conversation, and couldn't.

He returned to his father. "I think I might go home."

"What's the matter? Are you sick?"

"Tired."

"I told you Barrington Candies sucked people dry."

"The company's fine. I just want to be alone."

"You should see that place," his dad said, turning to the other people in their conversational circle. "It's a scrappy little town, full of people who will bleed you dry if you give them half a chance."

Cullen's mouth fell open, and he answered before he could stop himself. "That's not true!"

His dad chuckled. "When we get home, I'll show you the letters I've gotten over the past five years."

"You've gotten letters?"

"Whining about no raises."

"You told me you didn't know they hadn't gotten raises!"

"Cullen," he said, using his voice like a reprimand. "Do you really think I wasn't watching over the details of that company? Why do you think I knew the plant couldn't run itself while Paul was on vacation and I'd have to send you up to run it?"

"*You* told Paul McCoy not to give them raises?"

"It's a candy factory. Not rocket science. It doesn't require brains to work there. They were getting paid what they deserved until you started to like that little admin assistant and pitched a fit. I only authorized those raises so she wouldn't spend enough time trying to coerce you into giving raises that you'd do something you'd regret."

Cullen crossed his arms on his chest. "Like what, Dad?"

"Do you really want to get into this in front of your friends?"

"You mean *your* friends?"

"What has gotten into you?"

"Maybe I'm just starting to see the truth for the first time."

"Oh, come on! Get a drink. Enjoy yourself."

"Did you ever stop to think, Dad, that the reason Mom felt she had to work so hard for her friends was that she knew you were working against them?"

"Your mother knew exactly what she was getting when she married me."

"I don't think so."

He set his empty champagne glass on the tray of a passing waiter. "I'm going home."

"Wait!"

"No. I think I've waited long enough."

* * *

Wendy finally fell asleep around four, and slept until nine. Christmas Eve morning, she found Harry in the living room, curled up with Creamsicle, watching cartoons.

"Good morning."

"Hey, Wendy!" he said brightly, no worse for the wear over losing Cullen.

Ambling up the hall to her kitchen, she wished she could get over Cullen as easily as Harry had, then reminded herself that making wishes was part of why she was so miserable. Caught in her reverie, she nearly tripped over Creamsicle. His bell jingled merrily and he looked up at her accusingly.

"Hey, I'm sorry about the whole bell thing. But this was Cullen's choice. Not mine. Like a big dope, I fell in love just like you and Harry wanted. So I'm in the clear. And since there's nothing we can do about Cullen, you can scram. Go play with Harry."

She stepped over the fat cat and pushed open the kitchen door. Instead of heading back to the living room, Creamsicle followed her inside and leaped onto a stool beside the center island, his bell ringing again.

She swallowed. "You've got to stop with the bell." Tears filled her eyes. She understood Harry's desperation when he wished on bells. Because right now, right at this very second, she wished Cullen would walk through that door, tell her he'd made a mistake, tell her he loved her and wanted to be with her, and that they'd be together forever.

Turning away from Creamsicle, she shook her head. She couldn't mean that. She couldn't wish him back into her life. She was just emotional. She was too smart to wallow in misery or wish him back into her life.

But suddenly she remembered how happy he had been with the candy packers, what a great job he'd done running the factory, how happy he'd been at the Christmas party. When he'd arrived he'd been quiet and sullen. The factory and its workers had made him happy. *She'd* made him happy.

If his problem was fear of repeating his dad's mistakes when he couldn't see that their situation was totally different, then was it so wrong to wish for him to come back to the life he seemed to love?

No. He needed help.

She reached down and brushed Creamsicle's fur enough that the bell rang.

"I wish he would come back. I wish he would give us a chance. Even if he doesn't love me yet, I know he was falling." She brushed Creamsicle's fur again. The bell jingled. "I wish he would come back."

Her wish was forgotten in a haze of preparations for the play in the park. That night, Wendy stood shivering a few feet away from the gazebo "stage." Wanting to be supportive of Harry, she made sure she was visible so her little boy would know that his life was on track. Secure. He was hers. And she was here for him.

Rubbing her mitten-covered hands together, as she waited in the sea of parents and grandparents for the play to begin, she let her gaze ripple around the crowd. A flash of black leather stopped her heart.

Cullen.

He had a coat like that.

But as quickly as she thought she saw the swatch of coat, it disappeared.

Cullen raced into the park, searching for Wendy. The crowd unexpectedly parted and there she was. Standing to the right, twenty or so feet from the large stage-size gazebo where the children were performing, Wendy glowed with excitement.

His heart tripped over in his chest. The cold air had turned her cheeks a bright pink. Her eyes sparkled. The yellow scarf around her neck highlighted the cinnamon red of her hair. She was so beautiful, so happy, so alive, so real that he stood frozen. Why would she want him back when he'd hurt her? When he'd been confused over things that should have been obvious?

Harry Martin was an adorable star. Wendy could barely contain her happiness at his performance. As she jumped up and down, clapping for Harry, hands on her shoulders brought her back to the present, and she spun to see who was behind her.

"Boo."

"Boo?"

Cullen?

"You scared the devil out of me." And also stopped her heart. He looked amazing in his black leather jacket with the white wool scarf tied around his neck. There was just enough wind to ruffle his hair and color his cheeks. He looked so damned good she could have jumped into his arms. But she'd made that mistake at least twice already. Wouldn't make it again.

"Happy Christmas Eve." His words formed a white mist around him. A light snow began to fall. He lifted his face into it. "I'm so glad I'm home."

His referring to Barrington as home almost tripped her up, but she decided it must have been a slip of some sort. She refused to make anything of it.

"Did you come back to see Harry in the play?"

"Yes. And wasn't he funny? I've never seen a kid happier to be a star. But I also came back because Tom Ross couldn't take the job after all. When he put in his notice, his employer doubled his salary." He pulled in a breath. "So, Barrington Candies lost him."

Not knowing what else to say, she said simply, "That's too bad."

"Not really. I want the job."

She stifled the urge to squeeze her eyes shut in misery. She couldn't work with him, knowing he didn't love her—*couldn't* love her—when she was head over heels in love with him.

"Yep. I'm going to take over the company and keep my dad out of it."

The tone of his voice hinted that there was a story behind that decision and Wendy itched with curiosity. But she said nothing.

"Yeah. And with it being Christmas Eve my hotel's booked. So it looks like I'll be staying with you tonight."

"Not on your life." That broke her vow of silence. "There's no ice storm. And don't you dare mention this to Harry. He won't understand why I can't let you stay and he'll be upset with me, when you're the culprit."

He put his finger over her lips to silence her. "Not really. I got my priorities straightened out really quickly on a yacht last night, and I had a little something made for you." He produced a ring box from his jacket pocket and handed it to her. "Open it."

She swallowed hard. Her heart pounding in her chest, she forced her trembling fingers to open the box. A brilliant diamond winked at her.

"Will you marry me?"

Her eyes widened in shock and she gaped at Cullen. "Marry you? You leave me one day, and two days later you come back and ask me to marry you?"

"I know the timing seems a bit quick. But I think I fell in love with you the night I stayed at your house and toasted marshmallows. Unless I miss my mark, you love me, too. So I really can't see a reason to wait. Especially when we have Harry to consider. God only knows what he'd tell his teacher if I spent too many nights before we made it official."

She laughed through her tears. "I thought you didn't believe in marriage."

Taking the ring box from her hand, he said, "I've had some revelations in the past twenty-four hours." He slid the ring out and slipped it on her finger. "My dad spent his adult life telling me love never lasted. But I think what he was really saying was that *his* love hadn't lasted. I think ours will."

She looked down at the sparkling ring. "I know ours will."

"You're sure enough to put up with me every day for the next fifty or sixty years?"

She laughed. "It will be my pleasure."

"Then it looks like we're getting married."

Harry skipped over. "Hey, Cullen!"

"Hey, kid."

"I knew you'd come."

Cullen laughed and ruffled Harry's hair. "Why? Did you wish on a bell again?"

"No, Wendy did."

Cullen threw his head back and laughed.

"Harry, you and I are going to have to work on your secret-keeping abilities."

Harry just grinned.

"Doesn't matter," Cullen said, sliding his arm around Wendy's waist as he took Harry's hand.

Harry looked up at him. "It doesn't?"

"Nope, Wendy and I are going to get married. None of us will be keeping secrets anymore."

The church bells began to chime out the hour, and Cullen leaned over and kissed Wendy.

Harry grinned. There were some things about adults he would never understand, but he did understand the power of wishes. He raised his eyes to the sky and whispered, "Thanks."

Cullen pulled away from Wendy and caught her hand. "Let's go home."

Harry had never heard better words.

EPILOGUE

CARRYING a tray holding three servings of scrambled eggs and toast, Cullen led Harry up the stairs on Christmas morning.

"Can I give her my present first?"

"Yes," Cullen answered, dropping his voice to a whisper. "But keep your voice down or she'll know we're coming. It won't be a surprise."

Harry stage-whispered, "Okay."

Stifling a laugh, Cullen finished the climb up the stairs and walked to the bedroom he'd shared with Wendy the night before. When she fell asleep, he'd been so overcome with love that he'd slipped out of bed and awakened Harry.

Neither one of them had bought Wendy a Christmas gift. After one phone call to the jeweler who'd made her engagement ring, banking on his festive goodwill and promising him it would be a large purchase, he and Harry had bounded out into the night.

As he stepped into the bedroom, Harry raced past him and bounced on the bed. "Get up! It's Christmas."

Wendy stirred.

"Really, Wendy, get up! I have a present for you and Santa left presents for me and I want to open them."

Cullen set the tray across her knees. "You don't want breakfast first?"

Harry peered at Cullen over his glasses. "No."

Wendy sat up. "You're at least having toast."

Cullen bent across the tray and kissed Wendy. "Good morning."

She smiled. "Good morning."

Harry bounced across the bed to kneel beside her. He grabbed a piece of toast. Before stuffing most of it into his mouth he said, "Open mine first."

"I think I'd rather have coffee first."

Harry's face fell comically. "But I want to open my presents."

Wendy laughed and relented. "I was teasing." She ruffled his soft yellow hair. "So what do you have for me?"

He thrust the small package at her. "You're gonna love it."

"I'm sure I will," she said, ripping off the paper. When she saw the logo on the elegant box, she glanced over at Cullen. "How did he get something from Smithmeyers?"

Cullen shrugged. "I don't know. Maybe Santa took him."

Harry giggled.

"You snuck out in the middle of the night, didn't you?"

Cullen shook his head, looking as innocent as a newborn babe. Harry giggled merrily.

Wendy glanced from one to the other, then pulled the lid off the box to reveal a sterling-silver Christmas-tree ornament, engraved with the words *Our First Christmas as a Family* and the year.

Tears blurred Wendy's vision. "It's beautiful." She reached out and hugged Harry. "Perfect."

Cullen pulled a long, thin box from his trouser pocket. "Well, since you're already crying, here's mine."

She took the little box that was all but hidden by curled

ribbons and opened it. A diamond necklace caught the morning light streaming in through her bay window and winked at her.

"Oh, my gosh!" She looked up at Cullen. "You do know I have nowhere to wear this, right?"

He laughed. "I have a home in Miami, lots of friends in New York."

She swallowed. "I'm…I'm…"

Obviously seeing his opportunity, Harry filled in the blank, saying, "Ready to go downstairs so I can open my presents?"

Wendy laughed through her tears. "Okay. You go ahead downstairs, Harry. Cullen and I will be down in a minute."

Harry sighed. "Okay, but don't kiss too long."

The second Harry was out of earshot, Cullen said, "We may live and work in Barrington, but I'd like to show you the world."

She looked up at him. They'd talked and talked the night before, listened to each other's hopes, learned each other's dreams. So she knew this was important to him. "I'd like to see the world."

"Good." He kissed her, then rose from the bed. "We'd better get down to the living room before Harry starts making wishes on Creamsicle's bell again."

Wendy laughed and tossed back the covers. "Heaven only knows what he'd wish for now."

Catching her hand, Cullen led her from the bedroom. "Probably brothers and sisters."

As he said the words, Cullen stopped. Turning to face Wendy, he grinned as if something miraculous had just occurred to him. "We could have kids."

"As many as you want."

His grin grew. "This is going to be fun."

"Greatest adventure ever."

With that they left the bedroom, raced down the stairs and watched Harry open more presents than Wendy had ever seen under a tree.

She would never be alone again.

Neither would Cullen.

And neither would Harry.

CHRISTMAS TREATS

For an early Christmas present Susan Meier would like to share a little treat with you…

"I got the idea for Harry's cookie-painting fun from my mother, Helen Petrunak. Every Friday after Thanksgiving, rather than battle shoppers, she hosts a 'cookie-painting party' for her grandkids.

"She bakes sugar cookies and the kids paint them with colorful icing. They paint faces on Santa cookies, stained-glass windows on church cookies and red noses on reindeer cookies.

"When dry, the cookies are hung on a Christmas tree in the family room. The 'goodie' tree is decorated with cookies, bubble gum and candy canes. The kids wait eagerly for the day they can plunder the goodies hanging from the bright-green limbs."

CHRISTMAS CUT-OUT COOKIES

1 cup butter, softened
1 cup sugar
1 egg
2 tbsp orange juice
1 tbsp vanilla
2 ½ cups all-purpose flour
1 tsp baking powder

Combine butter, sugar and egg in large bowl. Beat with mixer on medium speed, scraping bowl often, until creamy. Add orange juice and vanilla; mix well. In a separate bowl, sift together flour and baking powder. Add flour and baking powder mixture to sugar, butter and egg mixture in easily blended increments, mixing with mixer on low speed. Beat until well blended.

Divide the dough into thirds; wrap in plastic wrap. Refrigerate until firm (two to three hours). When dough is firm, heat oven to 400°F. Remove one-third of dough from refrigerator. On lightly floured surface, roll out to ⅛" to ¼" thickness. (Keep remaining dough refrigerated.) Cut with 3-inch cookie cutters. Place 1 inch apart on ungreased cookie sheets.*

Bake 6 to 10 minutes or until edges are lightly browned; cool completely. "Paint" with colorful icing.

* If you're using the cookies for decorations and need a way to hang them, a drinking straw will cut a perfect hole for hanging. After cookies are placed on cookie sheet, cut a hole

in the top of each cookie using a drinking straw. Press the straw into the dough, leaving approximately 1/4 inch of dough around the hole. Bake as above and cool. After the cookies are painted, run ribbon through the hole and tie in a bow to create a loop to hang the cookie on the tree.

GRANDMA'S SHINY ICING FOR COOKIES

2 egg whites
1 tbsp lemon juice
1 to 1 ½ cups powdered sugar
(extra ½ cup only used as needed)
Food coloring

Mix egg whites, lemon juice and most of the cup of powdered sugar. If the mixture is too thin, continue to add the remainder of the first cup of powdered sugar in increments until you have a consistency of icing that can be spread or painted onto the cookies. If it is still too thin after an entire cup of powdered sugar, add increments of the extra powdered sugar until you get the correct consistency. It can't be too thick or too thin. If it's too thick, add a few drops of water.

Separate the icing into several small bowls. Dye the icing in each of the bowls using enough food coloring to create the colors you desire. Icing can be spread on cookies, or painted on with a thin brush, depending on how fancy you intend to make your cookies.

HIS MISTLETOE BRIDE

BY
CARA COLTER

Cara Colter lives on an acreage in British Columbia with her partner, Rob, and eleven horses. She has three grown children and a grandson. She is a recent recipient of an *RT Book Reviews* Career Achievement Award in the Love and Laughter category. Cara loves to hear from readers, and you can contact her, or learn more about her, through her website at www.cara-colter.com.

To Pat Walls,
a man dedicated to family,
and a true romantic even after forty years!

CHAPTER ONE

OFFICER BRODY TAGGERT decided he was upgrading his mood from cranky to just plain foul.

"As good a time as any to go see Miss L. Toe," he said, out loud, heavy on the sarcasm as he said the name. Tag's dog, Boo, the only other inhabitant of the police cruiser, who was stretched out comfortably in the backseat, woofed what Tag took as agreement.

Actually, Tag thought, given his mood, now was probably not the best time to go see Snow Mountain's newest business owner, resident, budding author and pain in the butt.

Unfortunately the new-in-town Lila Grainger, aka Miss L. Toe, unlike most people Tag ran into who had an alias— an *also known as*—was not a criminal at all. She was the chief of police's niece.

Which was the reason Tag had to go see her.

Directly ordered.

Tag's boss, Chief Paul Hutchinson "Hutch," was notoriously mild-mannered, but he had a core of pure steel and he had not been amused that Tag had missed the first ever meeting of the Save Christmas in Snow Mountain Committee last night.

"She's up to something," the chief had muttered. "She's crafty, just like my sister, her mother. And you missed the meeting, so now we're in the dark."

Tag decided not to point out that *in the* dark was a particularly bad choice of phrase, since that was what had ignited the Christmas fervor in Snow Mountain in the first place.

Town Council had decided to turn off the lights. The Christmas lights, that was. And the traditional Christmas display in the tiny Bandstand Park that was at the end of Main Street was to be no more.

Every year since 1957, the park had been transformed into Santa's Workshop. Ingenious motorized elves made toys and wrapped gifts, reindeer cavorted and Santa ho-ho-hoed and waved. But those particular models of elves and reindeer did not have fifty-year life spans.

Santa's ho-ho-ho had gone into slow mo. Last year one of the elves had seriously overheated and burst into flames. Unfortunately, someone with a cell phone camera had caught on film a child wailing in fear, his face dramatically backlit by the flickering blaze, and Snow Mountain had been put on the map.

The whole issue had been causing heated debates since last January. But at the October Town Council meeting, Leonard Lemoix, who was not Tag's favorite councilor, had gone where no one had gone before. Leonard had crunched the numbers. The cost of the much-needed repairs, setting up, and taking down of the display could, in three years, added up to enough money to buy a new police cruiser.

That didn't even include the cost of the power bill for running the Christmas lights, which were not the new energy-efficient variety, for between six and eight weeks every year.

Town Council had voted unanimously to shut down the

display and Leonard had gone up a notch or two in Tag's estimation.

"My niece thinks it's my fault," the chief had said glumly the day after the meeting. "I didn't know anything about the police cruiser. Now Lila's starting a committee to keep Christmas in Snow Mountain. You know what she said to me? *Uncle Paul, do you want Snow Mountain to be known as the town that canceled Christmas?*"

That's when Tag found out he'd been volunteered to be on the committee.

"We can't have the department looking like villains who want to trade Christmas for a new police cruiser," Hutch said. The chief's increasing concern about *image* seemed to coincide with the arrival of his niece, too.

Lila was a city girl from Miami, and was very savvy about what was and wasn't politically correct.

Despite the fact Tag was developing a dislike for the niece he had not yet met, he knew better than to bother to protest, *why me?* about his appointment to Lila Grainger's committee. After six years on the force he was still, unfortunately, its most recent recruit.

He had shaken the title of rookie, and finally refused to carry the humbling joke badge he'd been required to produce at the whim of anyone senior on the force that said, *Be patient, I'm new here,* but he still got every single assignment that no one else wanted.

Which described the committee to keep Christmas in Snow Mountain to a T. Karl Jamison, the oldest man on the force, kept threatening to retire, which meant there would be a new rookie someday, but not in time, obviously, to save Tag from being at the whim of Hutch's niece.

And now he'd missed her first damned meeting.

Tag had not bothered to offer excuses for his absence at the meeting. He felt his reason for not being there fell into the personal and very private category, and the truth was he would rather face his boss's wrath than his pity. After the death of his younger brother, Ethan, Tag had handled about all the sympathy he could for one lifetime.

Still, he knew now there would be no acceptable excuse—short of an armed robbery in progress—for not going to see Miss L. Toe, aka Lila Grainger, now, tonight, immediately.

Tag swore softly. The dog moaned anxiously, able to detect the downward-spiraling mood in the patrol car.

"It's not your fault, Boo."

The coming of Christmas was not the dog's fault. But with Halloween only a few weeks past, and Thanksgiving not yet here, Tag could have ignored the inevitable coming of the season for a little while longer.

Okay, he'd been *glad* when the town voted against the Christmas display, and not entirely because of the possibility of a new cruiser, either.

In his line of work, Brody Taggert saw the *other* side of Christmas, the side that did not make the front cover of the holiday editions of all the glitzy magazines. He saw what no one ever wanted to acknowledge: the season of joy and faith and miracles had a dirty underbelly, fallout.

As a cop, even a small-town cop, Tag saw firsthand that it was a time of accelerated stress for the people he dealt with most. Soon, after the Thanksgiving turkeys were cleared away, Christmas drinking would begin in earnest. Earnest drinking led to serious trouble: arguments, fights, domestic violence, car accidents, hypothermia, drunken dismantling of business establishments and homes and lives.

This was the conclusion Tag had reached about

Christmas: poor people would feel poorer, lonely people would feel lonelier, desperate people more desperate, mean people meaner.

And of course, anyone who had ever known sorrow, as Tag himself knew sorrow, would feel the ache of that loss all over again, as if it were brand-new. This would be Tag's seventh Christmas without his brother. People had assured him that time would heal his wounds, but this seventh Christmas did not feel any different than the first: bleak, instead of joyous. There was an empty hole in his life that seemed to be made emptier by all the activity and excited anticipation building around him.

But that wasn't Lila Grainger's world.

He'd had a nauseating peek into her world when he'd received her first enthusiastic committee announcement via e-mail three days ago. Animated snowmen danced across a pink background that implored him: Save Christmas In Snow Mountain.

Action Meeting, Free Eggnog And Jeanie Harper's Nearly World Famous Shortbread Cookies.

The dancing snowmen had been particularly irritating to a guy whose computer skills ran to grave satisfaction that he had finally figured out the station's computers were equipped with spelling checkers.

But irritation at the whole concept, and dancing snowmen aside, Tag really had intended to go, and not just because he'd been told it was a good idea, either. The promise of Jeanie's shortbread was more bait than any bachelor could resist, particularly if they were the cookies that she dipped half in chocolate, which they almost always were at this time of year.

But life—real life, not the chocolate-dipped dancing

snowmen variety—had intervened. He sought out his dog in the rearview mirror. Tag had missed the meeting because he'd taken Boo to see a veterinary specialist in Spokane yesterday afternoon.

The truth was he'd been back in plenty of time to make the seven o'clock gathering, but after a man had heard the words, *You'll know when it's time,* he couldn't go. Not didn't want to—couldn't.

Tag was a man who had cleaned up the aftermath of a lot of ugliness, he prided himself on having total control over his emotions. But not even the world's best shortbread cookies could have enticed him off his couch last night. His forty-two-inch flat screen and a hockey game, Boo resting on his lap, had helped him block out his sense of helplessness in the face of the doctor's diagnosis.

Boo was dying. Boo, not just a dog, but a link to his brother; even more than that, a link to life. More than time, it was Boo who had healed in Tag what could be healed.

What Tag hadn't been expecting was how swiftly the chief would react to his absence to Lila's meeting.

He'd been called in to see the chief at the start of his shift, and told he'd better get with the program.

The Save Christmas in Snow Mountain program that was.

Tag was pretty sure if he read over his job description and contract there was nothing in there about having to cooperate with the fruitcake plans of the chief's niece, even if it was going to be good for the police department's image, as Hutch claimed.

The word *image,* up until this point in the department's history, had meant being nice to little kids, keeping a crisp uniform, polished shoes and a clean car and Tag would have been content if it stayed that way forever.

He was also pretty sure there was nothing in his contract about cleaning cells if he didn't comply, either.

On the other hand, Hutch *had* thrown Tag a lifeline, offering him a job on the police department when Tag had just about swamped himself in misery, had been heading down a wrong road *fast,* after Ethan's accident.

The chief had also known, without ever saying one word to indicate that he knew, that he and Boo were partners in the rescue of Tag's troubled soul and so he had turned a blind eye to the dog riding in the backseat. Tag knew he owed Hutch, and owed him dearly.

He turned the patrol car down Main Street. It was just dusk, and the icy winds of mid-November were beginning to blow down Snow Mountain, the black, jagged silhouette forming a backdrop for the town.

Dry leaves and a few newspapers blew down a street lined by single-story brick-and-sandstone businesses that had largely seen a better day. Tilley's Dry Goods had had Going Out Of Business soaped on the windows for at least ten years.

The "D" in the Mountain Drugstore sign was burned out, the odd summertime tourist ventured in there expecting rugs. There were no wintertime tourists, something the optimistic Miss Grainger thought would be a cinch to change.

According to her vibrant pink e-mail, Snow Mountain could not only revive its Christmas display of Santa's Workshop in Bandstand Park, but become a Destination, the capital "D" emphasized with both bold lettering and neon-green.

But as Tag watched the lights winking out, one by one, on Main Street, he thought this was probably the town least likely to ever be a Destination. In fact, he was aware of thinking it wasn't the prettiest picture of small-town U.S.A. that he had ever seen.

He was also aware of missing the garish display of lights and moving figurines in the park at the end of the street just the tiniest little bit.

Lila Grainger's store, of course, was a shining jewel in the middle of that street, the one-hundred-year-old limestone recently sandblasted back to soft, buffed ivory, the new sign hanging above it, green, red and white, saying in tasteful letters, Miss. L. Toe, and in smaller letters underneath it, The Christmas Store At Snow Mountain.

Miss. L. Toe. Cute. Nauseatingly so. Welcome to her world. The opening of the store lent itself to *motive,* too. Lila Grainger had a vested interest in keeping the Christmas in Snow Mountain, now that she'd invested her whole book advance in opening a store here.

When she'd signed a contract to write a book about Christmas, the chief had practically sent out announcement cards he'd been so pleased and proud. Then, unexpectedly, she'd decided to move here from Florida and invest her windfall in this old building.

Tag had yet to meet her, but he had formed a picture of the kind of person who opened a year-round Christmas store on what seemed to be a whim: scrawny, wire-rim glasses, flowered dress, blue eyes spilling over moistly with that do-gooder glow.

The store windows, cleaned until they sparkled, were filled with fairy tale like displays that confirmed his worst suspicions. Mrs. Santa incarnate had arrived in Snow Mountain. One gigantic window display contained an entire town in miniature, completely decked out for Christmas. A train moved through it; he could hear the muffled *choo-choo* of the whistle right through the plate glass.

The other window contained a tree, at least seven feet tall, decorated entirely and in his mind, hideously, in various shades of purple.

It was a fantasy, not appealing at all to a man who spent the days of his life dealing with harsh reality.

"I'm getting a headache," Tag admitted to the dog as he reached over to the seat beside him, put on his hat, pulled the shiny black brim low over his eyes.

The dog whined.

"You are not coming in."

Boo, who usually obeyed instantly and without argument, ignored him, hurtled over the seat into the front of the car and was out the door as soon as Tag opened it.

The dog sat on the sidewalk, and waited, her tail thumping enthusiastically. Tag looked at her, the world's ugliest dog, and felt the downward swoop of his heart.

Cancer. Who knew dogs got cancer?

Boo, the exact color of a mud puddle, had the head of a Great Dane, the body of a Chinese Shar-pei, and the legs of a dachshund. There was nothing the least bit "cute" about the combination of a wrinkled dog with a painfully oversize head waddling around on very crooked and too-short legs.

Tag knew darn well that the visit to the specialist's office, the promise that his Christmases were about to get worse than ever, rather than better, was the real reason his mood was blacker than the silhouette of Snow Mountain. Since he could change nothing, especially not the mood, there was no sense letting it go to waste. The rawness of his own hurt was under control tonight, as it had not been last night.

He felt a moment's sympathy for Miss L. Toe, having to face him when he was in this frame of mind, but then he quelled it.

He debated wrestling Boo back into the car, but the dog had an amazing instinct for people: Boo could tell good from bad with such telepathic accuracy it was spooky. Even before the dog saw a person, while Tag was still sitting in his cruiser running a license plate, Boo would be watching intently, sniffing the air, "sensing" things unseen.

The truth was people, even ones as cynical as Tag, could be fooled.

They could be fooled by a pretty face or an angelic air, by white hair and granny glasses, by adolescent awkwardness, by words, by body language.

Not Boo. The hackles on the dog's neck rose when something—or someone—needed a second look, and she grinned the silliest grin when everything was all right. Tag did not substitute her judgment for his own, but the world's ugliest dog had an uncanny knack for letting him know when he'd missed something.

She wasn't officially a K-9, but she was unofficially the mascot of the Snow Mountain Police Department.

So, why not see how she would react to the chief's niece? Just for interest's sake, nothing more. Lila Grainger's appearance and the opening of her store seemed mysterious and sudden, as if Tag needed to be any warier than he was of the woman he had never even laid eyes on. Still, the chief was usually a talker—you couldn't shut him up when she'd signed the book deal—but he'd said nothing about his niece's arrival in town until she had gotten here.

Tag ignored the big No Dogs Allowed sign posted on

the door, since just about everyone in Snow Mountain knew Boo was more human than dog anyway, and pulled the brass handle on the heavy walnut and glass door. He stepped in. A sleigh bell jingled a greeting and he was enveloped by smells of Christmas: candy cane, mint, pumpkin pie, incense, spices, pine.

Scent, he had found, was the most powerful of triggers and the aromas swamped him in memories of what his life had once felt like and had once been. A longing for the sweet, uncomplicated days of the past enveloped him. For a moment he could almost see his brother, Ethan, at about age six, tearing into a train set not unlike that one that chugged around the window.

He shook off the feeling of melancholy, liking crankiness better. A carol played loudly, old school Bing Crosby, and everywhere he looked Tag saw the highly breakable paraphernalia of the season. He warned Boo, with a finger, not to move.

At the far end of the store, a slight figure sat behind a counter had her back to the door and was typing furiously. She had not heard him come in over the high-volume crooning of Bing and her own intensity, and he studied her, frowning. No flowered dress?

In fact, the woman seemed to be wearing low-rider jeans that were slipping to show quite a bit of naked and very slender lower back. Tendrils of blond hair, the color of fall grass streaked with liquid honey, had escaped a clasp and teased the top of a delicate neck.

Tag's first thought was that it couldn't be the chief's niece. Hutch had a town full of relatives, not a niece or nephew under forty. This girl looked like she was about eighteen.

The wind picked that moment to send a vicious gust

down Main Street, and it sucked the door out of his hand and slammed it so hard even the dog flinched.

The woman, who had just reached for her coffee mug, started, and the glass dropped from fingers that had not quite grasped it, and shattered on the newly refurbished hardwood floor.

She leaped from the chair, and whirled to face him, one hand over her heart, the other reaching frantically for the three-foot-high striped candy cane decoration in a box beside her.

She held it like a weapon, and he might have laughed at what a ridiculous defense a candy cane was, except that somehow the picture of his brother ripping into Christmas parcels was still with him, as was his agony over Boo, and his laughter felt as dried up as those fall leaves blowing down Main Street.

Miss Mary Christmas was not eighteen after all, but midtwenties maybe.

And her eyes were genuinely fear-glazed, in sharp contrast to the pretty joy and light world she had created in her store. She registered his uniform and her hold on the candy cane relaxed, but only marginally.

She was dressed casually, but her outfit showed off feminine curves so appealing it pierced the armor of his hurt, which made him frown. She wore hip-hugging jeans, a red sweater over a white shirt, the tails and collar sticking out. She was sock-footed, which for some reason took him off guard, an intimacy at odds with the store surroundings.

"Sorry," she said, "you startled me."

No kidding.

He glanced down at Boo who did something he had never seen before: laid down and began to hum, deep in her throat, not a growl, a strange lullaby. He stared at the dog, flummoxed, hoping this was not the next stage in the diagnosis the doctor had given him yesterday.

He looked back up, as confused by her as he had been by the dog's strange humming.

She was young and beautiful, like one of those angels they sold to top the Christmas tree. Her Florida skin was only faintly sun-kissed, flawless as porcelain, her bone structure was gorgeous, but fragile, and eyes huge and china-blue fastened on his face. He could see where her pulse still beat frantically in her neck.

"You must be Miss Grainger," he said, despite the fact he'd been determined to address her as Miss L. Toe. Now he was aware of keeping his voice deliberately soft, his reasons for being here, nebulous to begin with, even more blurred by the fear he saw in her.

"Lila," she insisted brightly.

The chief's niece did not have the chunky build of the rest of the Hutchinson clan. In fact, he was aware of feeling guilty even thinking it about the chief's niece, but she was subtly but undeniably, well, *sexy*.

She was trying to make it look like she wasn't afraid anymore, but he could tell she still was, so he tried to tame his frown, and canned his plans to take out his bad mood on her.

He was in a business where he got thrown plenty of curveballs, but he had never developed a liking for being caught off guard, surprised, and the chief's niece was a surprise.

He'd been around enough fear to recognize the real McCoy, and to see wariness still haunted her eyes, despite his uniform. Or maybe because of it. Lots of people were afraid of police. He kept the space between them, but Boo began to wiggle forward on her belly, still humming happily. Tag snapped his finger at his dog, pointed at his feet.

Boo gave him a pleading look over her shoulder, then flopped over on her back and pointed all four feet in the air.

Lila Grainger's eyes left his face for the first time. Despite his uniform, he had the feeling she would bolt for the back if he made one move toward her. But when she looked at Boo, she smiled, and some finely held tension left her.

"What an adorable dog."

Maybe that explained her overreaction to the slamming of the door. Visual impairment. Boo was about the furthest thing from adorable on the planet!

An upside-down paw waved at her, and Lila Grainger laughed, proving she could see just fine, and that she was even sexier than he had first thought, which was unfortunate, because he'd rated her plenty sexy on that first glance.

"I missed the meeting last night," Tag said, getting down to business. He folded his arms over his chest, to make himself look big and remote, not a man in the least moved by the sexiness of strangers.

"Meeting?" she stammered, uneasily.

"I've been assigned to the Committee." He wanted to make that very plain. Assigned. Not volunteered.

"Oh, *that* meeting," she said too hastily, and tucked a wisp of that feathery hair behind her ear, "That's fine. We have enough people. More than enough. You look like a busy guy. No time for this type of thing. But thanks for dropping by. There's some leftover shortbread by the cash register. Go ahead and take some."

She was *trying* to get rid of him. Even with the distraction of the cookies, which he stole a glance at and saw *were* chocolate dipped, and with the further distraction of that wisp of hair popping back out from behind her ear, the policeman in him went on red alert as her eyes shifted uneasily to the right. The chief had been right. She was up to something. Something that she didn't want him to know about.

He was really watching her now. Every detail suddenly interested him, including ones that had nothing to do with what she might be trying to hide, like the fact she had faint circles under her eyes, as if she had trouble sleeping, and the fact that her ring finger was empty.

She was single. Miss L. Toe not Mrs. L. Toe. There was absolutely no reason he should feel uneasy about that. He didn't do the relationship thing. He'd become a master at ignoring that initial twitch of interest that could lead a man into that quicksand world of caring.

At his brother's funeral, six and a half years ago, the minister had said, *All love leads to loss.* Somehow it had become a credo Tag lived by—the dog had wormed her way by his defenses, but no one else.

And now, Boo, too, was going to drive the point home. That to develop attachments, to care about anything, even a dog, made a man vulnerable, stole his power from him as surely as Delilah had stolen Sampson's hair.

Not that he could indulge in such introspection right now. He made himself not look at Boo, who was still waving her paw engagingly at Lila Grainger.

"Well, nice of you to drop in, Officer, um—"

"Taggert," he supplied. What was causing her to feel such discomfort? He'd startled her, but there was more. He could sense it, even without Boo's help. Her uncle had been absolutely right.

She was up to something.

Or else the news he'd gotten yesterday, and that sudden poignant memory of his brother tearing into that gift, had rattled him badly enough that he was jumping at shadows.

After all, what could she be up to that she wouldn't want the police department—her uncle—to know about? She hardly looked like the type to decide to finance the saving of Christmas with a little illegal activity, like selling drugs or smuggling.

Still, Tag had a cop's gift. He knew instinctively when people were hiding something, and she was.

"Have you got some minutes from the meeting?" he pushed, just a little.

"Minutes?" her voice became suspiciously squeaky. "Of course not. It was very informal."

"So did you come up with a plan of action? For saving the Christmas display in Bandstand Park?"

"Oh," Lila said, her voice filled with bright and very fake cheer again, "we just bounced some preliminary ideas around. You know."

"I don't," he said uncooperatively.

"We changed the name. We're going to call ourselves Save Our Snow Mountain Christmas. SOS for short."

She looked at him like she expected his approval. When he said nothing she began to talk fast and nervously, another sure sign of a person who was being evasive.

"We might put up a tree. A big one," she said in a rush, "just to keep the Christmas spirit alive until we can come up with some money and get the Santa's Workshop display fixed. Or get the town to change their minds."

She blushed when she said that, as if she was planning

something *naughty* to get the town to change their minds, but just looking at her he could tell her idea of naughty and his would be completely different. He thought if she showed up in one of those red, fur-trimmed bikinis the town would do whatever the hell she wanted.

As if to prove how differently their minds worked, and that she was the girl least likely to ever wear a red fur-trimmed bikini, she said, "We might try putting a real Santa in the park on weekends."

"There are no real Santas," he said dryly, knowing with new conviction he was hearing only part of the story.

"I was thinking of asking that portly man who works with Uncle Paul. Do you think he'd do it for free?"

Portly was a very kind way to describe the most senior member of the Snow Mountain department.

"Jamison?" Tag asked, incredulously. "You want Karl Jamison to play Santa?"

Jamison, who was not portly, but obese, who chewed— and spat—tobacco, and who had the world's largest off-color vocabulary thanks to ten years in the Marine Corp, was the man least likely to play Santa.

"He just looked like he'd make a good Santa," she said wistfully.

Karl Jamison was the man most likely to kill Christmas forever on Snow Mountain should he ever be appointed a weekend Santa Claus.

"You wouldn't make a good Santa," she said, eyeing Tag speculatively before turning her eyes away, fiddling with the candy cane. "You're too—"

Despite the insult of being declared a worse Santa than Jamison, a number of ways to finish that sentence came to his mind: tall, dark, handsome, which just served to prove he had not been as successful at shutting down that initial spark of interest as he had hoped.

But she shot him another glance and finished her sentence with, "Unjolly."

He was not a literary giant like her, but he was pretty sure if he ran unjolly through the computer spelling checker at the station, it was going to make that noise he hated.

Still, *unjolly* was as accurate a description as any, so why was he vaguely annoyed that she had spotted his true nature, completely unsuitable in the peace and joy department, so instantly and accurately?

And since she had handed him his escape from her ridiculous committee practically gift-wrapped, why wasn't he gratefully bowing his way toward the door?

Instead he heard himself asking, "So besides that, did you come up with any other ideas for saving Christmas in Snow Mountain?"

He did not try to hide his cynicism, and her look of uneasiness increased.

"No, nothing at all," she said, way, way too quickly.

She was afraid of *him*. Or something. There were a lot of mysteries in Lila Grainger's eyes, and a man could be drawn to them, tempted to probe them, which was another reason to just get out of here, accept with grace and gratitude there was no room for cynical, Christmas-hating cops on the SOS committee.

But the chief wasn't going to believe he hadn't done something: kicked an elf, broken a manger, been rude and unreasonable, to get himself off the Save Christmas Committee hook. He slid one wistful look over his shoulder at the door, but sucked it up.

"You're sure you don't want me to do something?" he

asked gruffly. Damn. Now he was probably going to end up building a Santa throne that could hold Jamison without collapsing. Which would be a gigantic project.

But she was as eager to get rid of him as he was to leave.

"No, really, I can't think of a single thing." In fact, now she was backing away from him.

Only she'd forgotten the broken glass on the floor, and she was in her socks. She cried out, lifted her foot, the heel already crimson with blood.

"It's nothing," she said as he moved instinctively toward her. She slammed her foot back down with such conviction she nearly made herself faint.

She toppled, just as he arrived at her, and he managed to scoop her up before she hit the floor. She weighed practically nothing, perhaps a few pounds more than Boo, not that she was anything like Boo.

It had been a long, long time since he had held anything so close and so soft as Miss Lila Grainger. A yearning so intense it nearly stole his breath shot through him. Before he could stop himself, he had pulled her scent, wild summer strawberries, deep inside himself and it felt as if it was filling an emptiness he had not thought could be filled.

He wanted to drop her. He wanted to hold her tighter. He wanted to be the same man he had been thirty seconds ago, and was not sure he ever could be again.

"Oh, my," she moaned, her breath warm against his chest. "This has gone very badly."

He felt her sweet weight in her arms, saw the pulse going crazy in her neck, heard the dog humming at his heel with what he could suddenly and clearly identify as adoration, and thought, *You got that right.*

Out loud he said, without a single shred of emotion that might clue her in to how he felt about her softness pressed against him, "Where's your first-aid kit?"

CHAPTER TWO

LILA sat on the edge of the toilet in the bathroom, staring at the dark head bent over her foot.

Despite the fact Officer Taggert had perfected that policeman look of professional remoteness, he had actually flinched at the bathroom decor, which she knew to be fabulous: an imaginative creation of what Santa's washroom would look like.

There was a fake window, framed in snowmen-patterned curtains, looking out over beautifully hand-painted scenes from the North Pole. The towels had Christmas trees on them, the soap had glitter, the toilet paper, one of her top selling items, was printed with Ho, Ho, Ho.

In fact, before he had arrived, Lila had been sitting at her desk, contemplating starting her first ever book, *How to Have a Perfect Christmas,* with a really fun chapter on bathroom decorating for the holidays.

But now, despite the cheer of the bright red and white paint and the merry decor, the atmosphere in the close quarters of the bathroom seemed mildly icy. Taggert was remote, determined to keep his professional distance though, really, it seemed a little too late for that.

She had already *felt* him, felt the hard, unrelenting,

pure-man strength of him, and been as dazed by that as by the pain in her foot.

Dazed would describe her reaction to him, period—the reason she had stepped on broken glass.

After the initial fear had come something even more frightening. A feeling, unfounded because you could not *know* a person from simply looking at them.

But her feeling had been instant, and felt deeply.

The world is a better place because this man is in it.

She tried to thrust the thought away as soon as she had it. You could not know that about a complete stranger, even if he was wearing a police uniform. Despite making great strides since arriving in Snow Mountain, she was not sleeping well, and she knew her judgment was not what it once had been.

Naturally, now, she was doing her darnedest to be as perfectly poised and professional as he was, trying to act as though being picked up and carried down the hall by an extraordinarily appealing man was an everyday ho-hum kind of experience for her.

The dog seemed determined for them all to get cozy again. It had squeezed in between the toilet bowl and the sink, and was nuzzling her hand with its warm, damp nose.

"This really isn't necessary," she said again, her *world is a better place* feeling causing her to feel guilty about the secret she was determined to keep from him.

She was amazed that he had not seen the results of last night's meeting crammed into the dark corner by the bathroom: protest signs, freshly painted.

Lila had found out this morning that it was necessary to have a permit to assemble in Snow Mountain, a ridiculous formality given the tininess of the town, she felt. She had also found out that it took a number of weeks to get a permit, and she needed to draw attention to the fact Town Council had voted to cancel Christmas at Snow Mountain, *now*.

The unpermitted protest was scheduled for the Thursday before Thanksgiving. The SOS team was nearly delirious with delight over the plan to close down Main Street right in front of the town hall until some funding was reinstated for the Santa's Workshop display at Bandstand Park.

Her committee was not a bunch of hotheaded rebels, either, not the kind of people one would ordinarily expect at a protest. They were nice people, decent, law-abiding, hardworking people who were willing to stand up for what they believed in.

And they believed in Christmas.

Still, Lila was pretty sure her uncle would kill her if he knew. And this man in front of her? If the world *was* a better place because of him, it was probably because he would be exceedingly intolerant of schemes that fell even the *teensiest* bit outside of the law.

She shivered, still taken totally aback by her reaction of such total awareness to Officer Taggert. She, of all people, knew to be distrustful of instant attraction, since she had paid the horrific price of someone's totally unwanted and unencouraged attraction to her.

She'd been reminded of the consequences of that just a few minutes ago, when she'd once again experienced that horrible startled reflex, a reflex she had assured herself was almost gone—until the door had slammed tonight.

She had known as soon as she'd arrived in Snow Mountain that her doubts about opening the first storefront for her unexpectedly successful Internet Christmas company had been unfounded. It had been the right decision to pack up her life and move across the country.

Her healing, her return to normal, could begin here, in this sleepy little town nestled among forests and mountains.

Finally she was going to be able to overcome the block that she'd been experiencing ever since she'd been approached, because of the Internet success of her small company, to write *How to Have a Perfect Christmas* under the pseudonym, Miss L. Toe.

For weeks now, Lila had been experiencing excitement and hope instead of that horrible feeling of flatness, interspersed with anxiety. Except for the sleep problem, she was feeling so much better.

Snow Mountain had so much unrealized potential! It was a magical place, a town off a Christmas card. It was the place that could inspire her to write a *great* first book, to launch a *great* storefront for her Internet business.

But no lights? No Christmas display in the town square?

She remembered that display so clearly from the time her family had flown up here from their home in Florida to spend Christmas with her mother's oldest brother, Uncle Paul, the year she'd turned ten. She still remembered that Christmas more vividly than any other. The magic of snow, and real Christmas trees, the feeling in that small town.

Maybe that's what had pulled her back to this place when her world had fallen apart.

So, she just wasn't having Town Council squash her dreams before they even got started! She was giving herself over to creating the perfect Christmas store and the perfect Christmas town and the perfect book on creating the perfect Christmas. It gave her a sense of safety and control over the things that had been snatched from her.

Her arrival in Snow Mountain had returned to her a belief that there were places in the world that were wonderfully old-fashioned, where children still walked to school and played in the streets without their parents hovering, where women never gave a thought to walking alone, where violent things rarely happened.

But then the wrench—Town Council practically canceling Christmas!

Still, despite that challenge to her control over creating the perfect Christmas, Lila was aware of beginning to feel safe again. Tonight was a perfect example: She'd left her door unlocked even after store hours.

Lila was aware that her initial reaction of panic to the unexpected arrival in her shop had faded. It had not faded because she knew the man who had changed her world forever was in jail, but rather illogically because Officer Taggert radiated the strength and calm—the certain forbidding sternness—of a man who could be relied on to protect, to keep the world safe, to uphold standards of decency.

At first, she'd felt anxious that maybe he'd heard a whisper about the planned protest, especially when he seemed so suspicious, *probing*. Minutes of the meeting, for Pete's sake.

But it had soon become very apparent to her that, despite his offer to help, Officer Taggert's heart was not in it *at all*. He'd been ordered here by her uncle, and had put in an appearance.

Unless he saw the signs on his way out the door, the protest was safe.

She felt the tiniest little shiver of apprehension that she was on the wrong side of the law, but her purpose was so *right* that she felt justified.

Then it occurred to her that maybe the shiver she was feeling was not apprehension, but a treacherous little stirring of something else, despite the deliberate remoteness of the man who shared the bathroom with her.

Appreciation, primal compared to her rather philosophical thought that the world was a better place because he was in it. It was an almost clinical awareness of a healthy female for a healthy male. It didn't help that she had felt the strong bands of his arms around her, his easy strength as he had carried her to the bathroom.

He had seemed indifferent to their close proximity. But then again, he'd missed the protest signs, and he didn't look like a man who missed much, so maybe he'd felt a forbidden little stirring, too. He was a healthy male after all.

Taggert was at least six-one of pure male perfection: sleek muscle, long legs, deep chest, broad, broad shoulders, all accentuated magnificently by the crisp lines of his light blue on navy police uniform.

His face was astounding, chiseled masculine perfection, unconscious strength in the set of his chin, the firmness around his mouth, the lines around his eyes. His eyes, which had initially been shaded by the brim of his hat, were now fully visible since he had removed the hat.

While the rest of him was pure cop, one-hundred-percent intimidating and authoritative presence, his eyes were the softest shade of brown, shot through with threads of pure gold. His eyes did not reflect the remoteness of his demeanor, though there were walls up in them, walls that guarded a mystery…and most likely his heart.

He carried himself with the utter confidence of a man who knew his own strength and capabilities perfectly. No swagger, only pure, unadulterated self-assurance.

Now he was on one knee in front of her, focused on her foot. His hair was short, but incredibly thick and shiny, the rich color of dark chocolate. She was amazed by a renegade desire to feel its silk beneath her fingertips.

His hands were unbelievably sure on her ankle, and she stifled a gasp when he pulled her sock away and held her naked foot in the warm, hard cup of his hand. The shiver of appreciation she'd felt graduated to a betraying tingle of pure awareness. She felt terrified in a much different way than she had felt terrified the last two years of her life when she had become the victim of a stalker. He was a man she had worked with, and whose interest in her had seemed so benign…at first.

"Really," she managed to croak, "I can look after it."

"Look, either I'm taking a look at it, or I'm taking you to the hospital. You choose."

He glanced up, and she noticed just the faintest shadow of whiskers on his clean-shaven face, felt swamped by his closeness, his pure masculine scent.

"Are you all right?" he asked, genuine concern faintly overriding the professionalism in the masculine deepness of his voice. "You aren't going to faint, are you?"

"Faint?" she managed to say, inserting proud outrage into her voice, a woman determined not to be seen as weak ever again. "I am not the fainting kind."

But she had managed to sound more certain than she actually felt. Was she all right? Why did she feel as if she was standing in the open doorway of a plane, deciding whether to jump?

"I've been doing this a long time," he said patiently. "There is no fainting *kind*. I've seen a Marine faint at the sight of his own blood."

"Oh."

"Can I go ahead then? Or do you want me to take you to the hospital?"

The eyes were intent on her face, the voice no-nonsense, though his offering her a choice relaxed something in her, even though, logically, she knew it was not a *real* choice and he was very much in control.

"Go ahead," she squeaked.

"It's not so bad," he reassured her, lifting her leg so he could get a good look at the heel, gently swabbing away the blood with an alcohol pad. "I see a single cut, not very deep. I think there's a little piece of glass still in there."

He reached for tweezers, tugged, held up a tiny fragment of glass for her to see before he dropped it into the waste-paper basket that was painted like a toy drum.

"I'm just going to dress the wound," he explained, his voice deep, soothing, as if he was talking to a small child. "I don't see any more glass, no need for stitches. A wound to this part of the body just bleeds a lot."

The voice of a man who had seen many wounds and much blood, without ever coming even remotely close to fainting; a man who would be just this coolly and reassuringly competent in crises of any magnitude.

He placed a cotton gauze on her foot, held it in place by winding a bandage over her heel and up her ankle in a criss-cross pattern, all very professional, clinical, detached.

Not, apparently, being bothered by *tingles* the way she was.

"You're obviously used to doing this sort of thing," she said. "This is obviously your first trip to the North Pole, though."

He looked surprised, and then he smiled.

It was just the tiniest hint of a smile, but it changed the stern lines of his face completely. She glimpsed for a moment something of his past: something reckless, devil-may-care, mischievous. *Charming.*

He got up, picked up his hat and brushed off his knee with it. He glanced around at the bathroom decor, his eyes resting briefly on a jar of bright candies labeled Jolly Beans, For Medicinal Use Only.

The smile that had tickled his lips evaporated, and she was aware whatever he had once been, he was not that now. He actually winced, as if such adorable corniness hurt his eyes. He stepped quickly out of the bathroom and back into the hallway.

All she could think of was he had nearly brushed against the protest signs, and for the first time in her life she was completely unworthy of trust.

He clamped his hat back on his head, pulled it low, so his amazing eyes were once more shadowed. Then he whistled for his dog, and let himself out the front door.

She limped after him and locked it behind him, aware that even though Snow Mountain itself felt safer to her than it had half an hour ago, she herself did not feel as safe, as if she stood on the edge of something scary. And wonderful.

But that she of all people, she reminded herself with stern warning, should know how very scary a brief encounter with a strange man could become.

It was the reason she'd sworn off real life and chosen to embrace fantasy instead. Her beautiful store, this beautiful town, her literary adventures—those were going to be enough for her. It was going to fill every void, make her feel safe, fulfilled, *in control.*

A woman would never feel one hundred percent in control around a man like Taggert. Never.

Determined to make the creation of a perfect Christmas her life mission, she marched back to her computer.

Suddenly decorating a bathroom seemed like a terrible place to start *How to Have A Perfect Christmas*. Terrible.

"You have to start somewhere," she told herself, aware of a panicky little edge in her voice as she said it. She'd accepted the advance, and worse, she'd *spent* it. She had a deadline!

Obviously the writer's block was coming, at least in part, from her insomnia. But it wasn't helping one little bit that the place on earth most likely to be chosen for a poster of the perfect Christmas town had practically canceled Christmas. Once she looked after that, everything else was going to fall into place.

With a new sense of verve, Lila picked up the phone, took a deep breath and did the thing she had been debating about and putting off since the meeting last night.

"CLEM TV, Spokane," a voice on the other end answered.

"Could I speak to Jade Flynn, please?" She named the reporter who seemed to do the majority of the human interest stories for the station.

"Can I tell her what you're calling about?"

"The cancellation of Christmas," Lila said firmly.

Brody Taggert joined the other men at the window of the Snow Mountain Police Department, took a sip of his coffee and looked across Main Street at the fracas outside of Snow Mountain Town Hall.

The protesters had completely blocked the street, and were enthusiastically waving lovingly hand-painted signs.

Elves Have Rights, Too! Say Yes To Christmas. Save Our Snow Mountain. Save Santa. As they marched around in a circle, they chanted, "Heck no, the elves won't go."

It was an unlikely-looking group of protestors—not a dreadlock or pierced body part on any of them. Lots of gray hair out there, with one glaring exception, of course.

Her hair, where it showed beneath the brim of her fur-trimmed Santa hat, was catching the sun, and looked like it was spun through with gold.

It seemed to him Lila Grainger was as eye-catching in that hat, bundled up in a pink oversize parka that made her look like a marshmallow, as she would have been in a fur-trimmed bikini.

The CLEM TV mobile van from Spokane was pulling up. Bruce Wilkes from the *Snow Mountain News* was already happily snapping pictures.

"What are you going to do, Chief?" Randy Mulligan asked uncertainly.

Tag slid Hutch a look. *Have a heart attack,* came to mind. The chief looked apoplectic.

Of course, his niece, looking positively radiant, was in the very middle of the mêlée. When she separated from the other protestors to go and talk to Jade Flynn, who was getting out of the news van, it was more than obvious who was in charge of the protest.

Tag, instead of making the professional assessment *ringleader,* noticed that aside from the fact she looked cute as a button, she was still limping.

"You didn't even catch a whisper of this when you went to see her?" Hutch asked Tag accusingly.

"No, sir. She told me they were going to ask Jamison to play Santa—"

"Like hell I'm playing Santa," Jamison muttered indignantly, putting enough curse words between playing and Santa to do his Marine corps heritage proud.

"—and that they'd come up with a new name. That's it." Well, that wasn't it. Tag had known she was up to something *naughty*. He could now clearly remember the *guilty* blush when she'd mentioned getting city hall to change their minds. He felt he'd probably been distracted by *naughty* thoughts of his own, especially after he'd carried her down that endless hall to her bathroom, and then spent agonizing minutes administering first-aid to the cut on her foot.

You didn't admit to your boss you'd had naughty thoughts about his niece, thoughts that might have prevented you from seeing certain things coming, he told himself.

Besides, the grim news about Boo had been pretty fresh that night; Tag knew it had clouded his thinking, and still did, though he wore the mask of functioning perfectly.

"Go arrest her," Hutch said, thankfully to no one in particular.

Randy Mulligan obviously thought of some urgent work he had to do. He stampeded from the room as if the Hells Angels had arrived in town and he had to personally deal with them.

"Arrest her?" Pete Harper said. "Are you kidding? You know how that's going to look on the evening news? This town has barely recovered from the elf on fire last year."

"How's it going to look if I don't arrest her and she's my niece?" Hutch snapped. "Like I'm playing favorites, that's how. If I don't do something decisive right now every special interest group in Snow Mountain from the Grannies for Justice to Pals for Pooches is going to think they can shut down the town anytime they don't get what they want.

Pals for Pooches has been trying to get an animal shelter for a lot longer than Lila's been trying to save Christmas."

Unfortunately Tag could see his point.

"Well, I'm not arresting her," Pete said. "My mother would kill me."

His mother was out there right beside Lila, carrying a sign that showed a tombstone with Santa on it, RIP, and then Killed By Snow Mountain Town Council. Jeanie Harper was also dispensing cookies to the news crews, practically guaranteeing all stories would be slanted in favor of the protestors.

As if they wouldn't be anyway.

"I ain't arresting nobody, either," Jamison said. He jerked his thumb at Pete. "His mother wouldn't bake me cookies anymore."

Pete shot him a look. "My mother bakes *you* cookies?"

"Go arrest her, Tag," Hutch said wearily.

It fell neatly into that category of a job no one else wanted to do, and besides, he was the one who had missed the signs that this was going to happen. Now that he thought about it, hadn't there been something stuffed in that dark corner of the hallway by her bathroom?

Oh, yeah, signs.

"You mean arrest her?" Tag hedged uncomfortably, "Or just take her aside, and try to talk some sense into her?"

Her uncle sighed. "She's just like her mother. Talking sense to her is like trying to explain algebra to a chimp. Impossible. Besides, you think she's going to give in quietly? What kind of news story would that make?"

Unfortunately Tag could see his point. He took a deep breath, squared his shoulders, turned and lifted his jacket off the back of his chair, pulled on his hat. Boo, who had been snoozing under his desk, lifted her head and thumped her tail on the floor, hopeful for an invitation.

"Fat chance," he told her sourly, while silently searching for signs of the dog's deterioration. "I count on you to warn me about who I have to keep an eye on. You failed me on this one, Boo. You *loved* Lila Grainger."

He realized he did not want to be using the word love in any sentence addressed to Boo, especially one that also included the name Lila Grainger. She was just that kind of woman, the kind who could storm a man's defenses before he even knew he was under attack.

The kind of woman where you noticed the fact she was limping, rather than the fact she was leading an insurrection.

The kind of woman with a foot so enchanting, you overlooked the signs of revolt brewing all around you.

The dog sighed, put her head back down and closed her eyes. Almost easier to go out there and deal with *that* than the dog's easy surrender to being left behind.

Moments later, he was shouldering his way through a crowd worthy of a big-city Santa Claus parade, with the same attitude of excited anticipation in the air. There hadn't been this much excitement in Snow Mountain since the Snow Leopards, the high school football team, had made state finals three years ago.

Over the chanting, Tag could hear a tinny loudspeaker wailing out a sentimental rendition of the song, "You Light up My Life."

It seemed as if the entire population of Snow Mountain—plus most of the surrounding area—had known about the demonstration. This was a town that could not keep secrets, so how it had stayed below the police radar was something of a miracle.

The air of celebration toned down a bit as he shoved his way through to the center of activity. He tried to tell himself he had probably been in worse positions, but he could not remember when.

By the time he arrived in front of Lila Grainger, he was very aware of the hostility the crowd had toward him.

She saw him coming. So did the news crews. Every camera, cell phone and video recorder within a hundred miles had accumulated in front of town hall. And every single one of them was pointed at him.

"Hello, Officer Taggert," she said bravely, trying for, but missing, defiance. Hell, she was trembling slightly.

"Miss Grainger."

Damn it. She looked adorable in the ridiculous hat. The oversize coat made her look even smaller than she was.

He leaned close to her, could smell that heady scent of wild strawberries, tried to avoid the mistake he had made last time of breathing in too much of it. He fought back a sudden impulse to ask her about her damned foot. "Miss Grainger, would you come with me?"

He said it quietly, for her ears only. She looked like the type that buckled under to authority, but of course the wild-strawberry scent should have warned him of, well, a wilder side.

She took a step back from him, fixed the incredible deep sea-blue of her eyes on him, and squared her shoulders. "Am I under arrest, Officer Taggert?"

Jeanie Harper gasped, which probably meant a life sentence of no more shortbread for Tag, her son or Jamison. This was not something he wanted to be held responsible for, but he was the new guy. The flak always landed on him.

The cameras were snapping, the film rolling. The news crew moved in closer, and Jade Flynn flipped her hair and moistened her lips, her timing for the story impeccable. Microphones shaped like huge foam hot dogs dangled over them.

"You need a permit to assemble," he said quietly. "You're obstructing traffic."

"Am I under arrest?" she demanded again. She pointed her chin upward, stubbornly, but he could see she was shaking even more now.

And that she was all of five foot three and probably weighed about a hundred and ten pounds. He remembered that weight in his arms, struggled to keep his facial expression absolutely impassive.

Standing there in her Santa hat, she looked exactly like the girl who had probably not done one *naughty* thing in her whole life. She'd probably never even had a speeding ticket, never mind fur-trimmed bikinis.

She was just one of those people who became passionate about causes. Not that he wanted to be thinking about *her* and *passion*. What a waste. All that passion over a silly display in the park.

Though every time he drove by Bandstand Park, he had to admit he was aware of the black emptiness of it, instead of the lights, the little characters, Santa's reverberating ho-ho-ho. Suddenly, without warning, he remembered Ethan coming home when he was about twelve with Santa's hat, swiped from the park.

And he, the older brother, making him take it back, foreshadowing his career, which at this moment he hated.

"Are you arresting me, Officer Taggert?"

"Yeah," he said reluctantly, "you're under arrest."

A discontented hum began in the crowd. Jeanie called out, "Shame on you, Brody Taggert."

This was the problem with becoming a police officer in the small town where you had grown up. Jeanie Harper no doubt had memories of him raiding her garden, and knocking over her mailbox on Halloweens past.

He put a hand on Lila's shoulder, intending to guide her out of the crowd, but she shrugged out from under his hand, and stubbornly presented her wrists to him.

He bit the inside of his cheek, whether to keep his temper or to keep from laughing he wasn't quite sure. Miss L. Toe did look ludicrous, but since he had not laughed since Boo's diagnosis, he figured it was his temper.

He heard Jade Flynn say to her cameraman, "Oh, boy. Be sure and get this."

Everybody wanted a show to go with the storyline about the town that was canceling Christmas. And every show needed a villain. Jade Flynn didn't care who looked bad. Lila looked like she might, but not enough to let go of this opportunity to get the publicity she wanted.

And he was the *who* that was going to look bad.

He stared her down, she was obviously frightened, but not enough to back down. She was willing to sacrifice herself to her cause. He noticed she still had little circles of fatigue under her eyes.

"Okay then," he said, his voice deliberately flat, his expression hard. "Put your hands behind your back."

She did and he took the cuffs off his belt, and snapped them around her wrists, which were so small he had to adjust the cuffs. He was nearly blinded by flashes, and he felt like an idiot. If she was humiliated it didn't show one little bit in the proud tilt of her chin.

He told her she was being arrested for unlawful assembly and obstructing traffic, and told her her rights. She nodded that she understood, standing ramrod straight, her dignity intact while he felt his own was in tatters.

He spun her around, his hand on her elbow and marched her, her limp visible, through the crowd. He was aware of feeling as if he had to protect her from the crush of people, though it was him getting the looks. Several people clicked their heels and gave him straight-armed salutes.

Lila flinched more than he did from the insulting gestures.

As soon as he had his prisoner safely inside the police station, Hutch appeared.

"Was that really necessary?" he asked Tag of the cuffs.

Tag said nothing, but sighed inwardly. Who had ordered the arrest? Still, he was now aware this was something of a family dispute. No one ever wanted to be in the middle of *that*.

"Ask her," Tag said, and unlocked her wrists.

"He was just doing his job, Uncle Paul."

Tag shot her a look that clearly told her he didn't need a one-hundred-pound waif in a Santa hat and a marshmallow coat to defend him.

"Get into my office," Hutch said quietly to his niece. "Now."

She sent Tag an imploring look, which he ignored. He'd done his bit, and he wasn't the least bit proud of it, either.

"I'm not normally the kind of person who gets arrested," Lila said to him, ignoring her uncle's command, the only person Tag had ever seen do that.

"I kind of figured you for a virgin," he said, their department's lingo for a first-time offender.

It had slipped out, and it was a mistake. He knew it even before Hutch sent him a killing look and her blush went the color of a smashed raspberry.

Which of course made him entertain the extremely

naughty thought that maybe she was every kind of virgin it was possible to be.

"Sorry," he muttered. "I didn't mean that the way it sounded."

"Of course not," she said soothingly. "We're all rattled."

The thing was, he *shouldn't* be. He was no virgin. Of any kind.

"I hope we meet again," she said formally, "under better circumstances."

"Really? I was hoping the exact opposite." He knew as soon as he said it, it was way too harsh, a defense against everything she was making him *feel*. Rattled. Off-kilter. Guilty. Worried about her foot.

Boo chose that moment to waddle out from under his desk. She plopped down at Lila's feet and began humming.

Lila sat down on the floor beside the dog, wrapped her puffy pink marshmallow arms around Boo's neck and burst into tears.

She's exhausted, Tag thought, noticing the fatigue around her eyes again. And then, annoyed that he felt *sympathy* toward her, he told himself it was probably planning the little extravaganza outside that had exhausted her.

Then he noticed Hutch and Boo glaring at him with identical expressions of accusation. He threw up his hands in exasperation and went and found a cell to clean. Hopefully it would keep him busy until the crowd outside had dispersed, Lila had gone home, her uncle had cooled off and his dog had been returned to her senses.

Hopefully it would keep him busy long enough to forget the way he felt when he saw she was still limping.

CHAPTER THREE

"...DONATIONS are pouring in," Lila told her aunt Marla, tossing a raft of envelopes she'd been sorting through into the air. "And the best? A man, Henry, who retired in Spokane, but used to work in maintenance at a big California theme park, thinks he can fix the elves and the reindeer. He's sure he can save the Santa's workshop display!"

When Lila had accompanied Henry to the city storehouse, she'd been dismayed when the town maintenance man hadn't wanted to let her in, and had treated her vaguely as if she was the *enemy*.

When she had finally talked her way past the sentry, her dismay had deepened when she saw what sad shape everyone was in: it wasn't just the mechanics of the animated figurines that was in trouble. The paint had been neglected, and was faded, patchy and peeling. Rather than looking cheery, the elves looked downright spooky.

"Still, I'm trying to put together a work bee for the weekend. Henry's going to bring the special paint—"

She noticed suddenly that despite the good news, her aunt looked distracted. It occurred to her that Marla had not even mentioned the new display of sleds laden with fresh piles of holly and mistletoe at the front door of the store.

Her aunt *always* noticed the new things that came in. She was Miss L. Toe's greatest fan and Lila's biggest supporter.

"Is something the matter?" Lila asked.

Marla sighed. "Oh, Lila, all this is wonderful, but for every piece of mail you've received the Police Department has received one, too. Most of it's addressed to Brody. It's awful. Hate mail."

"He acts as if he couldn't care less, but Paul said he's called in sick twice this week. Brody Taggert has never been sick a day in his life. That poor kid. As if he hasn't had enough to deal with."

First of all, Lila was astonished that anyone would see Brody Taggert as a kid. To her he was one-hundred-percent pure intimidating man. And if she hadn't felt that way before, she certainly had while he *arrested* her.

She'd been so aware of his size, his power, his pure authority. He'd carried himself through that hostile crowd like the alpha male of a wolf pack: confident in his territory, unafraid, indifferent to the challenges of the lesser pack members. She had felt oddly protected, even though she knew the focus of the crowd's hostility had certainly not been on her, but on him.

Not that he deserved it. Her aunt was right. Poor guy. He had just been doing his job.

And that was what he'd looked like on the footage that had aired just a few days ago, first in Spokane, and then, luckily, a slow day for news, around the nation. The human interest aspect of the plight of Santa's Workshop in Snow Mountain had been picked up by media everywhere.

The camera had captured something she had not really been aware of at the time: that the mood in the crowd could have turned on a hair, that the smallest crack in Brody's confidence could have turned that situation very ugly.

But he had handled himself with astounding control. Brody had the look of a man who knew how to get the job done: the look of men who went into battle and gladiator's rings; a chilling calm, a thin veneer over a state of readiness. His expression had been flat and yet there was no mistaking the forbidding look on his features: *Don't mess with me. Don't even think it.*

She'd had that thought again, ridiculous, given the fact she'd been the one he was leading away in cuffs, but there it had been.

The world was a better place because of men like this one.

Lila, looking at herself in those video clips, wished she'd worn her black leather jacket instead of the warmer down-filled parka, and taken a miss on the Santa hat. She had looked tiny beside him, and frightened. The limp had made her look fragile. Still, when she looked at it, she didn't really see Brody *arresting* her. In fact, there was something protective about the way he put his body between her and that moody crowd. She'd felt the same *shiver* again when she reviewed the clips.

Unfortunately, then she had to remember bursting into tears when he'd said, perfectly understandably, too, that he hoped never to see her again.

She tried to tell herself it was the chronic insomnia, the emotion of the day, the disapproval in her uncle's eyes, the fact that the only being in the room who'd sympathized with her was a *dog.*

But in her heart she knew something about Brody Taggert called to her. It called to that place in her that *wanted:* heated looks and stolen kisses, brushes of hands, sizzling awareness.

Brody Taggert awakened the part in her she had deliberately put to sleep, deliberately walked away from: as too dangerous, too unpredictable, too painful, too unlike the world she created in her store, the world that she hoped to create in the town and in her book.

The book which, with all the excitement of the last week, she still had not started, though she was now contemplating beginning with a chapter called *How to Get Your Town to Care About a Perfect Christmas.*

But for now the important thing was that the story of Snow Mountain shutting down their Christmas display had had exactly the effect she intended. It had worked miracles. Three thousand dollars in donations so far!

And Henry. He thought he might be able to have the display ready to light up two weeks before Christmas. She was tentatively setting December 15 as the date they would reopen Santa's Workshop on Snow Mountain.

But this was the first Lila had heard that the Police Department was experiencing an equal and opposite reaction.

And the thought of Brody—she had started calling him that in her mind after Jeanie had called out his full name—getting hate mail made her stomach drop. She was frightened of him, or more accurately of her reaction to him, but to think of him getting hate mail was horrible.

She thought of his eyes: the brown shot through with gold, a glimpse of something she wouldn't quite call gentleness, but something in him that was tender, *hurting,* his mystery.

She could not shake the feeling of *knowing* him. Oh, not what he was showing her, not what he wanted her to believe about him, but who he really was.

"Town Hall's not faring very well, either," Marla said. "Some of the stations have dug up the footage from last year of the burning elf. These are not Snow Mountain's finest moments being aired for the entertainment of America."

That explained the chilly reception at the town storage facility. Lila had the sudden uncertain thought that maybe even if she did manage to get everything fixed, she still had to have the approval of Town Council to put the display back in the park. And she'd managed to alienate them.

Even though she wanted to ask her aunt exactly how mad she'd managed to make everyone, she had to know something else first.

"What do you mean Officer Taggert has had enough to deal with? What do you mean poor *kid?*" Because of the danger of his intrigue, Lila really knew she shouldn't be asking these questions. She considered herself to be a model of self-control, so she was stunned when the questions got asked anyway.

Of course, she reminded herself, the model of self-control had also been sitting on the floor of the police station, sobbing into the fur of a dog.

Insomnia, she excused her weaknesses.

It occurred to her there were parts of herself that she did not know, and that perhaps she could not control.

And when she thought of those *things* in relation to Brody Taggert the shiver inside of her intensified.

It was the wrong time to think of the firm line of his lips, to wonder about their taste, but again, she was aware of losing her hold on control.

If Marla now told her something that made her feel tender toward him and bashed down her wary defenses, she would be in trouble.

But Marla, thankfully, suddenly closed up. She was a

policeman's wife, who kept police business police business, who knew those taciturn kind of men who did that work did not like their personal lives shared, and who obviously knew no one would appreciate sympathy less than Brody Taggert.

"Lila," she said gently, "I really believe you can save Santa's Workshop. But I don't know if it's worth the public relations nightmare that's been created for the Police Department and for the town."

Marla could have said *the public relations nightmare you created for the police department and for the town,* and *for Brody Taggert.*

Lila looked at the distress in her aunt's face and knew, however unwittingly, she had managed to hurt the people who cared about her the most.

After her stalker had dismantled her life with unwanted telephone calls, and gifts and appearances for two years— and then taken her hostage for the six most terrifying hours of her life—who had been there for her? Who had unhesitatingly offered her refuge?

Her uncle Paul and her aunt Marla.

And just like her aunt Marla had protected Brody's personal history right now, she knew her aunt and uncle had done the same for her. There had not been a single whisper since she'd arrived here of what had driven her to this remote corner of the globe, about why she had appeared here so suddenly to open her store.

"What can I do?" she asked her aunt.

Marla smiled tiredly. "I think you've done quite enough, dear."

"No. I made this mess and I can fix it." How? Without tangling more with that man? Without putting herself more firmly in the danger zone, on the collision course with her secret untamable self?

"Some things can't be fixed," Marla said.

"Well," Lila said stubbornly, "most can. Look at the Christmas Display. Doomed. But now there's hope. Isn't there always hope?"

"I don't know," her aunt said. "Don't worry about it, Lila. It will pass. I'm sorry I mentioned it."

Don't do this, her rational side begged. But her wilder side begged, too: live a little dangerously. See what happens next. Put yourself in the path of the oncoming train. You can jump out of the way, just in time, just before disaster hits.

Think it through, her tame side demanded. *If it's a good idea it will still be a good idea tomorrow.*

But her wild side seemed to be all done with listening, with obeying, with being controlled.

Her wild side wanted to see Brody Taggert again, be with him, get to know him, dance with danger.

Not a shred of *that* showed in what she said next.

Oh, no, she did a perfect imitation of little Dorothy Do-Gooder, just trying desperately to right her wrongs.

"Aunt Marla, what if we all worked together to fix the display? The SOS committee, the Town, the Police Department? Wouldn't that make a great follow-up story? How the spirit of Christmas is bringing the whole town of Snow Mountain together? It's like a Christmas miracle. The media will eat it up! We can put Bro—Officer Taggert front and center. He'll be getting fan mail instead of hate mail!"

And I hope it isn't all from me.

Her aunt laughed. "I don't think Brody would go for that. He's the guy who least likes the front and center position."

"He doesn't even have to know the press is going to be there," Lila said stubbornly. "Just tell Uncle Paul to order him to help out."

It wasn't a very nice fact that a man she thought of way more often than she had any right to—a man who was as attractive as any other she had ever seen—would have to be *ordered* to spend time with her.

But he'd made it perfectly—painfully—clear at their last meeting he never wanted to see her again.

She didn't blame him. Not really. But this would be for his own good.

She didn't even want to contemplate the mess she had made last time she had decided that the means justified the end.

"Let me think about it," Marla said uncertainly.

"We have no time to think about it," Lila insisted. "The story will die, and then no one will care. Phone Uncle Paul. Tell him Brody Taggert and as many other police men as he can dig up have to be available Saturday morning at 10:00 a.m."

"Where?" Marla said.

"We need a place big enough to house at least twenty people, maybe more, twelve reindeer, eight elves and Santa Claus. It has to be a place that can handle a little grease and dropped paint."

"Taggert's barn is the only place I can think of that's that big," her aunt said. "That's where we built the Snow Mountain float for the Bloomsday Parade in Spokane."

"Brody Taggert's barn?" she asked.

"He lives on his family's place, just west of town. That's where the barn is."

Brody Taggert's barn. A peek into his personal life,

beyond the uniform. Her wild side was jumping up and down with glee. Her other side was frowning at her with prudish disapproval.

His barn, she told her inner prude, *not his bedroom.*

"If this doesn't go well, we've sent the press right to Brody's front door," her aunt said uncertainly.

"It will go well!" Lila pleaded. "I know it will."

But she wasn't feeling as certain as she made herself sound. Because really, she was sending *herself* to Brody Taggert's front door, and he had said very plainly he never wanted to see her again.

That was wishful thinking in a town this size, but still, she was probably pushing it by setting up shop in his barn.

Well, the barn hadn't been her idea. It wasn't her fault that was where the floats got built. She hadn't asked for a peek at his personal life: it had been handed to her. As if the universe was conspiring with her.

Still she felt a shiver of pure apprehension with toying with something as powerful as chemistry.

After a moment's hesitation, Marla looked at her, smiled ruefully, shook her head and picked up the phone. "Hi, Pete," she said. "Put me through to the chief."

Brody had been watching sourly from his kitchen window for the past few days as the elves arrived one by one at his barn, delivered by volunteers with pickups. And then the reindeer. And finally, before daybreak on Saturday on a big truck, Santa, and guess who was getting out of the truck with Santa, supervising the unloading?

The enemy at the gate.

Not that Lila Grainger was any kind of enemy. Jeez, he'd watched the news, too. She didn't even look like an opponent.

He understood perfectly why he was getting mail. It was a kind of David and Goliath story, him unfortunately being Goliath. Her unfortunately being a rather sexy version of David.

Which was where the *enemy* part came in.

Lila Grainger made him *feel* things, things he had been quite content not to feel for a long time.

The number one thing she made him feel was a longing…for, of all the crazy things, wild strawberries.

And the other thing was this weird desire to *protect* her, though as far as he could tell he was probably the one in need of protection.

He'd do well to remember how the David and Goliath story ended. Things did not go well for Goliath.

He watched her go to the barn, heave unsuccessfully on the doors. He frowned. She was still favoring one foot, he was sure of it.

Well, there was no sense letting her *know* how rattled she made him feel. He'd been in the cop business long enough to know you never let fear show, or uncertainty. Every man had weaknesses. Every man had moments when his courage failed him. But some men had a gift for not letting that show, and he was one of those men.

So, he'd confront her head-on. She would never know how badly he wanted to stay away from her, how badly touching her had made him aware of the hardness of his own world, the imbalance of a world where there was nothing soft.

Even this house, new, was all hard lines, modern and sleek, masculine and without frills. He *liked* it like that: orderly, easy to keep clean, free of knickknacks. Free of sentiment.

He'd succeeded in creating a life without softness, closing away all that tickled at those places in him, as easily as he had closed up the family home that now stood unused on the other side of the barn.

Except Boo, he thought as he shrugged on his jacket. Boo, his one *soft* thing, and now she was going.

A reminder of what *soft* things and tender feelings did to a man: left him vulnerable, stole his strength.

Love was Delilah stealing Sampson's hair.

That pesky word again. *Love.* He shook it from his mind, impatiently, a man shooing away an annoying fly. Boo was already at the back door, the one off the kitchen, humming happily as if she *knew* who had arrived.

His traitor dog usually *warned* him when he was about to get into trouble. Not this time, no sirree, the dog was leading him to the enemy at the gate with a wagging tail and eagerness he had not seen in her in days. Two days in the past week, Boo had been so sick he had not gone to work, not sure she would see the end of the day. Now she seemed improved again, and he was riding the roller coaster of denial and hope.

And that's what love did: made a man helpless when he most wanted to be powerful.

With that thought foremost in his mind, Brody stepped from the darkness of the yard into the light of the barn. Long ago, his father had taken the stalls out, leaving a cavernous space to store and work on farm machinery. That, too, was gone, now, and all that was left was space. Space that was filled right now with elves and reindeer, and one very large Santa.

"Hello," she said, coming out from behind an elf, Boo already attached to her heel. Her hair was caught back in a clasp and she was wearing pink earmuffs and matching mittens, as if it was forty below zero outside. Her nose looked almost as pink as her muffs.

Soft. Not made for this weather, he thought, aware of a certain hopefulness. *She'd quit this town, probably after Christmas, and his life could get back to normal.*

Though at the moment he couldn't think what it was he'd ever liked so much about normal.

That's what she did to him: made his thinking, always so clear, always so practical, now faintly scattered, a whole unexplored area of gray *uncertainty* edging into his nice black-and-white world.

"What a beautiful barn," she said, hugging herself against the chill. "How old is it?"

Was she avoiding looking at him?

He shoved his hands in his own pockets, decided to avoid looking at her, too. "It's been here since my family had the property. A hundred years or so."

"Imagine a family being in one place for a hundred years," she said wistfully. "Someday your children will play in that loft, just the way you did. I can practically hear them laughing."

Then she did look at him, and he at her.

And for a moment it sprang between them: that spark of heat, the life force needing to create, to bring another generation forward, that feeling between a certain man and a certain woman. *This could be it.*

He barely knew her, Brody told himself ferociously. *This couldn't be it, because he simply wasn't allowing it.* He did not think of the past. He did not think of the future. Especially not a future where his children laughed in a hayloft.

He survived by staying grounded in the now. She was not *connected* to him. She had not really heard laughter.

It was no big deal that she knew he had played in the hayloft. That's what kids did. But without warning he heard the ghost of his brother's laughter reverberating off the ancient timbers of the loft. He actually looked up toward that darkened place, then looked quickly away, frowning, *feeling*.

That was what she seemed to be bringing back into his life, whether he was ready for it or not, and he was pretty darn sure he was not. And that was after only a few brief, brief encounters with her.

He shivered.

"Are you cold?" she asked.

"No!" he said, *hating* that she wanted to see things about him that he did not want to show her. The place where he was not tough, not invulnerable, not able to withstand discomfort without flinching.

"I *love* the cold," she announced, just as if he had said *yes*, instead of no. "It feels so clean, so pure, don't you think?"

He had never given one thought to how cold felt. He didn't want to think about how cold felt now. He did not want her fooling with the way he saw his world.

But he bet her kisses would taste like snowflakes. Pure. Clean. Moist. Sweet. He looked at her lips, looked away before she noticed, shoved his hands deeper in his jacket pockets.

As if she hadn't noticed his lack of response, she said, "I can't wait to try skating. And sledding."

See? That was the thing about his thinking. Because he could picture doing those things with her, though he had not skated or sledded for years, and had felt no desire to do either activity. They were parts of his life left behind, that he could not reclaim without being swamped with memories of his brother.

She stuck out her hand rather formally. "Officer Taggert, thanks for the use of your barn."

Like he'd had a choice.

"Call me Brody," he said, but reluctantly, aware he had liked the barrier of his position between them. Liked it very much. Sought refuge in it.

"All right. Brody."

It sounded just as he had known it would, way too personal, like a blessing coming off her tongue. Then he made the mistake of taking her proffered hand.

Something happened. It was as if he had been cold, frozen cold, without somehow knowing it. Not the good kind of cold, either, not the pure, clean kind. And now warmth gnawed at the edges of his world, promising something.

Her hand lingered in his, her eyes met his and held.

They yanked their hands away at the same time.

"I'll make coffee," she stammered.

"I'll—" He looked around, saw a man tinkering with an elf, jerked his thumb at him. "I'll give him a hand."

Neither of them moved. The barn door heaved open and Mrs. Harper and Jamison came in.

Jamison loudly announced, "Cold enough to freeze off a monkey's—"

Jeanie gave Jamison a look.

"—eyelashes," he finished weakly. "Jeanie brought her cookies. I brought chili for lunch. Sounds like the whole fri—uh, darned—town is going to be here."

"You brought chili?" Brody asked, incredulous.

Jamison had brought chili? It was his secret recipe. He only made it for guys' poker night at his place.

"Yeah," Jamison said a little defiantly.

"With or without the secret ingredient?"

"What secret ingredient?" Lila asked innocently.

"Without!" Jamison sputtered.

"Well, that's good," Brody said.

"What's the secret ingredient?" Lila asked again, more insistently.

"Love," Jamison lied slickly.

The dog wasn't the only traitor. The dog wasn't the only one falling under her spell. Only Jamison slid Jeanie Harper a look. It wasn't Lila's spell he was under at all. It was the spell of those cookies.

"Oh, isn't that the sweetest thing?" Lila said.

Only Brody saw the look Jamison shot at him, not sweet at all. *Tell the real secret ingredient and I'll cut out your tongue.* The secret ingredient was supposedly ash from a Cuban cigar.

"Why'd you leave it out?" Jeanie teased him. "The world—or a pot of chili—always needs more love. I bake it into every batch of cookies."

So there they stood, two rough men, two soft women, something humming in the air, softly. Ever so softly.

Thankfully the barn door swung open and another group breezed in on a fresh cloud of cold air.

In fact within an hour, the barn was bustling with activity. As well as the entire SOS Committee, at least thirty people were there, including Marla and Paul. The mayor and most of Town Council came. A half a dozen or so Girl Guides had arrived, and their leader was trying to keep them away from five members of the Icemen, Snow Mountain's Junior B hockey team.

Soon, everybody had found a job: the women sanding and painting, the men gravitating toward where Henry showed them the mysterious workings inside the elves and reindeer. Somebody had brought a portable stereo and Christmas songs were playing. The barn was filled with laughter, joking, chatter.

Brody, after getting a few basics from Henry, had the back off a particularly grumpy looking elf. He didn't do social functions. The last town gathering he'd been at had been his brother's funeral. It seemed since then, when he went somewhere, someone always had to tell him how sorry they were. How much they missed Ethan.

He was aware, *suddenly,* he was missing Ethan.

Naturally he intended to blame Lila, since she had brought up the subject of children laughing in the hayloft.

Still, looking around, Brody was aware of how much Ethan had liked this kind of thing. Community. Service. He'd always been the volunteer counselor at the church summer day camp, the first one with a garbage bag on Highway Beautification Day. Painting a new smile on an elf would have been right up Ethan's alley. Ethan who had been artsy rather than bold, who had been sensitive rather than strong.

They had been opposites all their lives, really, Brody and his brother. It had never been a problem for them, not until Darla.

He shook off the unwanted thoughts, and as he did he became aware that even as he took apart the panels to get at the mechanical workings as Henry had instructed him to do he was more and more aware of *her.*

Of the way she fit in here. Of how wherever she was in the room the laughter followed.

And he was aware of Boo wagging with happiness as she went from person to person greeting them, accepting a pat on the head.

Someone called a coffee break, and Brody took a cup and joined the circle of the people he had lived with his whole life. For the first time in a long time he allowed himself to be a part of it. He told Jeanie Harper he would walk a mile barefoot through a blizzard for her chocolate dipped shortbread.

When he heard one of the hockey players tease Mary Beth Anderson about her new braces, he told her he'd been hearing all over town what a great piece she had played on the piano at the recital. He asked after Mrs. Olive's grandson who was serving with the armed forces overseas. He did not hold himself separate from them.

He had thought it was his job that kept him separate from them. How could you make friends with the guy you would be giving a speeding ticket to next week or next month? How did you chat casually with someone you knew had beaten his wife once?

But now, today, he was aware it was not his job that had kept him separate. It was his sorrow, his fear of connecting, of caring too deeply.

He looked again at the darkness of the loft, felt the warmth of Boo sitting right on top of his feet and surrendered, for the first time since the accident, to the life his brother would have wanted for him. For the first time in a long time he accepted the embrace of his small community, allowed himself to feel the warmth of belonging.

His community gathered around him as though he had never left them, never held himself apart, as if they had just saved his place for when he was ready to come back.

The women teased him, and asked how his folks were enjoying their retirement in Arizona, the men chatted about sports, and the weather and about hunting and fishing. He saw how children had grown and parents had aged. He *felt* his part in it, his history, knew this to be as much his family as his parents in Tucson.

He looked over at Lila. She smiled tentatively, and he could imagine *her* laughter in the hayloft.

A naughty thought. He ordered himself not to smile back, but he must have, because she blushed and looked away as if she was having a few naughty hayloft thoughts of her own.

But just when it felt good to let his guard down, just when he was wondering why he had held on to his aloneness so hard and so long, the barn doors swung open.

The television crew from Spokane had arrived, Jade Flynn breezing through the door, a cameraman, already rolling behind her.

He set down his coffee cup, got up and went out the back door. The cold air felt good. So did being by himself, except for Boo, who had trailed reluctantly out after him.

Boo, who never had a secret agenda, who never did something with a motive, wanting something else in return.

This great community project, this coming together of spirit suddenly felt as commercial as all the rest of it: a manipulation of the media. Not real at all. Just a big show to repair the damage of the last story.

The door squeaked open behind him, and shut again. He didn't turn around, because he didn't have to.

He could smell wild strawberries.

"Did everyone know they were coming except me?" he asked.

"No one ever knows if the media is coming for sure," she hedged. "They have to decide if the story is good."

He turned and gave her a look. "Oh, it's a good story.

Town divided. Town coming back together. What was my part in it going to be?"

"I just thought if you and I could be seen together looking like we were getting along, it might take some of the pressure off you."

"The pressure off me?"

"You know. The hate mail."

He snorted. Lila Grainger, little bit of nothing, was trying to look after *him?* It was insulting. He hated it that anyone, let alone her, would ever think he needed looking after.

"I don't think two letters from a nine-year-old in Connecticut who thinks I'm *nasty* qualifies as hate mail."

"You took two days off work because of it."

He went very still. That was something he didn't want anyone to know about. "Are you spying on me?"

"Of course not. But it's obvious to me you aren't even a teensy bit sick, so why were you off work?"

Something clawed at his throat. He could tell her. He could tell her about Boo. He could have a soft place to fall when it happened.

But there was the little trust thing. Poor cop losing his dog would probably make a great human interest story for the town, bring in even more donations for her stupid Save Our Snow Mountain Committee, bring more people out to her store.

"You know what a great ending to this story would be?" he said quietly. She didn't even recognize the danger in his tone.

"What?" she asked. She didn't even have the sense to back away from him.

"What if I kissed you?" he said. "Wouldn't that make a

nice ending? Arresting you one moment, kissing you the next?"

Her eyes went very wide. Too late, she took a step back from him.

He caught her, pulled her in close, took her lips harshly, angry, punishing. But her softness defeated him.

His clarity was gone.

He could taste wild strawberries and hear children laughing in haylofts. Her lips were like a homecoming to a man who had been at war. Her kiss could make a man forget how damned cruel life could be, her taste could fill him with the most dangerous thing of all: hope. Her lips held this power, even in the face of the fact she had betrayed him. Used his home to forward her cause, to create yet another media circus.

He put her away from him, while he still had the strength, before he believed the whisper of his heart above the stern warning of his head.

"How was that for an ending?" he said, trying to insert a caustic note into his voice when the truth was the sweetness of that kiss was taking the bitterness from him like sugar added to coffee. "Oh, just a sec. Too bad. The cameras missed it." He put enough swear words between them and cameras to do Jamison proud.

He wanted to wipe his lips to make his point, but he saw from the tears gathering like a storm in the blue of her eyes he already had made his point.

And besides, he wasn't quite ready to get rid of the taste of wild strawberries yet.

"And just when I was ready to concede you might be a nice guy," she sputtered angrily, in defiance of the tears that sparkled in her eyes.

"What would make you think that?"

"How nice you were to that little girl with the braces!"

"People can act like a whole lot of things they're not. They can make it look like they want to bring a town together, when all they really want is a story that will bring a whole lot of attention to a town that normally wouldn't get it. A town, that coincidentally, has a brand-new Christmas store in it."

He saw the arrow hit home, was not nearly as satisfied by the direct hit as he thought he would be.

Jade Flynn picked that moment to come out the back door, cameraman trotting behind her, camera on his shoulder. "Here's the two I was looking for. Lila, thanks for the heads-up, what a great story."

Lila sniffed, and scrubbed furiously at her eye. Brody stalked away. Was he going to make her cry every single time he saw her?

Or did she just cry so easily because she was tired? He'd still noticed the circles under her eyes today. It really bugged him that, as angry as he was, he still cared that he'd made her cry.

"I guess," Jade said catching on that the tension was pretty thick out here, "a picture of you two painting a new smile on an elf together is probably out of the question?"

The camera clicked on just in time to catch Brody's smoldering look over his shoulder, and then a careless salute, middle finger up.

Ignoring the activity in his barn, the overflowing of cheer and goodwill, Brody retreated to his house and his TV set. Boo threw up under the coffee table, and he told himself it was because people had been unable to resist her big brown eyes begging for cookies. It wasn't because her illness was progressing. It wasn't. But his explanation to himself held the hollow ring of a lie, of a man in denial.

Brody Taggert needed, almost desperately, to believe that kiss, delivered with such fierce anger, had ended whatever had been simmering between Lila and him.

But again he felt the hollow ring of a lie, of denial. In truth that kiss had opened another door, added another dimension to a relationship that was already way too complicated.

He wanted to feel *satisfied* that he had driven home his point that he was not going to have his life manipulated so that Lila Grainger could create her perfect story. He had definitely driven home that point. She'd been crying, hadn't she?

The problem was that he didn't feel satisfied.

Not at all.

He felt guilty. Of all the stupid reasons for a man to kiss a woman, anger would rate number one on his list.

And even worse than feeling guilty and stupid, he felt hungry. For another taste of those lips.

Brody Taggert realized, suddenly and uneasily, what had just happened to him. He had reacted to Lila Grainger with pure, unfettered emotion.

How was he ever going to face the shattering emptiness of another Christmas alone if his emotions got out of control? How was he going to face the stark loneliness of a life where his days did not begin with his dog licking his face in the morning in joyous greeting if he allowed himself to be emotionally weak?

He knew the solution: Lila was triggering emotional reactions. No more Lila. But somehow that resolution, instead of bringing him the comfort of a man firmly back in control, made him feel emptier than ever.

CHAPTER FOUR

SHE had such good intentions, Lila thought forlornly. After a week of hard work the fully repaired and painted elves were being brought in to Bandstand Park. The reindeer would arrive tomorrow, followed by Santa. She had not personally hazarded another visit out to Brody Taggert's barn, though.

That kiss had been a little too revealing. He had, she knew, intended for it to be punishing. Instead she had felt his stark loneliness so acutely it had brought tears to her eyes. Instead she had felt her own vulnerability to him so sharply it had felt like stepping on glass all over again.

So, she had busied herself here with other volunteers, rigging the park with enough new Christmas lights—LED, the energy efficient kind—that Snow Mountain would be seen winking and blinking merrily from space, with an energy bill that would have thrilled Scrooge.

On December 15, as dusk was falling, in a grand ceremony, everything would be plugged in and lit up. The high school band would play, the Baptist ladies' church choir would sing holding candles. Hot chocolate would be served. All the downtown businesses were staying open late. It was Snow Mountain just as she had wished it could be. Well, there was no snow yet, but the locals informed her it was too early for snow.

Why did she feel so hollow? As if she didn't care about the park anymore or lights that could be seen from space, or whether the choir had white candles or red ones?

It was because the book was still stalled, she tried to convince herself. She had thought maybe she could begin with a chapter on energy efficient Christmas lights, but it had turned out she couldn't think of that much to say about them.

She was lying to herself anyway. She wasn't feeling apathetic about bringing Christmas back to Snow Mountain because her book was stalled.

It was because of that kiss.

One little kiss, and she was ready to write off her whole life as an unmitigated disaster. Well, not just because of the kiss. First there had been her foot, then the arrest and then the kiss.

Something in her stomach dropped every single time she thought of the heat of his lips on hers, the fire in his eyes that had not been completely about anger, the answering fire in her belly that had not been about anger at all.

Thankfully Jade Flynn had taken pity on Snow Mountain, and had decided Brody's one finger salute was inappropriate, because the edited segment had showed Lila and her uncle and the mayor painting the new smile on the elf, and Brody's name and image had not been mentioned or shown.

To anyone looking closely enough, Lila's eyes might have seemed puffy, and her makeup a little smeared, but she was sure everyone thought she had cried tears of joy for the saving of Christmas in Snow Mountain.

Her eyes were always faintly puffy from lack of sleep anyway.

Brody had kissed her in fury. She knew that.

So it didn't say much for her that the memory of that kiss haunted those long hours in the night when she couldn't sleep anyway, made her torment herself with forbidden thoughts and dream impossible dreams.

Of smoldering eyes, and the magnificent beauty of the muscled male body. And gentler dreams, too, of little children laughing in haylofts.

"I think," her aunt Marla said, standing back, a string of LED lights over her shoulder, "it's missing a Christmas tree. Wouldn't that look nice? A twenty-foot blue spruce, decorated in all blue lights?"

"It's good enough," Lila said, desolately. "It's too late to get a tree."

Her aunt looked askance at her. "That kind of tree grows thick as hair on a dog's back in these parts. We'll just go pick one out and cut it down. I'm sure your uncle Paul will do it."

"Maybe I could go with him," Lila said, trying to at least act as if she had some enthusiasm, trying to at least pretend she was the person she had been three weeks ago. "I'd love to actually see a Christmas tree harvested."

And wouldn't that make a great place to start the book? Going out and getting the tree, the old-fashioned way, too. Not from the Christmas tree lot, not from the fake tree department of the local big-box store.

"Great. I'll get Paul to pick you up at around eleven next Saturday. Maybe pack a bit of a lunch. Just in case he's grouchy about it."

"If he's going to be grouchy about it, never mind." She said it reluctantly, because going to get a tree really could kickstart the book, and maybe it could occupy her enough that she would escape her preoccupation with Brody for a few hours. But on the other hand Lila felt like she had learned her lesson about asking people to do things for the greater good when they really didn't want to do them.

"Just pack a few of Jeanie Harper's shortbread cookies. The chocolate-dipped ones."

Brody liked those ones best, too. That little yearning, naked and helpless, leaped up in her.

"Chocolate-dipped shortbread," Lila said with false heartiness.

She turned away before she caught the fact her aunt was looking at her with far more knowing than she would have liked.

Brody pulled up in front of Lila Grainger's door. Nice part of town. Mature trees, big yards, old, well-kept houses. Hers, not surprisingly, looked like it could be the cottage from Snow White—a tiny house sat under a steeply pitched mossy roof. Deep windows were diamond paned and carved shutters bracketed them on the outside.

Brody resisted the temptation to honk the horn of the truck, which would be a betrayal of the irritation he felt that their paths were being forced to cross again.

"Go get a Christmas tree for the park with her," Hutch had ordered him. "And wipe that look off your face. Be cheerful about it, for God's sake."

Jamison had snickered in the background.

The chief had shot Jamison a look. "I wouldn't be so smug if I were you, Santa."

But Brody was lost in his own thoughts. *Be cheerful about spending more time with Lila Grainger, and her lips, and his own tenuous hold on his emotions around her?*

"I don't want to do it," Brody had said.

The answer was predictable. "Tough."

"Is there going to be a bunch of cameras there when I get back with the tree?" Brody asked, realizing he'd capitulated without too much of a fight considering what he had at stake.

"You just aren't that big a deal, boy," his boss had told him shortly. "The truth is Marla told me to go get a tree. A big one. I haven't handled a chain saw in over ten years. I'd probably limb myself instead of the damned tree."

That, unfortunately, was probably the truth, so Brody told himself he was doing it to save his boss's limbs as much as because he'd been told to. But be cheerful about it? *Sheesh.* He hadn't had one single thing to be cheerful about since he'd arrested Lila Grainger.

He was still getting hate mail, especially from one very persistent little kid in Connecticut who must have either missed the follow-up story, or been able to discern from Lila's distressed face that all was still not as it appeared to be in Snow Mountain.

Just as he'd predicted the pre-Christmas fallout was starting all over town. Last night, Tag had waited outside the bar to keep Mike Stevens from getting in his car and driving. Mike was generally a good guy: Tag had played hockey with him for years. Mike was strong, reliable and steadfast.

Mike and his wife were three weeks from having a baby. Everyone knew Mike had been laid off work at the mill and the financial pressure to provide for his new family was killing him.

"Do you know what a bassinet's worth?" he'd slurred drunkenly when Tag had driven him home last night. "That's what she wants for Christmas. A bassinet for the baby. I don't even know how I'm going to come up with rent."

Then, the Murphy girl, fifteen going on twenty, the one with trouble written all over her, had been caught shoplifting and he'd been sent to pick her up from the store.

In the back of the cruiser, her tough girl facade had broken. A video game for her little brother for Christmas. *Tower of the Rebels. Fifty bucks,* she'd said bitterly through her tears. *He might as well have wished for a ticket to the moon.*

And Brody's dog was fading by the day. This was the first time he'd brought her along with him for nearly two weeks.

And as if his life wasn't bad enough, he couldn't get the taste of Lila Grainger's lips or the look of her eyes out of his mind. Now he had to get a tree with her. Which he hoped he could do in about twenty minutes. Which was probably going to be the longest twenty minutes in his life now that he'd been fool enough to *taste* her.

Be cheerful?

How could he be cheerful when he could not be at all certain he was only here because he'd been ordered. Not at all.

Maybe he was here because the taste of her lips and the scent of wild strawberries drew him back, irresistibly, illogically, insanely.

Boo barely opened an eye when he got out of the truck.

"Stay here," he said unnecessarily, since the dog had not moved. "I'll be right back."

He rang the doorbell, and she came and answered. He stood looking at her, feeling awkward and tense, as if he was picking her up for a first date.

Not, he told himself sternly.

"Oh," she said, stopping dead in her tracks. "You."

"You were expecting?"

"My uncle."

"He couldn't make it." Cop loyalty prevented him from saying Paul was scared of cutting off his own limbs, because he was sure Paul didn't want his niece to know he was scared of anything.

"I'll go a different day. When he can make it."

"It'll only take twenty minutes. Half an hour. Let's get it over with."

He meant that in every possible way, as if by spending part of an hour with her, he could flush that kiss from his system, erase it with all the new ways she could be annoying.

For instance, right now, she had one earring in, the other dangled from her hand.

He could tell her earrings were not necessary for an excursion into the woods to chop down a tree, but then it would be way too apparent he had noticed, and then he couldn't be *annoyed* by it.

While he was noticing, her ears were dainty, and for a strange moment he had the forbidden thought of nipping one with his teeth.

And maybe that was the real truth of it: this thing between he and Lila Grainger would be over with when it had followed its path to its natural conclusion.

And he had a feeling that wasn't going to be getting a Christmas tree.

He took a step back, one foot resting on the top stair, now. "Maybe you're right. Your uncle. A different day."

"No," she said looking at him with regal dislike. "Maybe *you're* right. Let's get it over with."

"Okay," he said.

"Okay," she said.

Don't look at her lips, he ordered himself. *Or her ears.*

"You'll have to come in. Just for a sec. I'm not quite ready."

Before he could tell her he would rather wait in the truck, she had turned away, and he didn't want her to think he was *scared* to come in.

So that's how he found himself standing in the landing of her house, right inside the front door. He frowned as he watched her disappear. Was she still limping?

From where he stood he could see a real stone fireplace in the living room, already hung with socks. Out of range of his vision, he could tell she had her Christmas tree up because he could smell the pine.

He regarded her room with a policeman's eye. The way people lived could tell you an awful lot about them.

Not that he needed to know a single thing more about Lila Grainger. Her lips had pretty much said it all.

But her living room should have reassured him. No matter what that kiss had said about how compatible they might be in certain areas, it was more than obvious to him they were exact opposites.

A plump yellow sofa and a large ottoman took up most of the room. There were bookcases, and a single teacup on a side table. He craned his neck to see where the television was, and could plainly see there wasn't one.

It was the room of someone who liked solitary reading better than entertaining, he thought, and had to firmly stop himself from attaching a positive judgment to that.

Who cared if she threw a party every night?

He did, and he didn't like it one little bit that he did.

Somehow, in the small amount of time Lila had been in Snow Mountain she had managed to make her space colorful and warm, *homey,* a reflection of who she was.

Not a girl you stole kisses from, not even in anger.

Especially not in anger. Not a girl where you let things follow through to their natural conclusion.

She was the kind of girl who was wholesome, and decent, optimistic about life, probably a positive thinker.

A guy like him could probably wreck all those qualities pretty darn quick.

She was the kind of girl who was traditional: her house told him that. She would stand at the front of a church one day, dressed in white. She would never live with a man before exchanging vows with him. When she had kids, she would read them stories, and bake them cookies, volunteer at the school, teach them right from wrong.

She probably wouldn't even let them watch television!

There was nothing wrong with that. Nothing at all. He was glad Paul's niece was like that.

He just knew he himself could not be trusted with such wholesomeness, such sugarcoated dreams. He was too broken, too torn up inside, too much of a realist.

Lila Grainger needed someone nice like the preacher's son, who was working on his doctorate in Seattle.

Brody thought he'd put a bug in Paul's ear about that. Much relieved that he had managed, on the basis of her decor, to separate his life from hers, he looked around once more.

He had not lived in a place that felt *homey* since he had left home. A television went a long way in making a man feel at home. The bigger it was, the more at home he felt.

Still, Brody Taggert could have sworn he hadn't missed those homey little touches—paint and prints, throw rugs and knickknacks. But at this very moment, he was aware he had.

The memory came, as they all did, without any kind of warning.

Ethan, at eighteen. They'd been wrestling, Ethan having

something to prove all the time since developing a crush on Brody's girlfriend, Darla. Now they were standing there with Mom's broken cranberry glass wine decanter at their feet, wondering what the hell to do now.

Funny, he couldn't remember what they'd done, only the broken glass, the look of distress on his brother's face. Without warning, he felt lonely, and turned from the warmth of that cozy living room to look out at his truck, to see if the dog had her face pressed to the window, waiting for him.

She did, something so normal, he felt relieved.

But then he noticed Lila's front door.

And the locks on it. Lots and lots of locks. Most people in Snow Mountain couldn't be convinced to use the one lock they had on the handle of their door. He bent closer to inspect.

Four in all. Dead bolts. So brand-new that the metal was shiny. Plus, one of those chain things, and a newly drilled security peephole.

His first impression of her had been correct, that night he had startled her at her store. She was scared of something. Really scared.

What Brody Taggert wanted more than anything else was to move Lila Grainger right up to the number one position on his People I Find Annoying list. Or to make her the preacher's son's problem. But those locks made him *feel* something else.

Protective. Faintly angry at some unknown opponent.

She came back into the living room. Definitely still limping.

"I'm trying to figure out what to wear to go get a tree," she said. "I've never done anything like this before."

Which forced him to look at her way more closely than he wanted to because he was going to be responsible for her safety up there on the mountain, and she was from Florida, where they didn't know the first thing about dressing for even moderately cold weather.

She was dressed in snug jeans and a cable knit sweater, a fur-trimmed dark brown vest on top of that.

She held up a pair of bright pink-and-white-striped mittens for his approval.

First the *homey* house and now this: poster girl for a hot chocolate ad: wholesome, beautiful.

Girl least likely to be arrested. Most likely to be happy with the preacher's son. Least likely to have her front door locked up like Fort Knox.

"Yeah, that'll do," he said out loud. To himself he repeated the mission, *Let's get this over with.*

She suddenly was scrutinizing what he was wearing.

Jeans, T-shirt, sheepskin-lined jean jacket. He wasn't sure why he wished for his uniform. Something to hide behind, something to cut that awareness that suddenly tingled in the air between them.

Don't look at her lips, he ordered himself again. But he did.

"That doesn't look very warm," she said.

Don't look at her ears, he ordered himself, but he did that, too.

"It's thirty degrees Fahrenheit out there. Practically balmy for this part of the world," he pointed out as she slipped a toque, the same color as her mitts, over her ears. Even though he'd ordered himself not to look at them, he was disappointed when they were covered up.

"There's supposed to be a storm coming. If it's below

freezing that could mean snow at last!" She tried not to sound hopeful and failed. "You should dress warmer."

"I've been taking care of myself for a long time," he said flatly. "I don't need anyone to do it for me."

It was a warning and they both knew it.

She blushed, turned to her boots, which looked like they were Arctic rated to minus forty, with huge pom-pom things that looked like they had killed a few rabbits to make them.

Ridiculous things. Adorable.

"How's your foot?" he asked when she winced putting them on.

"My foot? Oh, *that*. Fine."

"You're still limping."

"I know. What an awful place to get a cut. It takes forever to heal."

Okay, he ordered himself, *leave it.* "Are you checking it? Making sure it's not infected?"

He regretted the show of concern immediately, because she folded her arms across her chest and looked at him with warning. A reminder that this was the woman—looking so innocent in her pink mittens—who was responsible for the fact he'd gotten a series of snotty letters from a little girl in grade five who wanted to let him know she thought he was *mean*. And also *nasty*.

This was the woman who was responsible for the fact the chief seemed to think Tag should now single-handedly rescue the image of the Snow Mountain Police Department, even though when he'd arrested her, he'd only been following orders.

"It's fine," she said. "My foot is fine. I've been looking after myself for a long time, too, Brody Taggert."

He liked her ears and her lips and her eyes, and the way his name sounded coming off her lips.

He wondered if that meant he was doomed.

More likely she would be the *doomed* one if she ever ended up with someone as cynical about life—and Christmas—as him. Not that he was ever going to let that be a choice. That they would end up together. Not ever.

He let himself out the door, watched with interest as she came behind him, carrying what looked to be a picnic basket. She set it down to lock the door, and his eyes slid over to it. A thermos. Sandwiches. Cookies. A damned outing.

His attention went back to the door. He watched with interest as she carefully locked two of the dead bolts.

She looked up, caught him looking, looked quickly away. "I figure anyone trying to get in would probably unlock two and lock the other two." He must have let his skepticism show because she said, firmly, "That's how criminals think."

"You don't even have a TV," he said. "Criminals like TVs." So did he, which sealed the fact they could never be together, him and her, not ever. Just too different. Thank God.

"I have a TV, I just keep it in a cabinet."

A TV that was hidden was almost as bad as not having one at all.

Now he was feeling a touch querulous. "And don't think your brush with the law made you any kind of expert on the criminal mind. They'd take one look at all those locks and smash in your basement window."

She became very pale.

"Sorry," he said, thinking she hadn't enjoyed his attempt at humor about her recent arrest. *So much for cheery, Chief.*

But she hadn't even noticed that. She was staring at her basement window with consternation.

"Isn't it awfully small?" she asked.

"You'd be surprised what people can squeeze through."

"Oh," she said in a small voice, standing frozen to the spot, staring at the window.

"Have you got something in there you're worried about?" Any TV that could be successfully *hidden* could not possibly be big enough to worry about.

She shook her head. "I guess I can get bars for it."

"What are you so afraid of?" he asked, that protective thing humming deep inside him, like a drumbeat calling a warrior to the fight. One of those *emotional* responses that he was so determined to be wary of.

She lifted her chin, the very same look she had given him when he'd arrested her.

"I'm not afraid of anything," she said.

But he knew now, just as he had known then, that it was a lie. He shrugged. So she didn't want to tell him. So what? He didn't really want to exchange confidences with her, either.

He held open the passenger side door for her, he had to shove Boo into the middle seat. Boo was thrilled at her arrival, the first show of enthusiasm he had seen from the dog in days.

And when Boo placed her big head on Lila's lap and began to drool happily, Lila didn't even say it was gross. He forgave her a little bit for the hate mail he was getting, for her lack of a television. But not for the fact she was making him *feel* again, when it felt so much safer not to.

"This was nice of you," she said finally, after the silence between them became oppressive. She must have decided it was time to change the tone of the day. "You must have volunteered to come on your day off."

Volunteered. Military style. You, you and you.

"I'm not a nice person," he said, setting up the defenses against future kisses. "You might as well not even think it."

"Ha," she said. "Tell it to someone who didn't see you save the day for a little girl who was self-conscious about her new braces."

"You're reading too much into that."

"How about lending your barn for a cause you don't even believe in?"

He didn't admit that he found himself being kind of glad the park would be back to normal soon. And hopefully his life.

But the dog sighing on the seat beside him reminded him there really was no normal. What was normal for him now would not be his normal by next year. Maybe even not by next week.

"Here's something that should renew your faith in humanity," she said, snapping her fingers, as if she'd totally forgotten the mission was to get this over with, not to restore his faith in humanity, "I've had five thousand dollars worth of donations come in."

He groaned. He flipped on the windshield wipers against the first flakes of snow. "I don't want to know about it."

"Why?"

"Are you a licensed charity?"

"Oh, for heaven's sake," she said, and then caught the grim cast of his face. "Are you always so cheerful?"

"Yes." He looked straight ahead, but the cab of his truck seemed to be getting smaller by the minute. The scent of wild strawberries was growing strong in here. He opened the window a hair.

"For the dog," he said, when she looked askance. She

pulled her scarf tighter around her neck, as if she was about to face a blizzard and forty below.

"Did you grow up here?" She was determined to get a conversation going.

"Yes." He offered nothing else. He didn't want to do this. Small talk. He was terrible at it, something he'd never regretted.

"What was it like growing up here?" she asked wistfully, looking out the window of the truck. "It's so beautiful. Look, snow!"

They were off the main highway now, moving up Snow Mountain on an old forestry road. At each clearing they reached, through a veil of faster and faster falling snow, they would see the valley stretched below them, like a postcard, fields, old barns and in the distance, the town.

Sudden pictures of him and his brother, always outdoors, hunting, fishing, climbing, hiking came into his mind. He longed for what his normal had once been.

"It was okay," he said, deliberately wanting to shut her out.

But she was not going to be shut out. "What was your favorite thing about growing up here?"

He could have said anything. He could have said hunting or fishing or swimming or climbing trees.

But he didn't. He said. "Picking wild strawberries." He didn't know why he said that, probably because of the scent in the truck.

"Strawberries grow wild here?"

He nodded. "A few. They're very small. You can spend a whole day looking for them and maybe get a cup. My mom used to love wild strawberries more than anything. If you offered her a glass of champagne or a handful of strawberries, she'd pick the strawberries."

Suddenly he remembered how they'd made up for busting the cranberry glass. On his last day with his brother.

"Your parents still live here?"

"No, they retired in Arizona." That wasn't the whole truth. The whole truth was when people got attached to what they thought *normal* was, when it changed they couldn't handle it.

His mother had never been the same after Ethan. Nothing had ever been the same. Not their house, not this town, not Christmas or Thanksgiving, or birthdays or the Fourth of July or the opening day of hunting season. Nothing had ever been the same.

Especially not his heart.

Because once upon a time, a long time ago, when he believed in normal and innocence, wouldn't his heart have been open to a girl exactly like this one?

"Do you have any family here?"

"No."

"Will you go spend Christmas with your parents, then?"

"I pulled duty."

"Didn't you work on Thanksgiving, too?"

"Yeah," he said, but he contemplated that she *knew.* Had she asked or had it just come up in conversation? She would have had dinner with Paul and Marla.

He *always* pulled holiday duty. He considered that to be just about the only perk of being the new guy on the job. After their first Christmas without Ethan, his father had taken him aside and said, "It's just too hard on your mother, trying to make everything normal. Next year, let's just get together after the holidays." And it had been like that ever since.

"Oh, that's too bad."

"Terrible," he said, and for some reason he thought of

the faraway look in his mom's eyes at this time of year, and his voice roughened with the memory.

He could feel Lila's eyes on him, full of questions. Like did he have brothers and sisters, and did he go to church on Sunday and did he drink beer, and all those *normal* little details two people getting to know each other wanted to find out.

Except that he did not want her to get to know him. And he did not want to get to know her.

He had been doing just fine with his heart in armor, and he planned to keep it that way.

So he slammed on the brakes so hard the dog had to scramble to stay on the seat.

"There's some good trees," he said.

Despite his optimism about the twenty-minute tree trip, it was more like an hour before she picked the tree she wanted: a huge blue spruce, twenty-feet high that was going to be a nightmare to get down and to load into his truck.

But a challenge was just what he needed right now.

He could feel her eyes on him as he started the chain saw, did the undercut, moved to the other side of the tree.

The tree fell without drama, slowly, and he cut the bottom of the trunk, then bucked the tree—cleared the lower branches—for her.

"I brought a snack. Hot chocolate. Some sandwiches." As if she sensed him weakening, "Jeanie Harper's cookies, chocolate dipped. You look like you need a break."

Her eyes were on him with *what?*

Interest. There it was. That dangerous little sizzle again. Time to winch the tree into the back of the truck and get out of here. The snow was falling in huge, heavy flakes now.

Lila tilted her head back, caught one on her tongue,

closed her eyes as if she was tasting heaven. Her enjoyment of that simple pleasure made it seem less urgent to leave.

Then Boo appeared from the trees, a pinecone in her mouth. She dropped it at Lila's feet and barked.

"What's she want?" Lila asked, laughing, when the dog barked again.

"She wants you to throw the pinecone for her," he said. He had not seen Boo play with a pinecone for a long time, and suddenly he was very aware his *normal* was going to be changing again very soon.

How many moments left like this? With his dog wagging her tail, chasing after a pinecone? He had to take these moments that were given to him.

Suddenly the moment seemed so beautiful it hurt his eyes. A young woman in a sweater and a vest and pink mittens throwing the pinecone for a dog who thought she was young again.

When Lila brought out the picnic basket and spread a plaid blanket on the thickening cover of snow, he didn't complain. He had lived here all his life and never, not even once, had a picnic in the snow.

Perhaps this, too, was a moment he was being given. One that, if he turned his back on, he might regret later.

So, he gathered branches and built a fire and then he sat, and took his dog's head in his lap and scratched her ears, and drank cocoa and ate ham sandwiches and chocolate-dipped shortbread cookies without letting one single thought about what the future held intrude on that moment.

Besides, there was simply no telling when or if he was ever going to get Jeanie's cookies again.

"This is so much fun," she said. "Do you know I've never done anything like this before?"

"Picnics in the snow not a big pastime in Florida?" he said.

She stuck out her tongue at him. "I meant getting the tree. Christmas trees are hard to come by in Florida. Real ones. My mom had an artificial tree that she left completely decorated in the garage. I hated that tree."

Don't ask, he told himself. "Is that why you came here? Real trees?"

"Don't laugh, but that's part of it. I remember coming here for Christmas once when I was ten. Everybody had a real tree. And there was real snow. That's what I remembered most about it. Everything seemed *real.*"

"I don't know why you're so anxious to bring the elves back then. They aren't real. As phony as it comes, actually."

She smiled. "Well, when I was ten they seemed real. I *loved* them."

"You're in a funny business for a lady who claims to like reality," he said. "You're kind of peddling fantasy, aren't you?"

She looked hurt. "I prefer to think of it as magic. Don't you think some things are magical and unexplained? Don't you think Christmas is one of those things? A time of miracles?"

He was silent, and then he said, "I had to arrest a little girl who was shoplifting a gift for her brother that was hopelessly out of the family's price range. A video game. *The Tower of the Rebels.* You know what? She didn't take one single thing for herself. I've arrested lots of teenage girls who are lifting lipstick or perfume, stuff for *themselves.* This was different. It makes it kind of hard for me to get the *magic.* Sorry."

Even as he said it, though, he was aware the sharing had not done what he intended. He had intended for her to get a glimpse of the real *real* world. But instead, he felt by telling her, a burden he carried, without even knowing how much it bothered him, was lifted a bit, not such a weight in his own heart.

"Oh, Brody," she said, "Oh, Brody."

He saw he had lightened his own load by giving it to her. He was annoyed with himself for telling her. Even more annoyed how he *felt*.

He hadn't had so many pesky feelings nipping at him like a small dog harassing a ball, since...

Since his brother had died.

That part of him had shut down. Thankfully. He didn't want it brought back to life, so he deliberately misunderstood her.

"I know. I'm an awful person, and I'm getting the mail every day to prove it."

"I never said you were awful. I meant it was awful about the little girl."

"See, that's the thing, Lila. While you're peddling the fantasy, elves in parks and purple Christmas trees in store windows, there's a reality out there that you wouldn't like one little bit. Even in Snow Mountain."

"That tree in my store window is not purple!" she said, evading the issue or deliberately not getting it. "It's lavender."

"Who cares?" he snapped.

The moment was gone, the sympathetic light doused in her eyes and so he kicked snow on the fire and doused that, too. The picnic was spoiled.

"The weather is turning," he said. "I better get that tree in the truck and get us down off this mountain."

Still, as he struggled with the tree, the dog pleaded with her to toss pinecones again. For a few brief moments, watching her taste snow on the tip of her tongue and toss pinecones for his dog, sitting sipping hot chocolate in the smoke of a fire, something in him had *hoped*.

For what, he wasn't quite sure. A life with laughter in it? Someone to share his burdens with? A life of simple pleasures: going out on a snowy day to get the tree, camp-fires, a good dog sniffing a picnic blanket for crumbs of the world's best cookies?

Things were always just a little more complicated than that. They were as *different* as two people could be, a fact that could be disguised by strawberry kisses, but only temporarily.

"Christmas is saved in Snow Mountain!" she said, when he'd finally loaded the tree, as if she was still annoyingly determined to *fix* his mood.

But he was aware Boo was slumped at her feet now, spent in a way a little pinecone chasing would not have spent a healthy dog.

"No, it's not," he said grimly. "Lila Grainger's fantasy is saved. The little kid who swiped a toy for her brother has the same day waiting for her as always."

My dog is still going to die, even though for a moment, watching her chase pinecones, maybe I really did want to believe in a time of miracles.

Hope could be a terrible thing in a hard world.

"You know what?" Lila said, "A person who spent too much time around you would probably catch grumpy from you like a bad virus."

Bingo, he thought. Out loud he said, "Get in the truck."

CHAPTER FIVE

LILA was not sure how things had turned so sour. One minute she'd been having a moment out of a Christmas dream: handsome man, hot chocolate, snowflakes, even a dog to complete the picture of holiday cheer. Every detail was perfect: even the air was laden with the sharp scent of the freshly fallen tree and the smoke from the fire.

For one suspended moment in time she had been allowed to enjoy perfection, a moment worthy of a Christmas card. She had even thought, relieved beyond belief, that she had been correct that this would be the perfect way to start her book. Of course having a perfect Christmas would begin with Chapter One: Getting the Perfect Tree.

But then she had looked at his lips, remembered their taste, the sizzling intensity of them taking her own lips, and the sudden dip of her stomach hadn't matched her wholesome holiday picture at all.

And then, Brody's mood had shifted as restlessly as the wind, which had also suddenly shifted, blowing smoke in her face. It had eased sneakily into her mind that despite how nice snow made everything *look* it was darned cold. Even with the blanket, her butt was starting to feel uncomfortably cold, tingly, then numb.

Plus, how could this be the starting point for her book: a book about innocence and wonder, tradition and family, when she was being totally captivated by thoughts that might be considered, well, *wanton*.

There was no way a woman could watch Brody Taggert fell a tree and be thinking strictly innocent thoughts afterward. Or even be admiring the tree, for that matter. Or even thinking about the tree for that matter, no matter how perfect it might be.

Brody felling the tree: a symphony of male strength, so sure of himself, so comfortable with his own power, so competent in his world.

Watching him cut down the Christmas tree had made her so aware of him. And then the moments on the blanket, him stretched out comfortably, lying on his back, staring up at the sky, letting the snowflakes gather in the thick tangle of his lashes, the dog draped across him with utter contentment.

And her preoccupied, not with pressing thoughts of her book or the fact fetching a tree might be an ideal starting point, but with wondering if they were going to kiss each other again. Not in anger this time, either.

Except, suddenly, without warning, his mood had shifted, he had kicked snow on the fire, and they were on their way back down the mountain.

Maybe starting with getting the tree was a bad idea, anyway.

"Do you think cutting down a live Christmas tree is controversial?" she asked him. Talking about anything would be better than the grim silence that filled the truck.

"Controversial?" He looked amazed and then annoyed.

"You know, not an environmentally sound idea."

"Cloning human beings is *controversial*."

"Artificial trees are probably better for the environment." Somehow starting her book with a chapter on selecting the perfect artificial tree was not as appealing, particularly in light of the ghastly white plastic needle one she had shared her childhood with.

"I guess how good an artificial tree is for the environment would depend on how it was made, wouldn't it? How many toxic substances the tree factory melted down and then pumped into the air afterward? And how people dispose of them when blue ones become more popular than green ones, or pink ones or white ones?"

The thing about a man like that was he would make you look at the world differently. He would challenge all your beliefs. You would be trying to write a book about creating the perfect Christmas, and thinking of a little girl stealing a gift for her brother.

A man like him could wreck a plan for a perfect life without half trying.

She shot him a look. He was squinting out through the thickening snow; she noticed he had both hands on the steering wheel.

She realized he *wanted* the animosity. He wanted distance between them. Which meant he had been feeling something, too.

She sighed. Her complicated way of thinking was probably why she was having so much trouble starting her book. It was really black-and-white: if he wanted distance between them, that was a warning sign.

A warning sign that she could get hurt, particularly if she didn't want distance between them.

Which, of course, she did!

They came to a steep incline, he geared down, the back end of the truck slid sideways.

She gasped, the feeling so unexpected, so out-of-control, and he glanced at her, looked right back to the road.

"Just a little slippery," he said, the edge gone from his voice, trying to calm her. "Nothing to worry about."

But why would he even mention there was nothing to worry about if there truly wasn't? If there was really nothing to worry about he might have said, "So what are you doing tonight for supper?" or "Doesn't Jeanie Harper make the best shortbread cookies ever?"

She watched him, his hands, the road, came to the conclusion that the driving was *challenging,* but nothing he hadn't handled a zillion times before.

"Is it going to be like this all winter?" she asked him. "I'll be scared to drive."

"Your uncle can give you a few winter driving lessons," he said. Her uncle, not him, reminding her just how unlikely it was that he would have ever said, "What are you doing for supper tonight?" or at least not in the context of what he was *also* doing for supper.

She took a deep breath, recognizing her mind was babbling to itself, nervous. She gasped again when the truck slid. Her heart felt like it was going to pound out of her chest.

Once, she had enjoyed new experiences. "Sorry," she muttered when he looked askance at her, "I was involved in an *incident* last year. I have a bad startle reflex now."

If he asked her what it was, she had the horrible feeling she would tell him, unburden herself right here and right now, as if he didn't have enough to think about just getting them safely off the mountain.

"Yeah," he said. "I kind of figured maybe you'd had something happen."

"Did my uncle say something?" she asked, aghast.

"No, ma'am, all the locks on your door did."

A man who missed nothing. But it was the lack of judgment in his firm voice, the unexpected compassion, that made her feel suddenly safe with him. As if she could trust him.

She looked at him, really looked. His face was calm, his hands light on the steering wheel. He even reached out and fiddled with the radio at one point.

But the reception mirrored the storm, static-distorted and thick.

Lila felt glad he was obviously so familiar with this area, because she could now barely make out the road against a sea of white. The tracks where the truck had come up the hill were completely erased by the snow. The world was turning white around them with astounding speed.

She began to feel quite safe: Brody so focused on the road, the dog unworried, fast asleep on her lap, the heat pumping out of the heater enveloping her in warmth. Even her butt was beginning to thaw out.

She should have known by now: it was always when she let her guard down that she got blindsided.

The deer jumped out from her side, a dark, swift shadow materializing just off the front bumper.

One minute there was nothing, and then he was there, a beautiful antlered male, monstrously large, blacking out the storm as he filled the view in front of them.

"Deer!" she cried out an unnecessary warning.

"Elk," he corrected her mildly.

She didn't see anyway they could avoid a collision, but

Brody slammed the truck into a lower gear, heaved on the steering wheel, as if his might and his will could prevent the unpreventable.

In that slowed down version of reality that happens during accidents, she saw the elk's eyes roll white with terror before it bounded away, seemingly unharmed though she could have sworn the truck glanced off of it.

Elk saved, the truck was sliding, so slowly its movement seemed benign. It went sideways across the road, the nose pointed to a steep embankment. The driver's side tire slipped over, and then hers followed. For a single second the truck hung suspended, and then it lurched, the front end plowed into hard ground, and they stopped hard.

Lila, pushed forward against the dash, her nose nearly on the windshield, was afraid to even breathe in case it sent the truck cascading farther down the embankment.

"Are you okay?"

His voice was deep, his calm could be reassuring if she was inclined to let it be.

She nodded, still afraid to move.

"We're hung up. Don't worry." Dead calm, a man who dealt well with calamity.

"D-d-don't worry?" she stammered. "We're hanging by a thread. We're in the middle of nowhere. We're in the middle of a blizzard. It's almost dark."

"Uh-huh."

He wasn't getting the seriousness of their predicament.

"We're out of cell phone range!" she told him, and could hear the squeaky note of panic in her own voice.

And then he laughed.

She was not sure she had ever heard a more reassuring

sound—his easy laughter surely meant they were not in as much danger as she thought they were in.

Though his laughter—bold, deep, full of life—awakened her to a danger of a different kind. She pulled back from where she was squished up against the dashboard of the truck and peeked at him.

This was the man she had glimpsed in his hint of a smile a long time ago.

Extraordinary. Something beyond handsome. Deep. Capable. A man who handled what life threw at him with a certain ruggedly appealing confidence in his own abilities and strengths.

"It's not as bad as you think it is," he told her. "Here put your arms around my neck."

If it hadn't been as bad as she thought it was before she put her arms around his neck, it certainly was after.

She was not just aware of his strength, of the steady beat of his heart as he lifted her easily from the truck.

No, she was aware of the heavily falling snow, and the deep silence, and the fact the light was now leeching from the air, even though it was barely four o'clock. She was also aware that truck was not going anywhere. They were stranded in a world of snow and cold and elements. A world as foreign to her as if she had journeyed to a brand-new and menacing land.

She was aware she was now totally reliant on him.

And that if there was ever a man a woman should be grateful for being totally reliant on, it was this one.

He set her down on the steep pitch of the bank, looked her up and down, hard, then reached in and pulled Boo from the truck.

The danger of her situation deepened, because Boo

reached up and licked at the bottom of her rescuer's chin. And for a moment in Brody's face she saw an unguarded tenderness so lovely it took her breath away.

"How long," he said, deliberate casualness in his voice, "until someone misses you?"

Her aunt and obviously her uncle had known she was going for the tree today. But she doubted that either of them would check to see if she had arrived home. Her aunt had done that at first, checked in on her, knowing how nervous she could be at night.

But as the hometown feeling of Snow Mountain had wrapped around her, as comfy as a favorite blanket, Lila had asked her to stop.

Would anyone notice the tree had not appeared in the square on schedule? The grand reopening was still days away. She doubted it.

"It could be a while," she said. "You?"

"Same. I'm on days off. Not scheduled to work again until Monday night."

The same. She understood just how much the same they were. Alone in a world of couples and families. Alone. No one to miss them if they didn't get back home right away. It was Saturday, no one would miss them for close to forty-eight hours.

And how exactly did a person like that, *alone,* write a book about how to have a perfect Christmas? she asked herself morosely. She was wanting to think about something like that, suddenly a *small* concern, rather than the harsh reality of the predicament they were in. Already, she missed the warmth she had so enjoyed inside the cab of the truck. The snow, driven by wind, stung her face.

"The upside is no one will be worried unnecessarily,"

he said easily, as if the swiftly deepening cold and night did not bother him one little bit.

"Excuse me if I don't exactly see that as an upside."

That smile again, reassuring, strong. "The guys will be really busy with a storm like this. I wouldn't want a whole bunch of manpower diverted to rescuing us when we don't need rescuing."

"We don't?"

"No. There's a hunter's cabin not far from here. It will be stocked with emergency supplies. We'll hole up there for the night. In the morning, I'll walk out. Did you see that farm we passed on the way up here? Bryce Hampton's place. He'll have a tractor. He can pull the truck out."

A night in a cabin. With a man whose laughter sounded like that. With a man who looked as if he would die protecting her if he had to. She refused to give in to her awareness of his lips, his *presence,* the thought that they were going to be alone, and that there was something between them that was so strong she was not sure she could fight it.

Instead she forced herself to think disciplined thoughts. *A cabin.* She latched on to it desperately. Maybe she could put a chapter on Christmas vacations in her book. Cabins: cozy fires, mulled wine, a popcorn string for the tree.

While she immersed herself in fantasy—always a safe defense from reality—Brody saw what he could salvage from the truck: the thermos, a few leftover cookies, the blanket, his chain saw.

Her ability to convince herself it was all a grand adventure, an opportunity to experience an alternate Christmassy locale, lasted about three minutes. Even the undeniable sensuality of the man faded into the background. Lila dismissed her fantasies and focused on the tasks at hand. Trying to get back up the incline was nearly impossible.

She fell and her mittens got wet, and Brody insisted she brush all the snow off her clothes before they moved again. Then he had to shove her from behind to get her up over the lip onto the road. At least she wasn't the only one struggling. She noticed Boo making a terrible gasping sound.

It seemed she was struggling endlessly through snow and darkness. In no time, she was exhausted, cold and hungry. She had tripped and fallen over logs and rocks hidden by snow at least a dozen times. Each time he had patiently helped her up, brushed her off, encouraged her. This was an amazing side to him that made her think—as if the ground she was on was not treacherous enough—he would make such a good father.

"Are you sure you know where the cabin is?" Her hands were so cold, the mittens like clumps of ice at the end of her sleeves. And the fabric of her jeans, frozen solid even though he had painstakingly brushed the snow from them after each fall, felt as if it was burning her legs.

What if he didn't know where the cabin was? How could anyone really know where it was? All the trees looked the same. They had left the road behind long ago. What if he was leading them farther and farther from safety? What if—

"I know where the cabin is." A voice a person could believe in. The kind of voice that instilled confidence in desperate situations. But then, that was what he was trained to do. Deal with crises. Car accidents. Bank robberies. Protests.

He could be *pretending,* she decided. He was making her go ahead of him, and she turned to scan his face.

Absolutely calm. A face incapable of any kind of pretense.

"Just a few more minutes," he said.

"I need a rest."

"No." He said it just like that, no gentleness this time. The firmness of a whip cracking. In other circumstances she might have resented his high-handedness, but she recognized this situation needed a leader, and he was it.

She cast one more glance back at him. When had he picked up the dog? He was carrying everything now: the basket, the blanket, the chain saw, the dog. And she was complaining?

"Move it," he said.

It was when she heard that tone of voice, entirely no nonsense, expecting obedience—as if their lives depended on it—that she understood he'd protected her all along from the precariousness of the position they were in.

When she really did not think she could go another slippery step down that path of snow booby-trapped roots and fallen logs, a shape loomed black and square against the darkness of the night.

How could she feel so painfully disappointed?

Because part of what had kept her going was her idea of a cabin: welcoming porch, golden logs, a chimney. A place a family might gather to enjoy a simpler Christmas and each other.

What was ahead of them was so obviously a shack.

She wanted to cry. Because it just underscored what he had said earlier. She had a problem with fantasy.

Still, when he shoved in the door and shut it behind them the space was nothing except unrelentingly black. It was at least as cold inside as it had been outside.

"What is that smell?" she asked weakly.

"Mice. Pack rats." He set down the dog, thudded into something and swore softly, but a moment later a lamp flickered to life and she saw the cabin in its humble entirety.

Most importantly, at the center of the single room, there was a stove, black and potbellied, with some wood stacked beside it.

But other than that welcome sight, the cabin was a horror: unpainted plywood floor and walls. No windows. A two-by-four single shelf, plywood, close to the floor, that she realized without enthusiasm was the bed. An old table was in the center of the room, flanked by two stump chairs. There was a plank countertop covered in white powder.

"Mice have been in the flour," he said matter-of-factly.

Mice in the flour. Some Christmas story that would make.

She turned and looked at him in the flickering light, and felt ashamed of herself. She had complained, but he was the one who was not dressed warmly, who had carried everything the whole way. This place might not be her fantasy, but the reality was it would help them survive a very bad night, and fairly comfortably, too.

His cheeks were becoming faintly whisker darkened, the snow melted in his hair and on the collar of his jacket.

His hands were bare.

"Your hands must be freezing," she said. "I had mittens on and mine are still cold."

"I'm okay."

He showed her, by reaching for her hands. He plucked her mittens off, one at a time, placed her hands between the amazing warmth of his.

She closed her eyes against the sensation: her whole world became not the storm outside, not the mice in the flour, but *this*. Warmth. Strength. Something to hold on to.

"I'm a terrible sissy," she said. "A liability. I'm sorry. I've never been lost in the wilderness before. I've never actually seen snow before. Except when I was ten. I remember it being *fun*. Not miserable."

There was a terrible catch in her voice. How could she ever write a book about Christmas now that she knew the truth: snow had a downside. It caused accidents. It caused loss of feeling to limbs.

"You were a trooper," he said, as if he really meant it, and then let go of her hands. "I was born doing this kind of stuff. And as dramatic as it sounds, I'm afraid we were never lost in the wilderness. My brother and I knew these mountains like the backs of our hands."

"I didn't know you had a brother."

He moved away from her, adjusted the lamp, moved with easy efficiency to the stove.

"In about five minutes," he said, ignoring her attempt at small talk, "you'll want to open the door, it will be so warm in here. It's amazing how a little heater like this can warm a small space."

And it did. But what she was newly amazed at was *him*. Taking each challenge in his stride, getting the fire going, checking the supplies. Soon he had a pot filled with snow heating on the stove, another bubbling with something that smelled so good.

He fed the dog some of the tinned stew he'd found in one of the cupboards, found a mattress rolled up tight against the mice, unfolded it and found bedding stored in tightly closed plastic boxes.

After he'd fed her and the warmth was creeping steadily

into her very bones, Lila realized she was actually starting to feel *happy* to be here. A funny kind of euphoria began to fill her up. A delayed gratitude for survival, she assumed.

"You know what's weird?" she said almost to herself. "I feel really safe. Isn't that crazy?"

"We were never in danger," he told her, giving her a quizzical look.

But she realized she felt as if she had been in danger for a long time, had lived with the finely held tension of one who had been hunted, and who could never forget what it meant to be prey.

Except here. Without any locks on the door, seemingly a million miles from any other human being, the snow wrapping her in a cocoon of security.

It occurred to her that even if it was irrational, she felt totally safe, really and truly safe, for the first time in two years. It occurred to her that not feeling safe, all those nights of listening, *waiting,* had exhausted her almost beyond comprehension. No wonder, she thought almost sleepily, that she hadn't been able to write a book!

It was a wonder she'd been able to open her store, organize the SOS committee.

No wonder her thoughts about Brody were confused, and out of control. No wonder she didn't know from one minute to the next what she wanted.

She was perpetually exhausted. She felt her gaze drift longingly to that uncomfortable-looking bed.

And then it occurred to her there were two of them and a single bed, and she was not safe at all.

And her sense of euphoria did not ease, not even one little bit.

* * *

The gods had it in for him. Brody Taggert knew that for sure. Because here he was, in a remote mountain cabin, with the woman he had sworn was the most dangerous to him, the one human being on earth he most had to stay away from.

Because of how he had felt for that moment after he had told her about the Murphy girl. The burden lightened.

Because of how he had felt when the truck started to slide, and as they had walked through the cold night here: as if he would lay down his life for her, without one thought, *gladly.*

Because of how he had felt, really, from the first moment he had met her, as if his world was tilting.

And mostly because of how he felt right now.

Strangely contented to be with her. Of course, being out here, far away from the trappings of civilization, had always had that effect on him. Soothed something in him. Made him aware of something bigger running the show.

So why had he not come here with his grief?

Because these places had always belonged to him and his brother *together.* He with his rifle, Ethan with his sketchbook.

He had thought he would feel nothing but pain returning to the places that had been theirs together, alone.

But he was not alone. And for a reason he could not fathom, he was not resentful of Lila's presence in this place that had been so special to him and Ethan.

He snorted at his philosophical turn. The truth about his contentment had not a thing to do with philosophy. He had been handed a bad situation, and was making the best of it. He had found them shelter from a storm that was going to get a lot nastier before it abated. That was something to feel grateful for. Lila had always made him feel protective, and now he was protecting her, and it was strangely satisfying.

Of course, in a few minutes the thing she was most

going to need protecting from was himself, since he was about to get Lila Grainger out of her jeans.

Okay, not in the way that a man usually thought of that.

Then again, he had a feeling things with Lila Grainger would probably never go quite the way a man thought they should or would.

He had fed her, and now she was drinking tea. The color was returning to her hands, and there was an expression of peace on her face that made him wish he could capture moments with a pencil, as Ethan had.

A few strokes of pencil or charcoal, and a moment saved forever. Brody had books full of those etchings at home, put away in boxes that he never opened.

But suddenly he felt ready to look at them again, to see the world through his brother's eyes.

Lila shivered, despite the warmth of the fire, and he knew she was never going to be warm as long as she had on those soaked jeans.

"Uh, you're going to have to take those pants off," he said.

She shot him a look, hugged her tea a little tighter, pretended she hadn't heard him.

"I'll turn my back. Here's the blanket from the picnic. It's dry now. Your pants aren't."

"What about yours?" she asked. "They must be wet, too."

"Damp. I didn't do quite as much rolling around in the snow as you. I'll be okay."

He passed her the blanket and turned his back, acting as if he expected to be obeyed, but he was still pleasantly surprised when she muttered, "Okay," and he turned around to find her with the blanket wrapped around her like a long skirt, the jeans in a puddle at her feet.

He picked them up, hung them deliberately by the fire,

trying not to notice how small they were, how straight: every curve they had appeared to have as he walked behind them had been added by her.

"Since I'm in the embarrassing position of having no pants, I guess now would be a good time to ask my most embarrassing question. Where's the bathroom?"

"Uh." It was his turn to blush.

The bathroom? Every tree was a bathroom to a guy. In hunting season, there was a log over a pit toilet behind here.

For the more delicate, he just wasn't sure. Especially now that he'd gotten her out of her pants. He didn't want to send her out into the snow with the blanket. That would get wet, too, and she was just starting to warm up.

"How would you feel about using a bucket?" he asked.

"Like I'd rather die first," she answered, and set down the tea with an accusing look as if he was personally responsible for the primitive lack of facilities.

"I won't think any less of you," he said uneasily. "I don't have any problems with bodily functions."

The wrong thing to say, obviously. She glared at him.

"Look," he said, struck by inspiration, "think of it as camping. Haven't you ever been camping?"

"No."

"Didn't you ever want to go?"

"We have alligators in Florida!"

"We have cabins with no plumbing in Washington," he said. "Life is full of hazards."

"I know that," she said somberly, and he thought of the locks on her door, the *incident* she had referred to when she had felt that first shiver of fear.

"I know you do. I do, too." He handed her the bucket. "I'll go outside. You might as well get it over with."

"When I write my book about creating the perfect Christmas, this is not making it into the chapter on Christmas cabins."

The dog, her stomach unsettled from the unfamiliar food, chose that moment to make a sound like air being released from a balloon.

"And neither is that," she said.

And then they were both laughing, and despite the unexpected twists and turns of life, he was aware it was the first time in a long time he had laughed like that. And it felt good, as if something that had been empty inside of him was filling up.

CHAPTER SIX

WARM. Safe. Cozy. Happy.

The snow fell unabated outside the cabin, Lila could hear the wind howling under the eaves.

But inside was only warmth. It was like the end to a perfect Christmas story, even though they were in a place with no tree, no lights, no turkey. There was a *feeling* in here, in this humble cabin, and it was exactly the feeling she'd been trying to create when she had started *Miss L. Toe* as an Internet business, and again when she had decided to open a storefront. It was exactly the feeling that she had wanted to create when she had agreed to write that book.

It was a feeling of being home.

Ridiculous to feel that way. No electricity. No plumbing. Not a single luxury or amenity.

And yet sitting at that small table, wearing a blanket, the dog on top of her feet, Brody Taggert dealing cards, that's how she felt.

Home.

It was because of him. Because he was a man you could come home to.

She snuck a look at him over the top of her cards, felt her breath stop. In the flickering, imperfect light of the lantern, he looked gorgeous, and faintly roguish with his whisker-roughened chin and cheeks.

"I've never seen anyone cheat at crib before," he said, throwing down his cards, stretching. His shirt lifted way up. She could see the taut line of his tummy.

"I didn't cheat!"

"You don't get three for a pair."

She looked down at the board, realized she had been so engrossed in all his taut lines, she might have taken the extra point. Since she wasn't about to admit that, she said, "Show me the rule book!"

"Why bother? You're the type that reads the rule book and then just does whatever you want anyway."

"How would you know that on our brief acquaintance?"

He lifted his eyebrows at her. She wished he wouldn't do that. In the flickering light it made him look wickedly sexy. In this primitive cabin it was easy to picture him as a renegade highwayman or a pirate. Rugged enough to make his own rules.

"Anatomy of a protest," he pointed out, reminding her he was on the *right* side of the law. "You knew you needed a permit."

"It was going to take weeks! It was for a good cause."

"Precisely my point. I bet you think winning at crib is a good cause, too."

"Right up there with saving Christmas trees," she said passionately.

He smiled. Something in him had relaxed. Surrendered.

Something in her had relaxed, surrendered.

"What made you become a policeman?" she asked, wanting to take advantage of this moment of surrender to *know* him. "I can picture you as a renegade."

"You can, hmm?" That smile deepened wickedly.

Visions of the highwayman became more clear. "I'm afraid I can," she admitted, "Quite clearly."

"I was a renegade when I was younger. Mostly mischief. Garden raiding, stealing mailboxes from the ends of driveways. But for a while it escalated. Some pretty hard drinking, fighting. I came to in a cell one morning, with Hutch sitting in the bunk across from me, waiting for me to wake up.

"I'd gotten tanked up the night before, hit one of his guys. I didn't even remember it."

"That's pretty serious, isn't it?" she asked.

"You're not kidding. Assault on a police officer? Given the fact I had collected a string of drunk and disorderlies by then, I knew a judge was not going to take pity on me."

"What happened?"

His face softened. "Hutch said he figured I was at a crossroads, a place where the choices I made were going to affect the rest of my life. He told me he'd been watching me. If I was going to choose a side, he wanted me on his side. And, instead of charging me, he threw down an application for the police department.

"It was a lifeline. And a turning point." He looked suddenly embarrassed, a man not used to talking about himself.

Sitting across from him, Lila could see exactly what her uncle had seen: integrity, honor, strength, but coupled with an almost amazing lack of ego. Even in a kid getting in trouble, all those qualities would have shone through.

"That's the kind of man your uncle is," he said gruffly. "That's why I'd do just about anything for him."

"Including go find a Christmas tree with his niece?"

"Yeah," he said with a small grin, "even that."

And then, a man who felt he had said way too much about himself, he got up from the table, and the next question hung in the air between them.

What now? Where was it going?

"Where are we sleeping?" she asked. It came out sounding faintly breathless, excited, hopeful.

"You can have the bed. Boo and I will take the floor." Every quality her uncle had ever seen in him was clearly visible now. Integrity, honor, strength. And he was going to use them all to fight the attraction, to be the man who could be trusted with another man's niece.

Even with the little wood heater cranked up to full blast, she could feel the chill rising up through the floor. They had the picnic blanket that she was wrapped in and two wool blankets that had been in the cabin, thin and frayed at the edges. He would need those both if he was going to be on that floor. She shivered at the thought.

"We could share the bed." She was glad for the light in here, because maybe it hid the stain that moved up her cheeks.

"No, we couldn't."

"Why not?" She told herself she was not suggesting they sleep together, not in an intimate way, only that they share the few comforts there were in the cabin. But she knew something in her was ready for more, hoping for more.

How much more? She was not going to find out.

"Boo snores," he said, deadpan.

But she knew that wasn't it. She knew that kiss outside his barn, a kiss he had bestowed on her in a fury, was in this room with them, and had been there, right below the surface, from the moment they had gotten in that truck cab together.

She licked her lips as if his taste lingered there, and somehow, even though it was weeks later, it felt as if it did.

He looked at her, his gaze brooding, simmering with passion that she wanted desperately to explore.

She got up, too, leaned toward him.

He took a step back, but he could not hide the reluctance with which he stepped back. He whistled to the dog, glanced once more at her lips and then turned on his heel and went outside.

A whoosh of cold air and snow blew in the door behind him.

She could wait for him. She could tempt him. But the truth was, she did not have that kind of confidence in herself or in her judgment. The pleasant exhaustion that she had been feeling almost from the moment she came in that door enveloped her now in a lethargy she could not fight.

Lila went to the bed, rearranged her blanket around herself, lay down on the lumpy mattress. Despite the fact it smelled of something—she hoped not mice—she could not keep her eyes open for even one second.

A moment later he came in from outside, shook the snow off himself, took off his boots. They thudded to the floor, she imagined his bare feet, but did not give in to the temptation to look at them. More rustling, his shirt whispering to the floor. That proved more temptation than she could handle.

She opened her eyes, but she had barely seen him—the ridges and lines of pure and intoxicating male beauty— when he blew out the lamp.

Blackness more complete than she had ever experienced enveloped her.

She heard him arranging the thin blankets on the floor, crawl in between them, the dog settling in beside him.

She could hear his breathing; it was all that prevented complete panic at the sudden impenetrable darkness.

"It's really dark in here," she whispered, trying to keep the wobble from her voice.

"Mmm."

"Really dark. I've never been in a room this dark in my whole life. I'm holding up my hand, I can't even see it."

Silence, and then softly. "Are you scared of the dark, Miss Lila Toe?"

His voice in the darkness, so soft, teasing her, using an endearment, was the same as his voice in a storm, a sound someone could hold on to, that could make them feel safe in a world that just wasn't.

"It's just there's always a streetlight," she said, avoiding his question. "Some kind of light. From the hallway. Or the bathroom."

"You're scared of the dark," he concluded, his voice without recrimination.

"Maybe a little," she admitted.

"Have you always been like that?"

It was her turn to hesitate. How vulnerable did she want to be to him? "No."

"Maybe you should tell me about *the incident.* Tell me what happened."

Suddenly the darkness made it feel safe to tell him, she *wanted* to. And so she told him, detail by detail.

"I was just starting *Miss L. Toe* as an Internet business. My love of all things Christmas had just been a hobby up until that point, so I was still working full-time as a research writer for a big marketing company. A new guy joined our department—Ken Whittaker."

Lila told Brody about Ken's growing but unwanted

interest in her, her trying to be polite and then having to be firm. The more she said no, the more he came at her: roses, invitations, poetry left on her desk.

"They finally fired him after he filled up every drawer in my desk with confetti," she said. "It was apparent to everyone it wasn't a harmless crush. He was harassing me. It triggered rage in him, as if I was responsible for the fact he'd been fired. The notes and poems kept coming, to my house, to work, but they turned nasty. He was in his car outside the office, outside my apartment building. Then one time I went for dinner with friends, and he broke into my apartment and stole some of my things. I finally got a restraining order."

"And it made everything worse," Brody guessed softly.

"How did you know?"

"It's one of the most frustrating crimes for a cop to deal with, stalking. In the worst cases, it seems like every attempt to control it just deepens the obsession, the rage, makes everything worse."

"Worse doesn't describe it." She stopped talking for a moment, took a deep shuddering breath. "He broke into my house. At night. I woke up with him hovering over top of me with a knife. He held me at knifepoint in my own kitchen for six hours."

Brody swore softly in the dark.

"He was raging and then crying and then raging again. To this day, I don't know what stopped him from raping me. Or killing me. Twice he held the knife against my neck so hard he drew blood."

"What did you do?"

She hesitated. "Lied my head off. Told him I loved him. Told him I wanted to spend the rest of my life with him. Told him—" her voice cracked "—I wanted to have his babies."

"Good instincts," Brody said approvingly.

"Afterward, when I thought about it, I felt sick that I had said things like that to him. Things that should be so sacred."

"They kept you alive. In my book that probably qualifies as sacred."

She was quiet, contemplating that. "A neighbor happened to be walking by. There was a back walkway past my apartment that went to the garbage. She was taking her trash out and happened to glance in my window.

"Later she told me she was only taking it out because she'd had fish the night before. Her garbage wasn't full. My life was probably saved because my neighbor had fish. Imagine. Amazing."

"I guess that qualifies as sacred, too," he said, his voice low and reassuring in the blackness of the night.

"It's why I moved to Snow Mountain. The Internet business was doing great, I had an advance on writing a book on Christmas that could get me started here, but the real reason was even after Ken was convicted, I couldn't stay there anymore. It seemed like the fear, the terror had seeped into the walls. I had to get to someplace new, I had to find something I could believe in."

"Christmas?" he guessed, and she could hear the calm in his voice, the evenness of his breathing. She thought she could hear acceptance, as if he did not for one minute blame her, the way she had blamed herself.

"Christmas," she said softly. "Or maybe what it stands for—peace, people loving one another, a time of miracles." She hesitated and then continued, "Maybe I'm looking for one myself, because when I moved I realized that the fear hadn't just seeped into the walls of my apartment. It had seeped into me."

"What miracle are you looking for, Lila?"

And it was the easiest thing in the world to trust him, which made her think maybe her miracle had already started to happen.

"I want to not be afraid anymore, to not have the knot in my stomach, to not startle at every loud noise. I want to be who I was before. And from the moment I walked in the door of this cabin, that's how I felt."

And suddenly, the exhaustion of two years of feeling that tension caught up with her.

"I want to sleep again, Brody. For a whole night. To not keep waking up with my heart pounding so loud in my ears it sounds like footsteps coming toward me."

"Lila?"

"Mmm-hmm?"

"You go ahead and sleep like that. I've got your back."

I've got your back. That was what she had not felt for a long, long time. As if she was not alone. Protected.

Amazingly, she buried her nose in the world's smelliest mattress and slept instantly for the first time in forever.

Brody lay awake, listening to the sound of her steadily deepening breathing, contemplating the killing fury he felt at a man who was already taken care of, supposedly paying his debt to Lila and society. But it seemed to Brody no matter how many years the perpetrator spent in jail he would never be able to fix what he had done to Lila.

Brody dealt with creeps. It would probably bug Lila to know that. Yup. They were everywhere. Even in Snow Mountain. He was always clinical in how he treated them, his personal feelings controlled, not an issue.

Now he realized he was a man capable of murder.

If that guy, Ken, got out and came after her, because they always came after the object of their obsession. They never quit until someone was dead. Brody knew he'd look after it. That simple.

The floor was hard and cold. He was uncomfortable and that was good. It kept his mind off all that softness just a few feet away. It kept his mind off the fact that when she had asked where they were going to sleep, he thought he'd detected the faintest hint of an invitation.

Brody was determined to be the guy Hutch thought he was, all those years ago when he'd given him a chance.

After what seemed to be a long, long time, Boo's breathing raspy in his ears, Brody fell asleep.

And woke to the sound of whimpering.

Not Boo's, either.

The whimpering intensified to a frightened cry, and he was already up by the time she started screaming.

"Get off of me! Get off!" Her voice had a hysterical edge, and Brody leaped toward the bed, tried to locate the source of her distress in the blackness.

Because of his last thoughts before sleep, he was ready to do murder in her defense if he had to.

But that was probably why the dream had come to her, too. Her last thoughts, thinking she was free of all that terror, hoping to be free, but her subconscious not quite ready to let go.

His eyes adjusted to the darkness. Lila was struggling under the weight of…his dog.

He bent and quickly lifted the dog off her. "Hey, it's okay. It was just Boo. She must have gotten cold."

Or she couldn't stay away. His dog was in love with

Lila, it was obvious, and Boo didn't have to control her attraction to people the way he did.

But Lila was beyond the point where she could be rational. She began to sob, punching away at an invisible enemy, her arms hopelessly tangled in the blanket, which seemed to be adding to her panic.

Brody hesitated, not knowing how strong he was. But then he decided to be strong enough to do what she needed done, not what was safest for him.

Because what he did was not safe at all.

He sat down on the edge of her bed and pulled her body, wrapped tight like a sausage, into his lap.

He loosened the blanket around her, her arms free, she flailed at him, and he let her flail, her blows landing harmlessly on his naked chest.

"It's all right," he said over and over, making no attempt to capture her hands. "No one's ever going to hurt you again, Lila. Never."

Slowly the panic subsided from her, the punches to his chest grew weaker. The sobs further apart and then soft, like a beaten puppy crying.

"Hey," he said, "hey, it's okay. He can't hurt you anymore. I won't let him."

At those words she finally stilled, took a long, deep breath, relaxed against him. He could feel her tears sliding, molten, down his skin.

"Brody?"

"Yeah, it's me."

"Sorry, I didn't mean to hurt you. I didn't know it was you. Even after you told me, all I could feel was panic. I'm sorry. I feel like an idiot."

"You didn't hurt me. You don't have anything to be

sorry about. It takes a long, long time for some wounds to heal. Some never do."

"Do you have a wound that's never healed, Brody?"

He could feel something catching in his throat and it took him a long time to answer. When he did, he said only, "I think everyone does."

She sighed her agreement against him, her breath warmer than fire on his chest.

"That's why I sleep with the light on. Not just the bathroom one, the one beside my bed, too."

"I can put the lantern on if you want."

She sighed, again. "It's okay. Brody, lie down beside me. The floor's cold."

He heard something else. She needed to be held. Maybe she needed to know a man could hold her without hurting her.

He lay her down on the bed, she scooted way over against the wall. He lay down beside her, stiffly, not wanting to touch her, not having any idea how much testing he could take.

She snuggled into him, laid her head once more on the nakedness of his chest. He hesitated and put his arm around the slenderness of her shoulders, tugged her into his side.

"Brody, will you kiss me?"

He knew all the reasons he shouldn't. All of them. He knew she was his boss's niece, and this couldn't go well.

He knew that he had so little to give, all the best parts of him buried with his brother, the part of him that might have been willing to risk again slowly shutting down since Boo had gotten sicker and sicker.

He knew she had come to trust and rely on him because of the situation they were in. He knew this could be temporary. A form of transference. As a first responder, he knew how desperately people could cling to their rescuer, he knew the strength of the bond that could be formed in those terrible seconds of crises.

He knew that after what she had been through, a man who was a cop—a professional defender and rescuer—could seem bigger than life to her, the ideal man, a hero, not a living, breathing person with lots of problems and baggage of his own.

He knew all this, but he also knew this was the limit he had asked to be shown; this, then, was how much testing he could take.

He took her lips in his, he didn't taste them, he drank them. He drank the heady wine of wild strawberries.

"Oh," she breathed against him. "Oh."

"I've wanted to kiss you like this ever since I kissed you like *that*," he admitted huskily.

And then he took her lips again, tenderly, and felt her welcoming answer, as if she had lived her whole life for this moment. Her lips parted beneath his, he felt the sweet curves of her body pressing against his, and he ached for that soft, soft world he had left so far behind him.

But that moment of surrender, of pure bliss was short.

Boo, left on the floor, jumped up on top of them. He tried to catch her, but Boo determined was a dog possessed. She scrambled and wriggled and wheezed her way right in between them. He was hanging on to the narrow bed by a thread, Lila was shoved up against the wall. Boo moaned her delight at having managed to occupy the tiny space between them.

"I think the chaperone has arrived," she said dryly, and then giggled.

Thank God, he thought. He reached past Boo, and touched Lila's cheek, still wet with tears.

When her lips found his fingers, he withdrew them.

She was in no frame of mind to be making decisions like the one he had very nearly asked of her. She was vulnerable. She needed protection, not someone who would take advantage of her.

His strength came back to him. He reached down and grabbed the blankets off the floor, tucked them around her, and around himself, and around Boo, the living, slobbering, snoring bolster.

"Let's go to sleep," he said.

He knew he had made the right decision when she did not argue with him, or press him to get Boo out of the bed.

She wasn't ready.

And God knew, neither was he.

Uncomfortable, but warm at least, he noticed her fragrance had released like a night blooming rose.

"What scent do you wear?" he asked her, when it tickled his nostrils, when he breathed it deep, even though he knew he was teasing himself.

"Scent?"

"Perfume."

"I don't wear perfume. I have sensitive skin. I even have to use unscented bath and laundry soap."

He contemplated that for a moment. All these weeks he'd *imagined* that she smelled like that? Like that last day with his brother? Summer sunshine, the fragrance of the damp woods and strawberries, their hands red with the juice, not eating a single one. Laughing at each find, a way to make amends to their mom for the broken cranberry glass vase.

In the dark of the cabin, with his eyes closed, he could see Ethan, his head thrown back in laughter, his quiet intensity as he sketched the wild strawberry plant.

He shook the vision away. He shook away the thought that the scent of wild strawberries was some kind of gift from his brother. Like a benediction on this woman he shared the darkness of this cabin with on a snowy night.

Ethan had thought like that: he had used his imagination like a bridge to spirit. Ethan had believed in larger purposes and signs from heaven.

Brody had not and did not.

No, he didn't have that good an imagination. She must eat strawberry candy or burn candles or use a strawberry shampoo, something that infused her with that fragrance. There was a logical explanation for why she smelled the way she did.

But he wasn't going to ask her.

He was tired. It had been a long, eventful day. He'd been woken from a deep sleep. A man's thoughts went strange places in the deepest part of the night.

"Good night," he said firmly. "Good night, Lila."

CHAPTER SEVEN

LILA woke to her nose feeling frozen, but unbelievable and delicious warmth everywhere else. The three of them, Brody, Boo and her were squished together in a bed made for one. Sometime in the night she had turned toward him, her hand had snaked by Boo and rested on Brody's shoulder. She let it linger there, awed by how right it felt to be touching him so intimately.

His skin was warm, smooth, resilient under her touch. Just beneath it, she could feel pure muscle, powerful, even when relaxed in sleep.

She looked at his face, and allowed herself the luxury of studying the fullness of his lips, the impossible length and tangle of his lashes, the stubble that darkened the lines of his cheeks and chin, making them seem harder and more pronounced, intimidating, and beautifully masculine.

She shivered. The air in the cabin was cold, making her snuggle deeper under the blankets.

No wonder it was cold in here. Now that morning had come, light was seeping through all the places the cabin was not sealed. There was frost on the wall behind her.

With a smile, she contemplated the fact that after the dream, she had slept until morning.

It had been a long, long time since she'd slept deeply. Until the night in his cabin, every sound had startled her awake, even the furnace whispering on, a cat outside, a branch scraping the window. She would come awake holding her breath, listening, her heart pounding, her hands clammy with fear. Sometimes she awoke, terrified, to such silence she would wonder if it was the tick of her bedroom clock that had awakened her.

Boo stirred beside her, opened an eye. She could have sworn the dog grinned at the position she found herself in, sandwiched neatly between the warmth of two humans. Lila freed one hand from the blanket, scratched Boo's chest and was rewarded with a slurp from an enormous pink tongue across her face.

She giggled and saw Brody stir, went very still as she watched him come awake. It was as breathtaking a thing to see him wake up as it had been to watch him sleep.

Slowly, a wrinkle in his forehead, his lips moving, then his eyes fluttering. An unconscious stretch of shoulders, and then his eyes opened, and he studied her with sleepy astonishment, a smile tickling the firmness of his lips.

But then he was all the way awake suddenly.

She realized her hand still rested on his shoulder, and she yanked it away, but he leaped from bed, ready for action.

She had caught a quick glance of him without his shirt last night before they had been plunged into darkness, and she had felt the magnificent strength of him as he had held her after she had woken, terrified, with Boo's weight on top of her.

This morning she gave herself over to the study of the perfect male form, just as she had given herself over to the study of his face.

His chest was solid, cut-marble perfection, the column of his throat, joining it, looked powerful. Then the mounding of pecs, the skin so taut over his rib cage that she could count the ridges there. The broadness tapered to a flat, hard stomach, more ridges, the stunning sexiness of his naked belly button, of his hip bones—just barely—holding up his jeans.

His flesh was completely stippled in goose bumps in seconds, and his nipples hardened to pebbles.

But he acted impervious to the cold, ran a hand through the tousled dark silk of his hair, squatted by the fire.

"I can't believe I let it go out." He began to feed wood into the fire. When the flames flickered healthily, he yanked on his shirt, whistled for the dog without doing up the buttons, shoved his bare feet into his boots, grabbed the water pot and went out the door.

He had barely glanced at her, and she couldn't think of anything that would be more humiliating than the strength of the attraction she felt for him not being reciprocated.

But she was pretty sure, her intuition intact for the first time in years, that he hadn't looked at her precisely because of what he was feeling—a pull as strong as the one she felt.

She wanted to stay in bed forever, or at least until the cabin was warmer, but she felt so invigorated. The woman she had been yesterday coming up the mountain, tired, frightened, that woman was gone.

She felt utterly rested, and with that feeling came a sense of clarity she had not enjoyed for so long.

She was glad she was here. She was glad she was here with him.

She got up and squeezed the legs of the pants he had hung up for her last night. They were dry, but still very cold when she put them on and did up the zipper.

By the time he returned, she had sorted through a number of cans and come up with breakfast. She used an ancient can opener to open a can and pour it into a pan.

"You won't believe this," she said, glancing at him, glancing again when she saw he had still not done up the shirt. She made herself look at the mess in the frying pan. "I found bacon for breakfast. Did you know bacon comes in cans?"

He stood there for a moment watching her, giving himself over to watching her as he had not done earlier, and then he motioned for her. "Come see this," he said.

He opened the door and they stood together on the porch and she felt her heart swell.

Not because he stood so close to her they were nearly touching, but because they were touching in a new way as they shared this sight together.

He had wanted her to see it. He had needed to share this with her.

Man created elves in parks and Santas who waved, man created beautiful homes and lovely gardens, and cities and paintings and museums.

Man created imitations of beauty.

Because looking out over the snow-covered world outside that cabin, her throat closed. They had come from the back of the cabin the night before, through the trees, in darkness. But today she could clearly see the cabin was located at the top of a sloping mountain meadow. The view was panoramic: mountain ridges folding in on themselves, a distant lake, a farm way down there in the valley, a thin plume of smoke coming out the chimney of the house.

The snow had stopped during the night and the world was blanketed in a sea of mounding white. The morning sun was coming out, tinged in pink, and it sparked off the snow as if thousands and thousands of tiny diamonds had been sewn onto that cotton-candy blanket. The branches of the trees dipped under the weight of white they carried.

And it was so silent, the world absolutely muted except for the breath of the man who stood next to her, and the crackle of the fire behind them.

She hugged herself against the cold, reluctant to go back inside to where it was warm.

"Is it colder this morning?"

"Always colder when it's clear like this," he said.

She turned to go back inside, but she suddenly saw it wasn't just the view he had brought her out here to show her. No, he was grinning, and nudging something with his toe.

It was a sled so old it could have been in the window of an antique store.

It had steel runners that might have been red once, but that were now rusty, a body shaped like a garden gate lying flat, an old piece of twine attached to the front steering bar.

"Before we go, I want to replace the wood we've used," he told her. "You can try this out."

Go. She didn't want to even think of that.

Yesterday, when they had arrived here, the cabin had not been anything that she had envisioned a cabin being. But today it felt different. As if it had given her gifts she could never repay: the gift of seeing just how little it took in material possessions to feel content. Full. Happy.

The gift of seeing you could put a thousand locks on your door and never feel safe until you had conquered the fear inside of yourself.

And one other unexpected gift: she could tell that he didn't want to leave, either, even if he said they were staying only because he wanted to replace the wood. It was just an excuse. To be here. To enjoy what they had found here just a little longer.

A bit of magic in a world without magic.

A hint of miracles in a humble cabin far, far from the nearest church.

"I think the bacon's burning," he said wryly.

She dashed back into the cabin, turned to see him standing in the open doorway, outlined in radiance by the morning light, the dog at his side.

And a look in his eyes as he watched her that stole her breath as surely as the scene outside the door.

An hour later, Brody stopped and wiped the sweat from his forehead. He had felled a dead tree behind the cabin. There was an unwritten law in these remote places that offered refuge: you left more than you took.

In his younger days he had been careless about such things, but Ethan never had. If his younger brother used one stick of wood, he put back two, if he drank one pouch of hot chocolate from the cabin's emergency supplies, he would bring back a whole box the next time they came.

Brody looked at the tree. He had used the chain saw to limb and section the tree, now he was using an ax that belonged with the cabin to chop the blocks of wood smaller. There would be a least a season's worth of wood here when he was done.

He contemplated the possibility he was a better man than he would have been if he hadn't had Ethan for a brother.

His attention turned to Lila. She was pulling the sled up the hill, yet another time, the dog glued to her heel. Apparently she wasn't going to get bored of that activity, every time she shouted with glee he found himself shaking his head and smiling.

He squinted at Boo.

Whatever was in this place, the dog was benefiting from it, too. Boo was almost puppylike in her joy, shoveling snow with her nose, bouncing, chasing imaginary squirrels, yapping at the heels of the sled.

People sometimes got sick and got better without any medical or scientific explanation.

His dog seemed better—clear-eyed, energetic, eating with more appetite than he'd seen in weeks.

So far Boo had chased the sled down the hill every time, barking with frantic happiness that reflected the shrieks of the woman going down the hill.

Lila was coming toward him now, puffing, a woman on a mission. She radiated joy and confidence, as if the experience of last night, of feeling safe and letting go, had freed her to be who she really was.

For the first time since he had met her, he was aware the faint circles of fatigue were gone from under her eyes.

He could see very clearly what Lila Grainger really was: a woman who vibrated with the life force, who shone with spirit, whose heart had not been broken by her experiences, but made braver.

He took up the ax and swung, cleanly halving a huge block of wood, not unaware of how her eyes rested on him.

Appreciative. *Hungry.* He knew he should not tempt fate by showing off for her, but he did anyway. He reset the halved piece of wood, swung, watched with satisfaction as the ax bit deep into it and it fell in two separate pieces.

"Come down the hill with me," she said. "Just once. Please."

He glanced at the piles of wood mounting around him, and at what was left of the tree. Another hour and he'd be done here. He felt no urgency to leave, despite the fact he had just shown off his strength for her was a clear warning it was time to go.

But they were probably going to have to dig up something to eat before they left now, too. She hadn't realized it, but she was going to have to dry her clothes all over again.

It would be early afternoon before they were ready to go. And that would be if he stayed on task, gathered the split wood, stacked it neatly outside the cabin.

"Please?"

Resist temptation, he ordered himself. So, naturally, he found himself setting down the ax, taking the sled string from her and pulling the sled up to the very top of the hill.

Somehow he was sitting on the front of that sled, his knees nearly touching his ears, and she was on it behind him, pressed so close to him he could feel the beat of her heart through her vest and through his own jacket. Her arms were wrapped around him, her head rested between the broadness of his shoulder blades.

And then they were flying down that hill, the dog racing beside them, the wind stinging his cheeks and making his eyes water.

She was shouting with laughter, and suddenly he was, too. He felt young again, carefree and unburdened, sweetly happy.

The sled veered unexpectedly, he tried to right it, but she threw her weight the wrong way.

He landed in a heap, and she landed with a fierce thump on top of him.

"Amateur," he teased her, choking on snow and laughter.

"Crazy driver," she said, giving his chest an indignant push. Neither of them made any move to, well, move.

He looked up into the laughter of her eyes, the joy on her face and he let himself have it. He let himself have this moment.

Something inside of him let go: his need to protect himself, his need to be in control, his need to not ever be hurt again.

There was a part of him that had decided it would be *wrong* to be happy when his brother was dead. But suddenly, in a moment of illumination, it felt as if it would be more wrong not to be happy, not to grab these unexpected moments of delight and embrace them wholeheartedly.

It suddenly was very clear to him that what would be wrong, what would truly dishonor his brother, would be to not live fully, as fully as he could.

He looked into Lila's shining face and he could clearly see she had risen to the challenge of allowing her heart to be made braver. She was *welcoming* whatever was happening between them.

He let go of his own desire to run from it. If this little chit of a woman could be so brave, then he could be, too.

It was not the kind of bravery that reached into the burning car and pulled out a woman stuck behind the steering wheel. It was not the kind of bravery that went into a dark building with a gun drawn.

It was not the kind of bravery that walked up to a ramshackle house, arms up, rifle pointed out the window at him and said, "Come on, Phil, we've known each other all our lives. Put the rifle down and put the coffee on. We'll talk."

No, it was not that kind of bravery.

That kind of bravery had its place. It was real.

But it did not hold a candle to the kind of bravery that

was being asked of him now. To put his heart at risk. To say *yes* to the mystery of something bigger than he could control. Say yes to what was in the laughter of her eyes, and the way she had rested against his chest last night.

To say yes to life.

He wrapped his arms around her and flipped so that now she was on the bottom and he was on top of her. He straddled her tummy, taking most of his weight on his own knees, but still effectively pinning her. He took a little snow and sprinkled it in her face, and then down the V of delicate skin that showed above her jacket. She struggled and sputtered, and laughed and begged him to stop.

But he didn't. He held her down and then he touched his lips to each place where he had put the snow, took the icy droplets that had melted instantly off her skin.

She went very still beneath him, her eyes wide with discovery, hunger…and welcome. Then he stood up, tugged her up behind him.

Her eyes were locked on his. She licked her lips. She leaned toward him. He leaned toward her.

She stuck a mittful of snow down his pants, and then shrieking with laughter dashed away from him.

They played like young children in the snow, as if they were completely unburdened. They chased each other and buried each other in snow, ran away, got caught on purpose. They made snow angels, and tried riding that sled every way you could ride it: laying down, with her on top of him, her in front, her back against his chest. They even tried riding the sled standing up, as if it were a surfboard. They tumbled off it so often they had snow down their pants and their socks and their jackets. He was pretty sure he had snow in his belly button.

They tasted each other, quick kisses, flitting warmth in the cold. But each stolen kiss, each breathless moment, seemed to last longer than the one before it.

Despite that, and despite the cold of the day, things were heating up.

She was in his arms, nipping at his lips and his ears. "Let's stay here," she said. "Just one more day. The store is closed Mondays, too."

And he didn't work until tomorrow night. Last night it had seemed prudent to stay, a smarter decision than braving the storm and the night for the long walk out to the farm.

"If Marla or Paul have noticed you aren't home, they'll be worried."

"I'm a grown woman!" she said indignantly. "I don't have to check in with anyone."

But he understood that was temptation talking. That was the power of the *thing* in the air between them, because she would never let anyone worry about her, cause distress.

And he understood the temptation. He understood it perfectly. This world was real in a sense: the cold of the snow melting down his neck, the laughter ringing through the quiet meadow, a man's strength and ingenuity being the forces that became most appealing in a world where nothing else mattered. But he understood that this place was insulated from reality, too, like being on a desert island with her.

"Let's go back to the cabin," she said. "We'll make some hot chocolate, dry our clothes, then decide."

But he knew if they made it to that cabin door, hot chocolate was probably going to be the last thing on either of their minds.

He heard it in the distance, and hoped it was not what he thought it was, but he turned to the noise.

"What is that?" she asked of the high-pitched whine that grew louder, desecrating the absolute silence of these high places.

"Look." He pointed. The machines were now visible, flying toward them across the meadow, five of them spread out, leaving a huge V of disrupted snow in their wake.

"What is that?" Lila asked, staring at the approaching machines as if Martians were landing.

"Sleds," he said, and when he saw she didn't understand the slang, he clarified, "Snowmobiles."

"Just when you think you're all alone in the world," she muttered, and he shot her a look at the undisguised resentment in her voice.

"I hope they are not looking for us," he muttered, thinking out loud.

But naturally they were.

And the decision about whether to stay or go was, thankfully or regretfully, taken from his hands.

Just as every other single decision since he had met her had been taken from his hands.

The snowmobiles pulled up, a bunch of local guys, avid sledders. Except for one of them. Hutch probably had not been on a snowmobile since the last time he had used a chain saw. Still, he had been leading the way, and he was first off his machine, unstrapping the helmet, and trying bravely not to look stiff.

"Uncle Paul," Lila said when Hutch's face appeared from under the visor. "What are you doing here?"

But Tag already knew. "You shouldn't have called out rescue," he said, annoyed and embarrassed. "We're okay."

"The snow angels aren't distress signals?" Hutch asked dryly.

Tag actually felt a surge of heat move up his neck.

Hutch was regarding the sled tracks, and the crash sites of messy snow at the bottom of the runs with grave interest.

"You've been sledding?" Hutch finally asked, faintly incredulous.

Tag shrugged, took an interest in moving some snow around with the toes of his boots. "Mostly Lila," he mumbled, like a grade seven boy who'd been caught peeking in the girl's locker room.

"She hasn't seen much snow," he rushed on when Hutch didn't say anything. "That's why we didn't head home as soon as day broke." Did he sound defensive? He sounded defensive. "Of course we didn't know anyone would come looking for us."

"Marla called Lila's place last night to see how it had gone with the tree. She started worrying when she wasn't home. She tried right up until midnight. Then I called your place, thinking—" Hutch glared at him just to know what he had been thinking, and what he would have thought, too, if his assumption of an inappropriate liaison had been correct.

So much for Lila declaring herself an independent adult. Hutch, old-fashioned on points of honor, would make any man who took advantage of her pay and pay dearly.

"When you weren't there, I figured a vehicle problem. The guys were going for a ride anyway, first great snow of the year, so I invited myself along to have a look around. We found the truck up the branch road, followed your tracks. I figured you'd be here. One of you and Ethan's old haunts."

"Whose Ethan?" Lila, who had been silent until that point—who actually looked like she was seething at the interruption—asked.

And Brody realized he really had allowed himself to live

in an insulated world. He could see the look of relief on Hutch's face that she didn't know who Ethan was. His boss assumed it meant nothing had happened, that they barely knew each other at all.

Was that a fair assumption?

He had not told Lila about Ethan. Or Boo. He had kept all his secrets. The snowmobiles had probably arrived in the knick of time.

He turned to Lila. "You go with your uncle," he said. "I'll finish up here. Hutch, if you can get someone to pull the truck out for me, me and Boo will walk out later in the day."

"I'll stay, too," Lila announced.

Which earned her, and him, a quizzical look from her uncle.

"No," Brody said. "I want you to go."

Yesterday, that probably would have made her cry. But she was leaving the victim role far behind her, and now she just looked mad.

He didn't have to fix that. He really didn't. Especially not in front of her uncle, who had started to frown.

"I'll call you," he said, suddenly not caring what her uncle thought. "I'll be home by early afternoon. I'll drop the tree off at the park for you. What are you doing for supper tonight?"

"No plans," she said, beaming at him in a way that he thought women reserved for diamond rings.

A stupid thing, to drag this out, to subject himself to more temptation, to ask her that in front of Hutch, who was glowering at him.

But Tag recognized the truth. He was a strong man, yes, but not strong enough to leave what he had found here on the mountain.

Hope.

A tiny hope had found a crack in his heart and taken up residence there like a spark that could become a flame.

For the first time in six and a half years, Tag was aware he wanted to do more than breathe in and out. He wanted to live.

CHAPTER EIGHT

LILA sat in front of her computer, aware she was only going through the motions of writing. What she was *really* doing was waiting for the phone to ring.

After being stranded on a mountain in the wilderness overnight—easily the biggest adventure of her life—it would be understandable if she took the afternoon off, even with the deadline looming.

But rather than being exhausted, Lila found she'd been wired when she got down off the mountain. She'd been practically buzzing with enthusiasm and joy. She had burst into her house, and thought she would put all this energy to good use.

She now knew *exactly* where to start her book on having the perfect Christmas. Chapter One: Christmas Fun in the Snow!

There was so much material: making snow angels, and even though the snow had not been sticky enough for building things, she could talk about snowmen and snow forts and snow carvings. Why not snow carvings for the front yard at Christmas time?

Then there was riding snowmobiles, which had been an exhilarating experience, one she wished everyone could have, the powerful machine cutting ribbons through un-tracked snow, the chance to see areas of pristine wilderness that no one else would ever see.

Then there were other outdoor cold weather activities that she had not yet tried, but couldn't wait to experience firsthand: tobogganing, skiing, skating, snowboarding, snowshoeing, ice fishing. The list was endless.

But with all that material, her computer screen remained completely, infuriatingly blank. *Start with what it feels like to go down that hill,* she ordered herself. If she could capture the thrill of careening down a snow-covered hill on a sled, she would have a runaway bestseller on her hands. She knew it.

She was not sure she had ever had as much fun in her entire life as riding that sled down that hill, her arms wrapped around Brody Taggert. It was wild and exhilarating, and that was before the tumbles.

She had a sudden flash: the solid weight of his body on top of her, the look in his eyes, the heat of his lips melting snow off the hollow of her throat.

"A little too hot for a Christmas book," she muttered.

She began to wonder how much of the thrill had been because of the snow and the speed and the wind in her face, and how much had been because she had been with him.

And then doubt raced in. How could you start a book about having the perfect Christmas with a chapter on snow activities when anybody who had ever been around snow would know no instructions were required? Snow, plus spontaneity equaled more fun than a day at the amusement park. Way more fun.

Besides, wasn't it possible quite a bit of her audience would not have access to snow? She went to a map site, looked at a map of America and sighed. It would seem a large percentage of people in the U.S. did not live in places where there was snow. Other places would experience it so rarely that she could hardly make it a component in planning their perfect Christmas.

I'm never going to get this book done. Never.

Lila's eyes went to the clock on her screen. It was nearly four o'clock. Would Brody be down off the mountain yet? Was he thinking of her? If he was, did his heart do a funny flip-flop?

She surrendered to what she really wanted to do. She got up, went to her bedroom closet and tried to decide what she would wear to grab a bite to eat or *something* in Snow Mountain. With Brody Taggert.

How could she write about creating the perfect Christmas when Christmas suddenly didn't seem to matter to her at all? When she had become like a giddy teenage girl waiting for that special boy to phone, the one she had had a secret crush on all year, who had suddenly noticed she was alive?

"Lila," she implored herself. "Grow up. Be mature."

But she really didn't feel like being mature. Would mature people have given themselves over with such wild abandon to making snow angels? To recklessly riding that sled down the side of that mountain, whooping with joy and laughter?

No, she didn't want to be mature. It implied a certain stodginess, an addiction to safety and security that might make life predictable, but that could also make people dull and humorless and no fun at all to be around.

Even though Lila had changed her whole life—picked up and moved across the country, opened a new business—it hadn't really been an adventure because she had not changed herself. Or risked herself. It had all been outer stuff.

She wanted to be alive. And unafraid.

What would someone alive and unafraid wear out for a bite to eat with a man like Brody? She scanned her wardrobe, chose casual jeans, but a bold red silk shirt. She could make it daring—an outfit worthy of one who was unafraid—by leaving that top button undone. By wearing her black bra with it, the one that actually gave the illusion that she possessed cleavage.

She had turned to dig that bra, rarely worn, out of the back of her drawer, and it was then that the truth hit her like an avalanche. It hit her so squarely and so hard that she reeled back from her dresser, dropped her favorite silk blouse on the floor and sank onto the edge of her bed.

She understood why she had not been able to start her book, had not made one inch of headway into an instruction manual on creating the perfect Christmas.

Because she had fully intended to write a book based on trappings and trinkets, decorating, trees and activities. Like her move across the country, her book about Christmas had focused on all the outer stuff.

She'd missed the truth that was as old as Christmas itself. She had missed the very soul of what she was trying to write about. Christmas was about love.

It wasn't about the elves in Bandstand Park, it wasn't about finding the perfect tree, it wasn't about all that *stuff* she had filled her store with. She could see so clearly she had been trying to escape from the emptiness in her life by filling it with things and activities, accomplishments and accolades.

The emptiness had been there ever since fear had left her guarded, unwilling to risk anything that really mattered.

Shocked, Lila realized she had been trying desperately to create the illusion of Christmas without touching the heart of Christmas at all.

Lila suddenly felt as if she couldn't breathe as she slowly recognized what had come knocking on her door.

Love. An opportunity to love. To live more richly, to feel more deeply, to reconnect with a spirit she had lost.

She was falling in love with Brody Taggert.

And if she was courageous enough to embrace what she had been brought, she would experience gifts such as she had never known.

The phone rang.

With her heart beating hard with equal amounts of fear and exhilaration, Lila ran to pick it up.

Brody thought it had probably been a mistake to take Lila to the Sunday night smorgasbord at Chan's. Not because the food was not good, because it was. He was willing to place money that the almond chicken here was the best in the state. And Mama Chan had a special place in her heart for him. Whenever she saw him come in—even if it was smorg night—she hustled back to the kitchen and made him something special.

Tonight she set it down with flourish. "Fire bowl," she announced. "Szechuan-style prawn. Lover's special."

Which was exactly why it was a mistake to have brought Lila here. Because it was the only decent restaurant open Sunday night, and the whole town was here.

Unless he was mistaken, it would be going out over the wires before they had finished eating. He and Lila would be an item by tomorrow.

"Lover's special?" Lila whispered leaning toward him,

wide-eyed with mirth. Her hair was loose, catching the light, touching the slender place where her neck joined her shoulders.

She was wearing a red shirt that clung to her, and when she leaned forward like that he saw a place he wished he would have dribbled a little snow on when he had the chance.

"You won't think it's so funny when your aunt hears we were here."

"She'll hear?"

"Before you get home," he said dryly. "Half the town will be driving down your block tonight to see if my truck's parked there."

And tomorrow he'd be interrogated by her uncle, and be taking elbow shots at his ribs all day from the other guys; lots of winks, too.

"No!"

"Welcome to small-town life." He lifted his drink and toasted her with it.

"I feel pressured now," she said, and plucked one of the prawns out of the fire bowl with a chopstick. He, of course, had requested utensils.

"How do you get to know a person with the whole town watching?" she asked, her voice hushed.

"We could play with them," he suggested wickedly. "Give them something to talk about."

She got it right away. She leaned toward him even more. He felt a little bead of sweat break out on his brow. That bra was black.

She held out a prawn to him right on the end of her chopstick.

He could practically hear a pin drop in that restaurant

when he leaned forward, and nipped the prawn off the end of her chopstick with his teeth.

Only the funny thing was, when he looked in her eyes, dancing with merriment, and felt the warmth of her smile, it didn't feel as if they were pretending. It didn't feel as if they were giving the whole town something to talk about.

It felt exactly the way it had felt in that cabin, as if the world just contained the two of them, nothing else.

And that world smelled not of spicy Szechuan fire bowl prawns, but of wild strawberries.

He was brought back to the real world when Mr. And Mrs. Anderson stopped by, congratulated Lila on her work on Bandstand Park. They promised to be at the opening on the fifteenth of December, which Brody realized was only a few days away.

"Will you be at the opening?" she asked. And then with endearing shyness, "I'd like for you to come."

"Are there going to be cameras there?"

"Most likely."

"Good story," he said dryly. "I already wrote the ending for it, only they didn't capture it on camera that time. I don't want the fact I'm dating you to be some great feel-good story for the whole world."

"Are you dating me?" she asked, putting one of the prawns into her own mouth, which was at least as sexy as her feeding one to him.

"That's what *they* think," he hedged, nodding toward the other customers, most of whom were barely able to conceal their interest in the new couple, and many who weren't even trying.

"I don't care what they think. I want to know what you think. Is this our first date?"

The problem seemed to be that around her at least, he didn't think clearly at all. Because it was a first date? A first date implied a beginning. A desire to get to know each other. A possibility it was going to go to a second date, and further.

Further, where? he asked himself, and he thought of children laughing in the hayloft, and the way it had felt to spend the morning with her as if he was a young man, carefree, full of laughter and energy. And hope.

"Yeah," he said gruffly, "I guess it is. A first date."

"It doesn't feel like a first date," she said.

"That probably has something to do with sharing a bed together with a smelly dog," he said, his voice very low, the tables suddenly seeming way too close together in here.

"Whatever it is, I'm glad. I don't feel awkward. I just feel—"

He waited, aware he was holding his breath.

"Happy," she decided.

Happy. He could analyze that and decide it was way too much pressure to make another person happy. But that was the man he'd been yesterday. Today, he had hope.

"Yeah," he said. "Me, too." And then he stabbed a prawn with his unused chopstick and held it out to her. Laughing, she took it.

They fed each other every single prawn in that big bowl.

"You didn't tell me if you were coming to the grand re-opening of Santa's Workshop at Snow Mountain," she said when they were done. He was aware he'd never been so sorry to empty a bowl of prawns.

"It really means a lot to you?"

"Really."

"Okay. Call it a second date. But I'm warning you, I'm bringing a gun."

"Very *unjolly* of you," she said disapprovingly.

"It shoots marshmallows. I'm going to aim it right at Jade Flynn if she comes anywhere near me."

They looked across each other over the empty dishes.

"Want to feed the rumor mill?" she asked him finally. "I have a video at my place. A Christmas movie. It's supposed to be hilarious."

He contemplated how her choice was telling him what kind of girl she was. And he realized he wanted to be exactly the kind of guy who could go watch a movie like that, and hold her hand, and laugh and go slow. Kiss her good-night on her porch when the movie was over.

"I don't like Christmas movies," he said and watched her pop open her fortune cookie.

She read it out loud. "You will travel to places you have never been," she said, and then smiled. "I think I already have. Read yours."

"Much joy in soup."

"It doesn't say that."

He passed it to her.

She read it. "It does say that." And then she broke up laughing, and so did he, and he could not remember a day in a long, long time where he had laughed so much. It felt so good.

"I have other movies," she said.

There was that *thing* again: *emotion* ruling him, wanting whatever it was he saw in her eyes.

"Okay," he said gruffly. "Let's go to your place and watch a movie."

In her house, her TV was hidden in a big cabinet on the end of the wall. He sorted through her DVD collection while she went and put on a pot of coffee. He snatched a recent action movie from the pile, noticed it was unopened.

He tore off the wrapper and set up the DVD player, then he wandered around, sniffing her candles to see if any of them smelled like strawberries. They didn't and he found himself at her tree. She'd brought it in too early and it was dropping needles all over the floor. He had never seen decorations like the ones on it. It was hung with perhaps a hundred little red and green velvet stockings, fur trimmed, each holding a tiny plush puppy. Only the puppies weren't cute.

"They're called Ugly Puppies," she said from behind him. "I just love them. There's one there that looks like Boo."

There was, too. He touched it, smiled. All that she was, and she loved ugly dogs, too. He'd better be careful or he was going to think she was the ideal woman. Or maybe he already did.

He turned to her.

"Is something wrong?" she said, and came and touched his face. "Brody, what is it?"

"Nothing. Put the movie on."

"What did you pick?"

He showed her the action movie DVD.

She shuddered a little. "I don't feel like watching it anymore. Let's talk."

"The most dreaded words a man can ever hear," he said wryly, but took a place on the couch. She sat right beside him, so close her knee was touching his. She poured coffee, took a sip, set her cup down and regarded him intently.

"Why do you hate Christmas so much, Brody?"

"I told you. I get to see the ugly underbelly of the season."

"So does my uncle Paul. He loves Christmas."

Brody sighed and closed his eyes. He wanted to tell her. Suddenly if felt like a burden he could not carry alone for one more second.

"My brother died," he said slowly. "This will be my seventh Christmas without him. It's not the same anymore. It's never going to be the same again. I don't feel any joy at Christmas. None. Only the space where he used to be."

It did feel good to say that because he wanted her to know the entire truth about him, before this thing went any further.

"That's what you should know about me," he said gruffly, "There's a hole in me so large nothing can fill it. I think maybe that hole is where my heart is supposed to be."

Lila's hand covered his, warm, surprisingly strong for such a small woman.

"Tell me about him," she said, and somehow it didn't feel like a request, but an order. Something she knew he had to do, something she knew she had to hear.

"Maybe some other time."

She was silent, and then she said softly, "Is this the brother you mentioned once before? You said his name was Ethan."

"Yeah, Ethan." Even saying his brother's name to her did not feel the way he had thought it would. It felt not as if he was sharing his sadness with her, but as if he was sharing something sacred with her. His memories of Ethan suddenly felt like water pushing behind a dam—it felt as if something would break if he did not let the pressure off, did not let something out.

She was silent, watching him, and he remembered how it had felt when he had told her about the Murphy girl.

As if the burdens he carried were lighter.

He closed his eyes, and told himself to shut up, but he

didn't. The scent of wild strawberries was so strong around him. If he just said one thing, let a little out, maybe the pressure he felt would fade.

"I was older than him. Three years. It seems like nothing now, but growing up I was the big brother. I was the leader, the instigator, the protector, the teacher."

Her hand tightened on his. "You feel guilty that he died," she guessed softly.

"Oh, yeah."

"Don't you think you might feel better if you told me?"

Brody opened his eyes and looked into the startling compassion of hers. He saw things there: wisdom and depth. He saw he could trust her, and he knew that being able to trust someone in a hard world was a rare and amazing gift, one he was not strong enough to throw back at her.

He saw that maybe, just maybe, she could move him toward the place he had never been able to arrive at: forgiveness of himself.

"We were really close," he said, closing his eyes again, remembering. "But really different. Ethan was quiet and thoughtful, artistic. I liked action movies or comedy, he liked drama and foreign language films. I liked playing hockey in the street, he'd rather read a book under a tree. If we went into the mountains together, I brought a rifle and bullets, he brought a sketchpad and charcoals.

"I was never afraid of anything—reckless, even. He was more cautious. Not timid, but he thought things through. He was always aware of consequences, I never gave them a thought.

"At the funeral I knew people were thinking that. They couldn't believe which brother had died.

"We didn't even look the same. I was dark, big, brawny,

a born football player, he was fair and kind of scrawny, like a long-distance runner.

"But given how different we were, we always got along. Always." He paused, knowing this was the turning point, the place where he gave himself over to what he saw in Lila's eyes or ran away from it.

The decision not to run filled him with the oddest warmth. "Until Darla," he admitted. This was the part of the tragedy he kept a secret within himself, that he had shared with no one, carrying the burden of his guilt and his shame alone.

"Tell me about that." She said it with a certain fierceness, as if she could see his soul, as if she knew intuitively this was the part that he needed to unload.

He swore under his breath, fighting with himself, wanting to get up and go home, *needing* something else entirely. Needing to be free of it.

"Tell me," she repeated.

He felt the surrender happen within himself, a sudden relaxing of tension that he had carried for more than six years.

"I was twenty that summer, working as a logger, full of myself. Making good money, strong as an ox. I started dating this girl named Darla. Honestly, looking back, I don't know what the attraction was. I think she asked for—and got—breast implants when she graduated from high school. She was the town 'It' girl. Blond, gorgeous, empty-headed. Probably my type, at that time, exactly."

The strangest thing was happening: Brody Taggert had always thought surrender would feel like an unbearable weakness. Instead, as he spoke, he felt stronger, as if he had been pinned under an enormous rock, under water, and now the weight was being lifted.

"Darla," he said, "was not Ethan's type at all. But he fell hard for her. From the first time I brought her home to have a hamburger before we went to the drive-in, he was smitten. After a few weeks, he started acting like he had something to prove—shoving me, tackling me from behind, yelling at me, calling me names."

With every word he spoke, damning as they were, Brody could feel himself rising up through murkiness, struggling toward light.

"That must have been hard for you. To go from being his hero, to *that*."

"I don't know. The summer of my colossal self-centeredness. I was irritated by it. Annoyed.

"In retrospect, I can see Ethan was really, really mad. As if he'd figured out guys like me were going to get girls like that, and guys like him weren't.

"If he'd lived long enough he would have figured out that girls like that always turn out to be more headache than you could ever imagine, and that the kind of guys who went for them, like me, ended up yearning for those wholesome, smart kind of girls that you could actually enjoy being with. Though by then Mr. Macho has usually managed to burn most of his bridges, and a nice girl wouldn't give him the time of day."

Brody was silent, and had Lila said anything he probably wouldn't have gone on, but she was silent, her hand warm and still on his knee, and the sensation of rising toward the light, of being suddenly freed, increased.

"Things came to a head and Ethan and I had a fight. I mean not really a fight. He wanted to come with Darla and I to the swimming hole, I'm sure I had something in mind that I didn't want little brother around for. I'm sure I'd said no to him before, but that time he just started swinging at me. I was kind of trying to hold him off while he was throwing wilder and wilder punches, getting madder and madder because I was egging him on by laughing at him. We broke one of my mom's vases. She collected cranberry glass. That vase was from 1854 or something.

"Ethan was so upset. We hid the broken vase. We were like brothers again, not like combatants, trying to figure out what to do."

He actually smiled, remembering. "We figured wild strawberries. We went to that hunter's shack, the same one you and I were at, and spent the night, and the next morning we went looking.

"It was the way things used to be. Just me and him. A truce between us. We joked and talked. He was such a good guy. Deep. Connected to spirit. We stayed one more night, I think both of us were a bit scared to tell Mom about that vase, even with an offering of wild strawberries.

"Ethan drew some pictures that night by the lamplight. The next morning we brought Mom the meager offering of wild strawberries, and even though they were her favorite thing, she was madder than a wet hen about her vase.

"So we decided to clear out for the day. I hoped the truce would last, I *wanted* to be with him. The day before had been so great. So I invited him to come, after all, with Darla and I to the swimming hole above Snow Peak Falls."

He shuddered, fell silent.

"Tell me," she said, insistent, and suddenly it felt as if her voice, her eyes were the light he was struggling toward.

"It used to be my favorite place in the whole world. A pool of green water between two rock faces. Ethan and I used to jump off the rocks into the water.

"The pool was in a kind of back eddy, the river went by there pretty swiftly. That pool was the last tranquil water before rapids and then the falls.

"So, we were spending the day there. A perfect summer day. And then, in one split second, it all changed. Everything changed. Forever."

"What happened?" Lila whispered.

"A puppy was being washed down the fast part of the river, we could hear it whining and crying in pure terror, then we could see its head bobbing in and out of the water. Darla started having hysterics.

"And this is the part no one knows except me: I remember my brother looking at her, and then at me, and this look came over his face, like finally, he was going to show her who was the better man. By the time I made a grab for him, he was already gone. He leaped into the rapids after that puppy, and was swept away before I had even registered completely what had happened."

"Brody," she whispered, and the fact that his pain had become her pain was the thing that finally made his head break water, finally allowed him to feel as though he could breathe again. He was not alone. Not anymore.

"Ethan didn't have the physical strength to hold out in that water. Once it hits the rapids, it's boiling. You can actually hear the water picking up boulders, they rumble around under the surface. Hell, I don't think I had that kind of strength.

"But the difference was, I knew it. I knew it couldn't be done. The puppy was doomed. That was another difference between us. He was a born optimist. I was a born realist."

He stopped, took a deep breath. Even the air tasted different: pure.

"A search team found him the next day," Brody said, quietly. "They said he probably died instantly, his head hit a rock. He didn't suffer. I guess suffering is for the living."

"You've suffered ever since, haven't you?" she asked softly.

"Nobody it touched was ever the same. All my mom could think of was that she'd been mad at him. Our family started to disintegrate. I couldn't stop asking all these questions. Why hadn't I gone after the dog? I was the bigger one, the stronger one. Maybe I could have pulled it off. Why hadn't I been able to grab my brother before he did something so stupid, and for such a dumb reason?

"Ethan, my cautious brother, died trying to win a girl. My girl. I went on self-destruct. Your uncle pulled me from my own rapids just before I went over the falls.

"Your uncle. And Boo."

"Boo?"

He felt his throat tighten. "Boo. The puppy survived. No one knows how. They found her right beside my brother's body, snuggled into him, nearly dead herself. But she had enough life in her that she growled and tried to bite the guy who tried to take her away from Ethan. She was in a bad way, her legs were broken, that's why they never grew properly.

"People didn't understand why I took her. Hell, I didn't really understand it myself. But I did take her, and she *needed* things from me. She needed me to feed her, and hold her, and take her outside. I had to learn to be responsible, and to put her needs ahead of my own. That was a lifeline, that I had to think of one little thing besides myself and my hurt and my anger.

"One day, I had set a beer mug on the floor—I was drinking hard back then—and she got her head stuck inside it. And I heard myself laughing. When I thought I would never laugh again, I heard myself laughing.

"Pathetic as it might seem, that dog gave me something to live for. In a way, she forced me to be a man my brother might have been proud of."

He stopped the story short. He stopped it short of the words that would totally threaten his control, that could take away every gain sharing his tragedy with Lila had given him.

I might lose Boo now, too, and I don't know what I'll do when that link to my brother is gone.

No, he wasn't going to lose her. Look at how Boo had been the last few days, so happy, so full of energy, eating with such appetite.

He looked at Lila for the first time since he had started talking. She was crying, great, huge tears slithering down her cheeks.

He felt something clawing at his own throat, something smarting behind his eyes.

Her arms went around him, and she pulled his head onto her breast and stroked his hair, her voice a healing balm that melted over him.

Like Lila, Brody realized he had not felt safe for a long, long time. He walked in the awareness that a good life could turn bad in a blink.

But in her arms he was aware that the opposite was also true: that a sad life could become happy again. That a man could feel safe even in an unpredictable world.

With her arms around him, with her whispering words in his ear, with the delight of the day at the cabin so fresh in his mind, he became aware that he was very close to believing in a miracle.

And that miracle had a name. It's name was love.

But right now he was exhausted and drained, and though he wanted to stay, he knew where it would go, and he knew he didn't want it to go there as a reaction.

When he made love to Lila, it was going to be because they had both made a conscious decision that was right for them. It wasn't going to be an impulse.

Still, he left her reluctantly.

When he got into his own house, for the first time in six and a half years, he was greeted with total silence.

"Boo," he called.

But she did not come. No careening around the kitchen corner, tail wagging, tongue hanging, eyes adoring on his face.

And he knew right then, in this brand-new emptiness, that she was gone. He had dared to hope, he had gambled on a miracle and he had lost.

Brody Taggert went down on his knees, and felt the break of his heart.

It broke for all his losses.

And for the loss of that thing he had grabbed on to so briefly: hope, a sense of the miraculous.

So, there were no miracles after all. He did not want to love again. Or hope again. Or believe again. Not ever.

Those things could bring a powerful man to his knees. Those things could make a powerful man realize he had no real power at all.

Asking a man like him to hope, to believe, to love, was like asking a warrior to face the world without his weapons. To trust there was a place safe enough for a man to be unarmed.

And life was reminding him there wasn't. There was no place that safe. Not even the sanctuary he thought he had glimpsed, briefly and beautifully, in Lila's arms.

CHAPTER NINE

BRODY stood before his boss in Hutch's office. He'd been summoned at the end of his shift, and he was pretty sure there'd been a complaint, maybe more than one. He felt ice-cold inside, not mean, but indifferent to people whining about getting tickets so close to Christmas.

Somehow they wanted *him* to be responsible for the fact they were piling Christmas gifts so high they couldn't see out the back windows of their vehicles, for the fact they were rushing here and there in frantic bursts of pre-Christmas activity.

"If you don't want a ticket," he'd told Herb Waters, "try not speeding through the school zone."

Herb hadn't liked that.

But if Herb had complained, Hutch said nothing about it.

"Karl Jamison wants to retire," Hutch said. "He said he's getting married."

That penetrated the icy wall around Brody slightly. "Jamison is getting married? Who would marry him?"

"Apparently, Jeanie Harper would."

For a moment, Brody hurt. Jamison, rough-spoken, tough as nails, was willing to give love a chance? Jamison was willing to do what it took not to be lonely anymore? For a moment he wished it was him.

But only for a moment, and then he shrugged off that thought by thinking of that fresh mound of dirt in his backyard, Boo wrapped in her favorite blanket with her favorite toy, a neon-orange Frisbee, in the bottom of that cold, cold hole.

"And like everything Karl wants to do, he wants to do it yesterday. He told me by the end of February he's going to be on his honeymoon cruise on the Caribbean."

The warmth of being with somebody you loved in the tropics tried to touch him, but again Brody shrugged, physically, told himself he *loved* the cold and had no wish to escape it. Hutch seemed to be expecting a comment, but Brody said nothing.

"You got any ideas about who could replace him?"

The icy shield came down just a bit. He knew a guy who needed a chance, a lifeline, just as he had once needed one. "Mike Stevens would probably be a good bet," Brody said.

Hutch grinned at him. "Funny you should say that. That's exactly who I had in mind." He noticed Brody wasn't smiling back, and his brow furrowed.

"The phone's been ringing off the hook all day. I'm being accused of having the world's biggest Scrooge on the department. And not Karl, either."

Brody said nothing.

"What's wrong, son?" Hutch asked him, his voice uncharacteristically gentle.

Please don't call me that. I'm just barely holding it together as it is.

Sooner or later someone was going to notice the dog wasn't tagging along at his heel, shedding hairs all over the backseat of the police cruiser. Sooner or later he was going to have to say it.

It might as well be sooner. "Boo died," Brody said grimly.

Hutch's mouth dropped open. "No," he said, and then gruffly, "How?"

"She had cancer."

"Aw, hell, Brody." The chief's eyes were tearing over.

Brody steeled himself. A voice that was not his own, cold and hard, said, "She was just a dog."

Hutch looked angry. "She sure as hell wasn't just a dog. She was one of us. Maybe we never officially made her a K-9, because they probably would have made her go to police dog school or some damn fool thing for insurance purposes, but Brody, that dog was one of us."

That pesky warmth was trying to penetrate the ice again. Brody did not trust himself to speak.

"Brody you know, probably better than most, that life gives us hard things to deal with. Really hard. But what I want you to know is that you're always given what you need to deal with those things. Always. But you got to look, son. You got to have a heart open enough to recognize them when they come."

It was a rare piece of philosophy from Hutch. Brody knew what his boss was saying was true. Boo had come along right when he needed her most.

And now an angel waited to help him through this. If his heart was open. But he was not sure it was. Or could be. Or ever would be again.

When the lifeline was tossed to him this time, he was not sure he would grab it. Because the price of grabbing it was opening up a heart that felt just fine frozen solid, where nothing could touch it and nothing could hurt.

"You let me know if there's anything I can do, Brody."

"I will," Brody said, but he knew he wouldn't.

"And now, ladies and gentleman, Snow Mountain welcomes you to A Celebration of the Season."

Lila watched as the ladies from the Baptist Church choir filed into the darkened park and up the stairs of the freshly painted bandstand. They wore their new long red robes, and the only light in the park came from the candles they held. The crowds, people all the way from Spokane and Coeur d'Alene, were three deep against the white picket fence that surrounded the park.

She scanned the expectant audience. Still no Brody. She hadn't talked to him since that night at her place when he had told her about his brother, but he had said he would be here, and one thing about Brody Taggert was that he was a man you could count on.

She shivered just thinking of him, of the way she felt when he looked at her, of the way she felt when his lips were on the hollow of her throat.

The ladies opened with "O Christmas Tree," and as they sang, the tree that Lila and Brody had harvested blinked on blue light after blue light, until finally the star at the very top winked on, shining brilliantly.

They sang "Deck the Halls," and the rest of the lights in the trees and on the fences, around the bandstand itself, lit all at once, colorful beacons of cheer. The crowd broke into applause.

Next came "Rudolph the Red-Nosed Reindeer," and spotlights shone on each reindeer in turn: this one rearing, that one kicking up his heels, one moving his head, another nudging a sleigh, one pawing the ground impatiently.

Where was Brody? Even he, as cynical as he pretended to be about this, would have to be impressed with this wonderful choreography of sound and light.

As the choir sang "Santa Claus is Coming to Town" all the elves lit up and began to move: this one wrapping a present, that one hammering a toy, this one filling boxes, that one picking his nose. The crowd howled with laughter, and the elf's eyes widened at them and then he smiled bashfully.

And then the park was plunged into darkness again, and only candles lit it. A solo voice began to sing "Silent Night," and then the crowd was joining in singing, too, the park and the street reverberating with the special miracle of that song.

When it was done, the lights came back on all at once to the thunderous applause of the audience. The choir left the bandstand stage, and it was empty save for a huge throne.

And then a child's high-pitched voice. "But where is Santa?"

It couldn't have been more perfect if there had been a script, which there wasn't. A hush went over the crowd. And then from behind the bandstand, waving and carrying a sack of toys, came a real live Santa.

Even though Brody had claimed there was no such thing, surely if there was it would look exactly like Karl Jamison did in this moment.

Brody was going to regret missing this for the rest of his life, Lila thought, casting another glance around for him. Even in this crowd she knew he would stand out. But he simply wasn't there.

"Hello, children," Karl roared. "Ho, ho, ho."

He was so fierce in his greeting that a child in the front row whimpered. But the older children were not the least intimidated, and yelled with excitement.

Jamison took his place on the throne in the middle of the bandstand and Jeanie Harper opened the gate to the red carpeted sidewalk that led right to his lap. Children, giddy with excitement, surged forward and lined up for their chance to tell Santa all their secrets and dreams, and wishes and hopes.

"Lila Grainger," Jade Flynn said to her, "you must be very proud of your town tonight."

Lila fixed a smile on her face as the TV lights were turned on her, but she was aware she did not feel like smiling.

Where was Brody? He had said he would be here. Maybe not quite promised, but she had always taken him completely as a man who could be counted on to do exactly as he said every single time.

Maybe Brody was watching from somewhere, waiting for the TV crew to disappear.

Lila forced herself to focus on Jade, talked about the community spirit that had come together for the park.

She concluded, "And I need to give special thanks to the Snow Mountain Police Department who provided us with Santa, and especially to Officer Brody Taggert for finding that beautiful Christmas tree. I also want to thank Town Council and all the people who sent donations and cards and letters so that Snow Mountain did not have to cancel Christmas."

Maybe that would stop Brody from getting the hate mail, not that, at this precise moment, Lila felt he deserved her intervention. And not that he had ever appreciated it in the past.

Jade asked her a few more questions, then wrapped it up. It was wrong to be disappointed that a marshmallow bullet had not zoomed in out of the darkness and knocked that silly red angora beret right off Jade's head.

But as the TV van pulled away there was still no sign of Brody. Lila went over to the hot chocolate stand and took her turn dispensing hot drinks to the crowd, reminding them Snow Mountain's stores would be open late tonight for their Christmas shopping convenience.

It seemed like hours later that the last child had sat on Santa's knee, the crowds around the park had dispersed to the downtown area.

Still, no Brody.

Lila decided to wait there just a little longer. She sat on a bench, pulled her coat tight around herself and tried to enjoy the light display, the antics of the repaired elves and reindeer. Later tonight, the city crew would bring the mechanized Santa in, and put him on that throne where Jamison had sat.

Something moved in the darkness, and she turned to look, her heart beating with hope. But it was her aunt who came and sat beside her.

"It's beautiful, Lila, better than ever. I missed it all more than I thought. Main Street just didn't seem right without it. Neither did Snow Mountain."

"Thanks." She hesitated and then said, "Do you know if Brody got called in to work unexpectedly?"

It became obvious her aunt was holding back tears.

"Is he okay?" she asked, stunned by the panic she felt, as if her world would never be the same if Brody Taggert was not in it.

Marla blinked back tears. "Boo died, Lila."

"Boo?" She felt the shock of it in the pit of her stomach. A fist closed around her heart. "Oh, no," she whispered. "What happened?"

"Brody told Paul she had cancer."

Lila felt the shock of that, too. Why hadn't Brody said something?

"Is Brody okay?" she asked.

Marla looked sad. "Probably not."

Lila got up off the bench. "I need to be with him. He needs someone to be with him."

Her aunt stayed her with a touch on Lila's arm. "Maybe you should give him some time, Lila. I don't think he wants to be with anyone right now. He won't want sympathy. He hates it."

Her aunt had been there when Brody had dealt with another tragedy. She would probably know. But still, in her heart, Lila thought, broken, *even me?* But if he had wanted her to go to him, wouldn't he have called her? Wouldn't he have told her Boo was ill?

A first date did not exactly mean their stars were joined.

But the things he had shared with her had made it feel as if he had trusted her, as if he knew his heart would be safe with her. If that was true, why hadn't he called?

Still, she took a miss on visiting the stores that were still open and went straight home to call him. His answering machine picked up after the second ring.

"Tag. Leave a message."

"Brody, it's Lila. I just heard about Boo. I'm so sorry. I didn't know her very long, but—" her voice cracked "—long enough to love her. Please call me."

But he didn't, and somehow even with Bandstand Park lit up so bright that its glow could be seen from a satellite, it felt as if her Christmas was going to be wrapped in darkness.

It was too soon to love him; rationally she knew that and accepted that. Their relationship had not deepened to a point where he wanted to share his sorrow with her, where he would invite her into his weakest moments, when he would surrender to leaning on her.

But even though she knew that rationally, her heart would not accept it as true. Her heart ached for him, and for his loneliness. Her heart waited for him to call, to invite her back into his world.

Her book on creating a perfect Christmas was now officially on hold. She couldn't give away something she did not have, and she did not have a joyous spirit.

It was two days before Christmas. Brody was alone, and he told himself that was exactly what he wanted and deserved.

He'd listened to Lila's message at least a dozen times, finding solace in her voice, *wanting* to call her, and yet not wanting her to see him like this.

Broken up over a dog, for God's sake. It had been over a week, and he was not mending, not healing, not moving on. Maybe *frozen* was the safest way to be, but it wasn't what he wanted to give Lila. He wasn't sure he had what he wanted to give her, and what she deserved.

What she deserved was a man with the ability to trust in life, a warrior who could protect her and be strong, yes, but who had the ability to put away the armor.

His house suddenly depressed him, even with the great television set. He hated the television offerings this close to Christmas, and he hated days with no football or hockey games scheduled.

After flipping through his three hundred channel options several thousand times, he finally threw down the channel changer in disgust. After a while, he went into the basement and pulled out a box.

Not quite sure what had drawn him here, he opened it.

Ethan's sketches. One by one, he went through them. Why not? He was depressed anyway.

But as he looked through the sketches, his depression did not deepen, it lessened. The ice seemed to fall a bit more from his heart with each sketch he looked at.

Somehow Ethan had captured not just the essence of their childhood—swimming holes and tire swings, the old barn at dusk, laundry on the line, two boys sitting on a rickety wharf, bare feet and fishing poles in the water—but the essence of *them*.

Carefree days, that had been so pure, so filled with the careless love that one brother had for another, so filled with their bond, a bond Brody had not fully recognized until it had been broken.

And then, nearing the bottom of the box, Brody found a drawing his brother had done of Darla. He started to go right by it, with no more than a glance, just as he went right by her with no more than a glance every time she drove by him with her vanload of kids.

But something stopped him, and he looked at the picture more carefully.

Just as his brother had captured the essence of brothers when he drew pictures of them both, so had he captured Darla's.

Brody had always seen Darla as his *ideal* girl at that time in his life—too much makeup and too little clothing, just as eager as him to get into the backseat of his car.

But Ethan had captured her looking off into the distance, something wistful and innocent in her face.

He suddenly realized he had completely misunderstood Ethan's anger at him that summer. Completely.

Ethan had seen who Darla really was, a girl, not quite

the woman she was determined to convince the world she was. In her eyes, in that sketch, were the dreams of the children she now hauled to hockey and soccer. Darla had wanted a life Brody had no intention of giving her and Ethan, with his uncanny ability to see people, had recognized that.

Ethan had seen his brother was completely unworthy of her. Ethan had known Brody would never see Darla the way he had shown her in this drawing. No, Brody had seen her only through his own self-serving lens: willing, eager to please in all the right ways, he had unabashedly *used* her. He had practically swaggered with his own arrogance that summer, so full of himself and testosterone and the self-centered restlessness of young men.

Unwillingly, Brody revisited those final moments on the river, and with this drawing in his hand, he saw it all differently. It was not that Ethan had been trying to *prove* who had been the better man.

Ethan *had* been the better man. He had seen Darla's innocence and wanted to protect it, and her, from the harsh reality of what was going to happen next if someone didn't do something. One quick glance at his brother had confirmed Brody sure as hell wasn't going to jump in that water for a measly little puppy.

Of course, in the end, Ethan had not accomplished what he wanted. Nowhere close. But there was pure *honor* in a man who would try to protect a young woman from a horrible experience, even if it put his own life at risk.

And it had taken that tragedy to humble Brody, to remove the arrogance from him, to take him to a place where he had realized slowly, and often painfully, the world was not there to serve him. He was there to serve the world.

Not that he was great at it. Or perfect. But at least today he was a man who could see the tragic beauty of a child who would steal a game for her brother.

Because he knew what it was to love a brother.

And at least today, he knew the value of a good dog.

At least today, he could look at someone like Lila Grainger, and *see* her.

But deserve her? He wasn't sure about that.

He set the drawing of Darla back in the box, gently, and took out the last two pieces of paper.

The last two drawings were spectacular.

One was a charcoal sketch of the hunter's cabin, and somehow, though Ethan showed only the building, you could hear the laughter coming from behind those walls, sense how many boys had become men in this place, sense how it had provided a place away, a place to be, a place to understand all that really mattered.

And the last drawing in the box was a wild strawberry plant, the only one of Ethan's drawings Brody had ever seen colored.

The strawberry hung beneath the broad, serrated edges of the plant's leaves, so bright red and shiny Brody could almost taste it. And he could certainly smell it.

He looked again at the picture of the cabin, thought of all the wood he had left there and the credo Ethan had lived by.

He put the rest of the pictures back in the box, but kept those last two out. He would have the strawberry picture framed to give to his mother when he flew down to see her and his dad in January.

In the emptiness of his house, he said out loud, "You left more than you took."

He didn't know if he was talking to Ethan or Boo or

maybe to both of them. He only knew that even though he was absolutely alone he didn't feel alone at all.

He felt as if he had been heard.

And he felt as if, finally, it was his turn. To leave more than he took. He only had one day left, and a lot to do, especially since he would be battling all those other self-centered guys who treated Christmas as if it was an inconvenience, who left all the things they had to do until the last minute.

Still, even with that, Brody was aware of feeling the first little tickle of happiness he had felt since Boo had gone. The first sense that maybe, just maybe, he was going to be all right after all.

Christmas Eve. The worst one of her life, Lila decided morosely. Oh, the store had done exceedingly well, and her Internet business had increased sales over last year by fifty-three percent.

People were coming in all the time to thank her for saving Christmas in Snow Mountain, and she was still answering mail generated by the news story Jade Flynn had done of the opening of Santa's Workshop at Bandstand Park.

But the book, *How to Have a Perfect Christmas,* was a complete loss. She had missed her deadline, and she did not really see the point in asking for more time.

She really had nothing to say on the topic of how to have a perfect Christmas.

Because really, hers *looked* perfect. Her house decorated beautifully, her business a success, the Santa's Workshop display not only saved, but attracting traffic and visitors to Snow Mountain from all over Washington and Idaho.

But her Christmas just didn't *feel* right.

She longed for Brody. She longed to crash through his silence, his rejection of her caring, and be there for him anyway, whether he liked it or not. Unfortunately she knew better than anyone what that felt like. She knew what it felt like to be the object of unwanted attention and affection. She could not chase Brody like some crazed stalker, ignore the boundaries he had set as if she knew better than he did what was good for him.

Just as Christmas was about what you could give, about the spirit rather than the trinkets and lights and presents, so was love.

It wasn't all about hearts beating fast, and heated looks, what to wear. It wasn't all about those fireworks elements that were so breathtaking. It wasn't like a storybook where everything just unfolded perfectly and everyone lived happily ever after.

Love was asking her to go deeper, to dig deeper within herself. Love was asking her to respect him, not to meet her own needs through him, but to trust that he knew what was best for himself.

"Though he obviously doesn't," she said out loud.

Brody wasn't going to come to her. It was not his nature.

She stood before her glorious tree, and felt her eyes mist over. "I want him to be happy," she whispered. "I wish him happiness even if that means he doesn't choose me."

There it was. The spirit of Christmas, and indeed the spirit of love.

Not about trinkets and lights, not about stolen kisses and heated looks: about a selflessness of spirit.

She went to her tree and looked at the Ugly Puppy ornament that looked so much like Boo. She removed it from the tree, and slipped it into her sweater pocket.

She would give it to her uncle Paul to give to Brody, just so he knew she was thinking of him, she wished him well. She would put her prayer for his well-being and happiness into it, and then she would let go.

Touching that ornament in her pocket, worth under four dollars, it felt as if it would be the purest gift she had ever given. A gift that asked nothing in return, that only gave.

There was an unexpected knock at her front door, and she noticed, with a small smile, that she did not startle. And that she did not feel afraid. She went and opened the door without looking out the peephole first.

And blinked back tears at how swiftly she had been rewarded for her awkward attempt at selfless love.

Because he stood there, Brody, gazing at her with a look in his eyes that she could only have dreamed of.

The look of a man who had been away to wars, and had found his way home through the sheer bravery of his heart.

"Hi," she said softly, the woman who had waited, and known, and done her best to trust that he would know what his own heart needed.

She reached out and touched his cheek with her fingertips, tenderly, looked deep into his eyes. "I'm so sorry about Boo."

He did not flinch or try to back away from her touch. He said, his voice hoarse, "I know, Lila. Thank you."

"Are you coming in?"

"I was hoping you'd come out. I want to show you something."

He waited while she pulled on her boots and jacket, and then he took her to his truck.

He opened the door, pulled out a package, handed it to her.

It was a tiny gift bag, silver, with a white bow on it. She

peeked in and saw a bottle of *Effervescence,* the scent this year, unbelievably expensive in Lila's mind.

She felt a surge of disappointment. She couldn't even wear scent. Just as she was trying to think of a way to thank him for the gift she didn't want, that said he had not listened to her as completely as she had thought he had, that didn't express what she wanted their relationship to be *at all,* he spoke, unusually uncertain for Brody.

"I need your advice. The lady at the drugstore said that a young girl would love this. What do you think? For a fifteen-year-old?"

Just when she thought she had got it, when she had accepted love wasn't all about her, she got this reminder what love was really about after all.

"Would that be for a fifteen-year-old girl who took something that didn't belong to her? A little girl who really loves her brother?" she asked softly.

He ducked his head, looked wildly uncomfortable. "Yeah."

"It's perfect," Lila told him, handing him back the bag.

"Are you sure?" he asked, frowning.

"Positive." How could you love a person as much as she loved Brody Taggert in this moment without shattering into a million pieces of dazzling light?

"Oh, good. I just thought I'd get your opinion. I trust your opinion."

"What's that?" she asked as he put the small silver bag beside another parcel on his truck seat. The other parcel, clumsily wrapped, was the exact size and shape of a video game.

"Ah, nothing."

The tears began to gather in her eyes as she recognized *him.* Saw exactly who Brody Taggert was. It was not what he showed people, not even what he wanted people to believe about him, but it was who he was.

Just as she had known all along, from the first moment she had set eyes on him, the world was a better place because he was in it, whether he knew it or not. And he so obviously didn't.

"Tower of the Rebels?" she asked him softly.

He shifted uneasily from foot to foot, didn't answer.

"Can I come with you? To deliver them?" Softly, "Santa?"

He snorted. "I'm not Santa, and I'm not good company right now."

"I know that," she said. "You don't have to be. You don't have to say a single word to me, Brody Taggert. I already know who you are."

And suddenly Lila Grainger knew exactly how you had a perfect Christmas. You found someone who needed your love and your gifts, and you gave them.

You gave them with no expectation of return, with not one single thought about what was in it for you.

You gave your love just the way Brody had given those gifts. Letting the truth of the universe pass through you, taking no credit at all.

And that, she thought with a sigh, was how to have a perfect Christmas.

Brody Taggert wasn't sure he should have brought Lila here. Clements Street didn't exactly fit with her storybook fantasies of Christmas.

Close to downtown, the houses were old, but not the lovingly restored kind of old. The falling-down kind of old.

He stopped his truck in front of a house with more tar paper than shingle showing on the side. The porch was leaning. A sign, brass and classy, as if in defiance of the poorness of the house, hung at the end of the walkway. *The Murphys.*

He took the gifts and went up the walk, slid open the outer door quietly, set the packages inside and came back down the walk without ringing the doorbell.

"That was one of the nicest things I've ever seen a person do, Brody Taggert," she said when he got back in the truck.

"Probably just plain dumb," he said. "You can't begin to make a dent in the sadness at this time of year."

He put the truck in gear and drove away. Somehow, without really intending to, he ended up at Bandstand Park. He turned off the engine.

"It looks great," he said, and then admitted, "I missed it. The town didn't *feel* right without it. It makes me think maybe you can put a dent in the sadness, after all. Anybody can come here and bring their kids here. It's free. It feels happy."

"Next year we'll make it even better," she vowed. "We'll make the tree a Secret Santa tree. We'll put a tag on it for every child in this town who needs a gift."

"I have something for you," he said, amazed by how shy, how uncertain he suddenly felt. "It isn't much. And I'm no gift wrapper."

In fact he'd used up the one sheet of Christmas paper he'd been able to unearth on *Tower of the Rebels,* so he'd wrapped this in brown paper. With a touch that he thought at the time had been decorative, but now just looked plain stupid, he'd tied it with a piece of hemp twine.

He handed her his gift.

She opened it carefully, as if she was unwrapping china, no ripping and tearing for her.

Inside that package was a framed charcoal drawing of the cabin where she and Brody had spent the night.

"It's beautiful," she breathed. "I can't believe how accurately it's captured the soul of that little sanctuary deep in the wilderness."

She looked at the signature on the drawing.

"Ethan," she said quietly, and even though he knew she had just read the name as it was signed, it sounded oddly and beautifully like a greeting.

And he understood, suddenly, what he was doing. Inviting her into a life, a life that held a past and a present, held light and darkness, held joy and sorrow. He was inviting her into a life where he'd had to fight and fight hard to stay strong, into a life where he had just realized sometimes being strong meant laying down the weapons, taking off the armor.

Sometimes, what took the most strength of all was to be vulnerable to another human being. To stop fighting. To surrender.

To say to love, *you have wounded me, but I am prepared to be wounded again. For to live without you is to live in a place so lonely and so empty it makes life a living hell.*

The cab of his truck became so filled with the scent of wild strawberries that he thought he might weep.

She looked him full in the face, and he realized she did know who he was.

He saw in her eyes that she knew him. That he would never be able to hide one thing from her, not even his weakness, not even his sorrow. He knew that if he ever lost himself, he would just be able to look in her eyes and find who he was all over again.

Instead of the intensity of the love shining from her feeling frightening, it felt good, like a man who had been lost in a storm suddenly sighting lights, and following them, drawing closer and closer to the place he could rest, the place where he could be home.

With the scent of wild strawberries all around him, he got it.

He got what the chief had been trying to tell him.

Boo, with her uncanny sixth sense, had known from the first moment she had seen Lila and begun to hum happily.

His dog had recognized in that way that dogs do, that love was there, and that the one she was leaving behind would be okay as long as love was there.

His dog, who had been sent to him, when he wanted her least and needed her most.

Life *was* hard. Love *was* hard. It made no promises, it offered no guarantees, it dished up its fair share of sorrow.

What had Hutch said? A man was always given what he needed. Always.

Tag slid Lila a look, and his heart sighed.

She pressed something into his hand, and he looked down to see the Christmas ornament that had hung on her tree that looked like Boo. He blinked hard, then hung it on his mirror, Boo watching over them.

He got it. The scent of wild strawberries. He got it. His brother, somehow, someway, letting him know. *Go on. Live.*

Not that Brody believed in that kind of thing.

But if he ever was going to, it would be in the cab of his truck as church bells struck midnight to remind the world it could only truly be changed by one thing.

Love.

Everything else—power, money, success, possessions, life itself, everything else—would come and go.

But love would remain.

It would remain and forever change the hearts of the

people it had touched. His brother was gone, but the lessons his brother had taught him would remain, and would go on through him.

"You know," he said to Lila, softly looking out over the park, "at my brother's funeral the minister said all love leads to loss. And for the longest time I believed that was true.

"But now I see something different. You might lose the person, but not the gift they've given you."

He thought of Ethan, and all the years they had shared. He thought of Ethan's wonderful, generous spirit, his sense of honor, the way he saw the world, how he saw straight past people's trapping and right to their souls. And he understood. He had been living in those moments of death, rather than appreciating all that Ethan had been while he lived.

He was ready, now, to make the next step.

"Ethan would want me to live again. Fully. He'd especially want me to love again." And then added softly, "Fully."

Lila sighed beside him, and he knew she understood.

He embraced the gift that was being offered to him. The true gift, the only real gift of the season of miracles.

"Lila," he said, "come on over here, squish right up beside me."

She did, eagerly, as if she had been waiting all her life to show him who he really was.

He put his arm around her, kissed her, drank in her sweetness and the absolute truth about himself.

And then he put the truck in gear and drove toward a future that held the laughter of children in haylofts. It was a future that shone like a star worth following, if a man had the strength and the faith to believe in what he would find at the end of it.

He heard himself saying words he had thought he would never say again.

"Lila, I love you. Fully." His voice was hoarse with emotion, but somehow along the road of this incredible journey he had embarked on, he had realized emotion was not the enemy. Not at all. Saying those words filled him, to the top, and then, when she said them back, his sense of well-being brimmed over, a well of liquid gold within him.

EPILOGUE

"COLBY ETHAN TAGGERT," Lila called, "you come down from that hayloft right now."

Silence.

"I mean it."

Chubby little legs appeared at the trap door, and Lila held her breath as her three-year-old son's legs hung suspended for a moment, but then, mercifully, touched the top ladder rungs.

She had just turned her back on him for a blink while she tried to find the toboggan that they were going to need when Brody got home, and Colby loved that hayloft unreasonably. She often heard him chattering away up there to his imaginary buddy.

Colby came down that ladder like a little monkey, dropped at her feet, looked at her with wide-eyed innocence, as if she had not told him a thousand times not to go up there unsupervised.

Did he have to be so like his father? His dark hair was tousled and woven through with hay, his eyes, green and gold and brown, danced with enough warmth to melt a rock. Her son was fearless, charming, devil-may-care, irrepressible. And he was only three! What would he be like at fourteen?

"Kitties up there, Mommy."

"Really?"

"Come see," he pleaded. "Please?"

She looked at the ladder, rested a hand on the enormous belly that meant she wasn't going to be joining the guys for any sledding anytime soon, sighed and gave in. At the top of the ladder, puffing, she paused, and let her eyes adjust to the light. Sure enough, playing in the hay of the loft were three exuberant kittens, a black, an orange and a calico.

She forgot the toboggan totally, found a piece of string and she and Colby played with the kittens until the rafters rang with their laughter.

That's what Brody heard, as soon as he entered the barn.

Laughter, as sweet as mountain brook water, washed over him, filled him with relief and peace.

He'd felt a moment's worry when he'd gone in the house after his shift to find it empty. His first thought had been that the baby had come, but then he remembered Lila had said she was going to try to find the toboggan so Brody could try to diffuse some of his son's frantic pre-Christmas energy.

He climbed the ladder quietly, so he could watch them for a moment or two undetected.

Sure enough, they did not see him right away, and he felt his heart expand when he saw Lila laughing at that calico kitten. How was it possible that she could seem more beautiful to him with each passing day? How was it possible that love had no limit, that a man could love more and more and more, endlessly?

Colby spotted him, whooped and tumbled across the loft

toward him. Brody braced himself so that his sturdy son's enthusiastic greeting wouldn't knock him right off the ladder.

"Daddy!" Colby Ethan cried, and leaped into his arms.

Was there any word in the world that made a man feel the way that one did? Ten feet tall and bulletproof?

And soon, another babe would be born. If the doctor was right, on Christmas Day.

Ethan smiled at Lila, and remembered once, it seemed like a long time ago, and a different man completely, he had not liked Christmas.

But now, with his son chattering daily about Santa Claus, and his daughter about to arrive like a special delivery gift just for him, he could barely remember the way it had once been.

Once, a preacher had said the words, *All love leads to loss.*

But now Ethan understood preachers did not know everything, and that one in particular had known less than most.

All love left a mark on the world that made it a better place than it had been before.

This thing inside him as he hugged his son to his chest could never lead to loss. It was the gift that would shape his children, so that someday they would give their gifts to the world. Love didn't lead to loss. Not ever.

"How's the world's bestselling author?" he said, crossing the hayloft with Colby riding in his arm. He sat down in the hay beside her, in no hurry to go anywhere. Home was where she was.

She leaned into him and kissed him right on the mouth.

"Yuck," Colby said.

They both laughed, and then talked about the little things that made up a life: the old farmhouse being freshened up for the arrival of Brody's parents; a postcard from

Jeanie and Karl Jamison that showed Santa's sleigh being pulled by "six white boomers" in Australia; Amanda Murphy, now twenty, and managing Miss L. Toe as if she had been born to it, in the throes of her first love; Mike Stevens flushing the *Be patient, I'm new here* badge down the toilet and flooding the whole police station.

Ordinary moments, ordinary people, ordinary lives.

But everything, especially at this time of year, seeming extraordinary, fused with a light that only a man who had walked in darkness so fully could appreciate.

Brody Taggert looked at his wife's face, felt the warmth of his son nestled in his arms, watched the kittens play and ever so fleetingly felt the whisper of a presence there with them in the hayloft.

Ethan. Love. Something so big and so good it could not be named. But it could be felt, clean through to a man's soul.

He lifted his face to it, closed his eyes and let the pure glory of the moment hold them all.

"You look so happy," Lila whispered, and her fingertips touched his face.

"Well," he said, with a smile, and kissed her fingertips, "You know how I get around Christmastime."

* * * * *

UNDER THE
BOSS'S MISTLETOE

BY
JESSICA HART

Jessica Hart was born in West Africa, and has suffered from itchy feet ever since, traveling and working around the world in a wide variety of interesting but very lowly jobs. All of them have provided inspiration on which to draw when it comes to the settings and plots of her stories. Now she lives a rather more settled existence in York, where she has been able to pursue her interest in history, although she still yearns sometimes for wider horizons. If you'd like to know more about Jessica, visit her website at www.jessicahart.co.uk.

PROLOGUE

'I WANT a word with you!'

Cassie almost fell down the steps in her hurry to catch Jake before he zoomed off like the coward he was. The stumble did nothing to improve her temper as she stormed over to where he had just got onto his motorbike.

He had been about to put on his helmet, but he paused at the sound of her voice. In his battered leathers, he looked as dark and mean as the machine he sat astride. There was a danger-ous edge to Jake Trevelyan that Cassie normally found deeply unnerving, but today she was too angry to be intimidated.

'You broke Rupert's nose!' she said furiously.

Jake observed her approach through narrowed eyes. The estate manager's ungainly daughter had a wild mane of curls, a round, quirky face and a mouth that showed promise of an interesting woman to come. Right now, though, she was still only seventeen, and reminded him of an exuberant puppy about to fall over its paws.

Not such a friendly puppy today, he observed. The nor-mally dreamy brown eyes were flashing with temper. It wasn't too hard to guess what had her all riled up; she must have just been to see her precious Rupert.

'Not quite such a pretty boy today, is he?' he grinned.

Cassie's fists clenched. 'I'd like to break *your* nose,' she said and Jake laughed mockingly.

'Have a go,' he offered.

'And give you the excuse to beat me up as well? I don't think so.'

'I didn't beat Rupert up,' said Jake dismissively. 'Is that what he told you?'

'I've just seen him. He looks *awful*.'

Cassie heard the crack in her voice and pressed her lips together in a fierce, straight line before she could humiliate herself utterly by bursting into tears.

She had been so happy, she had had to keep pinching herself. For as long as she could remember she had dreamed of Rupert, and now he was hers—or he had been. It was only three days since the ball, and he was in a vicious temper, which he'd taken out on her. It was all spoilt now.

And it was all Jake Trevelyan's fault.

'He's going to bring assault charges against you,' she told Jake, hoping to shock him, but he only looked contemptuous.

'So Sir Ian has just been telling me.'

Cassie had never understood why Sir Ian had so much time for a thug like Jake, especially now that he had beaten up his own nephew!

The Trevelyans were notorious in Portrevick for their shady dealings, and the only member of the family who had ever appeared to hold down a job at all was Jake's mother, who had cleaned for Sir Ian until her untimely death a couple of years ago. Jake himself had long had a reputation as a troublemaker. He was four years older than Cassie, and she couldn't remember a time when his dark, surly presence hadn't made him the kind of boy you crossed the road to avoid.

It was a pity she hadn't remembered that at the Allantide Ball.

Now Cassie glared at him, astonished by her own bravery. 'But then, I suppose the thought of prison wouldn't bother you,' she said. 'It's something of a family tradition, isn't it?'

Something unpleasant flared in Jake's eyes, and she took an involuntary step backwards, wondering a little too late whether she might have gone too far. There was a suppressed anger about him that should have warned her not to provoke him. She wouldn't put it past him to take out all that simmering resentment on her the way he so clearly had on Rupert, but in the end he only looked at her with dislike.

'What do you want, Miss Not-So-Goody Two Shoes?'

Cassie took a deep breath. 'I want to know why you hit Rupert.'

'Why does it matter?'

'Rupert said it was over me.' She bit her lip. 'He wouldn't tell me exactly what.'

Jake laughed shortly. 'No, I bet he wouldn't!'

'Was it…was it because of what happened at the Allantide Ball?'

'When you offered yourself to me on a plate?' he said, and her face flamed.

'I was just talking,' she protested, although she knew she had been doing more than that.

'You don't wear a dress like that just to *talk*,' said Jake.

Cassie's cheeks were as scarlet as the dress she had bought as part of a desperate strategy to convince Rupert that she had grown up.

Her parents had been aghast when they had seen it, and Cassie herself had been half-horrified, half-thrilled by how it had made her look. The colour was lovely—a deep, rich red— but it was made of cheap Lycra that had clung embarrassingly to every curve. Cut daringly short, it had such a low neckline that Cassie had had to keep tugging at it to stop herself spilling out. She cringed to think how fat and tarty she must have looked next to all those cool, skinny blondes dressed in black.

On the other hand, it had worked.

Rupert had definitely noticed her when she'd arrived, and that had given her the confidence to put Plan B into action. 'You need to make him jealous,' her best friend Tina had said. 'Make him realise that you're not just his for the taking—even if you are.'

Emboldened by Rupert's reaction, Cassie had smiled coolly and sashayed up to Jake instead. To this day, she didn't know where she had found the nerve to do it; he had been on his own for once, and watching the proceedings with a cynical air.

The Allantide Ball was a local tradition revived by Sir Ian, who had been obsessed by Cornish folklore. Less a formal ball than a big party, it was held in the Hall every year on 31st October, when the rest of the country was celebrating Hallowe'en, and everyone in Portrevick went, the one occasion when social divisions were put aside.

In theory, if not in practice.

Jake's expression had not been encouraging, but Cassie had flirted with him anyway. Or she had thought she was flirting. In retrospect, her heavy-handed attempts to bat her lashes and look sultry must have been laughable, but at the time she had been quite pleased with herself.

'OK, maybe I was flirting,' she conceded. 'That was no reason to…to…'

'To kiss you?' said Jake. 'But how else were you to make Rupert jealous? That *was* the whole point of the exercise, wasn't it?'

Taking Cassie's expression as an answer, he settled back into the saddle and regarded her with a mocking smile that made her want to slap him. 'It was a good strategy,' he congratulated her. 'Rupert Branscombe Fox is the kind of jerk who's only interested in what someone else has got. I'll bet even as a small boy he only ever wanted to play with someone else's toys. It was very astute of you to notice that.'

'I didn't.'

She had just wanted Rupert to notice her. Was that so bad? And he had. It had worked perfectly.

She just hadn't counted on Jake taking her flirtation so seriously. He had taken her by the hand and pulled her outside. Catching a glimpse of Rupert watching her, Cassie had been delighted at first. She'd been expecting a kiss, but not the kiss that she got.

It had begun with cool assurance—and, really, that would have been fine—but then something had changed. The coolness had become warmth, and then it had become heat, and then, worst of all, there had been a terrifying sweetness to it. Cassie had felt as if she were standing in a river with the sand rushing away beneath her feet, sucking her down into something wild and uncontrollable. She'd been terrified and exhilarated at the same time, and when Jake had let her go at last she had been shaking.

It wasn't even as if she liked Jake. He was the exact opposite of Rupert, who was the embodiment of a dream. Secretly, Cassie thought of them as Beauty and the Beast. Not that Jake was ugly, exactly, but he had dark, beaky features, a bitter mouth and angry eyes, while Rupert was all golden charm, like a prince in a fairy tale.

'Much good it'll do you,' Jake was saying, reading her expression without difficulty. 'You're wasting your time. Rupert's never going to bother with a nice girl like you.'

'Well, that's where you're wrong,' said Cassie, stung. 'Maybe I *did* want to make him notice me, but it worked, didn't it?'

'You're not asking me to believe that you're Rupert's latest girlfriend?'

Cassie lifted her chin. 'Believe what you want,' she said. 'It happens to be true.'

But Jake only laughed. 'Having sex with Rupert doesn't make you his girlfriend, as you'll soon find out,' he said. He reached for his helmet again. 'You need to grow up, Cassie. You've wandered around with your head in the clouds ever since you were a little kid, and it looks like you're still living in a fantasy world. It's time you woke up to reality!'

'You're just jealous of Rupert!' Cassie accused him, her voice shaking with fury.

'Because of you?' Jake raised his dark brows contemptuously. 'I don't think so!'

'Because he's handsome and charming and rich and Sir Ian's nephew, while you're just…just…' Too angry and humiliated to be cautious, she was practically toe to toe with him by now. 'Just an *animal*.'

And that was when Jake really did lose the temper he had been hanging onto by a thread all day. His hands shot out and yanked Cassie towards him so hard that she fell against him. Luckily his bike was still on its stand, or they would both have fallen over.

'So you think I'm jealous of Rupert, do you?' he snarled, shoving his hands into the mass of curls. 'Well, maybe I am.'

He brought his mouth down on hers in a hard, punishing kiss that had her squirming in protest, her palms jammed against his leather jacket, until abruptly the pressure softened.

His lips didn't leave hers, but he shifted slightly so that he could draw her more comfortably against him as he sat astride the bike. The fierce grip on her hair had loosened, and now her curls were twined around his fingers as the kiss grew seductively insistent.

Cassie's heart was pounding with that same mixture of fear and excitement, and she could feel herself losing her footing again. A surge of unfamiliar feeling was rapidly uncoiling inside her, so fast in fact that it was scaring her; her fingers curled instinctively into his leather jacket to anchor herself.

And then—the bit that would make her cringe for years afterwards—somehow she actually found herself leaning into him to kiss him back.

That was the point at which Jake let her go so abruptly that she stumbled back against the handlebars.

'How dare you?' Cassie managed, drawing a shaking hand across her mouth as she tried to leap away from the bike, only to find that her cardigan was caught up in the handlebars. Desperately, she tried to disentangle herself. 'I never want to see you again!'

'Don't worry, you won't have to.' Infuriatingly casual, Jake leant forward to pull the sleeve free; she practically fell back in her haste to put some distance between them. 'I'm leaving today. You stick to your fantasy life, Cassie,' he told her as she huddled into her cardigan, hugging her arms together. 'I'm getting out of here.'

And with that, he calmly fastened his helmet, kicked the bike off its stand and into gear and roared off down the long drive—leaving Cassie staring after him, her heart tumbling with shock and humiliation and the memory of a deep, dark, dangerous excitement.

CHAPTER ONE

Ten years later

'JAKE Trevelyan?' Cassie repeated blankly. 'Are you sure?'

'I wrote his name down. Where is it?' Joss hunted through the mess on her desk and produced a scrap of paper. 'Here—Jake Trevelyan,' she read. 'Somebody in Portrevick—isn't that where you grew up?—recommended us.'

Puzzled, Cassie dropped into the chair at her own desk. It felt very strange, hearing Jake's name after all this time. She could still picture him with terrifying clarity, sitting astride that mean-looking machine, an angry young man with hard hands and a bitter smile. The memory of that kiss still had the power to make her toes curl inside her shoes.

'He's getting married?'

'Why else would he get in touch with a wedding planner?'

'I just can't imagine it.' The Jake Trevelyan Cassie had known wasn't the type to settle down.

'Luckily for us, he obviously can.' Joss turned back to her computer. 'He sounded keen, anyway, so I said you'd go round this afternoon.'

'Me?' Cassie looked at her boss in dismay. 'You always meet the clients first.'

'I can't today. I've got a meeting with the accountant, which I'm not looking forward to at all. Besides, he knows you.'

'Yes, but he hates me!' She told Joss about that last encounter outside Portrevick Hall. 'And what's his fiancée going to think? I wouldn't want to plan my wedding with someone who'd kissed my bridegroom.'

'Teenage kisses don't count.' Joss waved them aside. 'It was ten years ago. Chances are, he won't even remember.'

Cassie wasn't sure if that would make her feel better or worse. She would just as soon Jake didn't remember the gawky teenager who had thrown herself at him at the Allantide Ball, but what girl wanted to know that she was utterly forgettable?

'Anyway, if he didn't like you, why ring up and ask to speak to you?' Joss asked reasonably. 'We can't afford to let a possible client slip through our fingers, Cassie. You know how tight things are at the moment. This is our best chance of new work in weeks, and if it means being embarrassed then I'm afraid you're going to have to be embarrassed,' she warned. 'Otherwise, I'm really not sure how much longer I'm going to be able to keep you on.'

Which was how Cassie came to stand outside a gleaming office-building that afternoon. Its windows reflected a bright September sky, and she had to crane her neck to look up to the top. Jake Trevelyan had done well for himself if he worked somewhere like this, she thought, impressed in spite of herself.

Better than she had, that was for sure, thought Cassie, remembering Avalon's chaotic office above the Chinese take-away. Not that she minded. She had only been working for Joss a few months and she loved it. Wedding planning was far and away the best job she had ever had—Cassie had had a few, it had to be admitted—and she would do whatever it took to hang on to it. She couldn't bear to admit to her family of super-achievers that she was out of work.

Again.

'Oh, *darling*!' her mother would sigh with disappointment, while her father would frown and remind her that she should have gone to university like her elder sister and her two brothers, all of whom had high-flying careers.

No, she had to keep this job, Cassie resolved, and if that meant facing Jake Trevelyan again then that was what she would do.

Squaring her shoulders, she tugged her jacket into place and headed up the marble steps.

Worms were squirming in the pit of her stomach but she did her best to ignore them. It was stupid to be nervous about seeing Jake again. She wasn't a dreamy seventeen-year-old any longer. She was twenty-seven, and holding down a demanding job. People might not think that being a wedding planner was much of a career, but it required tact, diplomacy and formidable organizational-skills. If she could organise a wedding—well, help Joss organise one—she could deal with Jake Trevelyan.

A glimpse of herself in the mirrored windows reassured her. Luckily, she had dressed smartly to visit a luxurious hotel which one of their clients had chosen as a venue that morning. The teal-green jacket and narrow skirt gave her a sharp, professional image, Cassie decided, eyeing her reflection. Together with the slim briefcase, it made for an impressive look.

Misleading, but impressive. She hardly recognised herself, so with any luck Jake Trevelyan wouldn't recognise her either.

Her only regret was the shoes. It wasn't that they didn't look fabulous—the teal suede with a black stripe was perfect with the suit—but she wasn't used to walking on quite such high heels, and the lobby floor had an alarmingly, glossy sheen to it. It was a relief to get across to the reception desk without mishap.

'I'm looking for a company called Primordia,' she said, glancing down at the address Joss had scribbled down. 'Can you tell me which floor it's on?'

The receptionist lifted immaculate brows. 'This *is* Primordia,' she said.

'What, the whole building?' Cassie's jaw sagged as she

stared around the soaring lobby, taking in the impressive artwork on the walls and the ranks of gleaming lifts with their lights going up, up, up…

'Apparently he's boss of some outfit called Primordia,' Joss had said casually when she'd tossed the address across the desk.

This didn't look like an 'outfit' to Cassie. It looked like a solid, blue-chip company exuding wealth and prestige. Suddenly her suit didn't seem quite so smart.

'Um, I'm looking for someone called Jake Trevelyan,' she told the receptionist. 'I'm not sure which department he's in.'

The receptionist's brows climbed higher. 'Mr Trevelyan, our Chief Executive? Is he expecting you?'

Chief Executive? Cassie swallowed. 'I think so.'

The receptionist turned away to murmur into the phone while Cassie stood, fingering the buttons on her jacket nervously. Jake Trevelyan, bad boy of Portrevick, Chief Executive of all this?

Blimey.

An intimidatingly quiet lift took her up to the Chief Executive's suite. It was like stepping into a different world. Everything was new and of cutting-edge design, and blanketed with the hush that only serious money can buy.

It was a very long way from Portrevick.

Cassie was still half-convinced that there must be some mistake, but no. There was an elegant PA, who was obviously expecting her, and who escorted her into an impressively swish office.

'Mr Trevelyan won't be a minute,' she said.

Mr Trevelyan! Cassie thought of the surly tearaway she had known and tried not to goggle. She hoped Jake—sorry, *Mr Trevelyan*—didn't remember her flirting with him in that tacky dress or telling him that she never wanted to see him again. It wasn't exactly the best basis on which to build a winning client-relationship.

On the other hand, he was the one who had asked to see

her. Surely he wouldn't have done that if he had any memory of those disastrous kisses? Joss must be right; he had probably forgotten them completely. And, even if he hadn't, he was unlikely to mention that he had kissed her in front of his fiancée, wasn't he? He would be just as anxious as her to pretend that that had never happened.

Reassured, Cassie pinned on a bright smile as his PA opened a door into an even swisher office than the first. 'Cassandra Grey,' the woman announced.

It was a huge room, with glass walls on two sides that offered a spectacular view down the Thames to the Houses of Parliament and the London Eye.

Not that Cassie took in the view. She had eyes only for Jake, who was getting up from behind his desk and buttoning his jacket as he came round to greet her.

Her first thought was that he had grown into a surprisingly attractive man.

Ten years ago he had been a wiry young man, with turbulent eyes and a dangerous edge that had always left her tongue-tied and nervous around him. He was dark still, and there were traces of the difficult boy he had been in his face, but he had grown into the once-beaky features, and the surliness had metamorphosed into a forcefulness that was literally breathtaking. At least, Cassie presumed that was why she was having trouble dragging enough oxygen into her lungs all of a sudden.

He might not actually be taller, but he seemed it—taller, tougher, more solid somehow. And the mouth that had once been twisted into a sneer was now set in a cool, self-contained line.

Cassie was forced to revise her first thought. He wasn't attractive; he was *gorgeous*.

Well. Who would have thought it?

His fiancée was a lucky woman.

Keeping her smile firmly in place, she took a step towards

him with her hand outstretched. 'Hel…' she began, but that was as far as she got. Her ankle tipped over on the unfamiliar heels and the next moment her shoes seemed to be hopelessly entangled. Before Cassie knew what was happening, she found herself pitching forward with a squawk of dismay as her briefcase thudded to the floor.

She would have landed flat on her face next to it if a pair of hard hands hadn't grabbed her arms. Cassie had no idea how Jake got there in time to catch her, but she ended up sprawling against him and clutching instinctively at his jacket.

Just as she had clutched at his leather jacket ten years ago when he had kissed her.

'Hello, Cassie,' he said.

Mortified, Cassie struggled to find her balance. Why, why, *why*, was she so clumsy?

Her face was squashed against his jacket, and with an odd, detached part of her brain she registered that he smelt wonderful, of expensive shirts, clean, male skin and a faint tang of aftershave. His body was rock-solid, and for a treacherous moment Cassie was tempted to cling to the blissful illusion of steadiness and safety.

Possibly not a good move, if she wanted to impress him with her new-found professionalism. Or very tactful, given that he was a newly engaged man.

With an effort, Cassie pulled herself away from the comfort of that broad chest. 'I'm so sorry,' she managed.

Jake set her on her feet but kept hold of her upper arms until he was sure she was steady. 'Are you all right?'

His hands felt hard and strong through the sleeves of her jacket, and he held her just as he had done that other day.

Cassie couldn't help staring. It was strangely dislocating to look into his face and see a cool stranger overlaying the angry young man he had been then. This time the resentment in the dark-blue eyes had been replaced by a gleam of amusement, although it was impossible to tell whether he was remembering that kiss, too, or was simply entertained by her unconventional arrival.

Cassie's cheeks burned. 'I'm fine,' she said, stepping out of his grip.

Jake bent to pick up the briefcase and handed it back to her. 'Shall we sit down?' he suggested, gesturing towards two luxurious leather sofas. 'Given those shoes, it might be safer!'

Willing her flaming colour to fade, Cassie subsided onto a sofa and swallowed as she set the briefcase on the low table. 'I don't normally throw myself into the client's arms when we first meet,' she said with a nervous smile.

The corner of Jake's mouth quivered in an unnervingly attractive way. 'It's always good to make a spectacular entrance. But then, you always did have a certain style,' he added.

Cassie rather suspected that last comment was sarcastic; she had always been hopelessly clumsy.

She sighed. 'I was rather hoping you wouldn't recognise me,' she confessed.

Jake looked across the table at her. She was perched on the edge of the sofa, looking hot and ruffled, her round, sweet face flushed, and brown eyes bright with mortification.

The wild curls he remembered had been cut into a more manageable style, and she had slimmed down and smartened up. Remarkably so, in fact. When he had looked up to see her in the doorway, she had seemed a vividly pretty stranger, and he had felt a strange sensation in the pit of his stomach.

Then she had tripped and pitched into his arms, and Jake wasn't sure if he was disappointed or relieved to find out that she hadn't changed that much after all.

The feel of her was startlingly familiar, which was odd, given that he had only held her twice before. But he had caught her, and all at once it was as if he had been back at that last Allantide Ball. He could still see Cassie as she sashayed up to him in that tight red dress, teetering on heels almost as ridiculous as the ones she was wearing now, and suddenly all grown-up. That was the first time he had noticed her lush mouth, and wondered about the woman she would become.

That mouth was still the same, Jake thought, remembering its warmth, its innocence, remembering how unprepared he had been for the piercing sweetness that just for a moment had held them in its grip.

Now here she was again, sitting there and watching him with a wary expression in the big brown eyes. Not recognise her?

Jake smiled. 'Not a chance,' he said.

Oh dear. That wasn't what she had wanted to hear at all. Almost reluctantly, Cassie met the dark-blue gaze and felt her skin prickle at the amusement she read there. It was obvious that Jake remembered the gawky teenager she had been all too well. Those kisses might have been shattering for her, but for him they must have been just part of her gaucheness and lack of sophistication.

She lifted her chin. 'It's a long time ago,' she said. 'I didn't think you'd remember me.'

Jake met her eyes blandly. 'You'd be surprised what I remember,' he said, and the memory of the Allantide Ball was suddenly shimmering between them. He didn't have to say anything. Cassie just knew that he was remembering her hopeless attempts to flirt, and her clumsy, mortifyingly eager response to his kiss, and a tide of heat seemed to sweep up from her toes.

She jerked her eyes away. 'So,' she began, but all at once her voice was so high and thin that she had to clear her throat and start again. 'So...' Oh God, now she sounded positively gravelly! 'What took you back to Portrevick?' She managed to find something approaching a normal pitch at last. As far as she knew, Jake had left the village that awful day he had kissed her on his motorbike and had never been back.

Jake's expression sobered. 'Sir Ian's death,' he said.

'Oh yes, I was so sorry when I heard about that,' said Cassie, latching on to what she hoped would be a safe subject.

'He was such a lovely man,' she remembered sadly. 'Mum and Dad went back for the funeral, but one of our clients was getting married that day so I was on duty.'

The door opened at that point and Jake's PA came in with a tray of coffee which she set on the table between them. She poured two cups and made a discreet exit. Why could *she* never be that quiet and efficient? Cassie wondered, admiring the other woman's style.

Jake passed one of the cups to her, and she accepted it gingerly. It was made of the finest porcelain, and she couldn't help comparing it to the chipped mugs she and Joss used to drink endless cups of tea in the office.

'I had to go and see Sir Ian's solicitor on Friday,' Jake said, pushing the milk jug towards her. 'I stayed in the pub at Portrevick, and your name was mentioned in connection with weddings. One of your old friends—Tina?—said that you were in the business.'

'*Did* she?' Cassie made a mental note to ring Tina the moment she left and demand to know why she hadn't told her that Jake Trevelyan had reappeared. It wasn't as if Tina didn't know all about that devastating kiss at the Allantide Ball, although Cassie had never told anyone about the second one.

Jake raised his eyes a little at her tone, and she hastened to make amends. Perhaps she had sounded rather vengeful, there. 'I mean, yes, that's right,' she said, helping herself to milk but managing to slop most of it into the saucer.

Now the cup was going to drip all over everything. With an inward sigh, Cassie hunted around in her bag for a tissue to mop up the mess. 'I am.'

That sounded a bit too bald, didn't it? *You're supposed to be selling yourself here,* Cassie reminded herself, but she was distracted by the need to dispose of the sodden tissue now. She couldn't just leave it in the saucer. It looked disgusting, and so unprofessional.

'In the wedding business, that is,' she added, losing track

of where she had begun. Helplessly, she looked around for a bin, but of course there was nothing so prosaic in Jake's office.

It was immaculate, she noticed for the first time. Everything was squeaky clean, and the desk was clear except for a telephone and a very small, very expensive-looking computer. Ten years ago, Jake would only have been in an office like this to pinch the electronic equipment, she thought, wondering how on earth the rebel Jake, with his battered leathers and his bike, had made it to this exclusive, perfectly controlled space.

She could see Jake eyeing the tissue askance. Obviously any kind of mess offended him now, which was a shame, given that she was banking her entire future on being able to work closely with him and his fiancée for the next few months. Cassie belonged to the creative school of organising, the one that miraculously produced order out of chaos at the very last minute, although no one, least of all her, ever knew quite how it happened.

Unable to think of anything else do with it, Cassie quickly shoved the tissue back into her bag, where it would no doubt fester with all the other crumbs, chocolate wrappers, pen lids and blunt emery-boards that she never got round to clearing out. She would have to remember to be careful next time she put her hand in there.

Jake's expression was faintly disgusted, but he offered her the plate of biscuits. Cassie eyed them longingly. She was starving, but she knew better than to take one. The next thing, there would be biscuit crumbs everywhere, and her professional image had taken enough of a battering as it was this afternoon.

'No thank you,' she said politely, deciding to skip the coffee as well. At this rate she would just spill it all over herself and, worse, Jake's pristine leather sofa.

Leaning forward, Jake added milk to his own coffee without spilling so much as a drop. He stirred it briskly, tapped the spoon on the side of the cup, set it in the saucer and looked up at Cassie. The dark-blue eyes were very direct, and in spite of her determination to stay cool Cassie's pulse gave an alarming jolt.

'Well, shall we get down to business?' he suggested.

'Good idea.' Delighted to leave the past and all its embarrassing associations behind, Cassie leapt into action.

This was it. Her whole career—well, her job, Cassie amended to herself. She didn't have a career so much as a haphazard series of unrelated jobs. Anyway, *everything* depended on how she sold herself now.

Reaching for her briefcase, she unzipped it with a flourish, dug out a brochure and handed it to Jake. 'This will give you some idea of what we do,' she said in her best professional voice. It was odd that his fiancée wasn't here. Joss always aimed her pitch at the bride-to-be; she would just have to make the best of it, Cassie supposed.

'Of course, we offer a bespoke service, so we really start with what *you* want.' She hesitated. 'We usually discuss what you'd like with both members of the couple,' she added delicately. 'Will your fiancée be joining us?'

Jake had been flicking through the brochure, but at that he glanced up. 'Fiancée?'

'The bride generally has a good idea about what kind of wedding she wants,' Cassie explained. 'In our experience, grooms tend to be less concerned with the nitty-gritty of the organisation.'

'I think there may be some misunderstanding,' said Jake, frowning. 'I'm not engaged.'

Cassie's face fell ludicrously. 'Not…? You're not getting married?' she said, hoping against hope that she had misheard.

'No.'

Then how was she to hold on to her job? Cassie wondered wildly. 'So you don't need help planning a wedding?' she asked, just to make sure, and Jake let the brochure drop onto the table with a slap of finality.

'No.'

'But…' Cassie was struggling to understand how it could all have gone so wrong before she had even started. 'Why did you get in touch?'

'When Tina told me that you were in the wedding business I was under the impression that you managed a venue. I hadn't appreciated that you were involved with planning the weddings themselves.'

'Well, we *deal* with venues, of course,' said Cassie, desperate to hold on to something. 'We help couples with every aspect of the wedding and honeymoon.' She launched into her spiel, but Jake cut her off before she could really get going.

'I'm really looking for someone who can advise on what's involved in converting a house into a wedding venue. I'm sorry,' he said, making to get to his feet. 'It looks as if I've been wasting your time.'

Cassie wasn't ready to give up yet. 'We do that too,' she said quickly.

'What, waste time?'

'Set up wedding venues,' she said, refusing to rise to the bait, and meeting his eyes so guilelessly that Jake was fairly sure that she was lying. 'Between us, Joss and I have a lot of experience of using venues, and we know exactly what's required. Where is the house?' she asked quickly, before he could draw the conversation to a close.

'I'm thinking about the Hall,' he relented.

'The Hall?' Cassie repeated blankly. 'Portrevick Hall?'

'Exactly.'

'But…isn't it Rupert's now?'

'No,' said Jake. 'Sir Ian left the estate in trust and I'm the trustee.'

Cassie stared at him, her career crisis momentarily forgotten. '*You?*' she said incredulously.

He smiled grimly at her expression. 'Yes, me.'

'What about Rupert?' she asked, too surprised for tact.

'Sir Ian's money was left in trust for him. He hasn't proved the steadiest of characters, as you may know.'

Cassie did know. Rupert's picture was regularly in the gossip columns. There was a certain irony in the fact that Jake was now the wealthy, successful one while Rupert had a reputation as a hellraiser, albeit a very glamorous one. He seemed to get by largely on charm and those dazzling good looks.

She forced her attention back to Jake, who was still talking. 'Sir Ian was concerned that, if he left him the money outright, Rupert would just squander it the way he has already squandered his inheritance from his parents.'

'It just seems unfair,' she said tentatively. 'Rupert is Sir Ian's nephew, after all. I'm sure he expected to inherit Portrevick Hall.'

'I'm sure he did too,' said Jake in a dry voice. 'Rupert's been borrowing heavily on exactly that expectation for the last few years now. That's why Sir Ian put the estate into a trust. He was afraid Rupert would simply sell it off to the highest bidder otherwise.'

'But why make *you* the trustee?' said Cassie without thinking.

'It's not a position I angled for, I can assure you,' Jake said with a certain astringency. 'But I owe Sir Ian a lot, so I had to agree when he asked me. I assumed there would be plenty of time for him to change his mind, and he probably did the same. He was only in his sixties, and he'd had no history of heart problems. If only he'd lived longer…'

Restlessly, Jake pushed away his coffee cup and got to his feet. There was no point in 'if only's. 'Anyway, the fact remains that I'm stuck with responsibility for the house now. I promised Sir Ian that I would make sure the estate remained intact. He couldn't bear the thought of the Hall being broken up into flats, or holiday houses built in the grounds.

'Obviously, I need to fulfil his wishes, but I can't leave a house like that standing empty. It needs to be used and maintained, and somehow I've got to find a way for it to pay for itself.'

Coming to a halt by the window, Jake frowned unseeingly at the view while he remembered his problem. 'When I was down at Portrevick last week, sorting out things with the solicitor, she suggested that it might make a suitable wedding-venue. It seemed like an idea worth pursuing. I happened to mention it in the pub that night, and that's how your name came up. But, judging by your brochure, your company is more concerned with the weddings themselves rather than running the venues.'

'Normally, yes,' said Cassie, not so engrossed in the story of Sir Ian's extraordinary will that she had forgotten that her new-found career with Avalon was on the line. 'But the management of a venue is closely related to what we do, and in fact this is an area we're looking at moving into,' she added fluently. She would have to remember to tell Joss that they were diversifying. 'Clearly, we have considerable experience of dealing with various venues, so we're in a position to know exactly what facilities they need to offer.'

'Hmm.' Jake sounded unconvinced. He turned from the window to study Cassie, sitting alert and eager on the sofa. 'All right, you know the Hall. Given your *considerable experience*, what would you think of it as a wedding venue?'

'It would be perfect,' said Cassie, ignoring his sarcasm. 'It's a beautiful old house with a wonderful location on the coast. It would be hard to imagine anywhere more romantic! I should think couples all over the South West would be queuing up to get married there.'

Jake came back to sit opposite her once more. He drummed his fingers absently on the table, obviously thinking. 'It's encouraging that you think it would make a popular venue, anyway,' he said at last.

'Yes, I do,' said Cassie eagerly, sensing that Jake might be buying her spur-of-the-moment career shift into project management.

She leant forward persuasively. 'I'm sure Sir Ian would

approve of the idea,' she went on. 'He loved people, didn't he? I bet he would have liked to see the Hall used for weddings. They're such happy occasions.'

'If you say so,' said Jake, clearly unconvinced.

He studied Cassie with a faint frown, wondering if he was mad to even consider taking her advice. She had always been a dreamer, he remembered, and the curly hair and dimple gave her a warm, sweet but slightly dishevelled air that completely contradicted the businesslike suit and the stylish, totally impractical shoes.

There was something chaotic about Cassie, Jake decided. Even sitting still, she gave the alarming impression that she was on the verge of knocking something over or making a mess. Good grief, the girl couldn't even manage walking into a room without falling over her own shoes! Having spent the last few years cultivating a careful sense of order and control, Jake found the aura of unpredictability Cassie exuded faintly disturbing.

He had a strong suspicion, too, that Cassie's experience of managing a venue was no wider than his own. She was clearly desperate for work, and would say whatever she thought he wanted to hear.

If he had any sense, he would close the meeting right now.

CHAPTER TWO

ON THE other hand...

On the other hand, Jake reminded himself, Sir Ian had been fond of her, and the fact that she knew the Hall was an undoubted advantage.

He could at least give her the chance to convince him that she knew what she was talking about. For old times' sake, thought Jake, looking at Cassie's mouth.

'So what would need to be done to make the Hall a venue?' he asked abruptly. 'Presumably we'd have to get a licence?'

'Absolutely,' said Cassie with more confidence than she was feeling. 'I imagine it would need quite a bit of refurbishment, too. You can charge a substantial fee for the hire of the venue, but in return couples will expect everything to be perfect. All the major rooms would have to be completely re-decorated, and anything shabby or dingy replaced.'

Cassie was making it up as she went along, but she was banking on the fact that Jake knew less than she did about what weddings involved. Besides, how difficult could it be? She couldn't let a little thing like not knowing what she was talking about stop her, not when the alternative was losing her job and having to admit to her family that she had failed again.

'Naturally you would have to set it up so that everything is laid on,' she went on, rather enjoying the authoritative note in her own voice. She would convince *herself* at this rate! 'You need to think about catering, flowers, music; whatever a bride and groom could possibly want. They're paying a lot of money for their big day, so you've got to make it very special for them.

'Some people like to make all the arrangements themselves,' she told Jake, who was listening with a kind of horrified fascination. 'But if you want the Hall to be successful you'll have to make it possible for them to hand over all the arrangements to the staff and not think about anything. That means being prepared to cater for every whim, as well as different kinds of weddings. It might just be a reception, or it might be the wedding itself, and that could include all sorts of different faiths, as well as civil partnerships.'

Cassie was really getting into her stride now. 'Then you need to think about what other facilities you're going to provide,' she said, impressing herself with her own fluency. Who would have thought she could come out with this stuff off the top of her head? All those weddings she had attended over the past few months must have paid off.

'The bride and groom will want somewhere to change, at the very least, or they might want to take over the whole house for a wedding party. You'll need new kitchens too. Loos, obviously. And, of course, you'll have to think about finding staff and making contacts with local caterers, florists, photographers and so on.

'There's marketing and publicity to consider as well,' she pointed out. 'Eventually, you'll be able to rely on word of mouth, but it'll be important until you're established.'

Jake was looking appalled. 'I didn't realise it was such a business,' he admitted. 'You mean it's not enough to clear the great hall for dancing and lay on a few white tablecloths?'

'I'm afraid not.'

There was a long pause. Jake's mouth was turned down, and Cassie could see him rethinking the whole idea.

Oh God, what if she had put him off? She bit her lip. That was what you got for showing off.

You always go a bit too far. How many times when she had been growing up had her mother said that to her? Cassie could practically hear her saying it now.

Anxiously, she watched Jake's face. It was impossible to tell what he was thinking.

'We're talking about a substantial investment,' he said slowly at last, and Cassie let out a long breath she hadn't known she was holding.

'Yes, but it'll be worth it,' she said, trying to disguise her relief. 'Weddings are big business. If you aim for the top end of the market, the house will more than pay for itself.'

Jake was still not entirely convinced. 'It's a lot to think about.'

'Not if you let us oversee everything for you,' said Cassie, marvelling at her own nerve. 'We could manage the whole project and set it up until it's ready to hand over to a permanent manager.'

It was a brilliant idea, even if she said so herself. She couldn't think why Joss hadn't thought of going into venue management before.

Jake was watching her with an indecipherable expression. Cassie lifted her chin and tried to look confident, half-expecting him to accuse her—accurately—of bluffing, but in the end he just asked how they structured their fees.

'I'd have to discuss that with Joss when we've got a clearer idea of exactly what needs to be done,' said Cassie evasively. Joss was much harder-headed when it came to money and always dealt with the financial side of things.

'OK.' Jake made up his mind abruptly. 'Let me have a detailed proposal and I'll consider it.'

'Great.' Cassie's relief was rapidly being overtaken by panic. What on earth had she committed herself to?

'So, what next?'

Yes, what next, Cassie? Cassie gulped. 'I think I need to take another look at the Hall and draw up a list of work required,' she improvised.

Fortunately, this seemed to be the right thing to say. Jake nodded. 'That makes sense. Can you come to Cornwall on Thursday? I've got to go back myself to see the solicitor, so we could drive down together if that suits you.'

It didn't, but Cassie knew better than to say so. Having bluffed this far, she couldn't give up now. A seven-hour car journey with Jake Trevelyan wasn't her idea of a fun day, but if she could pull off a contract it would be worth it.

'Of course,' she said, relaxing enough to pick up her coffee at last, and promptly splashing it over her skirt. She brushed the drops away hastily, hoping that Jake hadn't noticed. 'I can be ready to leave whenever you are.'

Jake watched Cassie practically fall out of the door, struggling with a weekend case on wheels, a motley collection of plastic carrier-bags and a handbag that kept slipping down her arm. With a sigh, he got out of the car to help her. He was double parked outside her office, and had hoped for a quick getaway, but clearly that wasn't going to happen.

He hadn't made many mistakes in the last ten years, but Jake had a nasty feeling that appointing Cassie to manage the transformation of Portrevick Hall into a wedding venue might be one of them. He had been secretly impressed by the fluent way she had talked about weddings, and by the way she had seemed to know exactly what was involved, but at the same time her lack of experience was obvious. And yet she had fixed him with those big, brown eyes and distracted him with that mouth, and before Jake had quite known what he was doing he had agreed to give her the job.

He must have been mad, he decided as he took the case from her. Cassie had to be the least organised organiser he had ever met. *Look at her*, laden with carrier bags, the wayward brown curls blowing around face, her cardigan all twisted under the weight of her handbag!

She was a mess, Jake thought disapprovingly. She was

casually dressed in a mishmash of colourful garments that appeared to be thrown together without any thought for neatness or elegance. Yes, she had grown into a surprisingly pretty girl, but she could do with some of Natasha's poise and sophistication.

He stashed the carrier bags in the boot with the case. 'What on earth do you need all this stuff for?' he demanded. 'We're only going for a couple of nights.'

'Most of it's Tina's. She came to London months ago and left half her clothes behind, so I'm taking them back to her. She's invited me to stay with her,' Cassie added.

Jake was sleeping at the Hall, and he'd suggested that Cassie stay there as well, but Cassie couldn't help thinking it all seemed a bit intimate. True, the Hall had bedrooms to spare, but they would still be sleeping in the same place, bumping into each other on the way to the bathroom, wandering into the kitchen in their PJs to make tea in the morning... No; Cassie wasn't ready to meet Jake without her make-up on yet.

'I thought I might as well stay for the weekend, since I'm down there,' she went on, talking over the roof of the car as she made her way round to the passenger door. 'I haven't seen Tina for ages. I might talk to some local contractors on Monday, too, and then come back on the train.'

Cassie knew that she was talking too much, but the prospect of the long journey in Jake's company was making her stupidly jittery. She had been fine until he'd appeared. Joss had given her unqualified approval to the plan, and Cassie had been enjoying dizzying fantasies about her new career in project management.

It had been a strange experience, seeing Jake again, and she'd been left disorientated by the way he looked familiar but behaved like a total stranger. In some ways, that made it easier to dissassociate him from the Jake she had known in the past. This Jake was less menacing than the old one, for sure. The surliness and resentment had been replaced by steely control, but it was somehow just as intimidating.

But at least she had the possibility of a job, Cassie reminded herself sternly as she got into the car. She had to concentrate on that, and not on the unnerving prospect of being shut up in a car with Jake Trevelyan. He had come straight from his office and was still wearing his suit, but, having slammed the boot shut, he took off his jacket, loosened his tie and rolled up his shirt sleeves before getting back into the driver's seat.

'Right,' he said briskly, switching on the ignition. 'Let's go.'

It was a big, luxuriously comfortable car with swish leather seats, but Cassie felt cramped and uneasy as she pulled on the seatbelt. It wouldn't have been so bad if Jake wasn't just *there*, only inches away, filling the whole car with his dark, forceful presence, using up all the available oxygen so that she had to open the window to drag in a breath.

'There's air conditioning,' said Jake, using the electric controls on his side to close it again.

Air conditioning. Right. So how come it was so hard to breathe?

'I was half-expecting you to turn up on a motorbike,' she said chattily, to conceal her nervousness.

'It's just as well I didn't, with all those bags you've brought along with you.' Jake checked his mirror, indicated and pulled out into the traffic.

'I always fancied the idea of riding pillion,' said Cassie.

'I don't think you'd fancy it all the way down to Cornwall,' Jake said, dampening her. 'You'll be much more comfortable in a car.'

Under normal circumstances, maybe, but Cassie couldn't imagine anything less comfortable than being shut up with him in a confined space for seven hours. They had barely left Fulham, but the car seemed to have shrunk already, and she was desperately aware of Jake beside her. Her eyes kept snagging on his hands, strong and competent on the steering wheel, and she would find herself remembering how they had felt on her arms as he had yanked her towards him.

Turning her head to remove them from her vision, Cassie found herself looking awkwardly out of the side window, but that was hard on her neck. Before she knew it, her eyes were skittering back to Jake's side of the car, to the line of his cheek, the corner of his mouth and the faint prickle of stubble under his jaw where he had wrenched impatiently at his tie to loosen it.

She could see the pulse beating steadily in his throat, and for one bizarre moment let herself imagine what it would be like to lean across and press her lips to it. Then she imagined Jake jerking away in horror and losing control of the car, which would crash into that newsagent's, and then the police would come and she would have to make a statement: *I'm sorry, officer, I was just overcome by an uncontrollable urge to kiss Jake Trevelyan.*

It would be in all the papers, and in no time at all the news would reach the Portrevick Arms, where they would all snigger. Village memories were long. No one would have forgotten what a fool she had made of herself over Rupert, and they would shake their heads and tell each other that Cassandra Grey never had been able to keep her hands off a man…

Cassie's heart was thumping just at the thought of it, and she jerked her head back to the side, ignoring the protest of her neck muscles.

Comfortable? Hah!

'Besides,' Jake went on as Cassie offered up thanks that he hadn't spent the last ten years learning to read minds, 'I haven't got a motorbike any more. I've left my biking days behind me.'

It would have been impossible to imagine Jake without that mean-looking bike years ago in Portrevick.

'You've changed,' said Cassie.

'I sincerely hope so,' said Jake.

Why couldn't she have changed that much? Cassie wondered enviously. If she had, she could be svelte and sophisticated, with a successful career behind her, instead of muddling along feeling most of the time much as she had at seventeen. She might look different, but deep down she felt just the same as she had done then. How had Jake done it?

'What have you been doing for the past ten years?' she asked him curiously.

'I've been in the States for most of them. I got myself a degree, and then did an MBA at Harvard.'

'Really?' said Cassie, impressed. In all the years she had wondered where Jake Trevelyan was and what he was doing, she had never considered that he might be at university. She had imagined him surfing, perhaps, or running a bar on some beach somewhere, or possibly making shady deals astride his motorbike—but *Harvard*? Even her father would be impressed by that.

'I had no idea,' she said.

Jake shrugged. 'I was lucky. I went to work for a smallish firm in Seattle, just as it was poised for expansion. It was an exciting time, and it gave me a lot of valuable experience. That company was at the forefront of digital technology, and Primordia is in the same field, which put me in a good position when they were looking for a new Chief Executive, although it took some negotiation to get me back to London.'

'Didn't you want to come back?'

'Not particularly. But they made me an offer even I couldn't refuse.'

'You were head-hunted?' said Cassie, trying to imagine a company going out of its way to recruit her. *Cassandra Grey's just the person we want for this job*, they would say. *How can we tempt her?*

Nope, she couldn't do it.

Jake obviously took the whole business for granted. 'That's how it works.' He pulled up at a red light and glanced at Cassie. 'What about you? How long have you been with Avalon?'

'Just since the beginning of the year. Before that I was a receptionist,' she said. 'I did a couple of stints in retail, a bit of temping, a bit of waitressing…'

She sighed. 'Not a very impressive career, as my father is always pointing out. I'm a huge disappointment to my parents. The others have all done really well. They all went to Cambridge. Liz is a doctor, Tom's an architect and even Jack is a lawyer now. They're all grown-ups, and I'm just the family problem.'

Cassie had intended the words to sound humorous, but was uneasily aware they had come out rather flat. Rather as if she didn't think it was such a funny joke after all. 'They're always ringing each other up and wondering what to do about Cassie.'

But that was all going to change, she reminded herself. This could be the start of a whole new career. She was going to turn Portrevick Hall into a model venue. Celebrities would be queuing up to get married there. After a year or two, they wouldn't even have to advertise. Just mentioning that a wedding would be at Portrevick Hall would mean that it would be the last word in style and elegance.

Cassandra Grey? they would say. *Isn't she the one who made Portrevick Hall a byword for chic and exclusive?* She would get tired of calls from the head-hunters. *Not again*, she would sigh. *When are you people going to get the message that I don't want to commit to one job?* Because, of course, by then she would be a consultant. She had always fancied the thought of being one of those.

Cassie settled herself more comfortably in her seat, liking the way this fantasy was going. All those smart hotels in London would be constantly ringing her up and begging her to come and sort out their events facilities—and probably not just in London, now she came to think of it. She would have an international reputation.

Yes, she'd get tired of jetting off to New York and Dubai and Sydney. Cassie smiled to herself. Liz, Tom and Jack would still be ringing each other up, but instead of worrying about her they would be complaining about how humdrum their sensible careers seemed in comparison with her glamorous life. *I'm sick of Cassie telling me she'd really just like a few days at home doing nothing*, Liz would grumble.

'And what's Cassie going to do about herself?' asked Jake, breaking rudely into her dream.

'I'm going to do what I'm doing,' she told him firmly. 'I love working for Joss at Avalon. It's the best job I've ever had, and I'll do anything to keep it.'

Even pretending to understand about project management, she added mentally.

'What does a wedding planner *do* all day?'

'It could be anything,' she said. 'I might book string quartets, or find exactly the right shade of ribbon, or source an unusual cake-topper. I love the variety. I can be helping a bride to choose her dress one minute, and sorting out accommodation for the wedding party the next. And then, of course, I get to go to all the weddings.'

Jake made a face. He couldn't think of anything worse. 'It sounds hellish,' he said frankly. 'Don't you get bored?'

'Never,' said Cassie. 'I love weddings. I cry every time— I do!' she insisted when he looked at her in disbelief.

'Why? These people are clients, not friends.'

'They feel like friends by the time we've spent months together planning the wedding,' she retorted. 'But it doesn't matter whether I know the bride and groom or not. I always want to cry when I walk past Chelsea register office and see people on the steps after they've got married. I love seeing everyone so happy. A wedding is such a *hopeful* occasion.'

'In spite of all the evidence to the contrary,' said Jake astringently. 'How many of those weddings you're snivelling at this year will end in divorce by the end of the next? Talk about the triumph of hope over experience!'

'But that's exactly why weddings are so moving,' said

Cassie. 'They're about people choosing to love each other. Lots of people get married more than once. They know how difficult marriage can be, but they still want to make that commitment. I think it's wonderful,' she added defiantly. 'What have you got against marriage, anyway?'

'I've got nothing against marriage,' said Jake. 'It's all the expense and fuss of weddings that I find pointless. It seems to me that marriage is a serious business, and you should approach it in a serious way, not muddle it all up with big dresses, flowers, cakes and whatever else goes on at weddings these days.'

'Weddings are meant to be a celebration,' she reminded him. 'What do you want the bride and groom to do instead—sit down and complete a checklist?'

'At least then they would know they were compatible.'

Cassie rolled her eyes. 'So what would be on your checklist?'

'I'd want to know that the woman I was marrying was intelligent, and sensible…and confident,' Jake decided. 'More importantly, I'd need to be sure that we shared the same goals, that we both had the same attitude to success in our careers… and sex, of course…and to little things like tidiness that can put the kybosh on a relationship quicker than anything else.'

'You don't ask for much, do you?' said Cassie tartly, reflecting that she wouldn't get many ticks on Jake's checklist. In fact, if he had set out to describe her exact opposite, he could hardly have done a better job. 'Clever, confident, successful and tidy. Where are you going to find a paragon like that?'

'I already have,' said Jake.

Oh.

'Oh,' said Cassie, unaccountably put out. 'What's her name?'

'Natasha. We've been together six months.'

'So why haven't you married her if she's so perfect?' Try as she might, Cassie couldn't keep the snippiness from her voice.

'We just haven't got round to talking about it,' said Jake. 'I think it would be a good move, though. It makes sense.'

'Makes sense?' echoed Cassie in disbelief. 'You should get married because you're in love, not because it *makes sense*!'

'In my book, committing yourself to someone for life because you're in love is what *doesn't* make sense,' he retorted.

Crikey, whatever happened to romance? Cassie shook her head. 'Well, if you ever decide that doing a checklist together isn't quite enough, remember that Avalon can help you plan your wedding.'

'I'll bear it in mind,' he said. 'I imagine Natasha would like a wedding of some kind, but she's a very successful solicitor, so she wouldn't have the time to organise much herself.'

Of course, Natasha *would* be a successful solicitor, Cassie thought, having taken a dislike to his perfect girlfriend without ever having met her. She was tempted to say that Natasha would no doubt be too busy being marvellous to have time to bother with anything as inconsequential as a wedding, but remembered in time that Avalon's business relied on brides being too busy to do everything themselves.

Besides, it might sound as if she was jealous of Natasha.

Which was nonsense, of course.

'I certainly wouldn't know where to start,' Jake went on. 'Weddings are unfamiliar territory to me.'

'You must have been to loads of weddings, mustn't you?'

'Very few,' he said. 'In fact, only a couple. I lived in the States until last year, so I missed out on various family weddings.'

'I don't know how you managed to avoid them,' said Cassie. 'All my friends seem have got married in the last year or so. There was a time when it felt as if I was going to a wedding every other weekend, and that was just people I knew! It was as if it was catching. Suddenly everyone was married.'

'Everyone except you?'

'That's what it feels like, anyway,' she said with little sigh.

'Why not you? You're obviously not averse to the idea of getting married.'

'I just haven't found the right guy, I suppose.' Cassie sighed again. 'I've had boyfriends, of course, but none of them have had that special something.'

Jake slanted a sardonic glance at her. 'Don't tell me you're still holding out for Rupert Branscombe Fox?'

'Of course not,' she said, flushing with embarrassment at the memory of the massive crush she had had on Rupert.

Not that she could really blame herself. What seventeen-year-old girl could be expected to resist that lethal combination of good looks and glamour? And Rupert could be extraordinarily charming when he wanted to be. He wasn't so charming when he didn't, of course, as Cassie had discovered even before Jake had kissed her.

Whoops; she didn't want to be thinking about that kiss, did she?

Too late.

Cassie tried the looking-out-of-the window thing again, but London was a blur, and she was back outside the Hall again, being yanked against Jake again. She could smell the leather of his jacket, feel the hardness of his body and the unforgiving steel of the motorbike.

In spite of Cassie's increasingly desperate efforts to keep her eyes on the interminable houses lining the road, they kept sliding round to Jake's profile. The traffic was heavy and he was concentrating on driving, so she gave in and let them skitter over the angular planes of his face to the corner of his mouth, at which point her heart started thumping and thudding alarmingly.

It was ten years later. Jake had changed completely. The leather jacket had gone, the bike had gone.

But that mouth was still exactly the same.

That mouth… She knew what it felt like. She knew how it tasted. She knew just how warm and sure those firm lips could be. Jake was an austere stranger beside her now, but she had *kissed* him. The memory was so vivid and so disorientating that Cassie felt quite giddy for a moment.

She swallowed. 'I had a major crush on Rupert, but it was just a teenage thing. Remember what a gawk I was?' she said, removing her gaze firmly back to the road. 'I have this fantasy that if I bumped into Rupert now he wouldn't recognise me.'

'I recognised you,' Jake pointed out unhelpfully.

'Yes, well, that's the thing about fantasies,' Cassie retorted in a tart voice. 'They're not real. I'm never likely to meet Rupert again. He lives in a different world, and the closest I get to him is seeing his picture in a celebrity magazine with some incredibly beautiful woman on his arm. Even if by some remote chance I did meet him I know he wouldn't even *notice* me, let along recognise me.'

'Why not?'

'Oh, I'm much too ordinary for the likes of Rupert,' said Cassie with a sigh. 'You were right about that, anyway.'

Jake looked taken aback. 'When did I ever say you were ordinary?'

'You know when.' She flashed him an accusing glance. 'After the Allentide Ball.' *After you kissed me.* 'Before you punched Rupert on the nose. I gather you took it upon yourself to tell Rupert I wasn't nearly sophisticated enough for him.'

It still rankled after all these years.

'You weren't,' said Jake.

'Then why were you fighting?'

'Not because Rupert leapt to defend your sophistication and readiness to embark on a torrid affair, if that's what you were thinking!'

'He said you'd been offensive,' said Cassie.

'Did he?' said Jake with a certain grimness.

It was typical of Rupert to have twisted the truth, he thought. He had been sitting at the bar, having a quiet drink, when Rupert had strolled in with his usual tame audience. Jake had found Rupert's arrogance difficult to deal with at the best of times, and that night certainly hadn't been one of those.

Jake often wondered how his life would have turned out if

he hadn't been in a particularly bad temper that night. The raw, piercing sweetness of Cassie's kiss at the Allentide ball had caught him unawares, and it didn't help that she had so patently been using him to attract Rupert's attention. Jake had been left feeling edgy, and furious with himself for expecting that it could have been any different and caring one way or the other.

And then Rupert had been there, showing off as usual. He'd been boasting about having had the estate manager's ungainly daughter, and making the others laugh. Jake's hand had clenched around his glass. He might not have liked being used, but Cassie was very young. She hadn't deserved to have her first experience of sex made the subject of pub banter.

Rupert had gone on and on, enjoying his audience, and Jake had finally had enough. He'd set down his glass very deliberately and risen to his feet to face Rupert. There had been a chorus of taunting, 'Ooohs' when he'd told him to leave Cassie alone, but he'd at least had the satisfaction of wiping the smirks off all their faces.

Especially Rupert's. Jake smiled ferociously as he remembered how he had released years of pent-up resentment. The moment his fist had connected with Rupert's nose had been a sweet one, and worth being banned from the village pub for. If it hadn't been for that fight, Rupert wouldn't have talked about assault charges, news of the fight wouldn't have reached Sir Ian's ears, and he wouldn't be where he was now.

Oh yes; it had definitely been worth it.

CHAPTER THREE

'It's my word against Rupert's, I suppose, but I can tell you, I was never offensive about you,' he said to Cassie. 'And being ordinary isn't the same thing as not being sophisticated. Believe me, you've never struck me as ordinary!'

'But I am,' said Cassie glumly. 'Or I am compared to Rupert, anyway. He's just so glamorous. Even you'd have to admit that.'

Jake's snort suggested he wasn't prepared to admit anything of the kind.

Of course, he'd never had any time for Rupert. Cassie supposed she could understand it. Rupert might be handsome, but even at the height of her crush she had recognised that arrogance in him as well. At the time, she had thought that it just added to his air of glamour.

The truth was that she still had a soft spot for Rupert, so good-looking and so badly behaved. In another age, he would have been a rake, ravishing women left, right and centre. Cassie could just see him in breeches and ruffles, smiling that irresistible smile, and breaking hearts without a flicker of shame.

Not the kind of man you would want to marry, perhaps, but very attractive all the same.

Cassie sighed a little wistfully. 'Rupert could be very charming,' she tried to explain, not that Jake was likely to be convinced.

They had barely got going on the motorway, and already overhead gantries were flashing messages about queues ahead. Muttering in frustration, he eased his foot up from the accelerator.

'What's so charming about squandering an inheritance from your parents and then sponging off your uncle?' he demanded irritably. 'Sir Ian got tired of bailing him out in the end, but he did what he could to encourage Rupert to settle down. He left his fortune to Rupert in trust until he's forty, in the hope that by then he'll have come to his senses.'

'*Forty?*' Cassie gasped. Rupert was only in his early thirties, like Jake, and eight years would be an eternity to wait when you had a lifestyle like Rupert's. 'That's awful,' she said without thinking. 'What's he going to do?'

'He could always try getting a job like the rest of us,' said Jake astringently 'Or, if he really can't bring himself to do anything as sordid as earning his own living, he can always get married. Sir Ian specified that the trust money could be released if Rupert gets married and settles down. He can't just marry anyone to get his hands on the money, though. He'll have to convince me as trustee that it's a real marriage and his wife a sensible woman before I'll release the funds.'

'Gosh, Rupert must have been livid when he found out!'

'He wasn't too happy,' Jake agreed with masterly understatement. 'He tried to contest the will, and when he didn't get anywhere with that he suggested we try and discuss things in a "civilised" way—which I gather meant me ignoring Sir Ian's wishes and handing the estate over to him to do with as he pleased.

'I was prepared to be civilised, of course. I invited him round for a drink, and it was just like old times,' he went on ironically. 'Rupert was arrogant and patronising, and I wanted to break his nose again!'

'You didn't!'

'No,' admitted Jake. 'But I don't know what would have happened if Natasha hadn't been there.'

'What did she make of Rupert?'

'She thought he was shallow.'

'I bet she thought he was gorgeous too,' said Cassie with a provocative look, and Jake pokered up and looked down his nose.

'Natasha is much too sensible to judge people on their appearances,' he said stiffly.

Of course she was. Cassie rolled her eyes as they overtook a van that was hogging the middle lane, startling the driver, who gave a grimace that was well out of Jake's field of vision. The van moved smartly into the slow lane.

'So how come she got involved with you if she's so sensible?' she asked, forgetting for a moment that Jake was an important client.

'We get on very well,' said Jake austerely.

'What does getting on very well mean, exactly?'

Ahead, there was a flurry of red lights as cars braked, and Jake moved smoothly into the middle lane. 'It means we're very compatible,' he said.

And they were. Natasha was everything he admired in a woman. She was very attractive—beautiful, in fact—and clear-thinking. She didn't constantly demand emotional reassurance the way his previous girlfriends had. She was focused on her own career, and understood if he had to work late, as he often did. She never made a fuss.

And she was classy. That was a large part of her appeal, Jake was prepared to admit. Years ago in Portrevick, Natasha wouldn't have looked at him twice, but when he walked into a party with her on his arm now he knew that he had arrived. She was everything Jake had never known when he was growing up. She had the assurance that came from a life of wealth and privilege, and every time Jake looked at her she reassured him that he had left Portrevick and the past behind him at last.

He didn't feel like telling Cassie all of that, though.

The traffic had slowed to a crawl and Jake shifted gear. 'I hope this is just sheer weight of traffic,' he said. 'I don't want to spend any more time on the road than we have to.'

Nor did Cassie. She wriggled in her seat. Quite apart from anything else, she was starving. Afraid that she would be late, she hadn't had time for breakfast that morning, and her stomach was gurgling ominously. She was hoping Jake would stop for petrol at some point, but at this rate they'd be lucky to get to a service station for supper, let alone lunch.

The lines of cars were inching forward in a staggered pattern. Sometimes the lane on their left would have a spurt of movement, only to grind to a halt as the supposed fast-lane speeded up, and then it would be the middle lane's turn. They kept passing or being passed by the same cars, and Cassie was beginning to recognise the occupants.

An expensive saloon on their left was creeping ahead of them once more. Covertly, Cassie studied the driver and passenger, both of whom were staring grimly ahead and not talking.

'I bet they've had a row,' she said.

'Who?'

'The couple on our left in the blue car.' Cassie pointed discreetly. 'Have a look when we go past. I can't decide whether she left the top off the toothpaste again, or whether she's incredibly possessive and sulking because he just had a text from his secretary.'

Jake cast her an incredulous glance. 'What's wrong with getting a text from your secretary?'

'She thinks he's having an affair with her,' said Cassie, barely pausing to consider. 'She insists on answering his phone while he's driving. Of course the text was completely bland, just confirming some meeting or something, but she just *knows* that it's a code.'

It was their lane's turn to move. Against his better judgement, Jake found himself glancing left as they passed. Cassie was right; the people both looked hatched-faced.

'They could be going to visit the in-laws,' he suggested, drawn into the fantasy in spite of himself.

Cassie took another look. 'You might be right,' she allowed. 'Her parents?'

'His, I think. She's got a face like concrete, so she's doing something she doesn't want to do. They don't really approve of her.'

'Hey, you're good at this!' Cassie laughed and swivelled back to watch the traffic. 'Now, who have we got here?' They were passing a hatchback driven by an elderly man who was clutching onto the wheel for dear life. Beside him, a tiny old lady was talking. 'Grandparents off to visit their daughter,' she said instantly. 'Too easy.'

'Perhaps they've been having a wild affair and are running away together,' said Jake, tongue in cheek.

'I like the way you're thinking, but they look way too comfortable together for that. I bet she's been talking for hours and he hasn't heard a word.'

'Can't imagine what that feels like,' murmured Jake, and she shot him a look.

'I wonder what they think about us?' she mused.

'I doubt very much that anyone else is thinking about us at all.'

'We must look like any other couple heading out of town for a long weekend,' said Cassie, ignoring him.

Perhaps that was why it felt so intimate sitting here beside him. If they were a couple, she could rest her hand on Jake's thigh. She could unwrap a toffee and pop it in his mouth without thinking. She could put her feet up on the dashboard and choose some music, and they could argue about which was the best route. She could nag him about stopping for something to eat.

But of course she couldn't do any of that. Especially not laying a hand on his leg.

She turned her attention firmly back to the other cars.

'Ooh, now...' she said, spying a single middle-aged man looking harassed at the wheel of his car, and instantly wove a complicated story about the double life he was leading, naming both wives, all five children and even the hamster with barely a pause for breath.

Jake shook his head. He tried to imagine Natasha speculating about the occupants of the other cars, and couldn't do it. She would think it childish. As it was, thought Jake.

On the other hand, this traffic jam was a lot less tedious than others he had sat in. Cassie's expression was animated, and he was very aware of her beside him. She had pushed back the seat as far as it would go, and her legs, in vivid blue tights, were stretched out before her. Her mobile face was alight with humour, her hands in constant motion. Jake had a jumbled impression of colour and warmth tugging at the edges of his vision the whole time. It was very distracting.

Now she was pulling faces at a little boy in the back seat of the car beside them. He crossed his eyes and stuck out his tongue, while Cassie stuck her thumbs in her ears and waggled her fingers in response.

Jake was torn between exasperation and amusement. He didn't know where Cassie got her idea that she was ordinary. There was absolutely nothing ordinary about her that he could see.

He glanced at the clock as they inched forward. It was a bad sign that they were hitting heavy traffic this early. It wasn't even midday, and already they seemed to have been travelling for ever.

Cassie had fallen silent at last. Bizarrely, Jake almost missed her ridiculous stories. Suddenly there was a curdled growl that startled him out of his distraction. He glanced at Cassie in surprise and she blushed and folded her arms over her stomach.

'Sorry, that was me,' she apologised. 'I didn't have time for breakfast.'

How embarrassing! Cassie was mortified. Natasha's stomach would never even murmur. At least Jake seemed prepared to cope with the problem.

'We'll stop and get something to eat when we get out of this,' he promised, but it was another twenty minutes before the blockage cleared, miraculously and for no apparent reason, and he could put his foot down.

To Cassie's disappointment they didn't stop at the first service-station they came to, or even the second. 'We need to get as far on our way as we can,' Jake said, but as her stomach became increasingly vocal he eventually relented as they came up to the third.

After a drizzly summer, the sun had finally come out for September. 'Let's sit outside,' Cassie suggested when they had bought coffee and sandwiches. 'We should make the most of the sun while we've got it.'

They found a wooden table in a sunny spot, away from the ceaseless growl of the motorway. Cassie turned sideways so that she could straddle the bench, and turned her face up to the sun.

'I love September,' she said. 'It still feels like the start of a new school year. I want to sharpen my pencils and write my name at the front of a blank exercise-book.'

Perhaps that was why she was so excited about transforming Portrevick Hall into a wedding venue, Cassie thought as she unwrapped her sandwich. It was a whole new project, her chance to draw a line under all her past muddles and mistakes and start afresh. She was determined not to mess up this time.

'It's great to get out of London too,' she went on indistinctly through a mouthful of egg mayonnaise. 'I'm really looking forward to seeing Portrevick again, too. I haven't been back since my parents moved away, but the place where you grow up always feels like home, doesn't it?'

'No,' said Jake.

'Really?' Cassie was brushing egg from her skirt, but at that she looked up at him in surprise. 'Don't you miss it at all?'

'I miss the sea sometimes,' he said after a moment. 'But Portrevick? No. It's not such a romantic place to live when there's never any money, and the moment there's trouble the police are at your door wanting you to account for where you've been and what you've been doing.'

Jake could hear the bitterness seeping into his voice in spite of every effort to keep it neutral. Cassie had no idea. She had grown up in a solid, cosy house in a solid, cosy, middle-class family. They might have lived in the same place, but they had inhabited different worlds.

Miss it? He had spent ten years trying to put Portrevick behind him.

'You must have family still there, though, mustn't you?' said Cassie. There had always been lots of Trevelyans in Portrevick, all of them reputedly skirting around the edges of the law.

'Not in Portrevick,' said Jake. 'There's no work in a village like that any more.' And there were richer pickings in places like Newquay or Penzance, he thought dryly. 'They've all moved away, so there's no one to go back for. If it wasn't for Sir Ian and the trust, I'd be happy never to see Portrevick again. And once I've sorted out something for the Hall I'll be leaving and I won't ever be going back.'

Cassie was having trouble keeping the filling in her sandwich. The egg kept oozing out of the baguette and dropping everywhere. Why hadn't she chosen a nice, neat sandwich like Jake's ham and cheese? He was managing to eat his without any mess at all.

She eyed him under her lashes as she licked her finger and gathered up some of the crumbs that were scattered on her side of the table. Jake had always been such a cool figure in her memories of Portrevick that it had never occurred to her to wonder how happy he had been.

He hadn't seemed unhappy. In Cassie's mind, he had always flirted with danger, roaring around on his motorbike or surfing in the roughest seas. She could still see him, sleek and dark as a seal in his wetsuit, riding the surf, his body leaning and bending in tune with the rolling wave.

It was hard to believe it was the same man as the one who sat across the table from her now, contained and controlled, eating his sandwich methodically. What had happened to that fierce, reckless boy?

Abandoning her sandwich for a moment, Cassie took a sip of coffee. 'If you feel like that about Portrevick, why did you agree to be Sir Ian's trustee?'

'Because I owed him.'

Jake had finished his own sandwich and brushed the crumbs from his fingers. 'It was Sir Ian that got me out of Portrevick,' he told her. 'He was always good to my mother, and after she died he let me earn some money by doing odd jobs for him. He was from a different world, but I liked him. He was the only person in the village who'd talk to you as if he was really interested in what you had to say. I was just a difficult kid from a problem family, but I never once had the feeling that Sir Ian was looking down on me.'

Unlike his nephew, Jake added to himself. Rupert got up every morning, looked in the mirror and found himself perfect. From the dizzying heights of his pedestal, how could he do anything *but* look down on lesser mortals? A boy from a dubious family and without the benefit of private schooling… Well, clearly Jake ought to be grateful that Rupert had ever noticed him at all.

'Sir Ian was lovely,' Cassie was agreeing. 'I know he was a bit eccentric, but he always made you feel that you were the one person he really wanted to see.'

Jake nodded. He had felt that, too. 'I saw him the day after that fight with Rupert,' he went on. 'Rupert was all set to press assault charges against me, but Sir Ian said he would persuade him to drop them. In return, he told me I should leave Portrevick. He said that if I stayed I would never shake off my family's reputation. There would be other fights, other brushes with the police. I'd drift over the line the way my father had done and end up in prison.'

Turning the beaker between his hands, Jake looked broodingly down into his coffee, remembering the conversation. Sir Ian hadn't pulled his punches. 'You're a bright lad,' he had said. 'But you're in danger of wasting all the potential you've got. You're eaten up with resentment, you're a troublemaker and you take stupid risks. If you're not careful, you'll end up in prison too. You can make a new life for yourself if you want it, but you're going to have to work for it. Are you prepared to do that?'

Jake could still feel that churning sense of elation at the prospect of escape, all mixed up with what had felt like a shameful nervousness about leaving everything familiar behind. There had been anger and resentment, too, mostly with Rupert, but also with Cassie, whose clumsy attempt to make Rupert jealous had precipitated the fight, and the offer that would change his life if he was brave enough to take it.

'The upshot was that Sir Ian said that he would sponsor me through university if I wanted the chance to start afresh somewhere new,' he told Cassie. 'It was an extraordinarily generous offer,' he said. 'It was my chance to escape from Portrevick, and I took it. I walked out of the Hall and didn't look back.'

'Was that when…?' Cassie stopped, realising too late where the question was leading, and a smile touched Jake's mouth.

'When you accosted me on my bike?' he suggested.

Cassie could feel herself turning pink, but she could hardly pretend now that she didn't remember that kiss. 'I seem to remember it was *you* who accosted *me*, wasn't it?' she said with as much dignity as she could, and Jake's smile deepened.

'I was provoked,' he excused himself.

'*Provoked?*' Cassie sat up straight, embarrassment forgotten in outrage. 'I did *not* provoke you!'

'You certainly did,' said Jake coolly. 'I wasn't in the mood to listen to you defending Rupert. He asked for that punch,

and it was only because he was all set to report me to the
police that Sir Ian suggested I leave Portrevick.

'That turned out to be the best thing that could have happened to me,' he allowed. 'And I'm grateful in retrospect. But
it didn't feel like that at the time. It felt as if Rupert could
behave as badly as he liked and that silver spoon would stay
firmly stuck in his mouth. I knew nobody would ever suggest
that *Rupert* should leave everything he'd ever known and
work for his living. I was angry, excited and confused, and
I'm afraid you got in the way.'

He paused and looked straight at Cassie, the dark-blue
eyes gleaming with unmistakable amusement. 'If it's any
comfort, that kiss was my last memory of Portrevick.'

That kiss... The memory of it shimmered between them,
so vividly that for one jangling moment it was as if they were
kissing again, as if his fingers were still twined in her hair,
her lips still parting as she melted into him, that wicked excitement still tumbling along her veins.

With an effort, Cassie dragged her gaze away and buried
her burning face in her coffee cup. 'Nice to know that I was
memorable,' she muttered.

'You were certainly that,' said Jake.

'Yes, well, it was all a long time ago.' Cassie cleared her
throat and cast around for something, anything, to change the
subject. 'I'd no idea Sir Ian helped you like that,' she managed
at last, seizing on the first thing she could think of. 'We all
assumed you'd just taken off to avoid the assault charges.'

'That doesn't surprise me. Portrevick was always ready to
think the worst of me,' said Jake, gathering up the debris of
their lunch. 'Sir Ian wasn't the type to boast about his generosity, but I kept in touch all the time, and as soon as I was in
a position to do so I offered to repay all the money he'd spent
on my education. He flatly refused to take it, but he did say
there was one thing I could do for him, and that was when he
asked me to be his executor and the trustee. He asked me if I

would make sure that the Portrevick estate stayed intact. You know how much he loved the Hall.'

Cassie nodded. 'Yes, he did.'

'I can't say I liked the idea of taking on a complicated trust, and I knew how much Rupert would resent me, but I owed Sir Ian too much to refuse. So,' said Jake, 'that's why we're driving down this motorway. That's why I want to get the Hall established as a venue. Once it's up and running, and self-supporting, I'll feel as if I've paid my debt to him at last. I'll have done what Sir Ian asked me to do, and then I really can put Portrevick and the past behind me once and for all.'

He drained his coffee and shoved the sandwich wrappers inside the empty cup. 'Have you finished? We've still got a long way to go, so let's hit the road again.'

Cassie studied Portrevick Hall with affection as she cut across the grounds to the sweep of gravel at its imposing entrance. A rambling manor-house dating back to the middle ages, it had grown organically as succeeding generations had added a wing here, a turret there. The result was a muddle of architectural styles that time had blended into a harmonious if faintly dilapidated whole, with crumbling terraces looking out over what had once been landscaped gardens.

It was charming from any angle, Cassie decided, and would make a wonderful backdrop for wedding photos.

Her feet crunched on the gravel as she walked up to the front door and pulled the ancient bell, deliberately avoiding looking at where Jake had sat astride his motorbike that day. She wouldn't have been at all surprised to see the outline of her feet still scorched into the stones.

Don't think about it, she told herself sternly. She was supposed to be impressing Jake with her professionalism, and she was going to have to try a lot harder today after babbling on in the car yesterday. Jake had dropped her at Tina's and driven off with barely a goodbye, and Cassie didn't blame him. He must have been sick of listening to her inane chatter for seven hours.

So today she was going to concentrate on being cool, calm and competent.

Which was easily said but harder to remember, when Jake opened the door and her heart gave a sickening lurch . He was wearing jeans and a blue Guernsey with the sleeves pushed above his wrists; without the business suit he looked younger and more approachable.

And very attractive.

'Come in,' he said. 'I was just making coffee. Do you want some?'

'Thanks.' Cassie followed him down a long, stone-flagged corridor to the Hall's vast kitchen. Without those unsettling blue eyes on her face, she could admire his lean figure and easy stride.

'Quite a looker now, isn't he?' Tina had said when they were catching up over a bottle of wine the night before. 'And rich too, I hear. You should go for it, Cassie. You always did have a bit of a thing for him.'

'No, I didn't!' said Cassie, ruffled. A thing for Jake Trevelyan? The very idea!

'Remember that Allantide Ball…?' Tina winked. 'I'm sure Jake does. Do you think you could be in with a chance?'

'No,' said Cassie, and then was horrified to hear how glum she sounded about it. 'I mean, no,' she tried again brightly. 'He's already got a perfect girlfriend.'

'Shame,' said Tina.

And the worst thing was that a tiny bit of Cassie was thinking the same thing as she watched Jake making the coffee.

Which was very unprofessional of her.

Giving herself a mental slap, Cassie pulled out her Netbook and made a show of looking around the kitchen. They might as well get down to business straight away.

'The kitchen will need replacing as a priority,' she said.

'You couldn't do professional catering in here. There's plenty of space, which is good, but it needs gutting and proper catering equipment installed.'

Jake could see that made sense. 'Get some quotes.' He nodded.

Cassie tapped in 'kitchen—get quotes' and felt efficient.

'We should start with the great hall and see how much work needs to be done there,' she went on, encouraged. 'That's the obvious place for wedding ceremonies.'

'Fine by me,' said Jake, handing her a mug. 'Let's take our coffee with us.'

The great hall had been the heart of the medieval house, but its stone walls had been panelled in the seventeenth century, and a grand wooden-staircase now swept down from a gallery on the first floor. At one end, a vast fireplace dominated an entire wall, and there was a dais at the other.

'Perfect for the high table,' said Cassie, pointing at it with her mug. Netbook under one arm, coffee clutched in her other hand, she turned slowly, imagining the space filled with people. 'They'll love this,' she enthused. 'I can see it being really popular for winter weddings.

'I always dreamed about having a Christmas wedding here,' she confided to Jake, who was also looking around, but with a lot less enthusiasm. 'There was going to be a fire burning, an enormous Christmas tree with lights, candles everywhere… Outside it would be cold and dark, but in here it would be warm and cosy.'

Funny how she could remember that fantasy so vividly after all this time. In her dream, Cassie was up there on the dais, looking beautiful and elegant—naturally—with Rupert, who gazed tenderly down at her. Her family were gathered round, bursting with pride in her, and Sir Ian was there, too, beaming with delight.

Cassie sighed.

'Anyway, I think it could look wonderful, don't you?'

Jake's mouth turned down as he studied the hall. 'Not really. It looks pretty dingy and gloomy to me.'

'That's because it's been empty for a while, and it needs a good clean. You've got to use your imagination,' said Cassie. Perching on an immense wooden trestle-table, she laid the Netbook down and sipped at her own coffee. It was cool in the hall, and she was glad of the warmth.

'It wouldn't be so different from the Allantide Ball,' she said. 'Remember how Sir Ian used to decorate it with candles and apples and it looked really inviting?'

Then she wished that she hadn't mentioned the Allantide Ball. In spite of herself, her eyes flickered to where Jake had been standing that night. She had been over by the stairs when she had spotted him. She could retrace her route across the floor, aware of the dark-blue eyes watching her approach, and a sharp little frisson shivered down her spine just as it had ten years ago.

And over there was the door leading out to the terrace… Cassie remembered the mixture of panic and excitement as Jake had taken her hand and led her out into the dark. She could still feel his hard hands on her, still feel her heart jerking frantically, and her blood still pounded at the devastating sureness of his lips.

Swallowing, she risked a glance at Jake and found her gaze snared on his. He was watching her with a faint, mocking smile, and although nothing was said she knew—she just *knew*—that he was remembering that kiss, too. The very air seemed to be jangling with the memory of that wretched ball, and Cassie wrenched her eyes away. What on earth had possessed her to mention it?

She sipped her coffee, trying desperately to think of something to say to break the awkward silence, and show Jake that she hadn't forgotten that she was here to do a job.

'What would you think about holding an Allantide Ball this year?' she said, starting slowly but gathering pace as she realised that the idea, born of desperation, might not be such a bad one after all. 'As a kind of memorial to Sir Ian? It would be good publicity.'

'No one would come,' said Jake. 'I'm not exactly popular in Portrevick. I went into the pub the last time I came down and there was dead silence when I walked in. I felt about as welcome as a cup of cold sick.'

Cassie had gathered something of that from Tina. Apparently there was much speculation in the village about Sir Ian's will, and the general feeling was that Jake had somehow pulled a fast one for his own nefarious purposes, in keeping with the Trevelyan tradition.

'That's because they don't know the truth,' she said. 'Inviting everyone to the ball for Sir Ian and explaining what you're planning for the Hall would make them see that you're not just out to make a quick buck. You need the locals on your side if the wedding venue is to be a success,' she went on persuasively. 'I think this would be a great way to kick things off.'

CHAPTER FOUR

'I'M DAMNED if I'm going to waste my time sucking up to Portrevick,' said Jake, a mulish look about his mouth..

'You won't have to. I'll do it for you,' said Cassie soothingly. 'You won't need to do anything but turn up on 31st October, put on a tux and be civil for two or three hours. You can manage that, can't you?'

'I suppose so,' he said grudgingly.

'It'll be worth it when you can walk away and know the Hall is established as part of the community and has local support,' she encouraged him. 'If you want to fulfil Sir Ian's wishes, then this is the best way you can go about it.'

Jake looked at her; she was sitting on the old table and swinging her legs. She was a vibrant figure in the gloomy hall with her bright cardigan, bright face and bright, unruly hair. She didn't look sensible, but he had a feeling that what she had said just might be.

'It's not long to Allantide,' he pointed out. 'You'll never get contractors in that quickly.'

'We will if you're prepared to pay for it,' said Cassie, gaining confidence with every word. 'We've got six weeks. If we aimed to have the great hall redecorated by then, it would give us a real incentive to get things moving.'

Narrowing her eyes, she pictured the hall decorated and full of people. 'It's not as if any major structural work is required. It just needs cleaning up a bit.'

She flicked open her Netbook and began typing notes to herself. This was good. There had been a nasty little wobble there when she'd remembered the time they had kissed, but she was feeling under control again now. Cool, calm, competent; wasn't that how she was supposed to be?

OK, maybe she wasn't *calm*, exactly—not with the unsettling feeling that seemed to fizz under her skin whenever she looked at Jake—but at least she was giving a good impression of competence for once.

'The more I think about it, the more I like the idea,' she said. 'We can use the ball to start spreading the word that the Hall can be hired for special occasions. We'll invite the local paper here to take some pictures…oh! And we can have some photos done for a website too, so people can see how fabulous the great hall can look. We can hardly put a picture up of it looking the way it does now, can we?'

'Website?' said Jake, a little taken aback at how quickly her plans seemed to be developing.

'You've got to have a website,' Cassie said as if stating the obvious. 'In fact, we should think about that right away. We can't afford to leave it until all the work's been done, or we'll miss out on another year.'

Fired with enthusiasm, she snapped the Netbook closed and jumped off the table. 'Come on, let's look at the other rooms.'

She dragged Jake round the entire house, looking into every room and getting more and more excited as she went.

'You know, I really think this could be fantastic,' she said when they ended up on the terraces outside. She gestured expansively. 'You've got everything: a wonderfully old and romantic place for ceremonies, enough space for big parties, plenty of bedrooms…

'We don't need to do them all at once,' she reassured Jake, who had been mentally calculating how much all these grand

plans were going to cost. 'At first, we just need somewhere
the bride can get ready, but eventually we could offer rooms
for the whole wedding-party.'

'Maybe,' said Jake, unwilling to commit himself too far at
this stage. He wanted the Hall to become self-sufficient so he
didn't need to think about it any more, but it was becoming
evident as Cassie outlined her ideas that it was going to prove
a lot more expensive than he had first anticipated.

'And the best thing is, there's no major structural work
required yet,' she went on. 'We just need to think about the
initial refurbishment for now.'

She pointed over towards the fine nineteenth-century stable
block with older barns beyond. 'Eventually you could have
more than one wedding at a time. The barns would be great
for an informal wedding.'

Her face was alight with enthusiasm, and Jake found
himself thinking that perhaps giving Cassie the contract might
not be such a big mistake after all.

Last night, he had bitterly regretted that he had ever taken
the advice to contact her. Cassie had talked all the way down
the motorway, barely drawing breath for seven whole hours.
She had an extraordinarily vivid imagination and was, Jake
had to admit, very funny at times. But she was much too distracting. He had been exasperated by the way she kept tugging
at the edge of his vision when he should have been concentrating on the road.

Now he was changing his mind again. Perhaps Cassie
wasn't as coolly professional as the people he normally did
business with, but she seemed to know what she was talking
about. Her speech was refreshingly free of business jargon, and
she had a warmth and an enthusiasm that might in the end get
the job done faster than one of his marketing team, however
sound their grasp of financial imperatives or strategic analysis.

She was leaning on the terrace wall, looking out over
garden, her hands resting on the crumbling coping-stones. In

profile, her lashes were long and tilting, the edge of her mouth a dreamy curve. The sunlight glinted on her brown curls—except that brown was too dull a word for her hair, Jake realised. Funny how he had never noticed what a beautiful colour it was before, a shade somewhere between auburn and chestnut with hints of honey and gold.

Unaware of his gaze, Cassie was following her own train of thought. 'I've just had a great idea!' she said, turning to him, and Jake looked quickly away. 'I've got contacts with a couple of wedding magazines. Maybe I could get them to do a story about how we're turning the Hall into the ultimate wedding venue? It would be fantastic promotion and get people talking about it. We could even start taking some advance bookings… What do you think?'

'I think I'm going to leave it all up to you,' said Jake slowly.

'*Really?*' The big brown eyes lit with excitement.

'Yes,' he said, making up his mind. He doubted that he would find anyone else as committed to the project, even if he had the time to find them. 'We can agree the fees when we get back to London, but in the meantime I'd like you to go ahead, make whatever decisions you need and get work started as soon as possible.'

'Er…it's me.' Cassie made a face at the phone. *Excellent, Cassie.* Stuttering and stumbling was always a good way to impress an important client with your professionalism. 'Cassie… Cassandra Grey,' she added, just in case Jake knew anyone else who went to pieces at the sound of his voice.

'Yes, so my PA said when she put you through,' said Jake with an edge of impatience.

'Oh yes, I suppose she did. Um, well, I just thought I'd let you know how things are going at the Hall.'

'Yes?'

His voice was clipped, and Cassie bit her lip, furious with herself for irritating him before she had even started. Why was she being so moronic? Everything was working out just as she'd planned, and she had been feeling really pleased with herself. Ringing Jake with an update hadn't seemed like a big deal when she had picked up the phone two minutes ago, but the minute he had barked his name her insides had jerked themselves into a knot of nerves.

He sounded so distant that she was tempted to put the phone down, but that would be even sillier. Besides, she needed his OK on a number of matters.

'We've been making progress,' she told him brightly.

'Yes?' he said again, and her heart sank. She had hoped they had reached a kind of understanding at the Hall. Jake had certainly seemed more approachable then, but he was obviously in a vile mood now—which didn't bode well for the idea she wanted to put to him.

She cleared her throat. 'There are one or two things I need to talk to you about,' she said. 'Are you free for lunch at all this week?'

'Is it important?'

What did he think—that she wanted to take him out for the pleasure of his company? Wisely, Cassie held her tongue.

'It is, rather.'

There was an exasperated sigh at the other end of the phone, and she imagined him checking his electronic organiser. 'Does it have to be this week?'

Clearly, he couldn't wait to see her again. 'The sooner the better, really,' said Cassie.

More tsking. 'Lunch might be tricky,' he said after a moment. 'Could we make it dinner instead?'

Oh, great. And there she had been feeling nervous at the prospect of an hour's lunch. 'Er, yes. Of course.'

'What about tomorrow?'

'Fine. I'll book a table,' said Cassie quickly, just so he knew that it was a business dinner and that she would be picking up the tab. Not that there was any question of a date.

She hesitated. 'As it's dinner, would Natasha like to join us?' she asked delicately.

There was a pause. 'Not tomorrow,' said Jake curtly.

'Oh, that's a pity,' said Cassie, although actually she was rather glad. She didn't fancy spending a whole evening being compared to the perfect Natasha, and besides she couldn't help feeling that her idea would be better put to Jake alone in the first instance.

They arranged to meet at Giovanni's, an Italian restaurant just round the corner from Avalon's office, where she and Joss were regulars. There was no way Cassie's expense account could rise to the kind of restaurants Jake was no doubt accustomed to, but the food at Giovanni's was good and the ambience cheerful, and in the end Cassie decided that it was better to stick to the unpretentious.

It was only when she arrived the following evening that she began to wonder if it had been such a good idea. Giovanni treated her and Joss like daughters, and the brides-to-be they took there were invariably delighted by him, but Cassie had a feeling Jake would be less charmed.

Still, it was too late to change now. Cassie hurried along the street, her heels clicking on the pavement. Anxious not to make it look as if she were expecting some kind of date, but wanting to make an effort for their now most-important client, she had dithered too long about what to wear. Eventually she had decided on a sleeveless dress with a little cardigan and her favourite suede boots, but they had proved to be a mistake, too. Fabulous as they were, it was hard to walk very fast in them.

Jake, of course, hadn't even had the decency to be a few minutes late and was waiting for her outside Giovanni's, looking dark, lean and remote. His suit was immaculately tailored, his expression shuttered. Oh God, now he was cross with her for not being on time.

Cassie's heart sank further. It didn't look as if the evening was getting off to a good start.

'I'm *so* sorry,' she said breathlessly as she clicked up on her heels. 'I hope you haven't been waiting long?'

'A couple of minutes, that's all. I was early.'

The dark gaze rested on her face and Cassie saw herself in his eyes, red-faced and puffing, her hair all anyhow. So much for cool professionalism. She had been so proud of herself recently, too, and had vowed that it would be the start of a whole new image.

'Well, let's go in.' Flustered, she reached for the door, intending to stand back and usher Jake through, but Jake was too quick for her. He reached an arm behind her and held the door, leaving Cassie no option but to go ahead of him. It was that or an unseemly tussle, but as it was she was left looking like the little woman rather than the cool, capable business-woman she wanted to be.

No, *not* a good start.

Giovanni spied her across the restaurant and came sailing over to greet her, his arms outstretched.

'Cassie! *Bella!*' His kissed her soundly on both cheeks before holding her away from him. 'You're looking too thin,' he scolded her, the way he always did, before turning his beady gaze on Jake. 'And who is this?' he asked interestedly. 'It's about time you brought a man here!'

'Mr Trevelyan is a *client*, Giovanni,' said Cassie hastily.

'Shame!' he whispered to her, plucking a couple of menus from the bar. 'He looks your type, I think.'

Cassie opened her mouth to protest that Jake was most certainly *not* her type, but realised just in time that she could hardly embark on an argument with Jake right there. She would just have to hope that he hadn't heard. He hadn't recoiled in horror, anyway. In fact, he didn't seem to be paying them much attention at all, which was a little irritating in one way, but a big relief in another.

So she contented herself with crossing her eyes and giving Giovanni a warning glare, which he ignored completely as he gestured them towards a table tucked away in a little alcove where a candle flickered invitingly. It looked warm and intimate, and perfect for lovers.

'My best table for you,' he said, handing them the menus with a flourish. 'Nice and quiet so you can talk to your *client*,' he added to Cassie with an outrageous wink.

At least the dim lighting hid her scarlet cheeks. Cassie was mortified. 'Did I mention Joss and I were thinking of taking our clients to the Thai restaurant next door in future?' she muttered, but Giovanni only laughed.

'I will bring you some wine and Roberto will take your order and then, don't worry, you can be quite alone…' Chuckling to himself, he surged off to the kitchen, leaving a little pool of silence behind him.

Cassie unfolded her napkin. 'I'm sorry about that,' she said awkwardly after a moment. 'He's quite a character.'

'So I gather,' said Jake.

'I mean, he's lovely, but he does go a bit far sometimes. We bring a lot of clients here, but it's usually at lunchtime, and they're usually brides, so it's become a bit of a standing joke that I never come with a boyfriend.'

She trailed off, horribly aware that she was babbling. Jake was making her nervous. There was a tightness to him tonight, a grim set to his mouth, and an air of suppressed anger. Surely it wasn't anything she had done, was it? Everything had been going so well down in Portrevick. Had he heard something?

'Er, well, anyway… We're supposed to be talking about the Hall,' she said brightly.

Jake seemed to focus on her properly for the first time. 'You said you had made some progress?'

'I have.' Cassie told him about the contractors she had engaged. A small army of them was already hard at work. 'They're mostly cleaners,' she explained. 'There's so much wood in the great hall that it doesn't need much decorating—

although they're repainting the roof—but the walls, the floor and the fireplace need a thorough clean and polish. It's all well in hand for the Allantide Ball.'

'Good,' said Jake absently. Cassie wondered if he had even been listening. He was frowning down at a knife he was spinning beneath one finger.

'I've also been in touch with various local caterers, florists, photographers and so on, and started to draw up a directory of our own.'

'It all sounds very promising,' said Jake as Giovanni's nephew appeared with a carafe of wine. Less expansive than his uncle, or perhaps just more sensitive to Jake's grim expression, he took their orders with the minimum of fuss.

'You've been busy,' Jake added to Cassie, folding the menu and handing it back to the waiter.

Well, at least he had been listening. She had wondered there for a minute. 'There's lots to do, but I'm enjoying it.'

Jake reached for the carafe, but, mindful that she was supposed to be the host, Cassie got there first, and he watched without comment as she filled two glasses. She didn't know about Jake, but she certainly needed one!

She drew a breath. 'I've been thinking about a promotion, too.'

If only Jake was in a more amenable mood, she thought. It was going to be tricky enough breaking the news of the deal she had made with *Wedding Belles* as it was. She took a sip of wine to fortify herself. 'Do you remember me saying it might be worth contacting a couple of magazines in case they wanted to run a piece about setting up the Hall as a venue?' she began cautiously.

'Vaguely.'

It was hardly the most encouraging of responses, but Cassie ploughed on anyway. 'Well, I did that, and one of them is very keen on the idea.'

There was a pause. Jake could see that she was waiting

for him to say something, although he wasn't sure what. 'OK,' he said.

'But they want a bit more of a human-interest angle.'

'Human interest?'

'Yes, you know, to personalise the story? So it's not just the story of how the building is being prepared, it's also about a couple preparing to get married there. The readers love real-life stories,' Cassie hurried on. 'The editor of *Wedding Belles*—that's the magazine—wants to follow a couple who are going to be married there. So the article will be illustrated with pictures of them choosing the flowers, planning menus, trying on wedding dresses and all that kind of thing.'

'But we haven't got any couples yet,' Jake objected. 'Surely the whole point of promoting the Hall like this is to *find* someone who wants to get married there?'

'Quite,' said Cassie, relieved that he at least could see the point of the article. 'We haven't got any punters yet, but we *have* got you and Natasha…' She trailed off, hoping that Jake would get where this was all going.

He had gone very still. 'What about me and Natasha?'

'OK, I *may* have stretched the truth a little bit here,' Cassie acknowledged, and took the final hurdle in a rush. 'But the editor was so keen on the idea that I told her that you were getting married at the Hall at Christmas.'

'*What?*'

Jake's voice was like a lash, and carried right across the restaurant. Diners on nearby tables turned to look at them in surprise, and behind Jake at the bar Giovanni clutched a hand to his heart with an exaggerated expression of sympathy for her.

Cassie glowered at him and turned deliberately back to Jake. She had been afraid he might react like that.

'I know it's a cheek,' she said, holding up her hands in a placatory gesture. 'But I really do think it would be great publicity for the Hall. And you don't have to go through with it if Natasha doesn't want to get married there. They'll only want pictures of a few set occasions, so I don't see any reason why we shouldn't set up a few shots and create a story for them.'

Jake was looking grimly discouraging, so she hurried on before he could give her a flat no. 'We don't need to tell them that it isn't actually the dress Natasha is going to wear, or those aren't really the flowers she'd choose,' she reassured him. 'You and Natasha would just be models, if you like, showing what a wonderful wedding-venue the Hall will be. I know you're both busy, but it shouldn't take up too much time. Just a few hours every now and then to have your photos taken.

'It would be a really effective way to promote the Hall,' Cassie went on when there was still no response from Jake. There was an edge of desperation in her voice by now. It had taken ages to get the editor of *Wedding Belles* to agree to feature Portrevick Hall, and it was only the promise of the human interest lent by the owner himself getting married there—another little stretching of the truth—that had swung it for her.

'You did say you wanted the venue to be self-sustaining as soon as possible,' she reminded him. '*Wedding Belles* is really popular with brides-to-be around the country, and its circulation figures are amazing. If they run a feature about the Hall, we'll have couples queuing up to book it, and you'll be able to hand the whole place over to a manager much sooner than you thought.'

Jake drank some wine, then put down his glass. 'There's just one problem,' he said.

'Just one?' said Cassie, trying to lighten the atmosphere. 'That doesn't sound too bad!'

He didn't smile back. 'Unfortunately it's quite a major one,' he said. 'I'm afraid Natasha isn't around to model anything any more. She's left me.'

Cassie put down her glass so abruptly, wine sloshed onto the tablecloth. 'Natasha's *left* you?'

'So it seems.'

'But…but…' Cassie was floundering. It was the last thing she had expected to hear. 'God, I'm so sorry! I had no idea…' No wonder Jake was looking so grim! 'When did all this happen?'

'When I got back from Cornwall.' Jake reached across with his napkin and mopped up the wine Cassie had spilt before she made even more of a mess. 'Natasha was waiting for me with her case packed. She said she was sorry, but she had met someone else and fallen madly in love with him.'

His first reaction had been one of surprise at her words. Natasha had never been the type to do anything *madly*. One of the things he had always liked about her was her calm, rational approach to everything, and now it seemed as if she was just as illogical and emotional as, well, as Cassie.

'How awful for you.' Cassie's round face was puckered with sympathy. 'How long had it been going on?'

'Hardly any time. She said he'd literally swept her off her feet. I'll bet he did,' Jake added grimly. 'He's had plenty of practice.'

'Gosh, he's not a friend of yours, is he?' That would make it twice as humiliating for him.

'A friend?' Jake gave a short, mirthless laugh. 'Hardly! Rupert Branscombe Fox is no friend of mine.'

'Rupert?' Cassie's eyes were out on stalks. Crikey, this was like something out of a soap opera! 'But how on earth did Natasha meet Rupert?'

'It was my own fault,' said Jake. Funnily enough, now that he'd started talking, he didn't feel too bad. He'd been so angry before that he could barely bite out a word. 'I invited Rupert round to discuss the trust at home, and Natasha was there. I didn't think she was that impressed with him at the time.'

Cassie remembered now. Perfect Natasha had decided that Rupert was shallow—or that was what she had said, anyway.

'What changed her mind?'

'Rupert did. He deliberately set out to seduce Natasha to get at me.' Jake's expression was set. 'I can't believe she fell for it,' he said, sounding genuinely baffled. 'I thought she was too sensible to have her head turned by Rupert's very superficial attraction. I can't understand it at all.'

Cassie could. Even as a boy, Rupert had been extraordinarily good-looking, and if he had turned the full battery of his sex appeal on Natasha he must have been well nigh irresistible. Perhaps Natasha had been tired of being told how admirably sensible she was.

But poor Jake. How hurt and angry he must have been!

'Rupert's very…charming,' she said lamely.

Jake tossed back his wine and poured himself another glass. 'He's *using* Natasha. I can't believe she can't see it for herself!'

'Maybe he's fallen in love with her,' Cassie suggested

'Love?' Jake snorted. 'Rupert doesn't love anyone but himself.'

'You don't *know* that—'

'Sure I do,' he interrupted her. 'Rupert was kind enough to explain it to me. Natasha was perfect for his purposes, he said. He was furious and humiliated by the trust Sir Ian had set up, and he's chosen to blame me for it. Breaking up my relationship with Natasha was doubly sweet. It hurt me, and it gives him access to the trust money, or so he thinks. He claims he's going to marry her because I won't have any grounds for arguing that Natasha isn't a sensible woman, as specified by Sir Ian. He was quite sure I would understand, *old chap*.'

Ouch. Cassie grimaced at the savagery in Jake's voice. She didn't blame him for being angry. She could practically hear Rupert's light, cut-glass tones, and could just imagine what effect they would have had on Jake.

'What are you going to do?'

'Well, I'm certainly not handing over the money yet. Natasha deserves better than to be married for such a cynical reason. The moment Rupert's got his hands on the money, he'll dump her like the proverbial ton of bricks,' said Jake. 'He's still got to prove to me that he's settled down, and I'll believe that when I see it!'

Under the circumstances, it was generous of him to still think about Natasha, Cassie thought. He must love her, even if she had proved to be not quite as perfect as he had believed.

Cassie pushed her glass around, making patterns on the tablecloth. It would be quite something to be loved by someone like Jake, who didn't give up on you even when you made a terrible mistake. She wondered if Natasha would realise that once the first thrill of being with Rupert wore off.

As it inevitably would. Cassie wasn't a fool, whatever her family thought. She had long ago realised that Rupert's appeal lay largely in the fact that he was out of reach. He was so impossibly handsome, so extraordinarily charming, so unbelievably glamorous, that you couldn't imagine doing anything ordinary with him. He was the kind of man you dreamed of having a mad, passionate affair with, not the kind of man you lived with and loved every day.

Not like Jake.

Cassie's fingers stilled on the glass. Where had *that* thought come from?

Looking up from her wine, she studied him across the table. Lost in his own thoughts, he was broodingly turning a fork on the tablecloth, his own head bent and the dark, stormy eyes hidden. She could see the angular planes of his face, the jut of his nose, the set of his mouth, and all at once it was as if she had never seen him before.

There was a solidity and a control to him, she realised, disconcerted to realise that she could imagine living with him in a way she had never been able to with Rupert. Bumping into Rupert again had been one of her favourite fantasies for years, but in her dreams they were never doing anything ordinary. They were *getting* married, not *being* married. They were going to Paris or sitting on a yacht in the Caribbean, not having breakfast or watching television or emptying the dishwasher.

How strange that she could picture Jake in her flat, could

see him coming in from work, taking off his jacket, loosening his tie, reaching for her with a smile…

A strange shiver snaked its way down her spine. It was just Jake, she reminded herself. But he was so immediate, so real, so *there*, that his presence felt like a hand against her skin, and all at once she was struggling to drag enough oxygen into her lungs.

And then he looked up, the dark-blue eyes locked with hers, and she forgot to breathe at all.

'Spaghetti carbonara.'

Cassie actually jumped as Giovanni deposited a steaming plate in front of her.

'And fettucine *all'arrabiata* for your *client!*'

She barely noticed Giovanni's jovial winks and nods of encouragement as he fussed around with pepper and parmesan. How long had she been staring into Jake's eyes, unable to look away? A second? Ten? Ten *minutes*? She hoped it was the first, but it was impossible to tell. She felt oddly jarred, and her heart was knocking erratically against her ribs.

She was terrified in case Jake was able to read her thoughts in her eyes. Of course, she would have known if he had, because he would look absolutely horrified. He probably couldn't think of anything worse than going home to her in an untidy flat every night.

Why was *that* a depressing thought?

CHAPTER FIVE

AND why was she even *thinking* about it? Cassie asked herself crossly as she picked up her fork. Disappointed by her lack of response, Giovanni had taken himself off at last. Jake was obviously still in love with the not-quite-so-perfect Natasha, who had had her sensible head turned by Rupert.

Twirling spaghetti in her spoon, she forced her mind back to the conversation. 'I'm really sorry,' she said when Giovanni had left. 'If it's any comfort, I don't imagine Rupert will be easy to live with. Perhaps Natasha will change her mind.'

'That's what I'm hoping,' said Jake.

That wasn't quite what Cassie had been hoping to hear. *I wouldn't take her back if she grovelled from here to Friday* was more what she had had in mind.

She sighed inwardly. Stop being so silly, she told herself.

'In the meantime, I'll go back to *Wedding Belles* and tell them that we'd still like a feature on the Hall, but we can't manage the human-interest angle.'

Jake's gaze sharpened. 'I thought you said they wouldn't do a piece without that?'

'No, well, it's not the end of the world. We can find other ways of promoting the Hall.'

'They won't reach the same market, though?'

'Probably not.'

Jake brooded, stirring his fork mindlessly around in the fettucine. 'To hell with it!' he said explosively after a while and looked up at Cassie, who regarded him warily. 'I'm damned if I'm going to let Rupert mess up my plans for the Hall, too. He's made enough trouble! I say we go ahead with it anyway.'

'We can't do much about it without Natasha,' she reminded him reluctantly.

'Unless…' Jake trailed off, staring at Cassie as if seeing her properly for the first time.

She stared back, more than a little unnerved. 'What?'

'Did you tell this editor Natasha's name?'

'No, I didn't go into details. I just said the owner of the Hall was getting married.'

'So I don't really need Natasha—I just need a fiancée?'

'Well, yes, but—'

'So why don't I marry you?'

There was a rushing sound in Cassie's ears. She went hot, then cold, then hot again. 'Me?' she squeaked. 'You don't want to marry me!'

'Of course I don't,' said Jake, recoiling. 'God, no! But you said yourself that it doesn't have to be a real engagement. If all we need is to have a few photographs taken, why shouldn't you be the bride-to-be?'

'Well, because—because—' Cassie stuttered, groping for all the glaringly obvious reasons why she couldn't, and bizarrely unable to think of any. 'Because everyone would know it wasn't true.'

'You just said you didn't give the magazine any names.'

'I wasn't thinking of them. I was thinking of all the people who know perfectly well we're not engaged.'

'Who's going to know?'

'Anyone who sees the article,' she said, exasperated, but Jake only looked down his nose.

'I don't know anyone who's likely to read *Wedding Belles*,' he said.

Cassie glared at him. 'It's not just about you, though, is it? I know masses of people who read it for one reason or another, and if one of my friends gets whiff of the fact that I'm apparently engaged without telling anyone I'll never hear the end of it!'

Jake couldn't see the problem. 'The article won't be published until next year,' he said dismissively. 'We can worry about what we tell people then. Rupert will never stick with Natasha for more than a few weeks, so there'll be no reason not to tell everyone the truth then. We'll say it was just a marketing exercise.'

'And what about when the *Wedding Belles* photographer comes down to take pictures of us supposedly planning our wedding at the Hall?' asked Cassie, picking up her spoon and fork once more. 'It'll be all over Portrevick in no time. You know what the village is like. We'd never be able to keep it secret. Rupert's got some fancy weekend place in St Ives; what's the betting he'll hear about it?'

'What if he does? It wouldn't do him any harm to think that I'm not inconsolable.'

'No, but if he gets wind of the fact that you're just pretending…' Cassie trailed off and Jake nodded.

'You're right,' he said. 'Rupert wouldn't hesitate to make trouble for me in whatever way he could.' He looked across the table at Cassie. 'In that case, let's make it true,' he said.

She stared at him. 'What do you mean?'

'Let's make it a real engagement,' he said, as if it were the most obvious thing in the world. 'Or, at least, not a secret one,' he amended. 'We can tell everybody who needs to know, and do the photographs for the article quite openly. We'll know it's not a real engagement, but we don't have to tell anyone else that.'

Let's make it a real engagement. Cassie was furious with

herself for the way her heart had jumped at his words, in spite of the fact that only a matter of minutes ago he had been recoiling in horror at the very idea. 'Nobody would believe it,' she said flatly.

'Why not?'

'Come on, Jake. I'm hardly your type, am I? Are you really going to ask people to believe you took one look at me and fell in love with me? They'd know it wasn't true.'

'Oh, I don't know.' Jake studied her over the rim of his glass. It was warm in the restaurant, and she had shrugged off the silky cardigan, leaving her shoulders bare. She was a warm, glowing figure in the candlelight. 'I can think of more unlikely scenarios,' he said.

His gaze flustered Cassie, and she tore her eyes away to concentrate fiercely on twisting spaghetti around her fork. 'Sure,' she said. 'And when was this supposed to have happened?'

'How about when you walked into my office and fell into my arms?'

Cassie felt her colour rising at the memory. 'And you thought, "I've been waiting all my life for someone clumsy to come along"?'

'Perhaps I've had a thing about you since I kissed you at the Allantide Ball,' Jake suggested. 'Perhaps I've been waiting ten years to find you again.'

It was clear that he was being flippant, but there was an undercurrent of *something* in his voice. Cassie did everything she could to stop herself looking up to meet his eyes again, but it was hopeless. Something stronger than her was dragging her gaze up from the fork to lock with Jake's. She could almost hear the click as it snapped into place.

His eyes were dark and unreadable in the candlelight, but still her heart began that silly pattering again, while her pulse throbbed alarmingly.

She swallowed. 'I don't think that sounds very likely either.'

'Well, then, we'll tell it exactly as it was,' said Jake, sounding infuriatingly normal. How come *his* heart wasn't lurching all over the place at the very thought of falling in love with her? He clearly wasn't having any trouble breathing, either.

'We met when you came to discuss developing the Hall as a wedding venue. Then we drove down to Portrevick together.'

'And on the way we fell madly in love and agreed to get married right away?' said Cassie, who had managed to look away again at last.

Jake shrugged away her scorn. 'You're the one who believes in that kind of thing,' he reminded her. 'If we say that's what happened, why would anyone believe it wasn't true?'

'I can't believe you're making it all sound so reasonable,' she protested.

How had they got to this point? It was as if the whole evening had been turned on its head. When she arrived, she had been cock-a-hoop at the idea of the magazine feature, and her only concern had been how to convince Jake to go for it. Now it was Jake talking her into an engagement just to make sure the article went ahead. How had that happened?

'Look, it makes sense.' Jake was clearly losing patience. 'You're the ideal person to feature in the article. You know all about weddings. You'll be able to say all the right things and make sure the Hall comes out of it looking beautiful.'

'That's true, I suppose.' Cassie looked at the fork she had laden so carefully with spaghetti and put it down. She had lost her appetite. 'But what about you?' she said hesitantly.

'What about me?'

'Won't you find it very difficult?'

'It might be a bit of a struggle to look interested in table decorations,' said Jake. 'But I expect I can manage if it's just one or two photo sessions. I won't be required to do much else, will I?'

'I wasn't thinking about that,' said Cassie. 'I was thinking about what it would be like for you to have to pretend to be happy with me when I know how you must be feeling about Natasha. I'd be devastated if it was me.'

'At least I won't look it,' said Jake, wondering how he did feel. Angry, humiliated—yes. But *devastated*? Jake didn't think so. His overwhelming feeling, he decided, was one of disappointment in Natasha. He had been attracted by her beauty, of course, but just as much he had liked her intelligence and composure. He couldn't believe that she would lose her head over someone like Rupert, of all people.

Jake remembered telling Cassie how well he and Natasha were matched. Natasha was perfect, he had told her. And she had been. She had never irritated or distracted him the way Cassie did, for instance. She was everything he needed in a woman.

More than that, when he looked at Natasha, Jake had felt as if he had left Portrevick behind him once and for all. With a beautiful, accomplished, sexy, successful woman like Natasha on his arm, he'd been able to believe that he had made it at last.

And then Rupert Branscombe Fox had lifted his little finger and she had gone.

Jake's jaw tightened and he stared down at the wine he was swirling in his glass. Rupert's condescension could still reduce him to a state of seething resentment. Rupert in return would never forgive him for humiliating him in that stupid fight, or for being the one his uncle had entrusted with his not-inconsiderable fortune.

'Rupert wants me to be devastated,' he told Cassie. 'He wants me to feel humiliated and heartbroken. He wants me to have to tell everyone that my beautiful girlfriend has dumped me for him. I've got no intention of giving him that satisfaction.'

Jake set down his glass and looked directly at Cassie. 'You asked if I'd find it difficult to pretend to be in love with you instead of Natasha—the answer is that it wouldn't be half as hard as losing face with Rupert. I'd do anything rather than do that. I'm sorry about Natasha, but this isn't about her. It's between Rupert and me.'

'Getting engaged to me would make it look as if Rupert had done you a favour by taking Natasha off your hands,' said Cassie slowly. She knew that Jake and Rupert had never got on, but she hadn't realised the rivalry between them was still so bitter.

'Exactly,' said Jake. 'You'd be helping me to save face, and that would mean a lot to me. I'm not proud. I'll beg if you want me to.'

'I don't know.' Cassie fingered the wax dribbling down the candle uncertainly. 'If we're pretending to be engaged in Portrevick, word's bound to get back to my parents. What are they going to think if they find out I'm apparently marrying you and haven't told them?'

Jake shrugged. 'Tell them the truth, then. What does it matter if they know? They're not going to rush off to *Wedding Belles* to tell the editor their daughter is telling a big fib, are they?'

'No, but they might rush to tell Liz and my brothers that I've got myself in a stupid mess again,' said Cassie, who could imagine the conversation all too clearly: *why can Cassie never do anything properly? When is she going to grow up and get a proper job that doesn't involve silly pretences?*

'I'm sick of being the family failure,' she told Jake. 'I wanted to show them that I could be successful too. That was why I so pleased when you gave us the contract to turn the Hall into a wedding venue. I rang my parents and told them I had a real career at last.'

She squeezed a piece of wax between her fingers, remembering the warm glow of her parents' approval. 'I don't want to tell them my great new job involves pretending to be in love with you.'

'Do you want to tell them you've lost your great new job because you weren't prepared to do whatever it took to make it work?'

Cassie dropped the wax and sat back in her chair. 'Isn't that blackmail?' she said dubiously, and Jake sighed impatiently.

'It's telling you to hurry up and make a decision,' he said.

'Look, if it's such a problem, say we really *are* engaged, then when we've finished with all the photos you can tell them you've changed your mind and dumped me. If they remember me at all, I'm sure they'll be delighted to hear it,' he finished in an arid voice.

Cassie turned it over in her mind. It might work. Of course, the best scenario would be that her family never got to hear about her supposed engagement at all, but if they did get a whiff of it she could always pretend that Jake had swept her off her feet. It was only three months to Christmas. She could easily find excuses not to take him home in that time.

Tina might be a little harder to fool, especially as she was on the spot in Portrevick, but there was no reason why she shouldn't tell her old friend the truth. Tina could be trusted to keep it to herself—and besides they might need her to pretend to be the bridesmaid.

Anyway, it didn't sound as if she had a choice. Cassie wasn't entirely sure whether Jake was serious about making the engagement a condition of the contract, but she wasn't prepared to push him on it. He had been hurt by Natasha, humiliated by Rupert, and was clearly in no mood to compromise.

And really, would it be so bad? Cassie asked herself. The article had been her idea to start with, and she still believed it would be just what they needed to kick-start promotion for the Hall. Of course, she hadn't reckoned on taking such a prominent role herself, but Jake was right. She would be able to decorate the Hall exactly as she wanted without having to take Natasha's wishes into account. She could recreate her dream wedding for the article.

Cassie felt a flicker of excitement at the prospect.

It might be fun.

It wasn't as if they were planning on doing anything illegal or immoral, after all. A mock engagement would save Jake's face, ensure a lucrative contract and her job at Avalon, if not a whole new career. Why was she even hesitating?

'All right,' she said abruptly. 'I'll do it. But, if we're going to pretend to be engaged, we're going to have to do it properly,' she warned him. 'That means that when the photographer is around you'll have to be there and be prepared to look suitably besotted.'

'Don't you think I can do that?'

Jake reached across the table for her hands, taking Cassie by surprise. 'I'm sure you can,' she said, flustered, trying to tug them free, but he tightened his grip.

'I can do whatever you need me to,' he said, turning her hands over and lifting first one palm and then the other to his mouth to kiss.

Cassie felt the touch of his lips like a shock reverberating down to her toes, and she sucked in a shuddering breath.

'See?' Jake said softly, without letting go of her hands. '*I* can do it. More to the point,' he said, 'can you?'

The challenge hung between them, flickering in the candlelight.

Cassie swallowed hard. It was hard to think straight with his warm, strong fingers clasping hers, and the feel of his lips scorched onto her palms, but she retained enough sanity to know that the last thing she needed was to let him know how his touch affected her.

He had recoiled at the very idea of marrying her. *Of course I don't*, he had said. Cassie suspected that Jake had been more hurt by Natasha's betrayal than he was letting on. This was partly to be his revenge on her, partly a game, a pretence, a strategy to save his face and solve the problem of his unwanted responsibility for the Hall. That was all.

Which was fine. All she had to do was treat it like a game too, and remember that her strategy was to turn the Hall into the most sought-after wedding venue in the South West. She would prove to her family that she was not just a dreamer, but could be just as successful in her chosen field as they were in theirs.

So she drew her hands from Jake's and laid them instead

on either side of his face. 'Of course I can, darling,' she said, shivering at the prickle of the rough male skin beneath her fingers, and she leant forward across the table to brush a kiss against his mouth.

She felt Jake stiffen in surprise, and, although a panic-stricken part of her was screaming at her to sit back and laugh it off as a joke, another more persuasive part was noting that his lips were warm and firm and that they fitted her own perfectly, as if their mouths had been made for each other.

It felt so good to kiss him, to touch him, that Cassie pushed the panicky thoughts aside and let her lips linger on his. But that was a mistake, of course. Beneath hers, his mouth curved into a smile, and the next moment she felt his hand slide beneath her hair to hold her head still, and he began kissing her back.

And then they were kissing each other, their lips parting, their tongues twining, teasing, and Cassie murmured deep in her throat, smiling too even as she kissed him again, lost in the dizzying rush of heat and the terrifying sense of rightness.

Afterwards, she never had any idea how long that kiss had lasted. But when they broke apart at last she was thudding from the tips of her hair to her toenails, and Giovanni was standing by the table wearing a broad smile.

'Client, huh?' he said to her with a wink, but it was Jake who answered.

'Not any more,' he said. 'We just got engaged.'

Cassie tossed and turned half the night, reliving that kiss. She had gone too far, just like her mother always said she did. A brief peck on the lips would have been enough to make her point, and she could have gone back to being businesslike—but, oh no! She had had to push it. She had had to *kiss* him.

She mustn't let herself get carried away like that again, Cassie told herself sternly. This was just a pretence, and she mustn't forget it. On the other hand, her job might have depended on pretending to be engaged to a man with wet lips and clammy hands. As it was, well, she might as well enjoy the perks, mightn't she?

So she was in high good humour when she bounced into the office the next morning. She had never been engaged before. OK, she wasn't *really* engaged, and she probably ought to be feeling more cross about having been effectively blackmailed into it, but at least it meant that she didn't have any choice in the matter. If anyone—for example her super-achieving family—ever asked her how she came to do such a crazy thing, she could hold up her hands and say, 'Hey, I was forced into it.'

Or perhaps it would be better to put a more positive spin on it. She didn't want to look like a victim. She could narrow her eyes, look serious and explain that she was someone who was prepared to do anything—anything!—to get the job done.

'Well, I hope you know what you're doing,' said Joss doubt-fully when Cassie tried this line on her. Joss, like Tina, had to know the truth. 'This Jake Trevelyan is a tough character. It was bad enough negotiating the terms of the contract with him!

'Don't get me wrong,' she said as Cassie's face fell. 'I'm delighted about the contract. But I'd hate to think you got hurt trying to save Avalon. I just think you should be careful about getting too involved with someone like that.'

'I'll be fine,' said Cassie buoyantly. 'Anyway, I'm not *involved* with Jake,' she said, firmly pushing the memory of last night's kiss away. 'Pretending to be engaged is simply a way to promote Portrevick Hall as a wedding venue. I'm just doing my job.'

She was still in a breezy mood when she rang Jake at his office later that morning.

'Hi!' she said when his PA put her through. 'It's me. Your brand-new fiancée,' she added, just in case he needed his memory jogging.

'Hello,' said Jake. He sounded cool and businesslike, and it was hard to believe that it was only a matter of hours since his lips had been warm and sure against hers.

'I think you mean "hello, *darling*", don't you?' Cassie prompted. 'We're engaged, remember?'

Jake sighed. 'Hello, *darling*,' he said ironically.

'OK, the darling is good, but you might want to work on your tone,' said Cassie, enjoying herself. 'You know? A bit lower, a bit warmer…a bit more like you're counting the seconds until you can see me again!'

'Darling,' Jake repeated obediently, and this time his voice was deep and warm and held a hint of a smile. Cassie's heart skipped just a little, even though she knew he was just pretending.

'Very good,' she approved.

'It's not that it's not wonderful to hear from you,' he said, reverting to his usual sardonic tone. 'But I've got a meeting in five minutes.'

'I won't keep you,' she promised. 'I just thought I'd tell you that I've spoken to *Wedding Belles* and broken the news that I'm the bride-to-be. I made up some story about being too shy to admit it before. I'm not sure if they believed me, but they're not asking too many questions, which is a relief.'

'Presumably they don't really care as long as they get a decent story.'

'Yes, that's right.' Cassie could feel his impatience to get off the phone. Just as well they weren't really engaged, or she *would* have been hurt. 'Anyway, we're committed now.'

'So what happens next?' asked Jake without much interest. Cassie imagined him scrolling through his emails while he listened to her with half an ear.

But she could do businesslike, too. 'I was just coming to that,' she said. 'It turns out that *Wedding Belles* is hosting a wedding fair at some fancy hotel this weekend. The opening party is on Friday night, and they want us to go. Apparently they're inviting all the couples who are going to be featured in the magazine next year, and we're getting a special preview of the show.'

She could practically see Jake grimacing at the idea. 'Do we have to go?'

'Yes, we do,' said Cassie briskly. 'This is the first part of the story. The photographer will be there, and we'll meet the editor, so we'll have to be on our best behaviour.

'Besides,' she said, 'the theme of the fair is Winter Wonderland Weddings, so we'll be able to pick up some ideas. Joss and I always to the shows, but I've never been to the preview or the party before. It should be great.'

'What goes on at a wedding show?' Jake asked, not at all sure that he was going to like the answer.

'Oh, they're fantastic,' Cassie assured him. 'There's everything you could ever need to plan a wedding under one roof. It doesn't matter if you're looking for a chocolate fountain or a tiara: you'll find someone who specialises in providing just what you want for every stage of getting married, from the engagement party to the honeymoon. Oh, and there's always a fashion show too. We don't want to miss that.'

'A fashion show,' Jake echoed dryly. 'Fabulous!'

'It'll be fun,' Cassie told him.

Jake thought that it sounded as much fun as sticking pins in his eyes, but he was the one who had insisted that they go ahead with the article, so he could hardly quibble now.

Since the hotel was almost exactly halfway between their offices, they agreed to meet in the lobby at six-thirty on the Friday.

'OK, I'd better go,' said Cassie in the same brisk tone. About to switch off the phone, she paused. 'Oh, nearly forgot,' she said, and cooed, *'Love you!'* in an exaggeratedly saccharine voice before spoiling the effect by laughing.

Jake put the phone down and sat looking at it for a long moment, her gurgling laugh echoing in his ears. Then he smiled unwillingly, shook his head, and pushed back his chair to go to his meeting, where everyone would be sane and sensible and dressed in shades of grey.

* * *

Jake looked at his watch as Cassie came tumbling into the hotel's ornate lobby through the revolving door. 'You're late,' he said.

'I know, I know, I'm sorry,' she panted, struggling out of her coat. 'I spent all afternoon trying to track down a carriage for one of our clients. It wouldn't be a problem, except that she wants four horses—all white, naturally—and the carriage has to be purple to fit the colour theme. Oh, and did I mention she wants it for next weekend? I finally found someone who was prepared to paint the carriage, but by the time we'd negotiated how much it would all cost it was nearly six…'

Still talking, she managed to get rid of her coat and checked it into the cloakroom, which gave Jake a chance to get his breathing back under control. It had got ridiculously muddled up at the sight of Cassie spilling through the doors, her cheeks pink, her eyes bright and brown, and the wild curls even more tousled than usual. She was like a crisp autumn breeze, swirling into the stultifyingly grand lobby, freshening the air and sharpening his senses. For a moment there Jake had forgotten whether he was supposed to be breathing in or breathing out.

How had he come up with a crazy idea like pretending to be engaged to her? Jake had spent the day wondering if Giovanni's wine had gone to his head. It wasn't the plan that bothered him, it was Cassie. It was that aura of turbulence that always seemed to be whirling around her, that sense that everything might tip into chaos at any moment. Jake, whose life now was built on rigorous order and control, found it deeply unsettling.

If only she could be more like Natasha, who was always calm, always neat, always predictable.

Except when she was running off with Rupert, of course.

The memory of Rupert was enough to make Jake's jaw tighten with resolve. He might not like muddle and chaos, but he disliked Rupert more. He mustn't lose his nerve about the plan now, he told himself. It made perfect sense. Pretending to be engaged to Cassie would deprive Rupert of his triumph and achieve his most pressing objective, which was to get the Hall up and running. If a little pretence was required for the purposes of promotion, well, Jake could handle that.

It wasn't as if anyone in London would ever know anything about it, either, he reassured himself. No; everything would be fine.

It had been fine until that damned kiss.

Natasha's defection had been a blow to his pride, true, but he'd had a plan. Life had been back under control. And then Cassie had leant forward in the candlelight, that dimple deepening enticingly as she smiled. *Darling*, she had called him, and then she had kissed him.

The moment her lips had touched his, control had gone out the window. Jake had forgotten everything but warmth, softness and searing, seductive sweetness. He'd forgotten Rupert, forgotten Natasha, forgotten the *plan*.

It had taken him all day to remember what was important and get himself back under control, and all Cassie had had to do was appear and he'd lost it all over again.

He was being ridiculous, Jake told himself savagely. It was just Cassie. He looked at her as she tucked the cloakroom ticket away in her bag. She was wearing loose trousers and a fine-knit top with a wide belt. She looked really quite stylish for once, although nothing like as elegant as Natasha would have seemed in exactly the same outfit.

She was just a girl. Pretty, yes—in fact, much prettier than she seemed at first glance—but a bit messy, a bit clumsy, a bit disorganised. Nothing special, in fact. Not the kind of girl you got yourself into a state about, that was for sure.

CHAPTER SIX

'YOU'RE looking very fierce,' Cassie commented, hoisting her bag back onto her shoulder. 'You're supposed to be deliriously happy at the prospect of spending an evening with me planning our special day together!'

She saw his mouth turn down at the corners. 'Look, this was your idea,' she reminded him. 'The editor of *Wedding Belles* is going to be in there. If you want to promote the Hall, you're going to have to convince her the way you convinced me the other night.'

Jake raised his brows. 'What, I have to kiss her?'

'You're not taking this seriously,' said Cassie. 'All you've got to do is look affectionate and not as if you can't decide whether to fire me or shoot me!'

She was right, Jake thought. He was the one who had insisted on doing this. He bared his teeth in a smile. 'Better?'

'A bit,' she allowed, glancing around for signs to the wedding fair. A notice board pointed them down to the lower floor. 'Come on, then,' she said. 'Let's go and find the party.'

'Shouldn't we hold hands?' suggested Jake.

'Er, yes, we probably should. Good idea.'

Cassie tried to sound casual, but she was desperately aware of the dry warmth of his palm and the firm fingers closing around hers. He had lovely hands, big, strong and safe, the kind of hands that could catch you if you were falling, the kind of hands that wouldn't let you go.

She was being fanciful, Cassie told herself as they made their way downstairs, where they found the party already in full swing. She wasn't falling anywhere, not even off her heels, and Jake would be only too keen to let her go as soon as possible.

The editor of *Wedding Belles* was greeting arrivals at the door, but they managed to brush through the introductions without rousing any suspicions, and were disgorged into the party. A passing waiter offered them champagne and Cassie accepted thankfully. Holding Jake's hand was making her jittery and self-conscious, and it was the perfect excuse to drop it and grab a glass from the tray.

Amazing how a gulp of champagne could make you feel better, she thought, looking around her and trying not to notice how tingly and somehow empty her hand felt now. She switched the glass to give it something to hold.

'We'd better try and circulate,' she murmured.

They were standing next to another couple, who introduced themselves after a few banalities as Mark and Michelle; it soon turned out that it was Michelle who did all the talking.

'We're getting married in April,' she told Cassie and Jake. 'Aren't we, Mark?'

Mark opened his mouth to agree but she was already sweeping on. 'We've been planning the wedding for two years. We got engaged on a cruise, so our theme is the sea.'

'Theme?'

'The theme of the wedding.' Michelle looked at Jake as if he were stupid. 'Blue is our main colour, of course, so all our favours will be blue, and we're having blue sashes on the chair covers. We had waves on the invitations, didn't we, Mark? And we're naming all the tables after different seas,' she finished triumphantly.

'Who are you putting in the Bermuda Triangle?' asked Jake, and Cassie nudged him.

'That sounds lovely,' she said quickly. 'Have you decided on a dress yet?'

Michelle had, of course, and described it at length. Then she went on to tell them about their matching stationery, the wedding website, the special, blue fascinators she had sourced for her five bridesmaids, the first dance they were practising already, and the personalised shells that she was trying to track down as place settings.

Her monologue was punctuated with requests for confirmation from Mark, although the poor man never got a chance even to agree. Michelle had a spreadsheet she was using to keep track of her budget, and kept all the paperwork to do with the wedding in a colour-coded filing system.

Weddings were Cassie's business, and she wouldn't have minded listening to Michelle drone on if she hadn't been aware that Jake was glazing over beside her.

'We're having a Christmas wedding,' she interrupted brightly at last.

'I think you mean a Christmas *theme*, don't you?' muttered Jake.

'We're getting married this Christmas, actually,' Cassie hurried on, trying not to giggle.

'Really? So, not long to go!' Michelle looked from one to the other. 'You must be excited!'

'I'm beside myself,' Jake agreed, deadpan.

'Don't mind him,' said Cassie, taking his arm and leaning into him. 'He's thrilled, really—especially since we found him a Regency-buck outfit.' She smiled winsomely up at him. 'You're going to look *soooo* gorgeous in those breeches!'

She turned back to Michelle. 'We're going for the Mr Darcy look, you know? But he's worried he won't be able to tie his cravat properly.'

'I'm sure you can get instructions on the Internet,' said

Michelle, completely missing Jake's expression at the very thought of a cravat. 'So, are you going for a Regency dress as well?' she asked Cassie.

'I haven't got it yet,' Cassie admitted.

'You're getting married at Christmas and you haven't got your *dress*?' Michelle fell back in horror. 'You're leaving it very late!'

'Maybe I'll find something here tonight. Perhaps you're right; I could go for a period look and wear a bonnet.' She pretended to muse.

'A muff's very nice at a Christmas wedding,' offered Michelle.

That was when Cassie made the mistake of catching Jake's eye. 'Now, there's a thought,' he said, and waggled his eyebrows at her. It would have been fine if she hadn't just lifted her glass to her lips to hide her smile, and at that she spluttered champagne all down the front of her top and started choking.

Jake patted her none too gently on the back. 'Here, let's go and find you a glass of water,' he said, taking her by the arm and bearing her off with barely time for a goodbye to Michelle and the silent Mark.

'Look, my top is all stained,' Cassie complained, brushing champagne from her cleavage. 'And it's all your fault for making me laugh!'

'*My* fault? I wasn't the one who started on the Regency bucks!' said Jake. He had his hand on her back and was steering her firmly to the other side of the room. 'I couldn't stand it any longer. Poor Mark looked like he had lost the will to live, and I don't blame him. And what the hell is a "favour", anyway?'

'It's a little thank-you gift for your guests. It usually goes on the table as a memento of the day that they can take away.'

Jake snorted. 'Well, the only favour *I* want is for you to get me out of here!'

'We can't go yet,' said Cassie. 'We've only just arrived. Besides, they haven't opened the show. I think there are going to be some speeches first.'

Putting her empty glass down on a passing tray, she took another one and turned to see who else they could talk to. Fortunately, the next couple they met was less obsessed with weddings than Michelle. 'We're only here for the champagne,' Kevin said.

'And for the draw,' said Victoria. 'First prize is a weekend in Paris as a break from the stress of planning a wedding, but the others sound worth winning too. Everyone here tonight is in with a chance.'

'Paris sounds lovely,' Cassie said wistfully, imagining strolling around Montmartre hand in hand with Jake. Then she caught herself up. What was she thinking? They weren't lovers. There would be no one to see them in Paris. Why would they be holding hands?

She forced a smile. 'Not that I ever win anything. Oh, I take that back,' she said. 'I once won a jar of pickled onions in the tombola at the village fête.'

Victoria laughed. 'Well, it looks as if you've won yourself a gorgeous guy,' she said with a meaningful glance at Jake, who was talking to Kevin about a new sports channel.

'Yes,' said Cassie, stifling a little sigh.

'Isn't it the best feeling when you find the right guy?'

Cassie looked at Jake, deep in blokey conversation with Kevin. She remembered the feel of his hand holding hers, the devastating sureness of his lips. 'Yes,' she said in a hollow voice.

'I'd almost given up on men,' Victoria confided. 'I thought it was never going to happen for me. Then I walked into work one day, and there he was! The moment I saw him, I knew he was the one.'

She showed Cassie her engagement ring. 'Every time I look at it, I feel so happy I want to cry,' she said.

Kevin obviously caught the end of her sentence as he broke off his conversation with Jake. 'Oh no, not the "I'm so happy I could cry" line again?' he said, rolling his eyes, but he put his arm around Victoria and pulled her close. 'Do you get that one?' he asked Jake.

'Not yet,' said Jake.

There was a tiny pause, when it suddenly seemed glaringly obvious that they weren't touching with the easy affection Kevin and Victoria showed, but then he slid his hand beneath Cassie's hair and rested it at the nape of her neck.

'You don't want to cry, do you?'

Actually, right then, Cassie did. Her throat had tightened painfully, watching Victoria and Kevin so obviously in love, and now the warm, comforting weight of Jake's hand on her neck only made her eyes sting with tears. She blinked them firmly away and mustered a smile. 'I probably *would* cry with happiness if I had a lovely ring like Victoria's!' She pretended to joke.

'Hasn't he bought you a ring yet?' Victoria tutted.

'We haven't been engaged very long.' Cassie excused him, and then sucked in a breath as Jake caressed the nape of her neck.

'Besides,' he said. 'I'm waiting to find something really special for her.'

The more couples they talked to, the more wistful Cassie felt. The others were all so happy, so much in love, so excited about their weddings; the happier they were together, the more conscious she was that she and Jake were just pretending.

'Doesn't it make you feel a bit sad?' she asked him when they found themselves alone for a moment.

'Sad? No. Why?'

'Oh, I suppose I'm just envious,' she said with sigh. 'Everyone else here is in love, and we're just promoting the Hall.'

Over Jake's shoulder, she could see a couple laughing together. Unaware that anyone was watching them, the girl hugged her fiancé's arm and lifted her face naturally for his kiss. They looked so comfortable together that Cassie's heart twisted and she jerked her eyes back to Jake.

'It must be even worse for you,' she said, and he lifted his brows.

'For me?'

'You might have been here with Natasha,' Cassie said. 'It's never easy, seeing everyone else all loved up when your own relationship has just fallen apart.'

And she ought to know, she thought glumly. Her relationships had a nasty habit of crashing and burning after a few weeks, and she had almost given up on meeting someone she could fall in love with, someone who would love her back.

'I can't imagine Natasha here,' said Jake, looking around him with a derisive expression. 'We didn't have that kind of relationship. If we had decided to get married, she wouldn't have had much time for all of this.'

'All of what?'

'All this lovey-dovey stuff isn't a good basis for a strong marriage.'

He had given her that line before, Cassie remembered. She didn't buy it any more this time round. 'I would have thought love was the *only* real basis for a marriage,' she said.

'I don't agree with you,' said Jake coolly. 'Love is too random. It's a hit and miss affair, and even if you do get a hit it soon runs out of steam. How many times have you seen friends wild for their new partner, only to end up complaining about how they never put the top back on the toothpaste barely weeks later?'

All too often in her own case, thought Cassie.

'It doesn't always run out of steam,' she said. 'Sometimes it gets stronger. OK, the red-hot passion may not last, but it can change into something better, something that *will* last. When you love someone completely, you accept their little quirks as part of who they are. You certainly don't throw away a good relationship because they squeeze the toothpaste in the middle instead of rolling up the ends neatly!'

'Are you talking from your own experience?' asked Jake, and she lifted her chin.

'Not personally, no,' she said with dignity. 'But I've seen

plenty of other relationships where both partners learn to compromise because they love each other. It *can* work.'

'Not often enough.' Jake shook his head. 'Marriage is too serious a business to be left to love,' he said. 'It should be about shared interests, shared goals, about practicalities and the things that can't change. If you can add in sexual attraction as well, *then* you've got yourself a winning formula.'

'You can't reduce love to a formula, Jake.'

'What else is it?'

'It's—it's finding someone who makes your heart beat faster. Someone who makes your senses tingle.'

Hang on, that sounded alarmingly like the way Jake made her feel, Cassie realised uncomfortably.

'Someone who makes the sun shine brighter.' She hurried on into unfamiliar territory. Jake didn't do that, did he?

'That's just chemical attraction,' said Jake dismissively.

'It isn't chemistry that makes someone the first person you want to talk to in the morning and the last person you want to see at night,' Cassie said hotly. 'The person who believes in you, however bad things are, who will take you in their arms and make you feel that you've found a safe harbour.'

Her voice cracked a little. She had never found that person, but she wasn't giving up on the belief that he was out there somewhere, whatever Jake Trevelyan said. 'It's got nothing to do with chemistry,' she said, recovering.

'And how long does that feeling last?' Jake countered. He gestured around the room with his head. 'How many of these loving couples are going to feel like that a year from now, let alone in ten years, twenty years? Relying on how you feel is too random a way to choose a partner for life. Call it a formula, if you like, but if you're interested in the long haul you're better off sticking to what you know works.'

'The formula didn't work for you and Natasha, though, did it?' Cassie retorted without thinking.

There was a short, not entirely pleasant silence. 'No,' Jake said just as she opened her mouth to apologise. 'The formula isn't foolproof, sure. But if you find someone who fits your specifications I'd say your chances of a successful marriage are much greater than investing all your happiness in someone you don't really know.'

'Well,' said Cassie, draining her glass of champagne defiantly. 'I couldn't disagree with you more. It looks as if we're completely incompatible on that front, anyway. It's just as well we're not really getting married!'

'Just as well,' Jake agreed dryly.

At the front of the room, a microphone was spluttering into life. The editor of *Wedding Belles* was up on the little stage, making a speech and announcing the winners of the prize draw to much ooh-ing and aah-ing from the crowd. The happy couple who had won the trip to Paris was called up and had their photo taken, beaming from ear to ear.

It gave Cassie a chance to get a grip. There was a time, when they'd been chatting to other couples, when it had felt quite normal being with Jake. It had felt more than normal, in fact. It had felt strangely right to have him at her side, talking, laughing, being able to catch his eye and know that he would find the same comments amusing. For a while there, she had forgotten how different they were.

But the conversation just now had reminded her. Jake, it seemed, had a completely different idea of love. He was looking for someone who fitted his specifications the way Natasha had.

The way *she* never would. Cassie didn't need to ask what kind of woman Jake wanted. She was fairly sure the answer wouldn't be someone scatty, messy or with a poor time-keeping record. No, he would be looking for someone poised, quiet, elegant. Someone who would slot into the carefully controlled life he seemed to have built for himself since he'd left Portrevick.

And why is that a problem, Cassie?

It wasn't; Cassie answered her own question firmly. It wasn't as if she wanted a man like Jake either. Control freaks weren't her style. It didn't matter that they were completely incompatible. It wasn't as if they were actually having a relationship. This was just a pretence, and the less seriously they both took it the better.

Clutching their tickets to Paris, the winners of the first prize were leaving the stage, and more prizes were announced. Cassie was getting tired of clapping politely, and her thoughts were wandering so much that when she heard their own names called she hadn't even heard what they had won.

Perhaps her luck was changing at last, she thought buoyantly.

She dug Jake in the ribs with her elbow. 'Come on. We're on. Don't forget to smile!'

Together they climbed the stage; Cassie accepted a voucher from the editor, and they posed obediently for the camera.

'A bit closer,' called the photographer, and after the tiniest of hesitations Jake put his arm around Cassie, who had little choice but to snuggle in to his lean, hard body.

'Perfect,' said the photographer, and for a dangerous moment there it *felt* perfect too. Jake was warm and solid, and his arm was very strong. It felt wonderfully safe, being held hard against him, and Cassie found herself wishing that he would hold her like that for ever.

The moment the shot was taken, she straightened and pushed the treacherous thought aside, cross with herself. There was no point in thinking like that. Hadn't she just decided that they were incompatible?

'What have we won?' Jake asked out of the corner of his mouth as they left the stage and the next winners were called up.

Cassie opened the envelope and started to laugh. 'It's vouchers for a his 'n' hers day at a luxury spa, including treatments.'

'Treatments?' he asked nervously. 'What sort of treatments?'

'Oh, you know, pedicures, massages, waxing.'

Jake paled. '*Waxing*?'

'I believe a certain wax is very popular with men nowadays,' said Cassie naughtily, enjoying his expression of horror. 'You want to look your best for our wedding photos, don't you?'

'Not if it involves wax of any kind *anywhere*!'

'Oh well, if you're going to be such a baby…'

'Why don't we just give the voucher to someone else?'

'We can't do that. *Wedding Belles* might want photos of us enjoying our prize for the article.'

'If they think they're getting a photo of me having any hairs ripped out, they've got another think coming!' said Jake firmly.

'Don't worry; I'm sure we can find you something less painful,' Cassie soothed him as she flicked through the brochure that had come with the voucher. 'Maybe you could have a facial— or, I know, a seaweed wrap! That wouldn't hurt.'

Jake was looking aghast. 'A *wrap*?' Then he caught Cassie's dancing brown eyes, realised that she was teasing and relaxed into a laugh. 'If you *dare* book me in for anything like that, Cassie…!'

'What, and risk you cancelling our contract? No way— although it would be almost worth it to see your face.'

It was a good thing they had had that discussion about love earlier, Cassie decided. She had been in danger of forgetting that theirs wasn't a real relationship for a while, but now that she'd remembered she could relax and enjoy herself again.

She tucked her hand into his arm. 'Worry not,' she said. 'I wouldn't do anything like that to you.'

'So, can we go now?'

'Go? We haven't even started yet!' Cassie pointed to where a set of doors was swinging apart to revel a huge ballroom crammed with stalls. 'The show's just opened, and we've got a whole winter-wonderland of weddings to explore…'

'Have you got a moment?'

'Jake!' Cassie looked up in astonishment as he appeared

in the doorway. It was the following Tuesday, and she was sitting on the office floor surrounded by fabric samples. She scrambled to her feet, ridiculously breathless. 'What on earth are you doing here?'

He was looking uncharacteristically hesitant. 'I wanted to ask a favour. In the circumstances, it seemed only fair that I should come to you, but I can go away if you're busy.'

'No, no. It's fine.' Cassie swept a pile of magazines off a chair. 'Sit down. I'm sorry it's all such a mess.'

She grimaced, looking at the office through Jake's eyes. They really ought to tidy up some time. Every surface was piled high with magazines, fabric books, photographs, brochures, and samples of everything you could think of from thank-you cards to lip salves to artificial flowers. A wedding dress in a protective bag hung from a door, and the walls were covered with photos of all the weddings Avalon had planned. It was a colourful, cheerfully chaotic place, but, coming from his immaculately cool and contemporary office, Jake was unlikely to be impressed.

'Coffee?' she offered, and then wished she hadn't. They only had chipped mugs, and the milk was probably off.

'No. Thank you.'

Phew. Cassie lifted a pile of cake-design brochures off another chair and sat down. A favour, he had said. 'So, what can I do for you?'

She was rather proud of how normal she sounded, not at all as if her heart was bouncing around in her ribcage and interfering ludicrously with her breathing. She was disconcerted, in fact, by how pleased she was to see Jake.

In the end, they had had a good time at the wedding fair, and the weekend had seemed, well, a bit *empty* without him. Jake had said goodnight as they parted, but hadn't mentioned meeting again. Why would he? It was her job to get things going at the Hall, and she had that well in hand. They would need to arrange a photo session at some point, but the Hall wasn't ready for that yet.

As it was, the week stretched drearily ahead. Cassie had even caught herself wondering if she could invent an excuse to call him, and had had to give herself a stern talking-to, reminding herself about key words like 'contract', 'professionalism', and 'incompatibility'.

Jake seemed to be having trouble deciding where to start. 'Remember that voucher we won on Friday?' he said at last.

He had taken so long that Cassie had begun to worry that he was about to give her bad news. Relief made her laugh. 'Look, there's no need to worry,' she assured him, relaxing. 'I won't book anything.'

'It's not that.' Jake wanted to get to his feet, but the office was so crowded with stuff that there was nowhere to step, let alone pace. How on earth did Cassie manage to work in all this clutter?

He brought his attention back to the matter in hand. 'It turns out that one of the accountants at Primordia is getting married next year, and she was at the *Wedding Belles* party.'

'Ah,' said Cassie, seeing where this was going at last.

'I didn't recognise her, but she thought she recognised me, apparently, and when our names were announced as winners of that bloody voucher that just confirmed it. So she trotted in to work yesterday and mentioned to someone she worked with in finance that I was engaged.'

'And word went round faster than you can say "seaweed wrap"?'

Jake nodded heavily. 'That's about it. The next thing I know, Ruth, my communications director, is congratulating me and saying I must bring you to some fund-raising event we're sponsoring on Thursday.' He sighed. 'I can't believe how quickly it's all got out of hand. I didn't think anyone in London would need to know about our so-called engagement,' he confessed. 'I obviously didn't think things through properly.'

'You weren't to know anyone from work would be at the wedding fair,' Cassie pointed out consolingly.

'No.' Jake brooded, trying to work out where it had all gone wrong. He wasn't used to his plans going awry. He spent so much of his life keeping things under rigid control; this was way out of his comfort zone.

'Perhaps I should have laughed it off when Ruth first mentioned it,' he said. 'But it seemed humiliating to admit that my engagement was just a marketing exercise. Ruth knew Natasha, too. She would have felt sorry for me.'

He didn't need to tell Cassie how much he would have hated that.

'The upshot is that I let her believe that you and I really were engaged,' he went on, looking directly at Cassie. 'I'm sorry about this, but I wondered if you would mind putting on an appearance at this do on Thursday, and any other similar events in the next couple of months?' He took a breath. 'If you don't want to do it, I'll understand, of course.'

'What, no more blackmail?' said Cassie, brown eyes dancing.

Jake set his teeth. 'No. This wasn't part of our agreement. I'm just asking you to help me.'

'Of course I will,' said Cassie, regretting now that she'd teased him. He so obviously hated the whole situation. 'It'll be fine. Honestly, I don't mind.'

'It's not likely to be a big deal,' Jake said. 'Just a couple of outings.'

'There you go, then. No problem.'

'Well…thank you.'

Jake was taken aback by how relieved he was, and he had a nasty feeling it wasn't just because Cassie was prepared to save his face at work. It was barely two weeks since she had—literally—tripped back into his life, and already she had changed things more than Natasha had in six months.

That wedding fair on Friday…Jake had thought about it all weekend. Cassie had dragged him round every stall. She had tried on tiaras and sampled cupcakes. She had sighed over shoes and chatted to other brides-to-be about make-up and hen parties and how to keep children entertained at a reception.

It should have been Jake's worst nightmare, but oddly he'd found that he was enjoying himself. He'd liked watching Cassie's animated face as she talked and waved her arms around, her intent expression as she'd studied the dizzying array of goods and services on offer, and the way she'd licked her fingers after trying a piece of fruit at the chocolate fountain.

They had wrangled over table decorations, pretended to choose a honeymoon destination, dodged behind stalls to avoid Michelle and the ever-silent Mark, and generally laughed more than Jake could remember since… Well, he couldn't remember the last time he had laughed like that. And all the time he had been aware of Cassie, of her bright face and her warm smile, and the memory of her kiss was like a hum underneath his skin.

So when Ruth had congratulated him on his engagement, instead of quietly admitting that it was all a mistake he had imagined seeing Cassie again, and he had found himself playing along.

It was only after Ruth had gone that he'd realised how much he had taken it for granted that Cassie would agree. He had blackmailed her into this charade, for goodness' sake! That didn't happen to nice middle-class girls like her. Jake wouldn't have blamed her if she had told him to stuff his pretence.

After all, it wasn't as if she could like being with him. They'd got on well enough at the wedding fair, but in lots of ways being there had just pointed out the differences between them. Cassie was ridiculously romantic, he was rigidly practical. She was warm, vibrant and spontaneous, he was cool and controlled. The only thing they could agree on was that they were completely incompatible.

Jake had told himself he would deserve the humiliation of admitting to Ruth that he had lied if Cassie didn't agree.

But she had agreed. 'It'll be fine,' she had said easily, and Jake had felt his heart lift.

'Thank you,' he said again.

'When do you want me?'

Now. I want you now. Unbidden, the words hovered on the tip of Jake's tongue. He clamped his lips together, aghast at how close he had come to opening his mouth and letting them spill out without any idea of where the thought had come from.

Cassie misunderstood his silence. A blush unfurled in her cheeks. 'On Thursday, I mean.'

'Can you come to my office at six?' said Jake, recovering. 'The reception starts at half past. We may as well go together and look like a proper couple.'

CHAPTER SEVEN

'Don't say anything!' Unbuttoning her coat, Cassie collapsed onto one of the sofas in Jake's office. 'I was so determined I was going to be on time for once, but it's really not my fault this time,' she told him. 'I've been stuck on the tube for *forty* minutes!' She groaned at the memory. 'Some problem with the signals, they said. I thought I was never going to get here.'

Jake didn't sit down. He needed a few moments to readjust. Had he actually been worrying about her? He had certainly started looking at his watch a good half-hour before she was even due to arrive, and as the minutes ticked past six o'clock he had looked more and more frequently.

And now she was here, lying on the sofa in a pose of exaggerated exhaustion, looking extraordinarily vivid. Her coat had fallen open to reveal a party dress. Jake had an impression of a vibrant blue colour, and some kind of satiny material, but all he really noticed was that it was rucked up over Cassie's knees, and in spite of himself his eyes travelled over the legs sprawled over the leather. His mouth dried. Had Cassie always had those spectacular legs? Surely he would have noticed if she had?

Clearing his throat, Jake made himself look away. 'If you're too tired, we can always give the party a miss.'

'Absolutely not.' Cassie sat up. 'How can we convince everyone we're engaged if we don't turn up? I'm fine,' she said, pushing back her hair.

Getting to her feet, she crossed to the window, and looked down at the street below. The traffic was nose to tail, the pavements choked with umbrellas, everyone anxious to get home or heading for the nearest pub. Thousands of people, all with somewhere to go and something to do, even in the rain. She loved London like this, busy, purposeful and pulsating with energy.

Jake was reaching for his coat when he stopped. 'Oh, I nearly forgot…' He patted his jacket and pulled a small jewellery-box from the inside pocket. 'You'd better have this.'

Cassie turned from window. 'What is it?'

'Open it.'

Jake handed the box to Cassie, who opened it almost fearfully and found herself staring down at a ring set with three large square-cut rubies separated by two dazzling diamonds.

'Oh…' she said on a long breath.

Watching her face, Jake found himself rushing into speech. 'I remembered how all the other brides at the wedding fair had a ring,' he said. 'I thought you needed one for tonight. It would be odd if we'd got as far as announcing our engagement and you didn't have one. Do you like it?' he finished abruptly.

Cassie raised her eyes from the ring to look directly into his, and Jake felt as if a great fist was squeezing his heart. 'It's beautiful,' she said.

'Perhaps I should have gone down on one knee.' He tried to joke in a weak attempt to disguise his relief. He didn't want to admit even to himself how long he had spent choosing the damn thing, or how determined he had been to find exactly the right ring for her.

The brown eyes flickered and dropped again to the ring. 'There's no need for that,' she said. 'It's just a prop.'

A prop he had spent a whole afternoon agonising over. 'Yes,' said Jake.

Cassie pulled the ring out of the velvet and slipped it onto her finger. She couldn't help imagining what it would have been like if this was a real engagement ring, if Jake had bought it for her because he loved her.

She swallowed the tightness from her throat. 'It's really lovely,' she told him. 'It must have been terribly expensive. Will you be able to take it back when this is all over?' she said, just to reassure him that she hadn't forgotten that they were just pretending.

Jake was shrugging himself into his coat. 'I expect so,' he said.

'I'll take great care of it,' Cassie promised, overwhelmed by the feel of the ring on her finger.

She had never worn anything remotely as beautiful or as valuable, and the thought that Jake had chosen it for her made the breath snare again in her throat. He could have picked out a plain diamond, which would have done the job just as well, but instead he had bought *this*.

'It's gorgeous,' she said, turning her hand so that the gems flashed in the light. 'Look what a beautiful warm glow it has.'

Jake didn't need to look. The glowing warmth was the reason he had bought the ring. It had reminded him of her.

'Does it fit?' he asked.

'It's a tiny bit loose, maybe,' said Cassie, turning the ring on her finger. 'But it'll be fine just for a couple of evenings. How on earth did you know what size to get?'

'One of the assistants in the shop had hands about the same size as yours.'

Cassie didn't think Jake had ever noticed her hands. The thought that he had felt like a tiny shiver deep inside her.

'Well…thank you,' she said.

An awkward silence fell. If it had been anyone else, Cassie wouldn't have hesitated to kiss him. Just on the cheek, of course; it was the obvious way to thank him for choosing such a lovely ring for her to wear, even if only temporarily.

But Jake had stepped back after giving her the box, and now he wasn't close enough for her to give him a quick hug or brush her cheek against his. She would have had to walk across to him, and that would have made too much of a big deal of it, wouldn't it? It wasn't as if he had given her the ring because he loved her. He had agreed that it was just a prop.

Jake put an end to her dithering by looking at his watch. 'We'd better go,' he said. 'We're late.'

Outside, it was still raining. The tyres of the passing cars hissed on the wet tarmac, and the pavements gleamed with puddles. Cassie huddled into her coat. It was only the middle of September, but the temperature had dropped over the last few days, and there was an unmistakable smell of autumn in the air.

'Where are we going?' she asked.

'The Strand,' said Jake, and her face fell.

'That's miles!'

'It's too far for you to walk in those shoes, certainly,' he said, nodding down at them.

'What shall we do? We'll never get a taxi in this weather.'

The words were barely out of Cassie's mouth when Jake put two fingers in his mouth and produced a piercing whistle that had a taxi heading in the opposite direction, turning instantly and ignoring the blare of horns to cut right across the traffic and pull up in front of them.

'Well, that was annoying,' said Cassie as Jake opened the door with a mocking bow. 'But a relief too,' she decided, sinking back into the seat and fastening her seatbelt.

'The Savoy,' Jake told the taxi driver, and sat back beside her. 'Why don't you wear something more sensible on your feet?' he said, half-relieved to find something to irritate him again. He scowled at her shoes. 'Look at them—they're ridiculous!'

'They're not ridiculous!' Stung, Cassie stuck her legs straight out in front of her so she could admire her shoes. Perhaps the heels weren't *that* practical, but she loved the sling backs, and the cute, peep-toe effect, and the hot pink was a fabulous colour. 'They're party shoes. I couldn't wear sensible shoes with a party dress, now, could I? That really *would* be ridiculous!'

Jake wished she'd put her legs down. They were distracting him. *She* was distracting him.

He had to keep reminding himself that this was Cassie. He'd known her as an eager child, as an ungainly adolescent. She had never been cool, clever or graceful, or any of the things he admired in a girl. She was an unstable force, chaotic and uncontrollable.

And now that force was bouncing uncontrollably around in his carefully constructed life.

Jake didn't like it one little bit. He had spent ten years fighting his way to the top, ten years making sure he never had to go back to Portrevick. He had changed himself quite deliberately. He had had enough of being the child wearing cast-offs, the troublemaker, the one who made eyebrows twitch suspiciously whenever he walked along the street. He had made himself cool, focused, guarded. Invulnerable.

Until Rupert Branscombe Fox had cracked his defences by taking Natasha from him, and Cassie had kicked them down completely the moment she'd laid her mouth against his.

Dragging his eyes from Cassie's legs, Jake made himself look out of the window. They were driving along the Embankment, and the Thames gleamed grey and oily in the rain, but he didn't see the river. He saw Cassie—her eyes dark and glowing in candlelight. Cassie perched on the table at Portrevick Hall, swinging her legs. Cassie laughing as she tried on a fancy tiara. Cassie looking down at the ring on her finger.

He was disturbingly aware of her warm, bright presence on the other side of the taxi. Her perfume was already achingly familiar. When had that happened? His careful life seemed to be unravelling by the minute, and Jake didn't like the feeling at all.

Completely unaware of the desperate trend of his thoughts, Cassie was patting her hair, trying to smooth it into some kind of shape. Jake's hands itched to do it for her, to slide into the soft curls, the way they had in the restaurant before that buffoon Giovanni had interrupted them. He imagined twisting its silkiness around his fingers, tucking it neatly behind her delicate ears, and then he could let his hands drift down her throat, let his lips follow…

'Is this it?' said Cassie, leaning forward to peer through the window as the taxi drew up outside the hotel, and Jake had to unscramble his thoughts enough to pay the taxi driver.

At least he had a few minutes to pull himself together while Cassie disappeared into a cloakroom to leave her coat and check her make-up. Adjusting the knot of his tie, he made himself think of something other than Cassie and the strange, disturbing way she made him feel. He remembered Portrevick instead, and the grim house where he had grown up. That was always a good way to remind himself of the importance of control. He thought about his mother's worn face, and the long, silent bus rides to visit his father in prison.

And then he thought about Rupert's supercilious smile and his jaw tightened. If it wasn't for Rupert, he wouldn't be in this mess. If it wasn't for Rupert, he and Natasha could have posed for a few photographs for this damned article and that would have been that. If it wasn't for Rupert, he would never have kissed Cassie, and he wouldn't be standing here now, unable to shake the feel of her, the taste of her, the scent of her from his mind.

Jake gave his tie a final wrench and looked at his watch. What the hell was Cassie doing in there? He was just getting ready to storm into the Ladies and drag her out when she appeared, smoothing down her dress. It was short and simply cut, and held up with tiny spaghetti-straps that left her shoulders bare. The colour—less a blue than a purple, he could see now—was so vivid that it dazzled the eye—or maybe that was just Cassie, Jake thought as the breath leaked from his lungs. She looked warm, lush, bright and unbelievably sexy. As she walked towards him he couldn't help remembering another time, ten years ago, when she had walked towards him in a different dress.

Cassie was smiling as she walked towards him, but as she got closer and her eyes met that dark, deep-blue gaze she faltered and the smile evaporated from her face. All at once, the air seemed to close around them, sealing them into an invisible bubble and sucking the air out of her lungs. The babble and laughter from Reception inside the big doors faded, and there was just Jake, watching her with unfathomable eyes, and a silence that stretched and twanged with the memory of how it had felt to kiss him.

Suddenly ridiculously shy, she struggled to think of something to say. Something other than 'kiss me again', anyway. 'How do I look?' was the best she could do.

'Very nice,' said Jake.

He couldn't have said anything better to break the tension, thought Cassie gratefully. 'No,' she told him, rolling her eyes. 'Not "very nice". You're in love with me, remember? Tell me I look beautiful or gorgeous or sexy—anything but *very nice!*'

'Maybe I won't say anything at all,' said Jake. 'Maybe I'll just do this instead.' And, putting his hands to her waist, he drew her to him and kissed her.

His lips were warm and persuasive, and wickedly exciting. Afterwards, Cassie thought that she should have resisted somehow, but at the time it felt so utterly natural that she melted into him without even a token protest. Her hands spread over his broad chest, and she parted her lips with a tiny murmur low in her throat.

It wasn't a long kiss, but it was a very thorough one, and Cassie's knees were weak when Jake let her go.

'Sometimes actions speak louder than words,' he said.

From somewhere, Cassie produced a smile. It felt a little unsteady, but at least it was a smile. At least she could pretend that her heart wasn't thudding, that her bones hadn't dissolved, and that her arms weren't aching to cling to him. That she didn't desperately, desperately want him to kiss her again.

'That's better,' she said, astonished at how steady her voice sounded. 'See how convincing you can be when you try?'

'Let's hope we can convince everyone else too,' said Jake. 'Ready?'

Of course she wasn't ready! How could he kiss her like that and then expect her to calmly swan into a party and act like a chief executive's fiancée—whatever one of those was like?

But she had agreed, and to make some feeble excuse now would just make it look as if she had been thrown into confusion by a meaningless kiss. Even if she had, Cassie didn't want Jake to know it.

She drew a deep breath. 'Ready,' she said.

Jake kept a hand at the small of her back as they made their way through the crowd. Cassie was intensely aware of it, and even when he dropped his arm she could feel its warmth like a tingling imprint on her skin burnt through the fabric of her dress.

She was nervous at first, but Jake seemed to know a lot of people there, and everyone was very friendly. There was quite a bit of interest when he introduced her as his fiancée, and Cassie wondered how many of them had known Natasha. It soon became clear, in fact, that they should have prepared their story more carefully.

'So, where did you pop up from, Cassie?' someone asked, and Jake put an arm around her waist.

'We knew each other years ago,' he said. 'We met up again recently.'

'Oh, so you've found your first love again? How sweet!'

'Well, not really,' said Jake, just as Cassie said,

'Yes. Jake was the first boy who ever kissed me.'

There was a tiny silence. 'Jake wasn't in love with me.' Cassie rose to the occasion magnificently. 'But I had a thing about him for years. Didn't I?' she said to Jake, but he was looking so baffled that she swept on, feeling rather like Michelle at the wedding fair. 'Anyway, the moment we met up again, it just clicked.'

She chattered on, inventing an entire love-affair while Jake watched her distractedly. He had been completely thrown by that kiss out there in the lobby. What had possessed him to kiss her like that? But she had looked so warm and enticing, he couldn't help himself. Now he could still taste the soft lips that had parted in surprise, still feel her body melting into his.

As the party wore on, Jake was achingly aware of Cassie by his side, a vibrant, glowing figure chatting animatedly to whoever they met. She was behaving beautifully—much better than him, anyway, Jake thought. *Look at her*, showing off her ring, turning a laughing face to his, leaning into him as if it was the most natural thing in the world for her to be here with him.

It was obvious that everyone found her so charming that Jake began to feel almost resentful. He didn't want Cassie to be able to play her role so well. He wanted her to be as disconcerted by him as he was by her.

She seemed to be managing perfectly well on her own, so he joined a neighbouring group in the hope that a little distance would help. But it was almost impossible to concentrate on chit-chat when he could feel Cassie somewhere behind him, not touching him, not talking to him, not even looking at him, but her presence as immediate as if she had laid a hand against his bare skin.

Jake finished his champagne in a gulp and looked around for a fresh glass, only to find himself face to face with the two people he least wanted to see. They saw him at the same time. Natasha looked appalled, Rupert predictably amused.

'Well, well, look who's here,' said Rupert. 'We'd no idea you'd be here too, Jake—but it's inevitable we had to meet some time, I suppose. Much best to get the first meeting over in civilised surroundings, I can't help feeling. After all, we're a little old for pistols at dawn, don't you think?'

Jake ignored that. 'Rupert,' he acknowledged him curtly. 'And Natasha.' It was odd, he thought, how much of a stranger she seemed already. 'How are you?'

'I'm fine,' she said, but Jake didn't think that she was looking her best. She was still beautiful, of course, but after Cassie she seemed a bit muted. She had none of Cassie's vitality, none of her warmth. It was hard to remember now how bitter he had felt at losing her.

Rupert put his arm around her. 'We've just been talking about getting married, haven't we, darling?' The question was for Natasha, but the words were aimed squarely at Jake. Rupert's smile was slyly triumphant. 'It's an awkward situation, knowing how much Natasha meant to you, but we hope you'll be pleased for us.'

'Or are you just hoping that I'll end the trust?' Jake asked.

'I believe marriage to a sensible woman *was* the condition—and Natasha is certainly that, aren't you, sweetheart?'

'Settling down was also a condition,' said Jake. 'When you've been married a year or so, I'll consider it.'

There was an unpleasant silence. Jake and Rupert eyed each other with acute dislike, and Jake found himself longing for Cassie. He could hardly go and drag her away from the conversation she was having just because he was confronting Rupert and Natasha on his own.

But suddenly there she was anyway, almost as if she'd sensed that he needed her, touching his rigid back, tucking her hand into his arm. Jake felt something unlock inside his chest.

Cassie studied Natasha. She was very lovely, with immaculate, silvery-blonde hair, green eyes, flawless skin, and intimidatingly well-groomed. From her perfect eyebrows to the tips of her beautifully manicured nails, Natasha was a model of elegance and restraint. She was wearing a simple top and silk trousers, but the combination of subdued neutrals and striking jewellery was wonderful.

'Classy' was the only word Cassie could think of to describe her, and her heart sank. Next to Natasha, she felt like a garish lump.

Why hadn't she thought to wear black or elegant neutral

colours like every other woman here? Cassie wondered miserably. She should have known this would be a sophisticated party. She looked ludicrously out of place in her vivid, purple dress and pink shoes. No wonder Jake had been distracted since they'd come in. He must be horribly embarrassed by her. He was used to being with Natasha, who fitted into this world in a way she never could.

How awful for Jake, to come face to face with the woman he loved on the arm of a man he hated, and to realise just what he had lost. Cassie had sensed his sudden tension somehow, and had turned to see him with Rupert and a woman she had known instantly was Natasha. His shoulders were set rigidly, and his back when she had touched it to let him know that she was there had been as stiff and as unyielding as a plank.

Well, she might not be Natasha, but she was here, and she could help him through this awkward meeting if nothing else.

Forcing a smile, Cassie turned her attention to Rupert. Even if she hadn't seen his photo in the papers over the years, she would have recognised him. He was still astonishingly good-looking, with golden hair, chiselled features and mesmerising blue eyes. It was only when you looked a little closer that you could see the lines of dissipation around his eyes.

And the faint bump in his nose where it had been broken. Cassie hoped Jake could see it, too.

'Hello, Rupert,' she said pleasantly.

Rupert looked at her, arrested. 'Do we know each other?'

'We used to,' said Cassie. 'Portrevick?' she prompted him. 'Cassie Grey? My father was Sir Ian's estate manager.'

'Good God, *Cassie*! I do remember now, but I would never have recognised you.' Rupert's eyes ran over her appreciatively. 'Well, well, well,' he drawled, evidently remembering how she had looked the last time he'd seen her. 'Who would have thought it? You look absolutely gorgeous! How lovely to see you, darling.' Taking his arm from around Natasha, he kissed her warmly on both cheeks.

The force of his charm was hard to resist, but Cassie felt Jake stiffen, and she made herself step back. 'How are you, Rupert?'

'All the better for seeing you,' he said, eyeing her with lazy appreciation. 'Where have you been hiding yourself all these years?'

How odd, thought Cassie. Here she was with Rupert, who hadn't recognised her, and was doing a very good impression of being bowled over by her looks. It was just like her fantasy.

But in her fantasy she hadn't been aware of Jake beside her, dark and rigid with hostility. She could see a muscle twitching in his jaw. He must be hating this.

'Growing up,' she said, and for the first time realised that it was true. She could look at Rupert and see that he was just a handsome face, a teenage fantasy, but not a man you could ever build a real relationship with. Had Natasha come to realise that as well? Cassie wondered. It seemed to her that the other woman's eyes were on Jake rather than Rupert, and when Cassie took Jake's hand Natasha's gaze sharpened unmistakably.

Jake's fingers closed hard around hers. 'Cassie, this is Natasha.' He introduced her stiffly.

Natasha smiled, although it looked as if it was a bit of an effort. 'You've obviously met before,' she said.

'We all grew up together in Cornwall,' said Cassie cheerfully. 'I was madly in love with Rupert for years.' She laughed. 'You know how intense adolescent love is? I promise you, I adored him.'

'You mean you don't any more?' said Rupert with mock disappointment, and with one of his patented smiles guaranteed to make a girl go weak at the knees.

Ten years ago, Cassie would have dissolved in a puddle at a smile like that. This time her knees stayed strangely steady. 'Not since I discovered what real love is,' she said, smiling at Jake, who looked straight back into her eyes; for a second the two of them were quite alone.

And then her knees *did* wobble.

Rupert's brows shot up. 'You and Jake…? How very unlikely!' His voice was light and mocking, but Cassie refused to be fazed.

'That's what we thought, didn't we, darling?' she said to Jake, and to her relief he managed to unclench his jaw at last.

'We thought we were completely different,' he agreed. 'And it turns out that we are made for each other.'

'What do your parents think about that?' Rupert asked Cassie smoothly. 'The Greys and the Trevelyans used to move in rather different social circles, as I remember.'

Cassie lifted her chin. 'They're delighted,' she told him. 'They're coming back to Portrevick for the wedding,' she added, and heard Natasha's sharp intake of breath.

'Wedding?'

'We're getting married at Christmas.' Cassie held out her hand to show her the ring, and then wished she hadn't. Her nail polish was bright-pink and chipped, and looked slatternly compared to Natasha's perfect French manicure. She pulled her hand back quickly.

'Engaged?' said Rupert. 'That's very sudden, isn't it?'

'It must seem that way to other people,' said Cassie, annoyed by his mocking expression. Anyone would think he didn't believe them. 'But to me it feels as if I've been waiting all my life to find Jake again.'

Slipping an arm around his waist, she leant adoringly into him. 'I can't believe how lucky I am. I always thought about him, but I never dreamt we would bump into each other again, and as soon as we did…bang! That was it, wasn't it, darling?'

'It was,' said Jake. 'It's enough to make you believe in fate. Cassie came along just when I needed her. I should thank you,' he said to Rupert and Natasha. 'I didn't think so at the time, I must admit, but you both did me a huge favour. If it hadn't been for you, I might never have found Cassie again.'

'So pleased to have been of help,' said Rupert a little tightly.

Natasha managed a bleak smile. 'Christmas is very soon.

I thought you didn't believe in rushing into things,' she said to Jake.

'I didn't until I met Cassie. But I know I want to spend the rest of my life with her, so there doesn't seem much point in waiting.'

Cassie saw the stricken look in Natasha's eyes and for a moment felt sorry for her. But only for a moment. Natasha had hurt Jake. She had left him for Rupert, but it was clear she wasn't at all happy to see him with someone else. It wouldn't do her any harm to think about just what she had thrown away, Cassie decided.

'It's going to be a bit of a rush to get everything organised in time,' she said, with another adoring look at Jake. 'But you're all for it, aren't you?'

'Absolutely,' he said, and a smile creased his eyes as he looked back at her. 'I'm just worried about where I'm going to get that Regency-buck outfit.'

'Regency buck?' echoed Rupert with a contemptuous look as Cassie smothered a giggle, and Jake met his eyes squarely.

'Cassie has always had a Mr Darcy fantasy. If she wants me in a cravat, I'll wear one,' he lied. 'Actually, Rupert, you might be able to give me a few tips about how to wear one. You look like the kind of man who knows his way around a cravat.'

Rupert's eyes narrowed dangerously. Clearly he couldn't decide whether Jake was joking about what he was wearing, but he knew a snide attack when he heard one. 'I'm afraid not, old chap,' he said. 'Natasha, there's Fiona—didn't you want to have a word with her? We'd better move on. Congratulations, and it was *marvellous* to see you again, Cassie.'

He produced a card as if by magic and handed it to her, as Natasha nodded to them both and headed off as if grateful to escape. 'We should meet up and talk about old times,' he said caressingly in her ear as he kissed her goodbye. 'I know Jake works all hours, but, as you're so in love, I'm sure he trusts you off the leash! Why don't you give me a ring some time?'

Cassie looked after him, fingering the card. By rights she should have been thrilled. Rupert Branscombe Fox wanted her to ring him! He was as devastatingly attractive as ever, but she couldn't shake the feeling that he had only shown an interest in her to rile Jake. Years ago, Jake had pointed out that Rupert was only interested in girls who belonged to someone else, and it seemed as if he hadn't changed very much. He had taken Natasha from Jake. Did he really think he could seduce her away, too?

She glanced at Jake, who was wearing a shuttered expression. 'Don't worry,' she said, 'I'm not going to ring him.'

His face closed even further. 'It's up to you,' he said abruptly. 'We're not really engaged. Keep the card, and you can call Rupert when all this is over.'

Cassie stared at him, hurt. She had forgotten about the pretence for a while, but clearly Jake hadn't. Then she remembered how difficult it must have been for him to pretend, with Natasha looking so beautiful with Rupert, and she felt guilty for not realising how embarrassing it would be for him if he suspected that there was a danger of her taking this all too seriously.

She tucked the card away in her bag. 'Maybe I will,' she said.

CHAPTER EIGHT

'IT'S coming on well, isn't it?' Cassie watched anxiously as Jake looked around the great hall. She badly wanted him to be impressed with the progress they had made, but to his eyes it must still look a bit of a mess.

'That scaffolding will come down as soon as the decorators have finished that last bit of ceiling,' she said. 'And then the sheets will come up so you can see the floor. That still needs to be cleaned, but the fireplace and the windows have been done—see?—and they've made a good start on the panelling, too.'

Cassie had a nasty feeling that she was babbling, but she was feeling ridiculously nervous. This was the first time she'd seen Jake since the reception at the Savoy. It had been a busy couple of weeks, most of which she had spent running up and down between London and Portrevick so that she could keep an eye on the work at the Hall. But there had still been rather too much time to think about Jake and remember how it had felt when he had kissed her.

To wonder if he would ever kiss her again.

Not that there seemed much chance of that. Jake hadn't asked her to appear as his fiancée again. She had obviously been much too crass. Cassie felt hot all over whenever she thought about how garish she had looked that evening. She must have stuck out like a tart at a vicar's tea-party. It wasn't surprising that Jake wasn't keen to repeat the experience. He only had to look at her next to Natasha's immaculate elegance to realise just how unconvincing a fiancée she made.

Their only contact since then had been by email. Cassie sent long, chatty messages about what was happening at the Hall, and Jake sent terse acknowledgements. She couldn't help wishing that he would show a little more interest. Email was convenient, but she wanted to hear his voice. She needed to know what he thought about the decisions she was making. It was lonely doing it all on her own.

But that was what he was paying her for, Cassie had to keep reminding herself. What was the point in a consultant you had to encourage the whole time, after all? Still, she had thought that they had more than a strictly businesslike relationship. They had laughed together. They had pretended to be in love.

They had *kissed*.

Whenever she thought about those kisses—and it was far too often—Cassie's heart would start to slam against her ribs. The memory of Jake's mouth—the feel of it, the taste of it—uncoiled like a serpent inside her, shivering along her veins and stirring up her blood.

It was stupid.

It was embarrassing.

It was pointless.

Time and again, Cassie reminded herself that Jake only cared about saving face with Rupert. The engagement was a tactic, that was all, one that had the added advantage of promoting the Hall so that he could rid himself of an unwanted responsibility. He hated Portrevick and all it represented. Once the Hall was up and running as a wedding venue, he would settle their fee and that would be that. She had to keep things strictly professional.

That didn't stop her heart lurching whenever she saw an email from him in her inbox, or sinking just a little when she read the brief message. It didn't stop her hoping that he would come down at the weekend, or being ridiculously disappointed when he decided to stay in London instead.

But he was here now. Cassie had—rather cleverly, she thought—arranged with *Wedding Belles* that they would supply photos themselves rather than have the magazine send a photographer all the way from London to Cornwall. It would be cheaper for the magazine, and much more convenient for them.

Tina's boyfriend was a photographer, Cassie had explained to Jake in one of her many emails. He and Tina were in on the secret, and Cassie had organised for him to take some photographs to illustrate the article. They needed some shots of the two of them apparently working on the renovation of the Hall and preparing for the wedding together, Cassie had told Jake. Could he come to Cornwall that weekend?

He would come down on Saturday, Jake had agreed, and Cassie had been jittery all day while she'd waited for him to arrive. She had changed three times that morning, and hours before there was any chance that he would turn up she would jump every time she heard a car. It was impossible to concentrate on anything, and even the most prosaic of conversations had her trailing off in mid-sentence or unable to make a decision about whether she wanted a cup of tea or not.

'What on earth is the matter with you this morning?' Tina had asked with a searching look.

'Nothing,' Cassie had said quickly. 'I'm just thinking about how much there is to do. I might as well go up to the Hall now, in fact. There's plenty to be getting on with. When Jake arrives, can you tell him I'm up there already?' she'd added casually, as if she wasn't counting the minutes until she saw him again.

She'd given herself a good talking-to as she walked up to the Hall. She'd hauled out all those well-worn arguments about being cool and professional, and concentrating on making the Hall a success, and had been so stern that she'd been feeling quite composed when she'd heard Jake's car crunching on the gravel outside.

So it had been unnerving to discover that all he had to do was walk in, looking lean and dark and forceful, for the air to evaporate from her lungs in a great whoosh. How could she think coolly and professionally when every cell in her body was jumping up and down in excitement at the mere sight of him?

Cassie swallowed and made herself shut up.

Jake was still inspecting the hall. 'It looks much better than it did,' he agreed. 'Are we still on target to have this room ready for the Allantide Ball? We're in October already,' he reminded her.

'It's only the fourth,' said Cassie. 'That gives us nearly a month until Hallowe'en. It'll be fine.'

It'll be fine. That was what she always said. Jake wasn't sure whether he envied Cassie her relaxed attitude or disapproved of it. There was so much about Cassie that made him feel unsure, he realised. Like the way he hadn't known whether he was looking forward to seeing her again or dreading it.

Jake didn't like feeling unsure, and that was how Cassie made him feel all the time. Ever since he had met her again, he seemed to have lost the control he had fought so hard to achieve.

Take that reception at the Savoy, when he had been so distracted by her that he had hardly been able to string two words together. Having to stand and watch Rupert kissing Cassie goodbye and slipping her his card had left Jake consumed by such fury that it was all he'd been able to do to stop himself from breaking Rupert's nose again. He'd had to remind himself that Cassie was probably delighted. She had told him herself of how she had dreamed of Rupert for years.

And, when it came down to it, she wasn't actually his fiancée, was she? Why was that so hard to remember?

Hating the feeling of things being out of his control, Jake had retreated into himself. He would focus on work. Work had got him where he was today, and it would see him through this odd, uncertain patch.

He had been glad when Cassie had said that she was going

down to Portrevick. It had felt like his chance to get some order back into his life—but the strange thing was that he had missed her. Her message about the photographs Tina's boyfriend had agreed to take had pitched him back into confusion again, but he hadn't been able to think of an excuse not to come, and then he had despised himself for needing an excuse. What was wrong with him? It was only Cassie.

Now he was here, and so glad to see her his throat felt tight and uncomfortable. At least she was dressed more practically today, in jeans and a soft red jumper, but he had forgotten what a bright, vibrant figure she was. It was like looking at the sun. Even when you dragged your eyes away, her image was burned onto your vision.

Jake cleared his throat. 'So, what's happening about these photos?'

'Oh, yes. Well, it's not a big deal. Rob is just going to take a few pictures of us inspecting the work here, maybe pretending to look as if we're making lists or looking at fabric samples. The idea is to have some "before and after" shots, but we don't need many now. We'll have to pull out the stops for the supposed "wedding" photos, but we'll do those after the Allantide Ball, when the great hall is finished and we can decorate it as if for Christmas.' Cassie looked at him a little nervously. 'Is that OK?'

'I suppose so,' said Jake. 'I can't say I'm looking forward to it, but we're committed now. We may as well get it over and done with.'

'Tina and Rob said they'd be here at five.' Cassie glanced at her watch. 'It's only three now. Do you want me to ring them and get them to come earlier?'

'What I'd really like is to stretch my legs,' said Jake. His gaze dropped to Cassie's feet. 'Those look like sensible shoes for once. Can you walk in them?'

Outside it was cool and blustery, and the sea was a sullen grey. It heaved itself at the rocks, smashing in a froth of white spray as they walked along the cliff tops. The coastal path was narrow, and the buffeting wind made conversation difficult, so they walked in silence—but it wasn't an uncomfortable one.

When at length they dropped down onto the long curve of beach, they were sheltered from the worst of the wind. Although Cassie's curls were still blown crazily around her head, it felt peaceful in comparison with the rugged cliffs.

'This was a good idea,' she said as they walked side by side along the tide line, their heads bent against the breeze and their hands thrust into their jacket pockets.

'It's good to get out of the car,' Jake agreed. 'Good to get out of London,' he added slowly, realising for the first time in years that it was true. He had been feeling restless and uneasy, but now, with the waves crashing relentlessly onto the shore, the wind in his hair and Cassie beside him, he had the strangest feeling of coming home. 'It's been…busy,' he finished, although the truth was that he had deliberately created work for himself so that he didn't have time to think.

'Has anyone said any more about our engagement?' Cassie asked after a moment.

'Nobody seems to talk about anything else,' said Jake. 'My staff are giving me grief that I haven't introduced you, and you've been specifically included in endless invitations to drinks and dinner and God knows what else. I'm running out of excuses.'

'I don't mind going,' said Cassie. 'But you probably don't want me to,' she added quickly. 'I know I don't exactly fit in.'

Jake stopped to stare at her. 'What do you mean?'

'I was so out of place at that reception,' she reminded him. 'I know I looked crass and ridiculous compared to everybody else there. It must have been really embarrassing for you.'

'I wasn't embarrassed,' he said. 'I was proud of you. You didn't look crass. You looked wonderful. Nobody could take their eyes off you. Do you have any idea of how refreshing you were?'

'Really?' she stammered, colouring with pleasure.

Jake began walking again. 'You ought to have more confidence in yourself,' he told her. 'You might not have a profession, but you've got social skills coming out your ears, and they're worth as much as any qualification. Look at what you've achieved down here.'

'I haven't really done anything,' said Cassie. 'The contractors are doing all the work.'

'They wouldn't be doing it if it wasn't for you. You had the idea; you're getting them all organised. It's time you stopped thinking of yourself as such a failure, Cassie.'

'Easy to say,' she said with a sigh. 'But it's hard when you've spent years being the under-achiever in the family. Social skills are all very well, but it's not that difficult to chat at a party.'

'It's difficult for me,' Jake pointed out. 'I never learnt how to talk easily to people. There were no parties when I was growing up, and precious little conversation at all. We didn't do birthdays or Christmas or celebrating.'

He walked with his eyes on the sand, remembering. 'My mother did her best, but there was never enough money, and she was constantly scrimping to put food on the table. She was a hard worker. She didn't just clean for Sir Ian, but at the pub and several other houses in the village. When she came home at night she was so tired she just wanted to sit in front of the television. I don't blame her,' he said. 'She had little enough pleasure in her life.'

And how much pleasure had there been for a little boy? Cassie wondered. Starved of attention, brought up in a joyless home without even Christmas to look forward to, it was no wonder he had grown up wild.

'It was hard for her trying to manage on her own,' Jake went on. 'I barely remember my father being at home. He was sent to prison when I was six. After he was released, he came home for a couple of weeks, but nobody in Portrevick was going to employ him. He went off to London to find a job, he said, and we never heard from him again.'

'I'm sorry,' said Cassie quietly, thinking of how far Jake had come since then. From village tearaway to chief executive in ten years was a spectacular achievement, and he had done it without any of the support she, her brothers and sister had taken for granted from their own parents. 'I can't imagine life without my dad,' she said. Her father might be a bit stuffy, but at least he was always there.

'You're lucky,' Jake agreed. 'I used to wish that I could have a father at home like everyone else, but maybe if he had been around I would have ended up following in his footsteps. As it was, I inherited his entrepreneurial spirit, but decided to stick to the right side of the law. But it was touch and go,' he added honestly. 'I was getting out of control. When you've got no money, no family life and no future, it feels like there's nothing to lose.

'Sir Ian's offer came just in time,' he said. 'It made me realise that I could have a future after all, and how close I'd come to throwing it away. I knew then that if I was going to escape I had to get myself under control. I built myself a rigid structure for my life. I worked and I focused and I got out of Portrevick and the mess my life had become, thanks to Sir Ian.'

He glanced at Cassie. 'But there wasn't much time along the way to learn about social niceties. You said you felt out of place at that reception, but you belonged much more than I did. I'm the real outsider in those situations. It's one of the reasons I was so drawn to Natasha,' he admitted. 'She fits in perfectly. I could go anywhere with her and be sure that she would know exactly what to do and what to say. It sounds pathetic, but I felt safe with her,' said Jake with a sheepish look.

'But you look so confident!' Cassie said, unable to put a lack of confidence together with her image of Jake, who had always been the coolest guy around. 'You were always leader of the pack.'

'In Portrevick, and the pack was a pretty disreputable one,' said Jake. 'And I can talk business with anyone. It's a different story in a smart social setting, like that reception, where you're supposed to know exactly how to address Lord This and Lady That, how to hold your knife and fork properly, and chit-chat about nothing I know anything about.

'You could do it,' he told Cassie. 'You chatted away without a problem, but I can't do that. It makes me feel…inadequate,' he confessed. 'It's one of the reasons I resent Rupert so much, I suppose. He's colossally arrogant and not particularly bright, but he can sail into a social situation and charm the pants off everyone. Look at what he was like with you,' said Jake bitterly. 'All over you like a rash, and never mind that you're supposed to be my fiancée and I'm standing right there.'

'I think it's just an automatic reflex with Rupert,' said Cassie, hugging this hint of jealousy to her. 'He flirts with every woman he meets.'

'Does he give them all his number and tell them to call him?'

'Probably,' she said. 'And most of them no doubt will ring him. But I'm not going to. I've thrown his card away.'

Jake felt a tightness in his chest loosen. 'Good,' he said, and when he looked sideways at Cassie their eyes snagged as if on barbed wire. Without being aware of it, their steps faltered and they stopped.

Cassie was intensely aware of the dull boom of the waves crashing into the shallows, of the familiar tang of salt on the air, and the screech of a lone gull circling above. The wind blew her hair around her face and she held it back with one hand as she finally managed to tear her eyes from Jake's.

He looked different down here on the beach, more relaxed, as if the rigid control that gripped him in London had loosened. She was glad that he had told her more about his past. It sounded as if his childhood had been much bleaker than she had realised, and she understood a little better now why he had been so insistent on a formula for relationships. If you had no experience of an open, loving relationship like her parents', fixing on a partner who shared your practical approach must seem a much better bet than putting your trust in turbulent emotions that couldn't be pinned down or analysed.

It was sad, though. In spite of herself, Cassie sighed.

Beside her, Jake was watching the wet-suited figures bobbing out in the swell. Even at this time of year there were surfers here. Portrevick was a popular surfing beach, and lifeguards kept a careful eye from a vehicle parked between the two flags that marked the safe area.

Following his gaze, Cassie saw one of the surfers paddling furiously to pick up a big wave just before it crested. He rose agilely on his board, riding the wave as it powered inland, until the curling foam overtook him and broke over him, sending him tumbling gracefully into the water.

'Why don't you surf any more?' she asked him abruptly.

'I can't.'

'But you were so good at it,' Cassie protested. 'You were always in the water. I used to watch you from up there,' she said, pointing up to the dunes. 'You were easily the best.'

Jake's mouth twisted. 'I loved it,' he said. 'It was the only time I felt really free. When things got too bad at home, I'd come down here. When you're out there, just you and the sea, you feel like you can do anything. There's nothing like the exhilaration you get from riding a big wave, being part of the sea and its power...' He trailed off, remembering.

'Then why not do it again?'

'Because...' Jake started and then stopped, wondering how to explain. 'Because surfing is part of who I was when I was here. I don't want to be that boy any more. When I left Portrevick, I cut off all associations with what I'd been. I wanted to change.'

'Is that why you gave up riding a motorbike too?'

He nodded. 'Maybe it's not very rational, but there's part of me that thinks the surfing, the bike, the risks I used to take, all of those were bound up with being reckless, being wild and out of control. It felt as if the freedom they gave me was the price I had to pay to get out of Portrevick and start again.'

'But you've changed,' said Cassie. 'Taking out a surf board or riding a motorbike isn't going to change you back.'

'What if it does?' countered Jake, who had obviously been through this many times before. 'What if I remember how good it felt out there? I'm afraid that, if I let go even for a moment, I might slide back and lose everything I've worked so hard for. I can't risk that. My whole life has been about leaving Portrevick behind.'

He was never going back, Jake vowed. No matter if here, by the sea, was the only place he ever felt truly at home. He had escaped, and the only way was forward.

'It seems a shame,' said Cassie. 'You can't wipe out the past. That wild boy is still part of who you are now.'

'That's what I'm afraid of,' said Jake.

Who was she to talk, anyway? Cassie asked herself as they turned and walked slowly back along beach. She didn't want to be the gauche adolescent she had been, either. Perhaps if she could put her past behind her as firmly as Jake had she too could be driven and successful, instead of muddling along, living down her family's expectations.

Tina and Rob were waiting for them back at the Hall, and Rob took a series of photos. 'Detailed shots are best,' Tina said authoritatively. 'I've been looking through a few bridal magazines, and that's what the readers want to see. A close up of a table decoration, or your shoes or something, so they can think, "ooh, I'd like something like that".'

'What about a close up of the engagement ring, in that case?' Jake suggested.

'That's a brilliant idea. Why aren't you wearing it, Cassie?'

'It feels all wrong to wear it all the time,' said Cassie, taking the box out of her bag and slipping the ring onto her finger. 'It's not as if it's a real engagement ring.' Unaware of her wistful expression, she turned her hand to make the jewels flash. 'It's just a prop.'

'Some prop,' said Tina, admiring it. 'It's absolutely gorgeous—and perfect for you, Cassie.'

'It's beautiful, isn't it?' Cassie's eyes were still on the ring. 'Jake chose it.'

Tina's sharp gaze flicked from her friend's face to Jake, who was watching Cassie. 'Did he now?'

Cassie was glad they had had that talk on the beach. Things were much easier between them after that, and they were able to chat quite comfortably when Jake gave her a lift back to London the next day.

She understood a little more why he was so determined to leave his old life behind him, and could admire the way he had transformed himself—but a little part of Cassie was sad too. Their conversation had underlined yet again how very different they were. She wished Jake could let go just a little bit, just enough to let him want someone a little muddled, a little messy.

A little bit like her, in fact.

Oh yes, and how likely is that? Cassie asked herself. Jake was used to a woman like Natasha, who was beautiful and clever and fit perfectly into his new life. Why on earth would he want to 'let go' for *her*? The best she could hope for was to be a friend.

And that was what she would be, Cassie decided. After the photo session, she had persuaded Jake to come to the pub with her, Tina and Rob. He had been reluctant at first, remembering the less-than-warm welcome he had had on previous occasions, but this time it was different. Cassie had made sure that Portrevick knew the truth about Sir Ian's will, and word had got round about the Allantide Ball too. She was determined to see Jake accepted back in the village, whether he liked it or not.

So the drive back to London was fine. Or, sort of fine. It

was comfortable in one way, and deeply uncomfortable in another. A friend would enjoy Jake's company, and that was what she did. A friend would ask him about his time in the States and about his job, and chat away about nothing really. A friend would make him laugh.

But a true friend *wouldn't* spend her whole time having to drag her eyes away from his mouth. She wouldn't have to clutch her hands together to stop them straying over to his thigh. She wouldn't drift off into a lovely fantasy, where Jake would pull off the road and rip out her seatbelt in a frenzy, unable to keep his hands off her a moment longer.

'Quick—where's the nearest Travelodge?' he would say— except a motel was a bit tacky, wasn't it? Cassie rewound the fantasy a short way and tried a new script. 'Let's get off the main road and find a charming pub with a Michelin-starred restaurant and a four-poster bed upstairs,' she tried instead.

Yes, that was more like it, she decided, almost purring in anticipation. There would be a roaring fire and they would sit thigh-to-thigh in front of it with a bottle of wine...then Jake would take her hand and lead her up some rickety stairs to their bedroom. He'd close the door and smile as he drew her down onto the bed, unbuttoning her blouse and kissing his way down her throat at the same time.

'I've been thinking about this for weeks,' he would murmur, his lips hot against her skin, his hands sliding wickedly over her. 'I'm crazy about you.'

'I love you too,' she would sigh.

'Did you mean what you said?' said Jake, startling her out of her fantasy at just the wrong point.

'What?' Cassie jerked upright, her blood pounding. Good grief, she hadn't been dreaming aloud, had she? 'No! I mean...when? What did I say?'

'On the beach yesterday. You said you wouldn't mind coming along to various events as my fiancée again?'

Cassie fanned herself with relief. 'Oh...no, of course not.'

Willing her booming pulse to subside, she pulled at her collar in an attempt to cool herself. She had got a bit carried away there. *I love you too*. What on earth was that about? She wasn't in love with Jake. What a ridiculous idea. She just… found him very attractive.

Yes, that was all it was.

On the other hand, friendly was all she was supposed to be, she reminded herself sternly. 'I'm always up for a party.'

Keep it light, Cassie had told herself. But it didn't stop her spending hours searching for the definitive little black dress when Jake rang and asked if she could come to a drinks party later that week.

She should have spared herself the effort. Jake hated it. 'It's boring,' he said when Cassie presented herself with a twirl and made the mistake of asking what he thought. 'Why didn't you buy a red one? Or a green one? Anything but black!'

Cassie was crestfallen. 'I thought you'd like it if I wore what everyone else was wearing,' she said. 'I didn't want to stand out.'

'I like you as you are,' said Jake.

When Cassie thought about it afterwards, she realised that it was actually quite a nice thing for him to say, but the words were delivered in such a grumpy, un-lover-like tone that at the time she was rather miffed. She had thought she looked really smart for once.

She didn't bother dressing up for the day at the spa. To Jake's horror, *Wedding Belles* had decided to send a photographer along to take a picture of them enjoying their prize, so Cassie had to hurriedly arrange a day when they could make the most of the voucher. Jake was furious when he heard that he had to take a day off work.

'It'll be good for you,' Cassie told him. 'You need to relax. I'll book some treatments.'

'There had better not be any seaweed involved,' warned

Jake as they signed in to the spa, which promised them 'utter serenity'…'a time out of time'.

'Don't worry,' said Cassie. 'I knew you didn't like the idea of seaweed, so you're going to be smeared in mud from the Dead Sea, and then wrapped in cling film instead.'

'What?'

She rolled her eyes and laughed at his aghast expression. 'Oh, don't panic. You're just getting a back massage. It'll help you unwind.'

Jake was deeply uncomfortable about the thought of a massage at all, but in the end it wasn't too bad. He couldn't say he found the spa a relaxing experience, though. There was nothing relaxing about spending an entire day with Cassie, dressed only in a swimming costume and a fluffy robe which she cast off frequently as she dragged him between steam rooms, saunas and an admittedly fabulous pool.

How could he relax when Cassie was just *there*, almost naked? Jake couldn't take his eyes off her body. She wasn't as slender or as perfectly formed as Natasha, but she had long, strong legs and she was enticingly curved. She looked so *touchable*, thought Jake, his mouth dry.

He had to keep dragging his eyes back to her face as she sat on the edge of the pool, dangling her legs in the water, or stretched out on the pine slats in the sauna, chatting unconcernedly. The photographer took a snap of them in their robes, and Jake had a feeling that he was going to look cross-eyed with the effort of keeping his hands off that lush, glowing body.

Utter serenity? Utter something else entirely, in Jake's book!

He told himself that it would be a relief when Cassie went back to Portrevick to prepare for the Allantide Ball. But as soon as she had gone he missed her. It was almost as if he was getting used to her colourful, chaotic presence; as if a day without seeing her walk towards him on a pair of ridiculously unsuitable shoes, or hearing her laugh on the end of the phone, was somehow dull and monochrome. Cassie enthused by email from Portrevick:

Wait till you see the great hall! It's looking fab. As soon as ball is over, will redecorate as if for a Christmas wedding and Rob is all teed up to come and take some photos of us. Will send them to *Wedding Belles* in January, and then it'll all be over, you'll be glad to know! Cxxx

Jake spent a long time looking at those three kisses. Kiss, kiss, kiss. What kind of kisses did she mean? Brief, meaningless, peck-on-the-cheek kisses? Or the kind of kisses that made your heart thunder and your head reel? The kind of kisses you couldn't bear to stop, but were never enough? She had added,

P.S., We're having an evening wedding (just so you know!) so don't forget your tuxedo!

But all Jake saw was 'it'll all be over'. He wasn't sure that he wanted it to be over, and not being sure threw him into turmoil. For ten years now he *had* been sure. He had known exactly what he needed to do. Now Cassie had thrown all that into question with three little kisses.

CHAPTER NINE

'WHAT do you think?' Cassie gestured around the great hall, and Jake turned slowly, staring at the transformation she had wrought.

From the ceiling hung a mass of paper lanterns, gold, red, russet and orange, their autumn colours investing the great hall with a vivid warmth. Everywhere else in the country rooms were being decorated with pumpkins, ghoulies and ghosties for Hallowe'en, but here in Portrevick Hall there were candles in every stone niche and great bowls piled high with Allan apples, just as there had been in Sir Ian's time.

Outside, it was cold and damp. Fallen leaves were lying in great drifts and the air held an unmistakable edge, with the promise of winter blowing in from the sea, but inside the Hall was warm and inviting.

'It looks wonderful,' said Jake sincerely. He couldn't believe how Cassie had transformed the Hall in such a short time. He couldn't quite put his finger on what she had done. It was as if she had waved a wand and brought the old house to life again. 'You've done an amazing job,' he told her.

Cassie coloured with pleasure. 'I'm glad you like it. I think it'll look good in the photos. The local paper are sending someone to cover the ball, and they're going to mention the fact that the Hall is being developed as a venue—so that should get us some coverage locally, at least.

'Oh, by the way,' she said, carefully casual, 'word has got out about our supposed engagement, so I thought I'd better move into the Hall with you. It's not as if we're short of bedrooms here, and it might look a bit odd if I was engaged to you but still staying chastely with Tina.'

'Fine,' said Jake, too heartily. The idea of Cassie moving in with him was like a shot of adrenalin. He knew quite well that she wouldn't be sharing a bedroom with him, but still there was a moment when the blood roared in his ears and he felt quite lightheaded. 'Good idea.'

He cleared his throat, wondering how to get off the subject of bedrooms. 'How many people are you expecting tonight?' he asked Cassie.

'I'm not sure. Probably about a hundred and fifty or so,' she guessed. 'More or less the same as usual. Everyone I've spoken to in the village has said they're coming.'

She didn't add that she suspected that most of them were curious to see Jake again. 'I've put notices up in the local pubs, the way Sir Ian used to do, so we may have some people from round about, too.'

Jake ran his finger around his collar. 'I'm not sure how I feel about confronting so much of my past in one fell swoop,' he admitted.

'It'll be fine.' Cassie laid a hand on his arm, her brown eyes warm. 'Everyone knows the truth about Sir Ian's will. They're prepared to accept you for how you are now.'

Jake didn't believe that for a moment, but he was too proud to admit that he was dreading the evening ahead. 'What time are they all coming?'

'Seven o'clock.' Cassie looked at the old clock still ticking steadily after all these years. 'We'd better get changed.'

'I hope you're not wearing that black dress again,' said Jake as they moved towards the stairs.

'No,' she said. 'You made such a fuss about that, I thought I'd wear a red one this time.'

'A red one?' Jake paused with one foot on the first step. 'Like the one you wore to the last Allantide Ball?'

Their eyes met, and the memory of how they had kissed that evening shimmered in the air so vividly that Cassie could almost reach out and touch it. A tinge of colour crept into her cheeks. 'I hope this one is a little more classy.'

'Shame,' said Jake lightly. 'Does that mean you're not going to flirt with me again?'

'I might do,' said Cassie, equally lightly, but the moment the words were out she wanted to call them back. If she was going to flirt with Jake, was she going to kiss him too? The question seemed to reverberate in the sudden silence: *did flirting mean kissing…kissing…kissing?*

She swallowed and set off up the stairs. 'Only if I have time—and nothing better to do, of course.' She tried to joke her way out of it.

'Of course,' Jake agreed dryly.

'Use this bathroom here,' he said, leading her down a long, draughty corridor. He pointed at a door. 'It's the warmest, and the only one with halfway decent plumbing.'

Cassie tried to calm her galloping pulse as she showered and changed into the dress she had bought after Jake had so summarily rejected her foray into black elegance. This one was a lovely cherry-red, and the slinky fabric draped beautifully over her curves and fell to her ankles. It had a halter neck and a daringly low back. Her mother would have taken one look at it and told her that she would catch her death and should cover up with a cardigan, but Cassie wasn't cold at all. The thought of Jake in the shower just down the hall was keeping her nicely heated, thank you.

She leant towards the mirror to put on her make-up, but her hand wasn't quite steady; she kept remembering the look in Jake's eyes when he'd asked if she was going to flirt with him the way she had ten years ago.

She was no good at this 'just being friends' thing, Cassie

decided. A friend would have treated his question as a joke. Had she done that? No, she had given him a smouldering look under her lashes. *I might do*, she had said.

Cassie cringed at the memory. Good grief, why hadn't she just offered herself on a plate while she was at it? She would have to try harder to be cool, she decided. But she couldn't stop the treacherous excitement flickering along her veins and simmering under her skin as she slid the ruby ring onto her finger, took a deep breath and went to find Jake.

He was still in his room, but the door was open. Cassie knocked lightly. 'Ready?' she asked.

'Nearly.' Jake was fastening his cuffs, a black bow-tie hanging loose around his neck. Glancing up from his wrists, he did a double take as he saw her standing in the doorway, vibrant and glowing in the stunning red dress.

For a moment, he couldn't say anything. 'You look…incredible,' he said, feeling like a stuttering schoolboy.

'Thank you.'

Mouth dry, Jake turned away. 'I'll be with you in a second,' he managed, marvelling at how normal he sounded. 'I just have to do something about this damned tie.' He stood in front of the mirror and lifted his chin, grimacing in frustration as he attempted to tie it with fingers that felt thick and unwieldy. 'I hate these things,' he scowled.

'Here, let me do it.' Cassie stopped hovering in the doorway to come and push his hands away from the mess he was making with the tie. 'I deal with these all the time at weddings. Stand still.'

Jake stood rigidly, staring stolidly ahead. He was excruciatingly aware of her standing so close to him. He could smell her warm, clean skin, and the fresh scent of her shampoo drifted enticingly from her soft curls, as if beckoning him to bury his face in them.

In spite of himself, his gaze flickered down. Cassie's expression was intent, a faint pucker between her brows as she concentrated on the tie with deft fingers. He could see her dark lashes, the sweet curve of her cheek, and he had to clench his fists to stop himself reaching for her.

'OK, that'll do.' Cassie gave the tie a final pat and stood back. And made the fatal mistake of looking into his eyes.

The dark-blue depths seemed to suck her in, making the floor unsteady beneath her feet, and her mind reeled. Cassie could feel herself swaying back towards him, pulled as if by an invisible magnet, and her hands were actually lifting to reach for him when Jake stepped abruptly back.

'Thank you,' he said hoarsely, and cleared his throat. 'That looks very professional.'

Cassie's pulse was booming in her ears. She moistened her lips. 'I should go down—see if the caterers need a hand.'

She practically ran down the stairs. Oh God, one more second there and she would have flung herself at him! It had taken all her concentration to fasten that tie when every instinct had been shrieking at her to rip it off him, to undo his buttons, to pull the shirt out of his trousers and press her lips to his bare chest. To run her hands feverishly over him, to reach for his belt, to drag him down onto the floor there and then. What if Jake had seen it in her eyes?

Well, what if he had? Cassie slowed as she reached the bottom of the staircase. It wasn't as if either of them had any commitments. They were both single, both unattached. Why *not* act on the attraction that had jarred the air between them just now?

Because Jake had felt it too, Cassie was sure.

The prospect set a warm thrill quivering deep inside her. It grew steadily, spilling heat through her as she helped a tense Jake greet the first arrivals, until she felt as if she were burning with it.

Cassie was convinced everyone must be able to see the naked desire in her face, but if they could nobody commented. There was much oohing and aahing about the decorations instead, and undisguised curiosity about Jake and their apparent engagement, of course. But nobody seemed to think that there was anything odd about the feverish heat that must surely be radiating out of every pore.

She kept an anxious eye on Jake, knowing how much he had been dreading the evening. He might not think he could do social chit-chat, but it seemed to Cassie that he was managing fine. Only a muscle jumping in his cheek betrayed his tension. She had felt him taut beside her at the beginning, but as he relaxed gradually Cassie left him to it. Standing next to him was too tempting, and it wouldn't do to jump him right in front of everyone.

Smiling and chatting easily, she moved around the Hall. Having grown up in Portrevick, she knew almost everyone there, and they all wanted to know about her parents, brothers and sister. Normally, Cassie would have been very conscious of how unimpressive her own achievements were compared to the rest of the family's, but tonight she was too aware of Jake to care. She talked about how Liz juggled her family and her career, about Jack's promotion, about the award Tom had won—but her attention was on Jake, who was looking guarded, but obviously making an effort for the village that had rejected him.

Cassie was talking to one of her mother's old bridge friends when she became aware of a stir by the main door, and she looked over to see Rupert and Natasha stroll in, looking impossibly glamorous. Her first reaction was one of fury—that they should turn up, tonight of all nights, to make the ball even more difficult for Jake than it needed to be.

Jake had his back to the door and hadn't seen them yet. Cassie excused herself and hurried over to intercept Rupert and Natasha. 'I'm surprised to see you here,' she said, although she was more surprised at how irritated she was by Rupert's ostentatiously warm greeting.

'I saw the ball advertised, and thought we would drop in for old times' sake,' said Rupert. 'After all, Sir Ian *was* my 'uncle.' He looked nostalgically around the great hall. 'Besides, I wanted Natasha to see the house where I grew up.'

'You only came for part of the summer holidays,' Cassie pointed out, knowing that what Rupert really wanted to do was flaunt Natasha in front of Jake and remind him of his humiliation.

'Now, why do I get the impression you're not pleased to see me, Cassie?' Rupert smiled and leant closer. 'Or is it possible that you're not pleased to see Natasha?' he murmured in her ear.

Natasha, looking cool and lovely, was standing a little apart, her green eyes wandering around the great hall. She might have been admiring the architecture, but Cassie was sure that she was searching for Jake, and her lips tightened.

'Oh, dear, I suppose it was a bit tactless of us to come,' Rupert went on with mock regret. 'Jake did adore her so, and you can see why. She's perfection, isn't she?'

'She's very beautiful,' Cassie said shortly, thinking that that really was tactless of Rupert. As Jake's fiancée, she was hardly likely to want to hear about how much he had loved another woman, was she? 'But looks aren't everything, Rupert. Jake's in love with me now.'

'Is he?' Rupert's smile broadened as he looked down into Cassie's face. 'You don't think there could be a little touch of the rebound going on? Or even, dare I say it, a little face-saving, hmm? He did get together with you very quickly after Natasha left, after all.'

Cassie met his amused blue eyes as steadily as she could. Rupert might be extraordinarily handsome, but he wasn't stupid. 'Think what you want, Rupert,' she said as she turned on her heel. 'Jake loves me and I love him.'

She heard the words fall from her lips, and the truth hit her like a splash of cold water in her face: she *did* love Jake. Why hadn't she realised it before? It had snuck up on her without her realising.

Trembling as if she had had a shock, Cassie looked around for Jake and caught a glimpse of him through the crowd, standing almost exactly where he had been standing ten years ago. He was momentarily alone, looking dark and formidable, and the sight of him was like a great vise squeezing her entrails.

Cassie knew why she hadn't wanted to see the truth. It was impossible that a man like Jake could love her back. Rupert was right, of course. Jake had adored Natasha. He had told her so himself, hadn't he? If he had indeed felt the…*something* fizzing between them, Cassie was fairly sure that he would think of it as no more than a physical attraction.

Well, that might be enough, Cassie told herself as she wove her way through the chattering groups towards him, very aware of Rupert's mocking gaze following her. She would convince him that what was between her and Jake was real—even if it wasn't—and, if that meant seducing Jake, so much the better.

She wouldn't fool herself that it could last for ever, but she could at least make the most of the time she did have with him. She could save Jake's face and assuage the terrible need that was thudding and thumping in the pit of her belly at the same time.

So she smiled at Jake and ran her hand lightly down the sleeve of his dinner jacket, hoping if nothing else to distract him from the fact that Natasha and Rupert were here. 'I thought I'd come and see if my flirting technique is any better than ten years ago.'

Amusement bracketed his mouth, but his eyes were hot and dark as they ran over her. 'The thing about wearing a dress like that is that you don't need to flirt. You don't need to say anything at all. You just need to stand there and look like that.'

Cassie swallowed. 'Gosh, you're much better at flirting than I am!'

'You haven't even started yet,' Jake pointed out. 'I'm waiting for you to do your worst. Get those eyelashes batting!'

The dark-blue gaze came up to meet hers, and their smiles faded in unison. 'Come on—flirt with me, Cassie,' he said softly, and her breath snared in her throat.

Her heart, which had been pounding away like mad, had decelerated suddenly to a painful slam, so slow that she was afraid that it might stop altogether.

'I…can't,' she whispered, unable to tear her eyes from his, and Jake lifted a gentle hand to run a finger down her cheek, searing her skin with its caress.

'Shall we skip the flirting, then?' His voice was very deep and very low. 'Shall we just go straight to the kissing?'

Unable to speak, Cassie nodded dumbly. She had forgotten Rupert, forgotten Natasha, forgotten that they were surrounded by the whole of Portrevick. As far as she was concerned, they could sink right down onto the stone flags together and make love right there. But Jake, more aware of everyone around them, took her hand and pulled her out along the corridor and onto the side terrace, just as he had done ten years ago.

Like then, it was cold and drizzly, but neither of them noticed. The door banged behind them, and Jake was already sliding his fingers into Cassie's hair the way he had fantasised about doing for so long. His mouth came down hungrily on hers and they kissed fiercely, almost desperately.

Cassie grabbed his shirt, holding on to it for dear life; suppressed excitement was unleashed by the touch of his lips and rocketed through her so powerfully that she could have sworn she felt her feet leave the ground.

God, it felt so good to be kissing him! He tasted wonderful, he felt wonderful, so hard, so strong, so gloriously, solidly male. She slid her arms around him to pull him tighter, her pulse roaring in her ears, as Jake backed her into the wall, his hands moving possessively, insistently, over her, making her dress ruck and slither, smoothing warm hands down her bare back.

'I've wanted this for weeks,' he whispered unevenly in her ear, when they broke for breath.

'I think I've wanted it for ten years,' she said, equally shaky.

'Liar,' Jake laughed softly, but his mouth was drifting down her throat, making her gasp and arch her head to one side. 'You wanted Rupert.'

It was hard to think clearly with his lips teasing their way along her jaw and his fingers tracing wicked patterns on her skin. 'I don't want Rupert now,' she managed raggedly, clutching her hands in his dark hair. 'I want *you*.'

Jake lifted his head at that and took her face between his hands, looking deep into her eyes. 'Are you sure, Cassie?'

'Oh yes,' she said, reaching for him again. 'I'm quite sure.'

Cassie drew a long, shuddering sigh of sheer pleasure and snuggled closer into Jake. Her head was on his shoulder, and his arm was around her, warm and strong, holding her securely as they waited for their heart rates to subside and their breathing to steady. She suspected Jake had fallen asleep, but her blood was still fizzing with a strange mixture of peace and exhilaration. She could feel herself glowing, radiating, shimmering with such contentment that she was surprised she wasn't lighting the dark room. Plug her in and she could power a chandelier, if not a city full of street lights. They could keep her as an emergency back-up for the energy crisis. Who needed a nuclear power-station when all Jake had to do was make love to her like that?

Somehow they had got themselves from the terrace to Jake's room. Cassie had no idea whether anyone had seen them and she didn't care. Nothing had mattered but Jake: the feel of him, the taste of him, the sureness of his hands, the delicious drift of his lips, the hard possession of his body.

Cassie felt giddy just thinking about that heady blur of sensation. They had lost all sense of time, of place. Nothing had existed except touch—*there…there…yes, there…yes, yes*—need so powerful that it hurt, and excitement that spun like a dervish, faster and faster, terrifyingly faster, until they lost control of it and it shattered in a burst of heart-stopping glory.

Downstairs, Cassie could hear the muted sounds of the Allantide Ball still in full swing without them, and felt sanity creeping back. It wasn't entirely welcome, she realised, and wondered if Rupert was still down there.

And Natasha.

What was it Rupert had said? *A little touch of the rebound going on? Jake did adore her so.*

He had. Cassie remembered him telling her about Natasha the first time they had driven down here together. *She's perfect,* he had said. She was everything he'd ever wanted.

Which made her just someone to catch him on the rebound.

Cassie sighed and stroked the broad chest she was resting so comfortably against. What did she have to offer, after all? Look at her, the failure of her family. She wasn't beautiful, wasn't successful, wasn't accomplished, wasn't calm and sensible. She couldn't begin to compare with Natasha.

On the other hand, she was here, lying next to Jake, and Natasha wasn't.

She would have to keep her fantasies firmly under control for once, Cassie vowed. There was no point in getting carried away like she usually did. She wasn't Jake's dream, and she never would be. Best to face it now.

But she didn't have to think about the future yet. She had the here and now. Cassie rested her palm over Jake's heart and felt it beating steadily. For now that was enough.

'We'd better get on.' Cassie sighed and stretched reluctantly. November had dawned dark and dank, and she would have loved to stay snuggled up to Jake's warm, solid body all day. 'There's lots to do.'

Lazily, Jake slid his hand from the curve of her hip to her breast, and she caught her breath at the heart-stopping intimacy of the gesture. 'Like what?' he asked, pulling her closer.

'Like getting married,' she reminded him, and laughed as

he froze for a moment. 'I can't believe you've forgotten that Tina and Rob are coming tonight for another photo session!'

'I've had other things on my mind,' said Jake, rolling her beneath him, lips hot and wicked against her breast, making her arch beneath his hands. 'More important things—like reminding you what you've been waiting ten years for…'

Here and now, Cassie told herself as desire flooded her. Jake was right. What was more important than that?

It was much later when she finally forced herself out of bed, and nearly had a fit when she saw the time. 'There's so much to do!'

Fortunately the caterers had cleared up most of the debris from the party the night before, but they still had to take down the Allantide decorations and make the great hall look as if it was Christmas instead.

'Why don't we leave it until it *is* Christmas?' asked Jake as Cassie ran around putting up fairy lights and piling pine cones into bowls.

'Because I was trying to get everything over as soon as possible,' she said. 'I thought it made sense to do all the photos at once. Rob said he took some good ones last night, which we can use on the website, and I've arranged for him to come back tonight since you'd be down here anyway. I didn't think you'd want to come down more than you had to.'

'I don't mind,' said Jake, who couldn't quite remember now why he had been so resistant to the idea. He couldn't remember much about anything this morning except how warm, sweet and exciting Cassie had been the night before.

He felt as if he were walking along the edge of a cliff, knowing that a false step would send him tumbling out of control. Jake wasn't sure how he had got himself there, but he couldn't turn round and go back now. He had to keep going and not look down to see how far it was to fall.

They hadn't talked about the future at all, and Jake was glad. He had a feeling that even thinking about a future that accommodated Cassie, and the chaos she took with her wherever she went, would send his careful life slipping over the edge of that cliff.

The sensible thing, of course, would have been to remember that before he had made love to her. But he was here now, and Cassie's bright presence was lighting up the great hall. He could be sensible again when he got back to London.

'If we left it until December, you could have a Christmas tree,' he pointed out.

Cassie hesitated, picturing a tall tree in the corner by the staircase. 'It would look lovely,' she admitted. 'But everything else is ready now. I've got my dress on loan, as it's just going to be used for photographs, and Rob and Tina are all sorted too. We might as well go ahead,' she decided reluctantly. A Christmas tree would have been the perfect finishing touch.

She was setting a round table as if for a reception, and Jake was astounded by the detail. She seemed to have thought of everything, from carefully designed place-card holders to tiny Christmas puddings on each plate. A stunning dried-flower arrangement with oranges and berries in the centre of the table held candles, wine glasses were filled with white rose-petals, and silver crackers added a festive touch.

'How on earth did you think of all this?' he asked. He would have thrown on a tablecloth, and might have risen to a candle or two, but that was where his inspiration would have run out.

'Oh, it was easy,' said Cassie, straightening the last cracker and standing back to survey the table with satisfaction. 'This is my job, remember? Besides, all I had to do in this case was act out a fantasy I've had for years,' she went on cheerfully. 'I always wanted a Christmas wedding, and in my fantasy it was here at the Hall, so I didn't really have to think of anything. I knew exactly what I wanted.'

Of course, in her fantasy Rupert would probably have been the groom, Jake thought jealously.

Cassie was chattering on. 'Naturally, there would be lots

more tables if this was a real wedding. I'm hoping Rob will be able to take some pictures of us that will give the impression that hundreds of guests are milling around in the background. We'll feel complete prats, I know, but it's all in a good cause, and if Rob can get some good shots of details the Hall should look wonderful in that article.'

Ah yes, the article. Jake had almost forgotten why they were doing this.

'It does look surprisingly Christmassy,' he said, looking around. He wasn't sure how Cassie had done it. There were no snowmen or reindeer, no Santa Claus climbing down the chimney. Instead she had created a subtle effect with colour and light.

'Wait till we've lit the fire and the candles,' said Cassie. 'I've made some mince pies too, and some mulled wine to offer our guests as they come in from the cold. Rob can take a still-life shot and then we might as well enjoy them to get us in the mood.'

'All you need is some mistletoe,' said Jake.

'It's too early, unfortunately, but don't think I haven't tried to get some!'

'Let's pretend it's hanging right here,' he said, pointing above their heads and drawing Cassie to him with his other arm. 'Then I can kiss you right underneath it.'

Dizzy with delight, Cassie melted in to him and wound her arms around his neck to kiss him back.

'When are Tina and Rob coming?' Jake's voice was thick as he nuzzled her throat, making her shiver with anticipation.

Cassie opened her mouth, but before she could say anything the old-fashioned door-bell jangled.

Jake sighed. 'Now?'

'I'm afraid so.'

Tina gasped at the transformation Cassie had wrought on the great hall. 'It feels like Christmas already! I can feel a carol coming on… O come, all ye faithful,' she warbled tunelessly.

They left Rob taking photos of the table and decorations while they went to change. Tina had bought a black-evening dress, which they had decided would be suitable for a bridesmaid, and she helped Cassie into the borrowed wedding-dress. Made of satin and organza, it was fitted underneath with a floaty outer layer that was fixed at the waist with a diamond detail.

'Oh Cassie, you look beautiful,' Tina said tearfully as she fastened a simple tiara into Cassie's hair. The curls didn't lend themselves to a sophisticated up-do, and in the end Cassie had decided to leave her hair as it was and save on the expense of a hairdresser.

'Hey, I'm not really getting married,' she reminded Tina, but her expression was wistful as she studied her reflection. It was her dream dress, and it was impossible not to wish that she was wearing it for real.

Jake waited in the great hall with Rob as she and Tina headed down the grand staircase. Without the bother of make-up, it hadn't taken him long to change into his tuxedo again. He stood at the bottom of the stairs watching Cassie coming down, and looking so devastating. Her knees felt weak and her mind spun with the longing to throw herself into his arms.

And then she almost did as she missed a step and lurched to one side. She would have fallen if Tina hadn't grabbed her and hauled her upright. 'God, you're such a klutz, Cassie,' her friend scolded. 'It won't make much of a photo with you lying at the bottom of the stairs with a broken neck!'

Then Cassie was all fingers and thumbs as she attempted to pin a white-rose buttonhole on Jake. 'I'll do it,' he said in the end, and she turned away to pick up the bouquet she had ordered, only to fumble that too. Jake caught it just before it hit the ground, and shook his head. 'You're hopeless,' he said, but he was smiling.

Get a grip, Cassie, she told herself sternly.

'So, what's the idea?' said Tina, getting down to business. 'Are you having the wedding here too?'

'No, just the reception,' said Cassie who had managed to pull herself together. 'We've been married in Portrevick church, and we've just arrived in a horse and carriage.'

Jake made a face. 'A car would be much more sensible. It's a steep hill up from the village.'

'Yes, well, this is a fantasy,' said Cassie a little crossly. 'Who wants a sensible fantasy? It was a horse and carriage,' she insisted. 'A *white* horse, in fact. Or possibly two.'

'OK,' said Rob, breaking into the discussion. 'I've taken as many details as I can. Let's have the bride and groom looking into each other's eyes.'

He posed them by some candles Cassie had lit, and while he fiddled with his camera Cassie adjusted Jake's bow tie. 'You look very nice,' she said approvingly.

'And you look beautiful,' said Jake.

A jolt had shot through him as he had looked up to see her coming down the staircase, and he was feeling jarred, as if it was still reverberating through him. The dress was white and elegantly floaty. She looked glamorous and sexy and, yes, beautiful.

And then she had stumbled, and he hadn't been able to resist smiling, pleased to see that it was Cassie after all and not some elegant stranger.

Unable to resist touching her, he ran his hands up her bare arms. 'It's Christmas Eve. Weren't you a bit chilly in that carriage?' he said, trying to lighten the atmosphere, trying to loosen whatever it was that had taken such a tight grip on his heart when he had looked up to see Cassie as a bride.

'I had a *faux* fur stole to wear when we came out of the church,' she explained.

'And a muff, I hope?' said Jake, remembering Michelle at the wedding fair, and they both started to laugh at the same time.

They had forgotten Tina and Rob, who was snapping away. They had forgotten the article, forgotten why they were dressed up as a bride and groom. They had forgotten everything except the warmth and the laughter—then somehow they weren't laughing any more, but were staring hungrily at each other.

'That's great,' called Rob from behind his camera. 'Now, what about a…?'

He tailed off, realising that Cassie and Jake weren't even listening.

'A kiss,' he finished, but they were already there. Cassie was locked in Jake's arms, and they were kissing in a way that would have raised a few eyebrows at a real wedding, where kisses for the camera were usually sweet and chaste. There was nothing sweet or chaste about this kiss.

Rob looked at Tina, who rolled her eyes. 'Guys? *Guys!*' she shouted, startling Jake and Cassie apart at last. 'You're embarrassing Rob,' she said with a grin as they looked at her with identically disorientated expressions. 'These photos are supposed to be for a brides' magazine, not something they keep on the top shelf! They don't want pictures of the wedding night, just a sweet little peck on the lips so the readers can all go "aah".'

'Sorry, yes, I suppose we got a bit carried away,' said Cassie, flustered.

'A bit? We didn't know where to look, did we, Rob?'

'It must have been all the time shut up in that carriage,' muttered Jake, alarmed at how easily he lost control the moment he laid hands on Cassie.

They posed for a whole ream of photographs, but at last Rob decided that he had enough. 'I'll send you the link so that you can look at them online,' he told Cassie. 'And then you can pick a selection of the best to send to *Wedding Belles* after Christmas.'

Jake couldn't wait for Rob and Tina to be gone. He closed the door after them with relief and turned back to Cassie, who was blowing out the candles.

'Now, where was that mistletoe again?' he said, and she

beckoned him over so that she could put her arms around his neck and kiss him.

'Right here,' she said.

CHAPTER TEN

'I've got to go back to London this afternoon,' said Jake the next morning as they lay in bed. Realising how reluctant he was to go sent him teetering perilously on the edge of that sheer drop again, though, and he shied away from the thought. He smoothed the curls back from Cassie's face. 'Do you want a lift?'

Keep it light, he told himself. Offering a lift back to London wasn't the same as suggesting that she move in with him, have his baby or anything that smacked remotely of commitment. It was just saving a train fare.

'I can't,' sighed Cassie. 'I promised to meet one of the contractors tomorrow to talk about electrics. Now that the hall is done, we need to start work on the kitchens and bathrooms. There's still a long way to go before we can open as a venue. I really need to stay another couple of days.'

Jake was horrified by how disappointed he was at the prospect of three nights without her, but perhaps a few days apart wasn't a bad thing. It would give him a chance to get himself under control and start thinking clearly again. He wasn't himself when Cassie was right there, warm, soft and desperately distracting. It was too easy to lose control, too easy to forget what he risked by letting go of his careful, ordered life.

So when Cassie said that she would be back in London on Wednesday he made himself hold back. He didn't offer to meet her at the station, take her out to dinner or take her back to his apartment to see how she looked amongst his furniture, the way he really wanted to do. 'Give me a ring when you're back,' was all he said.

Right. Not 'I'll miss you'. Not 'I love you'. Not even 'I'll call you', thought Cassie. But what had she expected? Jake was a careful man nowadays. He might have made love to her with a heart-stopping tenderness and passion, but he wasn't about to rush into a relationship with her.

And quite right too, Cassie reminded herself. She had decided that the here and now was enough for her, and it was obviously enough for Jake as well. So she smiled as she kissed him goodbye after lunch and waved him off to London.

She ought to be happy, she thought as she went back inside and began the dreary task of taking down the Christmas decorations. She had had the most wonderful weekend. OK, so Jake hadn't said that he wanted to see her again, but he hadn't said that he *didn't* want to, either. He couldn't have made love to her like that if he didn't feel anything, could he?

They had all the photos they needed for the article, so there was no real need for him to come down to Portrevick again. But he might need her to be his fiancée again in London. It would look suspicious if they broke off their supposed engagement just yet. They had agreed that they would keep the pretence going until after Christmas, and that was still weeks away, Cassie reassured herself. It was only the beginning of November. Anything could happen in that time.

Just because Jake hadn't talked about the future didn't mean they couldn't have one.

Still, Cassie couldn't help feeling bereft now that he had gone. She wandered disconsolately around the great hall, taking down the fairy lights and dismantling the table she had laid so carefully the day before.

When the bell jangled, she hurried to open the massive

front door, relieved at the distraction. She hoped it would be Tina, who had promised to come and give her a lift back to the village. A good chat with her old friend was just what she needed. But when she threw the door open wide, the smile was wiped from her face. It wasn't Tina who stood there.

It was Natasha.

'Oh!'

Natasha smiled a little hesitantly. 'Hi,' she said.

'I'm afraid Jake isn't here,' said Cassie, unable to think of any other reason Natasha would be here on her own. 'He's gone back to London.'

'Actually, it was you I was hoping to see. Have you got a moment?'

The last person Cassie wanted to talk to right then was Natasha, but she couldn't think of a polite way to refuse. 'Sure,' she said reluctantly, and stood back. 'Come in.'

Gracefully, Natasha stepped into the hall. Swathed in a fabulous cream cashmere pashmina, she stood looking beautiful and making everything around her seem faintly shabby in comparison.

Including Cassie.

There was an awkward silence. 'Would you like some tea?' Cassie found herself asking to her own disgust.

'That would be nice, thank you.'

'We'll go to the kitchen. It's warmer there.'

Cursing her mother's training, which meant that you always had to be polite whatever the cost, Cassie led the way to the kitchen.

Natasha sat at the table, unwinding her pashmina to reveal an exquisite pale-blue jumper, also cashmere by the look of it, and Cassie sighed as she filled the kettle. If she tried to wear a top that colour, she would spill something down it and ruin it two seconds after she had put it on, but Natasha looked as if she had stepped out of the pages of a magazine.

Switching on the kettle, she turned and leant back against

the worktop and folded her arms. 'What did you want to talk to me about?'

'About Jake,' said Natasha.

Cassie stiffened. 'What about him?'

'I just wanted to know…how he is.' Natasha moistened her lips. 'I'd hoped to see him at the ball the other night, but I couldn't find him.'

Cassie thought about what Jake had been doing while Natasha had been looking for him, and her toes curled. 'He's fine,' she said shortly.

'I see,' whispered Natasha, and to Cassie's horror the green eyes filled with tears. 'I'd hoped…I'd hoped…'

'That he'd be pining for you?'

'Yes.' She nodded miserably. 'I've been such a fool,' she burst out. 'Rupert—he was like a madness. I've always been so sensible, and to be pursued like that by someone so glamorous and so exciting, well, I was flattered. You know what Rupert's like.'

'Yes, I know,' said Cassie. 'But I know what Jake is like too, and so should you. He's worth a thousand Ruperts, and he deserved better than being left without warning—and for Rupert of all people! You must have known how humiliating that would be for him,' she said accusingly.

Natasha bit her lip. 'I can see that now, of course I can, but at the time I wasn't thinking clearly.'

Dropping her head into her hands, she clutched her perfectly straight blonde hair with her perfectly manicured fingers. 'It sounds crazy now, but I just lost my head. I was tired of being clever and careful and doing the right thing all the time. Rupert was such fun and so seductive. Being with him seemed like my only chance to do something wild and spontaneous. It was like my own little rebellion.'

'A little self-indulgent, don't you think?' said Cassie, unmoved. 'Couldn't you have found a way to have fun and be *spontaneous* that didn't involve hurting Jake?'

'I never meant to hurt him, you must believe that!' Natasha lifted her head to look at Cassie with imploring green eyes. 'We never had a very demonstrative relationship. I suppose other people would have looked at us and thought we were cool, but I didn't appreciate what I had. I thought I wanted something different, but then I didn't like it. The truth is that I'm not a rebel. I'm conventional. I'm careful. I like a plan, just like Jake. With Rupert, I never know where we're going to be or what we'll be doing, and I hate it!

'I miss Jake,' she said on a sob, and the tears spilled over at last. 'When I'm with him, I feel so safe. We had so much in common. We were perfect together, but I treated him so badly, and now I don't know if he'll ever forgive me.'

Cassie poured boiling water onto two tea bags. Her face felt tight. Her heart felt tight. 'Why have you come to me?' she asked coolly, squeezing the bags with a spoon before fishing them out.

Natasha wiped tears from under her eyes. Predictably, she was one of those women who looked beautiful even when they were crying. When Cassie cried, she went all blotchy, her nose ran and her eyes turned piggy.

'Because Rupert said he doesn't think you're really engaged to Jake,' said Natasha in a rush. 'He thinks Jake is just saving face, and if…if that's true…then I would like to go to him, to tell him how desperately sorry I am that I hurt him, and ask if he'll give me another chance. I swear I would never do anything like this again,' she promised, an edge of desperation in her voice. 'I can be what Jake needs, I know I can.'

Tight-lipped, Cassie handed Natasha a mug and pushed the carton of milk towards her. She wasn't ready to prove Rupert right just yet, and besides there was last night. Everything had changed now.

Hadn't it?

'And what *does* Jake need?' she prevaricated.

'He needs someone who'll make him feel safe too,' said Natasha. 'I know what a struggle it has been for him to get where he is now. He needs someone who'll let him forget the past and love him for the person he is now. Someone who understands what drives him and doesn't try to challenge him.'

No, thought Cassie instinctively. She shook her head. 'I think you're wrong,' she said. 'Jake shouldn't forget the past. He needs to accept it, accept that it's part of him. You can't just pretend the past never existed.'

'If someone doesn't want to talk about their childhood, you should respect that,' said Natasha. 'Jake knew I would never press him about it. It's one of the reasons he felt comfortable with me.'

Cassie could feel herself prickling with irritation. 'Jake deserves more than comfortable, Natasha,' she said. 'He needs laughter and love and passion and—and *acceptance* of who he was and who he is.'

'I can give him all of that,' said Natasha defensively. 'I do accept him. If I didn't, I would want to change him, and I don't. He doesn't need to change for me.'

But perhaps he needed to change for himself.

Jake needed to let down his guard, to throw away his rule book and his specifications and let himself love and be loved—but that would mean him giving up control, and Cassie wasn't sure he would be able to do that.

He didn't believe in love. Jake had made that very clear. He thought all you needed for a successful relationship was a formula, and Natasha fitted his specifications perfectly. He had told her that.

They had agreed that they were completely incompatible. Two nights weren't going to change that, were they?

Cassie's heart cracked. She so wanted to believe that this magical weekend had been the start of something wonderful, but what, really, did she have to go on? When Jake kissed her, when his hands drifted lazily, possessively, over her body, she hadn't needed to hear that he loved her. Then, the here and now had been enough, but now he had gone, and she could feel her confidence leaking out of her in the face of Natasha's glowing beauty.

It was too easy now to wonder if he had turned to her on the rebound from Natasha, if he had simply been looking for someone different to distract him from the hurt and the humiliation of being left by the woman he really wanted.

Now, too late, she could remember that it had only ever been a pretence, and Jake had never suggested otherwise. Why hadn't she remembered that before?

Because it wasn't a pretence for her, not any more. Cassie loved Jake. She knew that she could give him what he really needed.

But what he needed wasn't necessarily what he wanted.

Stirring her tea, Cassie looked across the table at Natasha, who had dried her tears and was looking poised and elegant once more.

Looking exactly like the kind of woman Jake had aspired to for so long.

A lead weight was gathering in Cassie's chest as she remembered everything Jake had ever told her. He didn't want to take the risk of falling in love. He didn't want to lose control. He didn't want to change.

Natasha could give him so many of things he had said he *did* want. She wouldn't push him. She would let him keep his emotions all buttoned up—and wasn't that, really, all Jake wanted?

Strange that she and Natasha should love the same man when they were so different, Cassie thought. There was Natasha: so beautiful, so sensible, so classy and so cool, representing the future Jake had worked so hard for—and there was her; clumsy, messy Cassie who muddled through and did her best but would never be more than an also-ran. Who would always be associated with the past he resented so much.

Did she really think Jake would rather be with her than Natasha?

Better to face reality now, Cassie decided. She wasted too much of her life dreaming as it was. This time, she would be the sensible one.

Natasha had been watching her face. 'Is it true?' she asked quietly. 'Is Jake just trying to save face by pretending to be engaged to you?'

Cassie looked down at the ruby ring which she had never got round to taking off the night before. Very slowly, she drew it off and dropped it onto the table, where it clattered and rolled for a moment before toppling over.

'Yes,' she said. 'It's true.'

'You did *what*?' said Tina in disbelief. She had arrived about ten minutes after Natasha had left to find Cassie a sodden mess in the kitchen.

'I told Natasha the truth.'

'And sent her back to Jake with *your* ring? You're mad, Cassie! You and Jake had something really good going there.'

'We were just pretending,' said Cassie drearily, blowing her nose. Unlike Natasha, she wasn't a pretty sight when she cried, and she had just cried more than she had ever cried before.

Tina wasn't having any of it. 'Don't give me that. I saw the way you kissed each other last night. There was nothing fake about that. Good grief, the top of my head practically blew off, and that was just watching you!' She put her hands on her hips and shook her head at Cassie. 'I can't believe you'd just give up and let that drippy Natasha swan back to him. It's not like you to be so wet. You're crazy about Jake, and you just gave him up without a fight. What's that about?'

'Because it's not a fight I could ever win,' Cassie said miserably. Did Tina think she hadn't thought about it? 'We're completely incompatible.'

'You looked pretty compatible to me last night.'

Cassie's eyes filled with tears again and she swiped angrily at them with the back of her hand. 'We want different things, Tina. Jake thinks he can order a relationship like everything else, and I'm holding out for something he thinks doesn't exist. I want someone to love me, someone who needs me as much as I need him. Jake thinks that's a fairy tale.'

'I'm sure he does love you, Cassie,' said Tina, putting an arm around her shoulders. 'He may not realise it yet, that's all. I bet you anything he'll send Natasha away with a flea in her ear, and come roaring back down here with that ring as soon as he hears what you've done.'

But Jake didn't come. On Wednesday, Cassie sent him a brief, businesslike email saying that she was staying in Portrevick for a while to oversee work on the Hall. She didn't mention Natasha, and nor did Jake when he replied.

Thanks for update, was all he said. *Keep me posted. Regards, Jake.*

Regards? *Regards?* Was that all he could say after he had rolled her beneath him and smiled against her throat? After his hands had unlocked her, made her gasp and arch? After he had loved her slowly, thoroughly, gloriously, and held her, still shaking, as they spiralled back to reality together?

How dared he? Furious, Cassie stabbed at the delete button. How dared he send her *regards* after he had made her love him?

Sheer anger kept her going all afternoon, but when it leaked away it left her more miserable than ever.

'Tell him how you feel,' said Tina, exasperated. 'Put yourself in Jake's shoes. He's got no idea that you care for him at all. You have a great weekend together, and the next thing he knows you've tossed him back his ring and told Natasha he's all hers. What's the poor bloke supposed to think?'

'What am *I* supposed to think?' Cassie protested tearfully. 'He didn't even suggest meeting up in London.'

'He's probably terrified you'll think he's getting too heavy.

If you ask me, you're both being big babies,' said Tina. 'At least Natasha had the guts to go and tell him how she felt.'

The mention of Natasha was enough to plunge Cassie back into the depths. 'How can I go? He'll be back with Natasha by now.' She tortured herself by imagining the two of them together. How could Jake have resisted those green eyes shimmering with love and the promise of calm? When Cassie looked at herself in the mirror she saw eyes puffy with tears, awful skin and limp hair. There was no way Jake would want her now, even if he wasn't dazzled anew by Natasha's beauty.

At least work on the Hall was going well, she tried to console herself. Joss was pleased with the way the project was going, and as November was never a busy time for weddings she was happy for Cassie to stay in Cornwall for the time being. It was bittersweet, being up at the Hall every day, but Cassie threw herself into the job. It was all she had left.

Three long, wretched weeks dragged past. The days got shorter, darker and damper, and Cassie got more miserable. It was time to go back to London and pick up her old life, she decided grimly. She had been perfectly happy before, and she would be again. It wasn't as if she was likely to bump into Jake. London was a big city and their lives would never cross, unless he was tactless enough to ask her to plan his wedding to Natasha. Cassie couldn't see that happening. No, she would go back, stick to the job she could do and stop trying to be someone she wasn't.

'I'll be back tomorrow,' she told Joss, and went for a last walk on the beach. The sea was wild, the sky as grey as her mood. It was very cold, and the spray from the crashing waves stung her cheeks.

Head bent, Cassie trudged along the sand. There were no surfers today, no lifeguards, and she had the beach to herself. Except, she realised, for a figure in black leathers that was heading towards her from the dunes. Some biker who must have left his motorbike in the car park, and, not content with roaring through the villages disturbing everyone's peace, was now spoiling her solitude.

Cassie scowled. There were plenty of other empty beaches in Cornwall at this time of year. Why did he have to come here? She wanted to be miserable on her own, thank you very much.

And he was coming straight for her! Cassie glared at him, and was just about to turn pointedly on her heel when she stopped. Hang on, wasn't there something familiar about that walk? About that self-contained stride? She looked harder. The set of those shoulders, the darkness of the hair…. It couldn't be, could it?

All at once a great hand seemed to close tight around her, inside her, gripping her heart, her lungs and her entrails so that she couldn't breathe. She could just stand and stare, brown eyes huge with disbelief and desperate hope, as he came closer and closer until he was standing right in front of her.

'So this is where you are,' said Jake.

'Jake.' It came out as little more than a squeak.

Cassie was completely thrown, ricocheting around between astonishment, sheer joy and confusion at how different he looked. Standing there in black leather, he seemed younger, wilder, and the guarded look she had become used to had been replaced by a reckless glint. The wind ruffled his hair, and with the angry sea behind him he looked so like the old Jake that she could hardly speak.

'What…what are you doing here?' she stammered at last.

'Looking for you,' said Jake.

He sounded the same. He just looked so… Cassie couldn't think of a word to describe how he looked, but it was making her heart boom so loudly that it drowned out the crashing waves and the wind that was whistling past her ears.

She swallowed hard. This, remember, was still the Jake who had gone back to London without a word about the future, who had sent her his *regards*.

'What for?' she asked almost rudely.

'I bought a motorbike,' he said. 'I wanted to show you. Everyone thinks I'm having a midlife crisis, but I thought you would understand.'

'I would?'

'You were the one who said that riding a bike wouldn't change me, that I could let go just a little and I wouldn't lose everything I'd fought to be.'

Cassie eyed the leathers. They made him look lean, hard and very tough. Of course, he looked like that in a suit too, but now he was even more unsettling. 'I'm not sure I was right about that,' she said. 'You look like you've changed to me.'

'But I haven't,' said Jake. 'I'm still Chief Executive of Primordia. I still have my MBA, my experience, my career. My world hasn't fallen apart because I bought a bike. I really thought that it would,' he said. 'I was afraid that I might lose myself, but I've found myself instead. I've realised that I can't change the past. I have to accept that my family, my past, that difficult boy I was, all of them are part of who I am now.' A smile lurked in his eyes as he looked at Cassie. 'You were right about that too.'

Cassie moistened her lips. 'I don't think I've been right so often before,' she tried to joke, not knowing what else to do, not knowing what was happening, knowing only that all her certainties were being shaken around like flakes in a snow globe.

'You weren't right about Natasha,' said Jake. 'You sent her to me because you thought she was what I wanted, didn't you?'

'She is what you want.' It was cold in the wind, and Cassie hugged her jacket about her. By unspoken consent, they turned their backs to the wind and started walking back along the beach, the sand damp and firm beneath their feet.

Cassie dug her hands in her pockets and hunched her shoulders defensively. 'You told me she was,' she reminded him. 'You told me she was perfect.'

'I thought she was,' he admitted. 'I thought I needed

someone cool and careful, like I was trying so hard to be. I thought I needed someone who would help me fit in, who would help me forget what I'd been and where I'd come from.'

'Someone like Natasha,' said Cassie bitterly.

'Yes. I thought Natasha was exactly what I needed, but I was wrong,' said Jake. 'It took meeting you again to realise that what I really needed was someone who would make me laugh, who would give me the strength to let go of everything I thought I needed.' He slowed, and Cassie slowed with him, until they had stopped and were facing each other alone on the beach.

'Someone who would make me remember, not forget,' he said, his voice very deep and low. 'Someone who would force me to stop running away from the life I had here and accept it as part of who I am.'

He looked down at Cassie, whose hands were still thrust into the pockets of her jacket, and he could see the realisation of what he had come to say dawning in the brown eyes.

'Someone like you,' he said.

'But—but, Jake, you can't need me,' she said in disbelief, even as Jake was reaching for her wrists and tugging her hands gently from her pockets. 'I'm the last person you can want. I'm not sensible or clever or beautiful or—or *anything*,' she said, but her fingers were twining of their own accord around Jake's. 'I'm useless.'

'Useless?' he said. 'You've transformed the Hall, organised a ball, set up a wonderful marketing opportunity with a magazine, charmed the socks off everyone who met you in London. You're not useless at all,' he said sternly.

'My family wouldn't agree with you,' she sighed. 'I haven't achieved anything, not like the rest of you, with your degrees and your fantastically successful careers.'

'But you can do the things your clever, successful family can't.'

'Oh yes? Like what?'

'Like make the sun seem brighter when you smile,' said

Jake. 'Like making me laugh. Like making me happy.' He drew her closer. 'Like making me safe,' he said softly. 'Cassie, tell me I can do that for you too.'

Her eyes filled with tears. 'You can,' she whispered. 'You do.'

They didn't kiss, not at first. They just held each other, very, very tightly. Cassie's face was pressed into his throat, and she could smell the leather of his jacket, just as she had done ten years ago. But this time the shock and anger had gone and in their place was a ballooning sense of joy and relief, as if she had finally found her way home.

Safe—that was what Jake had said he felt. Cassie knew exactly what he meant.

'Tell me you love me, Cassie,' he murmured against her hair, and she tipped back her head to smile at him, her eyes still shimmering with tears.

'I love you,' she said. And then they did kiss, a long, intoxicatingly sweet kiss that dissolved the hurt and the uncertainty and left them heady and breathless with happiness.

'I love you,' said Jake shakily at last. Somehow they had made it to the shelter of the dunes, and sank down onto the soft sand as they kissed and kissed again. 'I love you, I love you,' he said again between kisses. 'I can't tell you how much.'

Cassie drew a shivery sigh of sheer contentment and rested her head on his shoulder, her arms wound tightly around him as if she would never let him go. 'What about the formula?'

'Ah, the formula,' he said with a wry smile. 'I clung to that formula like a life raft! It seemed to make sense,' he tried to explain. 'It worked, or at least it did until I met you again. You don't know what you did to me, Cassie. You turned my world upside down. I had constructed such a careful life, and suddenly everything was out of control.

'You made me *feel* again, and I was torn. I wanted you, but I didn't want you. You were part of the past I'd been running away from for so long. I thought if I could just hold onto my sensible, practical formula I'd be all right, but I can see now that it was just as much a fantasy as the fairy tale that you believe in.'

'Yes, I've learnt that too,' said Cassie, snuggling closer as they lay in the sand. 'I held on to the fairy tale, just like you held on to the formula. I suppose I was always such a dreamer that it was natural for me to fantasise about the perfect relationship, the perfect wedding, the perfect everything.'

She ran her hand over his abdomen. Even through the leather, she could feel the muscled strength of him. 'I don't think you're perfect, though.'

'Oh?' Jake pretended to sound hurt, and she softened the blow by leaning up on her elbow and smiling down at him as she dropped a kiss on his lips.

'No, you're not perfect. You're impatient and practical and oh-so-sensible—or you were until you went out and bought yourself a motorbike just to make a point! When I dreamed of the man I would love, I never imagined someone like you, but it *is* you. I've learnt to love what's in front of me, not a dream. Now I know that you love me back, well…' She smiled, kissing him again. 'I think this just might be the fairy tale after all!'

She settled back into the curve of his arm with a sigh of happiness. 'I've been so wretched for the last three weeks,' she told him. 'Why did it take you so long to come?'

'Because I thought you'd changed your mind after I'd gone,' said Jake. 'I thought you'd just been amusing yourself that weekend, and that you didn't want to get any more involved. I thought you couldn't even be bothered to tell me yourself. You just sent Natasha instead.'

Cassie wriggled uncomfortably. 'I didn't *send* her. I thought you would be happy to see her.'

'Happy? Hah!' Jake snorted. 'There was one moment that day when I was wildly happy. The door bell rang and I convinced myself that it was you, that you'd told the contractors they could go to hell so that you could come up to London early and be with me.'

'Well, I don't know why you would think I would do that.' Cassie pretended to grumble. 'You never said a word. How was I to know you wanted to see me?'

'I know, I was a fool. I should have begged you to come with me.' Jake wound his fingers in the curls that were hopelessly tangled by wind and sand. 'But, Cassie, I was terrified,' he said. 'I'd fallen wildly in love with you. That weekend, when we made love, it all happened so fast. I felt as if I was losing control when I was with you, nothing else mattered. I could feel myself slipping back, becoming the reckless boy I'd been before, not caring about anything except the moment.

'It was as if everything I'd spent the last ten years working for had started to crumble,' he tried to explain. 'I thought I needed a day or two to get a grip of myself and decide what I really wanted.

'And I realised that I wanted *you*,' he told her. 'When I got to London, everything was colourless without you. That life I'd fought to keep under control was still under control, but it was flat and meaningless too. So I knew I wanted you, but I wasn't sure how to win you. You were always telling me how incompatible we were, and you clearly didn't need *me* to have a good time.'

Jake paused. 'There was a little bit of me, too, that was hung over from the past, a bit that didn't feel as if I was good enough for you. You come from such a nice, happy, middle-class family, and when all was said and done I was still one of those Trevelyans with a father in prison.'

'But you're more than that,' said Cassie. 'Your family doesn't matter. It's you I love, and as for my family, well, they're going to see a chief executive, not the wild boy who used to make trouble in the village. They like high achievers, remember? They'll approve of you much more than they do of me!'

'I hope so,' said Jake. 'I suppose I just lost my nerve in London. I told myself I had to take things carefully, so I planned to ask you out to dinner as soon as you got back and ask if you'd consider making that silly pretence of being engaged real. But Natasha turned up instead. She told me you'd admitted that it was just a pretence, and had sent back the ring to prove it.'

'I didn't think you'd be able to resist her,' sighed Cassie. 'She's so beautiful.'

'Well, yes, she is—but next to you she's just a little colourless. I never laughed with her the way I laughed with you. We never talked, or argued, or lost our cool with each other. Natasha's a nice person,' said Jake. 'But she was the last person I wanted to see that day. Once I'd got over my disappointment that she wasn't you, we had a long talk. I think the fact that she was ready to have an affair with Rupert made her realise that we weren't really right for each other. I hope she'll find the right man one day, but it's not me.'

'Why didn't you at least call me *then*?' asked Cassie, thinking of the weeks they had wasted being miserable apart.

'I was angry,' said Jake. 'With Natasha, with you, but mostly with myself—for letting myself fall in love with you, for throwing my whole life into disorder for someone who apparently didn't care enough about me to tell me she couldn't be bothered to carry on pretending. And then, when I *did* hear from you, it was just an impersonal email about the Hall!'

'At least I didn't sign it "regards"!' sniffed Cassie, and he laughed as he hugged her closer.

'I was trying to show you I cared as little as you did. God, I can laugh now, but at the time I was hurt and I was bitter. I was impossible to deal with for two weeks—my PA told me she was ready to shoot me, in the end—until I realised I couldn't go on like that. I used to take myself off for long walks around the streets, and one day I passed a guy on a motorbike. It was just like the one I used to have in Portrevick, and that's when I started to think about what you'd said about accepting the past and letting go of it at the same time.

'I can take a risk, I thought, and I went out and bought a

bike of my own. And then I took an even bigger risk. I thought you'd be back in London, so I went round to your office and Joss told me you were still here, so I got straight on my bike and drove all the way down here,' he said, unzipping a pocket to pull out the ruby ring.

He shifted so that he was lying over Cassie, smiling down into her eyes. 'I came to tell you that I love you and I need you, and that more than anything in the world I want you to take this ring back and say you'll marry me. Will you, Cassie?'

Cassie's smile trembled as she took the ring and slid it back onto her finger where it belonged. 'Oh yes,' she breathed, and her eyes shone as she put her arms around Jake's neck to tug him down for a long, long kiss. 'Oh yes, I will.'

The short winter afternoon was closing in, but it was only the first spots of rain that forced them to move at last. 'Have you still got that wedding dress you wore for the photos?' Jake asked as they brushed sand off each other.

'I took it back to the shop the next day.'

'Why don't you go and buy it?' he said. 'We can get married at Christmas.'

'Christmas!' said Cassie, startled. 'That's only a month away!'

'It's enough time for the banns to be read.'

'Just!'

'And the wedding's already planned,' he pointed out as they headed back to the car park. 'We've got the table decorations and we know the menu. We've even had the photos done already. Tina's got her bridesmaid's dress, and I've got my tuxedo—unless you want me in breeches and a cravat, of course! So all you need to do is buy the dress and tell your family.'

'Are you sure you don't mean next Christmas?' asked Cassie. 'What happened to Mr Sensible? I thought you'd be saying it was crazy to rush into marriage!'

'It is,' said Jake with a smile. 'But let's do it anyway.'

A gleaming, mean-looking motorbike had the car park to

itself. Jake handed Cassie a helmet when they got back to it and put on his own. 'Hop on the back,' he said, kicking the machine into gear. 'And we'll go and see if the vicar can fit us in for a Christmas wedding.'

EPILOGUE

Christmas Eve

CASSIE woke on her wedding morning to a glittering world. Under a thin, blue winter sky, a hard frost rimed every twig and every blade of grass. But by lunchtime the clouds had blanked out the meagre December light, hanging so heavily they seemed to be muffling the slightest noise, and Portrevick was enveloped in the stillness and strange, expectant silence that comes before snow.

In the pub, they were taking bets on a white Christmas at last, and the children were wild with excitement at the prospect of bulging stockings and presents under the tree. Cassie had always loved Christmas, too, but this was her wedding day, and all she was dreaming about was the moment she stood in front of the altar with Jake. Until then, she hardly dared let herself believe that it wasn't just all a dream.

At four o'clock it was already dark, but there were flares lining the path to the church, and the trees were strung with fairy lights. Tina took the *faux* fur stole Cassie had worn on the brief journey from Portrevick Hall with her father and laid it on the porch seat.

Cassie's father offered her his arm. 'You look beautiful, darling,' he said. 'Your mother and I are very proud of you,

you know.' His voice cracked a little at the end, and he had to clear his throat.

'Thank you, Dad.' Cassie's eyes stung with tears. 'Thank you for everything.'

'Promise me you'll be happy with Jake.'

'I will.' It was her turn to swallow a huge lump in her throat. 'I know I will.'

'In that case,' said her father, reverting to his more usual, reassuringly brisk manner. 'Let's go.'

And then they were walking up the uneven aisle of the old church. *How odd*, Cassie found herself thinking with a strange, detached part of her mind. She had spent so long planning weddings for other brides, so many years dreaming about her own, that she thought she would know how it would feel.

Everything looked exactly as she had always imagined it. Lit only by candles, the little church looked beautiful, and was filled with the people she loved. Her mother was there, trying not to cry. Liz had started already, and was wiping her eyes with a handkerchief as she smiled tremulously. Her brothers were doing their level best to look as if they weren't moved, and not quite succeeding.

The flowers were simple, stunning arrangements of white, and tiny wreaths hung at the end of every pew. Cassie had a blurred impression of warmth and colour as everyone turned to smile as they passed. Yes, it was just as she'd imagined it.

What she had never imagined was that none of it would really matter. The only thing that mattered was that Jake should be there, waiting for her at the altar.

And there he was. Cassie's heart gave a great bound of relief as she saw him turn. He was looking serious, but as she got closer she saw that he was not serious so much as anxious, and she knew with a sudden, dazzling certainty that he had been afraid she wouldn't come, that all that mattered to him was that *she* was there.

Her father lifted her hand to his lips and kissed it, and

Cassie smiled at him brilliantly before he stepped back to join her mother. Then she turned to face Jake at last.

He smiled at her as he took her hand, and she smiled back, twisting her fingers around his. All at once it was just the two of them in the warm candlelight. They had forgotten the church and the watching congregation, and Cassie could feel herself beginning to sway towards him, turning her face up for his kiss already.

The vicar cleared his throat loudly, and they turned to him with identically startled expressions. He smiled. 'If you could spare us few minutes of your attention…?' he murmured.

'Sorry,' they whispered back, and he raised his voice.

'Dearly beloved…'

The familiar words rang like a bell in Cassie's heart. This was what her wedding was about. It wasn't about the beautiful dress she was wearing, or the gasps when the guests saw the great hall. It was more than an excuse for a party. It was about Jake and about her, about the love they shared and the life they would build together.

Her eyes never left Jake's dark-blue ones. She was intensely aware of his hand, of his voice making his responses steadily, of the smooth coolness of the ring he slid onto her finger. At last she was in the right place at the right time. It wasn't a dream. This was where she was meant to be, and this was the man she was meant to be with.

Cassie's heart was so full, she could hardly say 'I do'. Even when she thought it couldn't possibly be any fuller, it kept swelling, and swelling until the vicar declared them man and wife, and then she was afraid it would explode altogether. Giddy with happiness, she smiled as Jake took her face between his hands and kissed her.

'You look beautiful,' he said.

Cassie had seen how radiant other brides looked, and now she knew exactly how they felt. She was brimming with joy. It felt as if it were spilling out of her, shimmering away into the candlelight.

In a blur, she dropped the pen twice before she managed to sign the register, and then she was sailing back down the aisle, Jake's fingers wrapped firmly round her own.

The church doors were thrown open and a magical scene awaited them. Great, soft snowflakes were drifting steadily to the ground, blurring the warm, flickering glow of the flares and glimmer of the tiny lights in the trees.

'Oh Jake, it's perfect!' gasped Cassie, and promptly tripped over the porch step. 'Just as well we decided not to have a video,' she muttered out of the corner of her mouth as Jake hauled her upright, and behind her she heard Tina smother a fit of giggles. 'Thank goodness I had you to hang on to, or I'd have gone flat on my face!'

Jake's hand tightened and he smiled down at her. 'That's the thing about being married,' he said. 'We'll always have each other to hang on to now.'

Cassie's smile widened. 'So we will,' she said, and then stopped, catching sight of a carriage drawn up outside the lych gate. In the light of the flares there, she could see that it was pulled by two white horses.

A car would be more sensible, Jake had said once, and it was a car she had expected to take them back to the great hall. But Jake, her sensible husband, must have remembered her fantasy and arranged the carriage for her instead.

Her eyes shone as she looked up at him. 'It's my dream!' she breathed, but Jake shook his head and smiled.

'It's not a dream,' he said. 'It's real.'

* * * * *

This season we bring you
Christmas Treats

For an early Christmas present,
Jessica Hart would like to share
a little treat with you...

JESSICA HART'S TOP TEN TIPS
FOR A SPARKLING CHRISTMAS PARTY!

1. Invite all your neighbours as well as your friends, even if you don't know them very well. Everybody loves to be invited to a party—and it's a great way to meet that person you smile at in the street every day but whose name you don't know…

2. It's much more fun if everyone is jammed in together, so put your guests in a room that's not quite big enough for them all. Don't let anyone sit down, either! It makes it easier for your guests to mingle and meet each other if everyone is standing up.

3. Don't forget to introduce guests to each other—it can be daunting to walk into a room full of people who all seem to know each other, and it makes a big difference if the hostess makes sure everyone has someone to talk to when they arrive.

4. At Christmas you can go to town on the decorations—a Christmas tree is a must, but fairy lights look wonderful strung around the room too. Keep the lighting flattering with candles and soft lamps, and put out piles of pine cones and crackers. A room fragrance scented with cinnamon, oranges and cloves will get everyone in the mood the moment they step through the door.

5. Greet guests with a glass of mulled wine and a mince pie as soon as they arrive, or impress them with a real Christmas cocktail—see below!

6. Cheese biscuits to nibble on are easy to make, and if you buy a box of Christmas pastry-cutters you can have holly,

stars, angels, Christmas trees and all sorts of other Christmassy shapes, or use letters to spell Noel or Happy Christmas on a plate. They can be made in advance, and will make it look as if you've gone to masses of effort even when you haven't.

7. Have a Secret Santa. Give all your guests a (very low) price limit and get everyone to bring a present to put beneath the tree. That way everyone will have a gift to take home—but much more fun will be had watching their reactions as they open their present!

8. Make sure you leave yourself enough time to make yourself look fantastic. It won't matter if nothing else is ready as long as you're there to greet people when they arrive.

9. Don't forget the music—the cheesier, the better. Bring out all the old Christmas favourites and your guests will dance the night away.

10. Have a good time and everyone else will too!

JESSICA HART'S CHRISTMAS COCKTAIL

Frost the glasses in advance by dipping the rims first in lightly whipped egg white, and then in caster sugar.

Put a sugar cube in the bottom of each glass and add enough brandy to cover. Let it soak for a while, then pour in some cranberry juice and top with sparkling wine.

Stand back and watch your party take off!

A sneaky peek at next month...

By Request

RELIVE THE ROMANCE WITH THE BEST OF THE BEST

My wish list for next month's titles...

In stores from 15th November 2013:

❏ *Her Secret, His Child* – Miranda Lee,
Anne McAllister & Christina Hollis

❏ *Untamed Billionaires* – Nicola Marsh,
Ally Blake & Trish Wylie

In stores from 6th December 2013:

3 stories in each book - only £5.99!

❏ *Marrying His Majesty*
– Marion Lennox

❏ *Christmas Miracle* – Caroline Anderson,
Shirley Jump & Linda Goodnight

Available at WHSmith, Tesco, Asda, Eason, Amazon and Apple

Just can't wait?

Special Offers

Every month we put together collections and longer reads written by your favourite authors.

Here are some of next month's highlights— and don't miss our fabulous discount online!

On sale 6th December

On sale 1st November

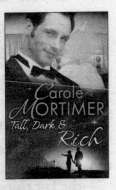

On sale 6th December

Save 20%
on all Special Releases

Wrap up warm this winter with Sarah Morgan…

Sleigh Bells in the Snow

Kayla Green loves business and hates Christmas.

So when Jackson O'Neil invites her to Snow Crystal Resort to discuss their business proposal… the last thing she's expecting is to stay for Christmas dinner. As the snowflakes continue to fall, will the woman who doesn't believe in the magic of Christmas finally fall under its spell…?

4th October

www.millsandboon.co.uk/sarahmorgan

Come home this Christmas to Fiona Harper

Make my Wish Come True

FIONA HARPER

From the author of *Kiss Me Under the Mistletoe* comes a Christmas tale of family and fun. Two sisters are ready to swap their Christmases—the busy super-mum, Juliet, getting the chance to escape it all on an exotic Christmas getaway, whilst her glamorous work-obsessed sister, Gemma, is plunged headfirst into the family Christmas she always thought she'd hate.

www.millsandboon.co.uk

1113/MB442

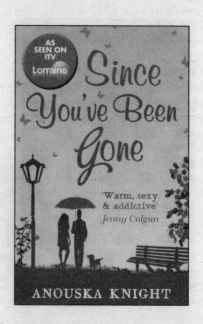